D0458624

9065
7/30/18

BEHELD

Also by
ALEX FLINN

BEHELD

ALEX FLINN

An Imprint of HarperCollinsPublishers

HarperTeen is an imprint of HarperCollins Publishers.

Beheld
Copyright © 2017 by Alexandra Flinn
All rights reserved. Printed in the United States of America.
No part of this book may be used or reproduced in any manner whatsoever
without written permission except in the case of brief quotations embod-
ied in critical articles and reviews. For information address HarperCollins
Children's Books, a division of HarperCollins Publishers, 195 Broadway,
New York, NY 10007.
www.epicreads.com

Library of Congress Control Number: 2016938971
ISBN 978-0-06-213456-1

17 18 19 20 21 PC/LSCH 10 9 8 7 6 5 4 3 2 1
❖
First paperback edition, 2018

Since this is a book about strong women,
I dedicate it to my daughters, Katherine and Meredith.

I know that children don't read fairy tales anymore. Oh, they see the movies—animated, sweet ones with helpful birds and talking raccoons, problematic ones where passive young women simply sleep and wait for their princes to come. But those are made-up stories. The real stories, stories that have recurred time and time again, are far more brutal. Stepmothers ordering their daughters' hearts brought to them to eat raw. Young women cutting off their toes to fit an idealized vision of female beauty. And those are just the romances!

I know, for I have been alive for much of this time. Not all, of course. These tales date back to the ancient Greeks, and I'm not *that* ancient. Still, I have lived as a witch since my birth in 1652, and as a teenager since I was one, over three hundred years ago.

In that time, I have sought love. Once, I found the man I thought would be mine forever. But I have lost him time and time again. This story is about how I found love and lost it. I don't know how it will end.

But it started in Salem, Massachusetts. I may, in previous accounts, have fibbed a bit when I said I wasn't there. It is *such* a cliché to claim one was in Salem. But I was. Most of those accused as witches there weren't actually witches, but a few of us were.

Or, at least, two.

Witches and Wolves
Salem, Massachusetts
January 1692

I might not have stayed in Salem had it not been for James. I might have been safer. But I have never been one to court safety above all, and I wasn't in 1692.

It was in 1692 that I fell in love with James.

Then I had been alive close to two score years, but like most magical beings, I did not look it. Nay, I did not feel it either. This was convenient, as few things in my life were, for appearing mature carries with it certain expectations—that the person will marry, have children, *be* mature. I wanted none of that, for few people were like I was. They would age. They would die, as my family had.

I would not, as long as I stayed clear of fire. Fire was the only thing that could kill a witch. Still is.

I knew not to play with fire.

I knew, also, not to play at love. Love would only lead to painful loss.

But then I met James.

It happened one morning, early, so early that my breath was a silver cloud on night black as my cloak. I was out chopping wood for the family's needs. I was a servant, but the Harwoods were not wealthy, so I was rather a maid-of-all-trades—chop the wood, darn the socks, watch the babes. It reminded me of life with my own family, back when I had one.

That morning, the spring breezes had not yet chased away the winter cold, but I was warm, for I was working. Goody Harwood kept a close watch on me, so I could not use magic. Not all the time, anyway.

If you think I was working like the mature woman I should have been, you do not know me well. I was slim, as I still am. Every swing of the ax was a herculean effort. I had been out close to an hour and had only two bone-thin logs to show for it. I knew that soon, she would be there, spying for me, accusing me (not incorrectly) of malingering. I had to move quickly.

I picked up the ax.

Just as I did, a black shape crossed my vision. Bird!

This was enough to make me stop again. The birds had left for winter and, thus far, had not returned. And this was no robin redbreast, but a crow.

I had a history with crows.

I examined the bird. It was a large one with a yellow bill. It flew around me just above my head and, finally, settled on the very log I had been about to split.

I laid down my ax, sighing as it sank into a snowdrift. My hands were bare and would surely freeze when I reached in.

I shooed the bird.

4

It did not move. Nor the second nor the third time, either. It merely stared with its black bead eyes, as if it intended to speak.

Finally, I reached for the ax. The blade was freezing. I meant to swing it just once.

When I rose, the bird had disappeared.

Not entirely pleased at the end of my excuse for idleness, I returned to my chopping.

"Mistress!"

A voice interrupted me, startled me.

I whirled to see where it came from, for I had been sure I was quite alone.

"Your humble servant," someone said, and he bowed.

He wore black, at least what I could see, from the toes of his shoes to his hat. With his face thus obscured, he might have been any man I had seen before, any man in Salem, farmers beaten down by the winter's struggle, old before their time.

But when he rose, I knew I had never seen him before.

I would have remembered.

The man staring back at me was beautiful in an unearthly way, with hair the color of fallen pine needles, skin that had never known harsh sun or harsher winter cold, and eyes a shade bluer than the bluest ocean. He was perhaps two years older than I—meaning two years older than I appeared, so still in the bloom of youth, tall and strong.

I hesitated. I wanted his help as much to keep him there as to get out of my work. But neither motive was proper for a girl my age, a girl any age in Salem. I glanced around. No signs of life anywhere except for the trickle of smoke from the chimney. I had built a fire when I'd risen. With any luck, the Harwoods would gather by it and Goody Harwood would not come looking for me when she needn't.

I nodded, trying to pull my gaze down like a proper young lady.

"If you please," I said.

He moved closer and, at first, I started at his nearness. Then I realized he meant to take the ax from me. I held it out to him, trying to lower my eyes.

I saw him notice, and his gaze upon me made me look down all the more. Yet I so wished to stare at him. I held my arms around my body, pretending only to be affected by the cold.

I knew it was more than that.

He took the ax, brushing each of my gloveless hands with his own. They were so warm, and I sank a bit when the weight was removed.

Finally, I glanced up, for he was very tall, and when I did, I saw him smile.

I pulled my eyes away, but his smile remained in my memory. He was *so* handsome.

"There now." He spoke with a bit of an accent, from Scotland. "You are too young and too lovely for such hard work."

I looked down harder.

"I am not as young as you might believe." I backed away.

"Nor am I." He made no move to chop the wood. "And I know things. Have you heard about what is happening in Salem?"

I had. At least, I thought I had. There were rumors of children bewitched by demons. But I did not want to admit that it concerned me. If I did, he might suspect how much it did. And why.

So I said, "I know little. I spend my days and nights just as you see me and my Sundays in worship."

The left corner of his mouth came up as if to call me on this lie. "Like any God-fearing young maiden."

I nodded. "Of course."

He nodded, half gravely. "Then I should tell you. It happened in town, at Reverend Parris's house. His daughter, Betty, and niece, Abigail, have been behaving . . . bizarrely."

I had heard it. Young girls barking like dogs, writhing and crying out as if in pain. I had not done it. Nor were there any other witches in these parts. Perhaps there was a fungus in their flour. Perhaps they just wished for attention. But I knew better than to say that.

"I see." I managed a nod.

"But did you know that in Boston four years ago, a young woman was stricken with similar symptoms?"

Aye. I had heard something of that.

I shook my head.

"She was, and a woman named Ann Glover was hanged as a witch based upon the suspicion that she had enchanted the girl."

"What has this to do with me?" I asked. "Why are you telling me this?"

I had stood out too long with too little work, and now my body was cold, so cold it felt as if the bones might snap.

His words did nothing to warm me. "Because it concerns you, Kendra."

"Why?" How did he know my name?

But then I heard the creak of the opening door. I whirled to make my excuses to Goody Harwood, but she smiled.

"Oh! I thought to hurry you along. The fire is waning, and you must make the breakfast still. But I see you have been harder at work than I suspected. I suppose I couldn't hear the thuds for the gusts."

As if to answer, the wind whipped through me, ruffling my hair. I turned away.

Goody Harwood had not mentioned the man who was there, and when I turned, I saw why. He was gone, gone as if he had never existed. But in his place was a cord of neatly stacked logs. A crow set atop them.

I took a shaky breath. I felt about to choke. "I will be but a moment longer."

Another gust shook the branches, and she shut the door against it.

When I turned back, the wood was still there, and the man. I had not imagined it, any of it.

"How did you . . . ?" A thousand questions leaped to mind, but I completed the one I had started. "How did you know?" *My name? That I was a witch?*

"I knew because I knew. James Brandon, at your service."

"I have to go inside, sir."

"Nay." His blue eyes were intense now. "You should leave Salem, and quickly. This place is not safe. For you. For any of us. But I will stay and see it out, to protect innocents. You should protect yourself."

Did he mean to say that he was a witch—a wizard—himself? I wanted to know, and yet my need to flee him was stronger. "I must go inside, sir. The family will wonder about me. I have to make the breakfast."

He gathered some of the wood and brought it to me. As he did, he met my eyes, and for a moment, the wind ceased and the air became first warm, then hot around me, until I felt like I might burn through the drifted snow and not be unearthed until springtime.

"Then I will see you soon, Kendra," he said. "I will see you every day until you agree to leave. Now go inside."

I could not turn away from him easily, but I forced myself. I had great experience in taking leave of people. I reached for the door-knob.

"One other thing." His voice interrupted me. "Beware of wolves."

I turned back, but when I did, he wasn't there. In his place was the black crow, staring at me with bright eyes.

It flew away.

The wind began to howl again and did not stop until I was inside the house.

Ann Putnam
A week earlier

Mother always told me to beware of wolves. They lurked in the forest, waiting to attack foolish girls who dared confront them. But, more than that, she warned me to beware of witches. Wolves, she said, feasted only upon the flesh. Witches were in league with Satan. Wolves hunted from hunger. Witches searched for souls to seduce then steal and bring back to their dark master. Wolves could be outrun. Witches were inescapable, materializing in the night, possessing their victims, forcing them to suckle at a demon's teat or to sign their souls away in an unholy black book.

Still, I feared wolves more. They were more real to me, more terrifying, when I walked alone in the woods to Reverend Parris's house.

By all that is right, I should not have been alone that day. I should have been with Mercy or Mary. But they had walked together, leaving me alone. They would say it was because they did not think I was coming. I knew differently. They wished to leave me. Although Mary Walcott was my cousin and, supposedly, my best friend, she preferred the company of Mercy, who was but a servant, to mine. They were older than I was, both seventeen, and could whisper of older girls' concerns, of men they hoped to marry. I was but a child to them. I bored them, so they treated me grievously.

But, of course, when Mother said they had gone, I ran to the door to try and catch up.

"You should not go alone." Mother's hand was a claw on my shoulder.

"Why not?" My hand twisted the doorknob. I knew why she wanted me to stay, to help her care for the little ones. Even now, she was holding the baby while Timothy tugged at her skirts.

"I do not like when you walk alone. There are people in Salem Village who wish us ill." She must have remarked my grimace, for she added, "And there may be wolves."

"There are no wolves in daylight. I hear them howling in the night." I shuddered, thinking of it.

"In the woods, they are out at all hours, and I know you mean to walk through the woods. Stay on the path and take your sisters, and you may go."

"Yes, Mother." I meant to do neither. "Let me just check the chicken coop for eggs. Mercy did not do that before she left."

Before Mother could answer, I grabbed the red woolen cape that had once been mine but was now my sister Elizabeth's. My reason for doing so was twofold. First, it was cold. But also, it would prevent Elizabeth from following me. I clutched it around my shoulders and was out like lightning, dashing toward the barn. As soon as I heard the front door slam, I detoured around it (for I had already checked the eggs) and ran for the woods.

By the time she realized what I had done, it would be too late. She was too covered in babies to pursue me.

I had no compunction about doing this. The new baby was colicky—at least that was Mother's excuse—and Timothy was merely a brat. I had listened to their crying and whining for days straight, and I had been helpful, doing more than my share of baby laundry in the freezing cold. Going to visit Reverend Parris and Betty and Abigail was a reward, and a small one at that. I did not mean to miss out. Of course I would be punished, but nothing could be greater punishment than to stay home.

The woods were freedom. I ran toward them, hearing my mother shouting my name beneath the wind, but ignoring her. The canopy of trees formed a doorway. Step through it. Be someone else. Though it was cold, the bright sun streamed down into the white snow, making it sparkle like diamonds. I kept running.

It was not Reverend Parris I wished to visit or, indeed, his staring daughter, Betty, who was only nine. It was Tituba. Tituba was Reverend Parris's slave from Barbados. She told the best stories, stories of exotic places, warm places, magic places.

The day was a bit less cold than the day before, and the snow was melting. In the wood ahead there was barely any, as the overhanging trees had prevented it falling. I felt the slush seeping through my shoes, but I kept running. I heard Elizabeth's voice in the distance. I did not stop. I knew if I reached the woods, I would be safe.

I did. My footsteps slowed, as did my heartbeat. The woods were strangely silent in the winter, neither birds nor even squirrels, the only movement the shadows of trees. The only sounds were my feet against the matted pine needles and the wind. I concentrated on my footsteps until they formed the rhythm of the hymn we had sung at church.

Sinners, the voice of God regard;
'Tis mercy speaks today.
He calls you by His sacred word;
From sin's destructive way.

I stomped my foot with each rhyming word, listening to nothing, save my head's music. This was how I did not see the wolf until it was nigh upon me. Then I froze, my heart beating so hard I feared it would shatter my ribs.

It was smaller than wolves look at a distance, but it was still far larger than I. It had fur of gray and white, puffed out against the winter cold, covered in a dusting of snow, and when it stared at me, its eyes were bright silver, almost white.

"Hello," I said, knowing not why. It was a dumb animal with no understanding. Yet its eyes said differently. I felt that I had to address it, that it would be rude not to. It was almost like a person, and my parents had taught me to be polite.

Also, I worried that the wolf might gobble me up.

But it did not seem hungry, at least at the moment. Rather, as it continued to stare at me with its intelligent eyes, I heard a voice say "Hello" in reply.

How was the wolf speaking? I backed away. My parents had also taught me to avoid wolves. And magic, for surely a talking wolf was magic.

Should I run? I knew, from watching our dogs and cats, that running was the worst thing to do. It motivated an animal to give chase. I must remain calm. I had to keep a cool head. I had to ignore my shaking knees. I had to stare him down. I had to . . .

I broke into a run. But only for a few steps. Then I slipped on a patch of ice and fell backward against a tree trunk.

For a moment, the world contracted and everything was black.

The earth vibrated beneath me, then stopped. I lay there, blinking, my beating heart sitting in my throat.

Then the wolf was upon me. Would it rip me apart?

"You should not run in such icy weather."

The wolf's voice was gruff yet surprisingly gentle, a male voice. I did not see his mouth move. I glanced around to see if there was anyone nearby. The wolf's breath blew hot in my face.

Mother had given me some cookies for Betty. Now I thought it would have been better had she given me a knife. Still, I reached for my basket. Perhaps the wolf would take a cookie.

But my basket was nowhere in my reach. I groped for it among the icy tree roots.

The wolf licked my face. It was slimy, and I shuddered for fear of his teeth.

"What is the matter, my dear child?" the voice said, and I felt the coldness where his warm tongue had been.

"Are you going to . . . to eat me?" I whispered.

The wolf chuckled. "Of course not."

Or had he said only "Of course"?

How was this? How was a wolf speaking to me? Yet he was. Perhaps I had fainted from the cold and was in a dream.

I pushed myself up onto aching arms. My head throbbed too.

"If you ate me, my parents would look for me. Father would get men to come, men with guns." I did not know if the wolf knew what a gun was. "They would search the forest for me, and when they found me"—I paused, wincing at the thought of what I might look like—"they would kill you."

The wolf seemed to consider this. His white eyes never left my own. I saw the gray fur ripple in the wind and snow fly off it. My fingers were frozen—I had forgotten my mittens—and I longed to touch the warm fur, but I dared not. Finally, the wolf said, "Perhaps."

I waited for more. When there was nothing, I asked, "Perhaps?"

The wolf moved his head, almost a nod. "Perhaps. Perhaps it is as you say, and your parents would be devastated at the loss of you, Ann Putnam."

I felt a chill when the wolf said my name. How did he know it?

"You, Ann Putnam, a girl whose parents have six other children, three of them boys."

"Of course they would." But I wondered.

"Girls are often prized by their parents." The wolf held my gaze, unblinking. "And you are always helpful, never shirking."

Had the wolf been watching as I snuck from the house? I remembered how Father had rejoiced last year when Timothy was a boy. This even though they had two others. A boy could help with the planting. A girl could only do tedious things like cooking and weaving and feeding the chickens. Father said that he wished to buy more lands, to have the largest farm in Salem Village, maybe in all Massachusetts. With three boys to do the work, he could.

"I help with the babies," I said, though it was lunacy to justify myself to a wolf. "Mother could never manage without me."

The wolf seemed to smile or maybe snarl, crinkling his nose and baring his teeth. He exhaled, breath turning to a cloud of smoke. What did he want from me?

"Of course you do. You are a lovely girl, a helpful girl. No one appreciates you, though."

That was true. The wolf came still closer. I cringed. Did he mean to bite me now? But no. The wolf sidled up against me, head level with my hand. My fingers shook. Almost without thinking, I sank them into the wolf's woolly fur. It was so warm, and he nuzzled my arm like a dog. I had never had a pet. Our farm had dogs to watch the animals or to warn us of intruders, human or not. But they were not pets, not my pets. Last year, my brother, Tom, had been given a puppy, a brindle bulldog that followed him around and slept at the foot of his bed at night. I tried to play with him sometimes, but he only liked Tom.

I scrunched the wolf's fur between my fingers.

"Where are you off to, little girl?" the wolf asked.

I was not a little girl, but this was a question with an easy answer. "To my friend Betty's. My cousin is there. They are . . . expecting me."

I pushed back the thought that they did not care whether or not I came.

"Off to play with witchcraft?" the wolf asked.

"What?" I must have misheard him. "No. We . . . talk, play games."

"What a shame." The wolf flipped his head upon my fingers, enjoying the petting. "I thought we could spend more time together."

And suddenly I wanted to, wanted to stay with the wolf or go where he was going. But that would be impossible, for I was not a wolf.

Still, I said, "Walk with me then."

Now that I knew—or, at least, thought—the wolf would not eat me, I grew bold.

"Very well." The wolf started in the direction I had planned to go. I trudged beside him, feeling his warmth at my side. "Why are you walking all alone through the woods?"

"I was supposed to go with Mary—my cousin. But she left without me." *She did not care.*

"The woods are dangerous," the wolf said. "Someone should have walked with you. There are wolves in the woods."

My nose was cold, and I sniffled a bit. Even though it was early, the overhanging trees and the clouds made the day dark.

The wolf continued. "No one pays you any mind, but you are superior to them all."

I started a bit at this, for I had always suspected as much. Yet how would the wolf know?

But admitting it would be sinful vanity. "Of course I am not superior."

"You are." The wolf's words left his mouth in a puff of smoke. "Smarter. Quicker on your feet."

It was true. I always won at games like hunt the slipper or charades, beating even older girls like Mary. My handwriting was much finer than theirs, and when I read, I had a clear, strong voice and did not hesitate at difficult words. Yet none of those skills were prized. Games were a waste of time at best, of the devil at worst. And Mother condemned my pride in my penmanship as a vanity. I knew that was because her own was not nearly as fine.

I only wanted to be good. No. I wanted to be good and have everyone *know* I was good.

"I do not know about that," I said.

"You are too modest," the wolf said. "You are the smartest and best girl. The others are simply jealous. That is why they left without you."

Once again, the wolf confirmed my own thoughts, or my deepest fears. I shivered.

"How can I make them not to be jealous?" It seemed wrong to admit that I wanted them to envy me.

The wolf did not answer for a moment, winding his body behind mine, warming me. Finally, he said, "I suppose you must look for opportunities."

"Opportunities?" I pulled Elizabeth's too-small cape around me. My boots squeezed my toes. They were too small as well. No one had thought to check, with two babies to care for.

"To impress them with something they value."

Something they value. "Like what?"

We had reached a clearing, and Reverent Parris's house lay ahead. I knew I must part company with the wolf, yet I wasn't sure I wanted to. The wolf's company was easy, easier than the company of my fellow humans.

Easy.

I wondered what it would be like to snuggle up against him and sleep at night like a cub.

"You will find the opportunity," the wolf said. "See what they care about, and use it."

"Will I see you again?"

He backed away, looking at me with his white eyes. The shadows of trees trembled against the ground like hands, grabbing.

"I am certain," he said.

I watched until he was gone, then turned and ran to Reverend Parris's house. When I reached the door, I heard a howl in the distance.

Had that happened? I shook my head and tried the doorknob.

But they were not inside. I searched around until I found them in a clearing behind a stand of trees, where Tituba had built a little fire. Mary, seeing me, acted happy. "Ann, you are here. God preserve you."

I thought that God had nothing to do with it. I had seen to my journey myself, since she had not waited. But I said, "Aye. I had to finish the chores." I glanced at Mercy.

"Tituba is beginning to tell us a story." Betty grasped my wrist. She was always trying to get my attention. She whispered, "My father is gone out. Will you sit with me?"

She pointed to a spot on a log that was barely large enough for her, but I followed and perched on the end nonetheless. Betty was crowded between Tituba and me as Tituba began her tale. She had an accent that made me think of a warm, wet night in an exotic place, a place overhung with fragrant yellow and red flowers I had never seen.

"I will tell you a tale," she said, "a tale so tall that it disappears into the sky and you cannot see it on a cloudy day."

I drew in my breath. We all did. Mary came and stood beside me, leaning against me.

"But though it is a tall tale, it is about a short, short man." Tituba leaned forward, confiding. I stared at her. She was so beautiful, with skin that seemed to gleam in the firelight and the whitest teeth I had ever seen. I shivered with anticipation.

"People call him Baccoo," she said.

Betty gasped. "What's a Baccoo?"

I rolled my eyes. Silly girl. Tituba was obviously going to tell us more.

"Shh!" Tituba put her long finger to lips. "All your questions will be answered, my little one." Her gaze took all of us in. Abigail, Mercy, and Mary giggled, but I was chilled. Tituba's stories frightened me, though I did not wish to admit it.

"Nobody ever sees Baccoo, but everybody hears of him. Everybody knows what he is like—a short, short, little, little man with a long, looong beard." Tituba gestured with her skinny fingers, as if stroking a beard of her own, and we giggled, or at least, the others did.

I remembered the wolf's words, *Off to play with witchcraft?* What had he meant?

Tituba continued. "The owner of the Baccoo keeps him in a bottle and feeds him on milk and bananas, and when there is mischief made, it is the Baccoo that makes it."

Tituba went on with her story about the spirit, who lurked in barns and pelted cattle with pebbles. I shivered, knowing my mother would not approve of my listening. I noticed Betty was staring ahead, at nothing. Or was there something? Betty's staring was so bizarre.

"If you hear rain on the roof on a summer night," Tituba said, "that is not rain—but the Baccoo."

I shuddered again.

And suddenly I could not stop shivering, like I would never feel warmth.

"Ann, quit it," Mary said when I bumped against her for the tenth time.

"I cannot . . . cannot help it," I whispered. And it was true. Tituba's stories had always scared me, but it was a good kind of scared, usually. Now, with the wolf's words in my head, I was not sure. Were there evil spirits? And would I be punished for communing with them? None of the adults knew the stories Tituba told us, the things she did with us. If they did, they would not allow it. It was more than mischief. It was witchcraft.

"What a baby," Mary muttered. "We were right to leave her."

"I am not," I said, but my teeth chattered, and they chattered more with the indignity of it all. They had left me on purpose. "I am just a little cold."

"You are just a little girl," Mary said. "Even Betty is not scared of Tituba's stories."

"I freeze." I ran from my seat to the fire Tituba had built, turning my head so no one could see my tears. I sat, shivering, and after a while, I stared into the fire.

Then I saw the wolf's face in it.

Off to play with witchcraft? he asked and stared at me with flame-white eyes.

I turned away, shuddering. No. It wasn't real. It wasn't.

I looked again. Only fire.

Still, I ran back to the girls and Tituba. They were all giggling as she finished her story, but Betty was crying. This happened often.

Betty stared. And cried. And sometimes screamed. I heard Mercy whisper something about the babies crying, and Abigail giggled.

"Shh, shh, shh." Tituba patted Betty's shoulder. "No scary stories then. We will do something else. We'll find out who you will be marrying."

Mary and Mercy squealed. They were older and thought of little else, Mercy especially.

I told myself that this was harmless. Tituba always had her superstitions, like laying a broom across the doorway at night, to keep the devil away, or never lending salt, for she said it was bad luck. I knew what my parents would say about such things, but Tituba lived with Reverend Parris, so it must be all right. Besides, I wanted to be with the other girls. And I wished to find out who I would marry, even if it was merely a silly game.

Yet the fact that I had encountered a talking wolf made it different. So different.

Mary went first. She sat across from Tituba on the log. Tituba took Mary's wrists in her hands, and then she threw her head back and began to hum with great concentration. It was stupid, really, a child's game. No one could tell the future.

Finally, Tituba opened her eyes, though her look was still far away.

"I see him." Her voice was a low hum. "Coming from the shadows."

"Who?" Mary giggled, but there was nervousness in her voice too. "Who?"

"A tall man," Tituba almost chanted, "with hair fair yellow."

Mary was fairly jumping in her seat, and I knew why. She had set her cap for Isaac Farrar. I had seen him gazing upon her at church, and his hair was the color of corn silk.

"And eyes . . ."

"What is his name?"

"Cannot see a name," Tituba said. "Just a part—like Ffffff."

"Oh!"

"That is so wonderful, Mary!" I exclaimed, but Mary grabbed Mercy's hand and they galloped round the clearing.

"Me next!" Mercy said. "Me next!"

But Betty had to go next, and since she was Tituba's pet, we let her, though she was a mere child with no thought of marrying. Tituba told her that she would marry a shoemaker with hair of black.

"A shoemaker!" Betty scoffed.

"Making shoes is a good trade," Tituba said, "and besides, yours are always scuffed."

"Perhaps she should marry a bootblack," I said, then regretted my meanness.

Next went Mercy, to find she would marry a man whose name began with *A*, but Tituba knew no more. She told Abigail that she would have so many men that Tituba could not tell which one was her husband. I thought this sounded awful and sinful, but Abigail was pleased.

I, of course, was last. Tituba's hands felt rough and calloused on my wrists, and it took her several minutes to speak up.

"Well?" I said.

"No husband for you." Her voice was confident.

"What?" Instantly, my stomach hurt, but surely I must have misheard her.

But she repeated. "No husband. No children." She stared ahead as if looking at something in the distance.

"But . . ." That was impossible. I was Ann Putnam, daughter of one of the most successful farmers in Salem Village. I would have many suitors, certainly more than Abigail.

Yet a thought frayed my mind. Not everyone liked my father. There was bad blood between our family and the Nurses, and Father said that the Howes wished him dead.

"Your father, your mother, I see their graves," Tituba chanted as if she was telling a tale.

In my mind, I saw them too, covered up with snow. I felt a chill that I struggled to control. The girls would make fun. But they were behind the trees, whispering. Were they talking about me?

"You will care for your sisters and brothers," Tituba said, "but no children of your own."

When Tituba had told the other girls' futures, she had sounded tentative. With mine, she had the certainty of an executioner.

And suddenly my skin felt as if an insect was crawling underneath it. Then many insects. I threw aside Tituba's hands and clutched at my arms. Then my legs, my stomach, creeping all over me. I wanted to cry out, to shriek, but Mary and Mercy would tease me. I shoved past Tituba, grabbed Elizabeth's cape around me, and ran from there.

I was still itching, still shaking. I ran as far as I could, that no one might see me, then fell to the ground, rolling like Tom's dog. Finally, the creeping feeling subsided. I lay there many minutes until the cold began to overtake me. Then, finally, I pushed myself up. My dress was damp and covered in dirt and pine needles. I thought to lie to Mother, tell her I had been attacked by an animal, even a wolf. Yet I knew if I did, she would blame me. I was always blamed for everything. I remembered Tituba's words. My parents would die. I would care for the children, which meant it would be soon.

I would be an old maid.

No. No, it was nonsense. Tituba knew nothing of me. If she had magical powers, why was she a mere servant? Why would the devil not make her a queen?

I brushed myself off best I could. I would walk slowly, in the hope that the dark would cover my disarray. Finally, I began to trudge home.

But where my footsteps had once played the exuberant marching rhythm of my favorite hymn, now they moved slowly, repeating, "Old maid, old maid, old maid." I stared at my feet, and that was how I did not see the wolf until he was upon me.

"Leaving so soon?" He licked his lips, and I wondered if he meant to eat me now.

"Not . . . s . . . so soon . . ." My teeth were chattering, but not from the cold. "The others left too. They are behind me." I glanced over my shoulder, as if Mercy and Mary would somehow be there, when I knew they would not.

"You have had bad news."

I wanted to run, cry to my mother, tell her all that frightened me. Yet how could I tell her about the prophecy of her own death? And she would blame me for counseling with a witch, for surely Tituba *was* a witch.

And she would blame me for speaking to the wolf.

So, instead, I spoke to the wolf again. "It was awful," I told him. "Tituba, she said my parents would die, die soon. She said she could see their gravestones. And she said . . ." My lip quivered. This was the most difficult part. "She said I would be an old maid."

The wolf slunk up to me, and then he rubbed against me. His fur was warm and soft. "It is not true," the wolf said.

"Then how . . . how can she say such things?" I had forgotten my nervousness. The wolf was the only creature to whom I could talk.

"She says it because she is a witch, an evil witch in league with Satan."

I hugged the wolf. It was as I had suspected.

"She casts spells on people," the wolf said. "She casts spells on Betty, which is what makes her act as she does."

I knew what the wolf meant. Betty was a strange child who often acted inappropriately, staring at nothing or sometimes crying out, even at church. But did the wolf mean Tituba would cast a spell on me? Or that she already had?

"What will become of me?" I asked.

"That," the wolf said, nuzzling my hand that I might pat its head, "remains to be seen."

"So you mean that she is wrong, that my parents will not die?"

The wolf stared at me. "Is that the part of her prophecy that concerns you most?"

"Of course." But was it? I knew it should be. For my parents to die before my siblings came of age would be horrible. I repeated, "Of course."

"Of course." The wolf's eyes were unblinking. "You are a dutiful daughter."

Was there mocking in his tone? "I am."

He held my gaze an instant longer than expected. "You are. And, as certain as I am that you are a dutiful daughter, I am equally certain your parents will not die."

His voice was calm, and I let out the breath I had not realized I was holding. If that part of Tituba's grotesque prediction did not come true, likely none of it would.

"But you must stay away from Tituba," the wolf said.

"Why?"

"For your own safety. And you must find a way to warn others of the havoc she may wreak. She and the other witches."

In the distance, I heard the crack of a branch. Was it Mary? Mary or Mercy, come to look for me? Nonsense. They cared little about me. If they cared, they would have pursued me when I left, not so long after. If they came now, it was for their own purposes. Still, it would not do for them to see me here dawdling, much less speaking to a wolf.

"I must go." I pulled away.

24

He bared his teeth. I started, then cringed, and gradually, his eyes regained their calm appearance. He said, "Go now, child, but be careful. And look for me again."

I heard a voice in the distance. In these empty woods, sounds carried far. Still, I ran down the path to my house.

But in the back of my head, I heard his words, *You must find a way to warn others of the havoc she may wreak. She and the other witches.* What other witches did the wolf mean?

Mary and Mercy followed a scant five minutes later. They were laughing when they barged through the door but stopped quickly at Mother's disapproving look. I was at my weaving and pretended to take no notice. I wished to punish them for the way they had treated me. I also wanted to hear what they had to say. If I was as quiet as falling snow, perhaps they would forget I was there.

And they did. "I was so worried for her," Mary said when they sat down to their sewing.

I looked up with only my eyes, lest they see I was noticing them. Did she mean me?

"I was not," Mercy said. "She does it for attention. She should not be rewarded."

This must be me, and I wanted to cry out at the unfairness. But still, I held my tongue.

"She has always been an odd child," Mary said. "Were she not our reverend's daughter, people would remark her behavior even more."

I looked down at my weaving, concentrating. It was Betty they meant, not me.

Confirming all this, Mary glanced about the room, then whispered, "You missed all the excitement, Ann. I do not know why you left."

I leaned toward her, away from Mercy, still trying to seem aloof but with much difficulty. "What happened?" I whispered.

"After you left, Betty began behaving strangely."

"Betty always behaves strangely," Mercy interrupted.

"But more strangely. She was staring, as usual. But after you left, she began to writhe around and bark like a dog. Abigail too. It was almost as if they were possessed by evil spirits."

"Possessed of the need for a good spanking, more likely," Mercy said.

I remembered the feeling I had had when Tituba held my hands, as if insects were crawling upon me, as if they might consume me alive.

"No," I said to Mercy. "There is evil in that house. We should not go there."

Mercy laughed. "Perhaps you should not go there, if you are so easily frightened," Mercy responded at the same time Mary said, "Evil at our reverend's house?"

I was framing my response when my father came home, so we could no longer speak freely. Mother asked Mercy to help her with the serving and me to gather the younger children. I had corralled Timothy, Deliverance, and Ebeneezer. They were pulling at me, pushing against me, wrapping themselves around my legs, and I remembered what Tituba had said.

Was Tituba right? And, if so, was she really a witch?

Kendra
About One Month Later

"What is a . . . witch cake?" I pretended simplemindedness, for of course I knew what a witch cake was. Any good witch would, and I was a very good witch. But I was not about to tell Betty Parris that. Nor would I tell her that witch cakes were silly superstition.

James Brandon had been at my side, as promised, informing me of the goings on at Reverend Parris's house (How he knew such details, I did not speculate). As predicted, Betty's symptoms had not been ignored. Rather, the doctor had been called, and when he found nothing, there was talk of witchcraft.

I had tried—oh, how I had tried—to ignore what was occurring, but it was impossible. Little of interest happened in Salem. On the rare occasion when it did, it was all people could talk about. The dry goods store, where I had walked to purchase buttons, had become a place of gossip and intrigue. And, dare I say, theatrics. Right now, young Betty was holding court with much of Salem's youth gathered around her.

"Since Abigail and I have been having so many ailments . . ." Betty shivered for emphasis. "Goody Sibley suggested that John Indian make a witch cake to find out who was afflicting us with such miseries."

I knew John Indian was one of Reverend Parris's slaves, along with Tituba. I wanted to find out what the witch cake had supposedly told them, but first, Betty went into a recitation of the nature of her various "miseries"—fever, crying out in pain, barking like a dog, convulsions.

"You were saying about the witch cake?" someone finally asked.

"Well." Betty smiled. "John Indian took the . . . contents of our chamber pots, Abigail's and mine, and baked them into a cake. Then he fed it to our dog. Goody Sibley said that, since a dog is a witch's familiar, once he ate the cake, the invisible particles that the witch sent to hurt us would make the dog hurt the witch."

"The witch sent invisible particles to hurt you?" a girl named Mary Warren asked.

"Of course, Mary," Betty said. "Everyone knows that! Invisible particles fly through the air and cause all our miseries. But when the dog ate the witch cake, the particles would come back to him, and make the witch suffer. So by her pain—Goody Sibley said—we would be able to tell who the witch was."

The assembled girls stood, slack-jawed at this brilliance, but I thought it was the stupidest thing I had ever heard. Particles? In piss? And those piss particles would make the *dog* sick and, in turn, make the witch sick, even if the dog did not belong to the witch?

"What if the witch does not like dogs?" I could not help but ask.

Betty looked around, for she had not been particularly speaking to me. "I . . . I do not know," she said. "Goody Sibley only said that witches had dogs as familiars."

"I had always heard that witches had different familiars," I said. "Like cats. Or wolves."

I heard a gasp from without the crowd, and a voice said, "Wolves?"

I looked to see young Ann Putnam. She seemed wide-eyed. I did not know why.

I stammered an explanation that would get me out of this. "Well, I had heard that witches in England, where I once lived, liked wolves. I have never heard of an American witch who kept company with a wolf. But a dog is a great deal like a wolf, is it not?"

The girls goggled at me, and I felt a hand pinching my upper arm. Then it tugged me away. "Can I help you now, miss?" a voice asked. James! He was employed with the shop.

I say this as if I did not know it, but in fact it was my reason for coming. My every excuse for going there.

"I have come to get buttons for a dress Goody Harwood is making," I said.

"What size buttons?" he asked, a bit more loudly than necessary, and before I could answer, he said, "Let us take a look," and pulled me as far from the assembled group as possible.

When we got to the corner of the shop, he whispered, "Are you insane?"

"I do not think so," I replied.

"Then why are you talking of witchcraft and familiars to the very girls who are likely going to be the ones . . ." He looked around, as did I. Betty was still giving her recital, but I noticed Ann Putnam was gone. When had she left?

James pulled me out the back door of the shop. "These may be the girls to accuse you."

I thought he was being a bit overly dramatic, though I did wonder why Ann had left. "I was trying to tell them how silly it was. Piss cakes—my goodness—and feeding them to dogs."

"Silly?"

"Aye. Silly. Those things are merely made-up stories."

"And you, of course, know what real witches do?" he said.

"Of course I . . ." I stopped, seeing his point.

"Has anything that you have heard in your life led you to believe that the people of this town—or any other—believe witchcraft to be silly?"

"It can be silly," I said. "For example, if I wanted to make an egg appear and crack itself onto your head right now, that would be quite silly."

I moved to conjure up an egg with a gesture of my hand. I had played such tricks on him before. But now, James caught my hand in the air.

"Do not do it, Kendra." His eyes were intense, and his fingernails dug into my wrist. "No witchcraft. It will put you at risk."

"Why do you worry so much?" I tried to laugh, but it was hard, for his grip was like a claw on my arm. Yet another part of me wanted to obey him. It was sweet, him being concerned for my safety. It had been a great while since anyone had been.

"Because I have seen what can happen." He pressed his lips together, and I heard him catch his breath.

"What do you mean?"

"I am a bit older than you, I suspect. You, I know, were alive for the English plagues."

"Aye. I lost my family to them. Thank you for reminding me."

"So if you saw someone about to be struck with Plague, I daresay you would warn them about it, so they might avoid it."

"Of course." I whipped my arm around, in an attempt to get away from him. To my surprise, he merely let go with a shrug. I looked down, pursing my lips.

"'Tis the same with me. I lost my family, my mother, at least, to witch trials in Scotland."

"Was your mother a witch?"

"Aye, she was. But not an evil witch who cast spells on people, merely a poor woman trying to support her children. She sometimes performed funny spells too, like making our cat appear to talk. But in 1590, the king of Scotland sailed to Copenhagen to marry his princess. The weather was bad, and when he finally returned, he looked for someone to blame for it."

"And your mother was implicated?" I asked. "How awful!"

"Aye. Along with seventy other women. Someone accused a neighbor, and then the neighbor named someone else, and soon, over a hundred people were on trial, my mother among them." He looked downward, not meeting my gaze. "They tortured her to get her to confess, pulled out her fingernails, and twisted her toes with thumbscrews. Such torture would have killed a normal person, but since she was a witch, she survived it." He shook his head.

I did too, imagining it, the horror. "But witchcraft does nothing for the pain."

"Nothing." James passed a hand across his face. "Finally, she confessed, just to stop the torture, though she was innocent."

"And that did not work?" I asked.

"Nay, of course it did not. After she confessed, they burned her alive. I can still hear her screams." He closed his eyes against the vision. "Someone else, someone who was not a witch, might have died from the smoke inhalation, but she was a witch, so only the flame itself could kill her. It probably was only minutes, but it seemed so much longer."

"I am so sorry." I imagined the pain he must have felt, losing her, the first of his family. I had lost my family, one by one. Only another witch would understand what it was to outlive everyone, to be alone. I wanted to take him in my arms, comfort him as I had once comforted my brothers and sisters when they were sad. But I dared not touch him.

And then his arms were around me, and he was weeping. "It has been over a hundred years. I was merely a boy. Yet I still feel that I could reach across the decades and stop it. But I cannot. I cannot."

"Poor James."

Suddenly he pushed me away with an intensity that shocked me. "Do not say that! Do not pity me. Save yourself. If you are called out as a witch, they may torture you. They may hang you. But, eventually, they will find the way to kill you. Or, if they do not, and if you do not die, you will provide the proof that witches are real. And then who knows how many innocent people will be killed for it."

Innocent people. Did he mean me? Was I an innocent person? Or did he mean only people free of the sin of being born a witch? I could not help it. What I was, was not a choice. If I could but have died with the rest of my family, I would have chosen that. As it was, the decades and centuries stretched before me with no promise of anything but heartbreak.

But James was right. It would not be fair to the other women of Salem for me to make their choice for them. And, if I gave them reason to know that witches were real, so many more might die.

I nodded. "I have to go. Goody Harwood will wonder what happened to me."

"Of course," he said. "Let me . . . you must have your buttons."

"Aye." I thought he meant to walk into the shop to get them for me, but I felt something in my hand, and when I turned it over, eight black buttons shone in my palm.

"Be on your way, Kendra," James said. "And remember what I said. No magic."

"But when . . . ," I whispered. "When can I see you again?"

He looked around. "I will find you."

Then, using the door like the mortal he pretended to be, he walked back into the shop.

I stole around the front. The position of the sun in the sky told me it was late, and even with James's shortcut with the buttons, I had taken longer than I should. I would have to walk through the woods to get back to the Harwoods'. I was not afraid of wolves or other wild creatures, but I had been attacked once in the woods, as a girl, and had to use my magic to defend myself. Since then, I had feared the people who might lurk in dark places.

Still, that day, I took off at brisk pace. It was early March, cold, and darkness was settling in. I stuck to the path. But then I saw something that startled me.

Another person. Someone in crimson.

Ann Putnam. But that wasn't what startled me. It was the creature to whom she was talking. Yes, creature, for Ann Putnam spoke to a wolf. A great, white one with snow-covered fur and eyes like pearls. Ann leaned in as if having a conversation with it.

"What should I do?" she said, and then she appeared to listen to the wolf's answer. I could not hear it myself, for it was muffled by the wind.

Ann Putnam, daughter of one of the town's wealthiest citizens, could talk to wolves? Or any animal? I knew that sometimes people—even ordinary people—spoke to their domestic animals, dogs, cats, or horses, even though the animals did not reply. But this was no cat nor even a dog. For Ann to be able to go up to a wolf in the wild . . .

Was Ann a witch?

Surely not. I would know if she was like me. I could sense it, as I had with James.

I remembered Ann's shocked reaction when I had said that wolves were a witch's familiars. Was it that she did not know that? Or that she did not wish it to be known?

33

Still, I determined to walk, quick as possible, back to town and take a more circuitous route home, a road that did not go through the woods or past Ann. If Goody Harwood questioned me, I would tell her I felt unsafe in the woods. It was true, after all. If she was angry, I would bear the consequences and, only later, put crushed-up insects into her food. But just as I started to turn on my heel, I felt the wolf's eyes upon me. Then Ann was looking at me too.

"Hello, Ann." I smiled best I could. "Did you, uh, get everything you wanted at the store?" I wondered if there was some sort of spell I could cast on Ann—or the wolf—to make them forget about me. I did not know one.

"Uh . . . I did," she stammered. "Just some sugar to make a cake."

A witch's cake? She must have thought it too, for she flushed and looked down.

"I only had to get buttons," I said. "I will be seeing you."

I turned and went down the path as I had been before.

But I was not quite out of earshot when I heard Ann say, "She saw us. She *saw* us talking!"

Ann Putnam

"She saw us! She *saw* us talking!" I said to the wolf as soon as the girl was out of earshot.

"Mmm." The wolf chuckled. "Do you want me to eat her?"

I felt hot, sweating around my temples, and my stomach seemed like a trapdoor, dropping to nothingness. I had been ill since that day at Betty's house, since the first time I had seen the wolf. I had chills every night, and sometimes, my body went stiff as a tree trunk.

My parents did not care. They spoke only of the farm, the town, what was happening to others, but not of me, their daughter. Salem had been in an uproar. Betty and Abigail had accused first Tituba, then two other women, of causing Betty's symptoms. Abigail had started to develop the same symptoms. There was evil afoot in Salem.

Some did not believe it. The night before, my parents had

returned from a town meeting. I was charged, of course, with watching the younger children, so I was allowed to stay up. Later, I overheard them speaking as they lay in bed, believing me to be asleep.

"She is going to get herself into trouble if she does not stop saying that," my father had said.

"Perhaps that is what she wants," my mother replied. "Martha always was contrary."

I had then been drifting off to sleep and was disturbed by their conversation. I covered my ears against it, but my father's voice was quite loud. Still, I didn't really hear his words until he said, "She is calling our reverend's daughter a liar."

"Reverend Parris—"

"Nay. I know. He is a hard man. But anyone can see how the poor girl suffers."

I knew Betty was not a liar, if for no other reason than that she was too stupid to lie believably.

My interest piqued, I had listened more intently.

"She says she does not *believe* in witches," Mother said. "Does not believe. As if it is for Martha Corey to decide whether witches exist."

Martha Corey. Martha Corey was an old woman whose children had grown and whose husband was known for having a temper. Martha herself was stern and unforgiving and quite frightening. When I saw her at church, I tried to avoid her gaze. What had she said about Betty?

My mother continued to speak. "But she is a God-fearing woman," she said.

"Sometimes, those who feign godliness are truly in league with the devil."

I shivered when my father said that and pictured Goodwife Corey with the devil. I knew it was the devil because he appeared the way Reverend Parris always said the devil would look, when he spoke of him in church, a dark man with horns. Goodwife Corey was with him, touching his hand, helping him, and he was counseling her on what to say, telling her to say Betty had lied, and as I was watching him, hearing him, I began to shiver and shake in my bed. Then my body was racked with pain, pain in my stomach, in my arms, as if I was being stuck with needles and knives or bitten by a million teeth, demons' teeth from hell. I wanted to run to my mother, to cry out, but my limbs were stiff, I could not move. My body and my hair were drenched in sweat.

Finally, I fell asleep. When I awakened in the morning, my father was already gone, my mother occupied with the children. They did not care about my ailments. That was why I went to town.

That was how the trouble had happened, how I had met the wolf, been seen by the servant girl.

"That girl has seen me speaking to a wolf," I told the wolf now. "She will think I am a witch."

"Perhaps you are," the wolf said.

"No. I am not!" I stamped my foot. I was not, was I? No. For one thing, the devil had never visited my bedside. But for another, witches had power, and I had none. If I were a witch, the first thing I would do would be to enchant Mercy Lewis to leave our house so I could have Mary all to myself. Next, I would make the babies behave. Or, perhaps, make there be fewer of them.

No, first I would make the pains in my stomach go away. It wasn't fair that I was always so kind yet suffered so. Perhaps Martha Corey was the one tormenting me. I could almost feel her nails digging into my skin. Was she bringing the devil to bite me?

"What should I do?" I asked the wolf.

The wolf stared ahead, his cool eyes reflecting the snow. "I do not know. But you must act soon, lest you pay the consequences for something that is not your fault."

"What do you mean?" Again, I felt a sudden chill.

"The girl," the wolf said. "Her name is Kendra Hilferty. She is the servant for the Harwood family, I believe."

"Aye." 'Twas true. She was merely a servant.

"But if she accuses you of witchcraft, it is possible someone might believe her."

I felt another stab of pain as the wolf said this.

"Perhaps you should run along home," the wolf said.

I did run along home, and I helped with the meal, stirred the stew, and set the table, but I could not stop thinking of the wolf's words. If Kendra accused me of witchcraft, if she said she had seen me speaking to the wolf, someone might believe her. They might believe the wolf was my "familiar." I could be taken to jail with Sarah Good and Tituba. I would be shamed, a laughingstock, perhaps hanged. Everyone would believe I was in league with the devil. It pounded on my mind, on my head.

But why *had* the wolf chosen me?

Finally, the table was set and all were gathered around it, and Father began the prayer.

I alone of my siblings loved to hear my father at prayer. My father had a voice better than any preacher or reverend. When he spoke at table, I felt at one with God.

"Oh lover of thy people," he began.

But today, I could not stop thinking about the wolf. Kendra Hilferty and the wolf.

"Thou has placed my whole being in the hands of Jesus, my commander, my redeemer . . . ."

I began to feel hot, as though coals pressed upon my shoulders. Was I too near the fire? But one look at Deliverance at my side told me that it was not hot. It was March.

"Keep me holy, harmless, undefiled, separate from sinners."

Separate from sinners. Was this happening to me because I had consorted with Tituba, because I had believed in her powers? Now I felt an icy claw, clutching at my throat. The devil's hand! I began to shiver.

"May I not know the voice of strangers but go to Him where He is, follow where He leads."

I trembled. The bench below me shook from my quivering, shivering body. I tried to stop it, to concentrate on the prayer, on following where He led.

"Stop it, Ann," Tom said.

"Shh." Mother gave us a stern look.

Father kept praying. "Thou has bathed me once for all in the sin-removing fountain. . . ."

The hand on my throat strangled me now. I could not breathe. I was choking, struggling to swallow.

"Cleanse me now from the day's defilement, from its faults. . . ."

No breath. No air. No air.

"That I may exhibit a perfect character in Jesus," Father prayed.

I fell to the floor, gasping for breath, my heart feeling the twist of a knife.

Mother sprang from her seat. I heard the straight wooden chair fall over beside me.

"What is it? Ann! What is happening?"

Father kept praying. "O, master, who did wash thy disciples' feet . . ."

"Thomas! She is having some sort of fit!" My mother's voice seemed to be coming through a wall of water, and my body was a world of pain, my stomach, my head, my heart.

"What is it, Ann? Ann! Speak to me!" To my father, she said, "It is bewitchment!"

"Ann?" My father knelt beside me now, and I could hear Deliverance crying. "Ann! What is happening?"

I writhed from side to side, clutching my stomach to my knees to hold in the pain, gasping, glad of the little breath I had.

"They . . . hurt . . . me!" I gasped out.

"Who does?" Mother took hold of my shoulders. "Who has done this to you?"

I coughed, choked, tried to form the words, for I knew the source of my trouble. "Kendra!" I finally gasped. "She sticks me with pins! She pushes the breath from my lungs!"

"Who?" Father asked.

"I think she means the Harwoods' girl," Mother said. She peered into my face. "No one else?"

"And Martha Corey," I said, for I knew it was true, knew she was in league with the devil, knew she tormented me, knew they would believe it.

And then the pain became too much for me, and I could not speak, could not move. My body went stiff, and the world went blank.

Kendra

That night, I could not sleep. I huddled on my pallet, which was near the window and thus subject to the freezing cold. I clutched the buttons James had given me, turning them over and over in my hands.

And then I found myself pressing my hands together. What if James was right? The girl had seen me. She could implicate me as a witch. They would rip out my fingernails to make me confess. Should I run away?

But I did not want to. There was some part of my personality that did not run away, that did not want to be defeated. I had done nothing wrong, so why should I leave Salem?

The wind whistled through the cracks in the window frame.

Also, I could not leave James.

James. When I had seen him in the shop, something stirred in me.

No, not *that*. Not merely that. Certainly, he was handsome. I could not recall when I had been more drawn to a man. But it was more than that. I also could not recall when someone, *anyone*, had been so concerned for my well-being. Not since my parents had died so many years before.

The Harwoods had also become something of a family to me. In the end, I did not wish to leave Salem. Salem was my home. I was tired of running and wanted to be in one place. I was tired of giving up and letting others—awful others—have their way.

The wind whistled outside, wailing to come in, and then I heard a rapping on the window across the room. I gathered the thin quilt around myself and pulled it over my head. I had to go to sleep. There was a world of wood to chop and chickens to kill for dinner. I could not do it on an hour's sleep.

Yet the rapping continued. It was too regular to be a branch. But what else could it be? I rose, clutching the quilt around me. I traversed the room. I slept on the first floor, while the family slept on the second, so it was up to me. My plan was to open the window, find the delinquent branch, and snap it in two.

When I reached the window, there was no branch, only a crow.

I undid the latch, but it would not retreat. Instead, it stared at me.

"James?" I whispered.

It continued to stare. The wind howled behind it, burning my hands.

"James, is that you?"

At this, the crow flew a few feet away and landed near the woodpile. Through the snow and tree branches, I saw it become a man. He beckoned to me.

Quick as I could, I shut the window, donned my shoes and coat, and ran out the door. I pulled it shut behind me. I ran to the woodpile.

He was not there. I looked around, the snow whipping at my

face. Finally, I spied him, as a crow still, perched atop that woodpile. He flew away.

I turned myself into a crow and followed him.

We flew, higher, higher, over the houses and trees and fields, over the church and the little shops of town. It was glorious, for I had seldom flown with another of my kind before. Finally, we reached the woods. I saw James look back at me, and I imagined him as a boy, playing in the snow. I flapped to catch up to him, but when I was close, he dove down under a branch. He was too quick for me to follow. I flew around him, swooping at him, and finally, we reached the thickest, darkest part of the forest, away from any homes. It was there that he landed. I set down too, about ten feet away.

He started toward me.

I ran. "You cannot get me!" I shouted over my shoulder.

"I will catch you!" he hollered back, and he ran after me. The snow was shallow, for little of it could pass through the looming trees. Still, I was not a fast runner. But neither was he.

"Why are you running from me?" he yelled. "You followed me out here!"

Just for fun, I waved my arm at him. "Catch me!"

I hastened my step, hearing his footsteps like thundering hooves behind me. I wanted him to catch me. But, more than that, I wanted to run. I wanted to be free like the little girl I once was back in Eyam, before I lost everything and found my powers.

My foot hit a rock, and I stumbled. I fell to the ground, only the snow breaking my fall.

"Kendra!" James screamed behind me. "Kendra! Are you all right?"

Then he was beside me, gathering me up me into his arms. He lifted me toward him.

"Tell me you are not hurt."

"I am not hurt," I whispered, leaning into him. I felt his warm breath on my face, and I longed to be closer to him, to have not even my thin coat between us. To have him kiss me.

He did. He kissed me. He kissed me.

He kissed me.

Finally, he stopped.

"I have been wanting to do that since I first laid eyes upon you."

I laughed. "Why?"

"You are lovely. Is that not reason enough?"

I shook my head, no, for I knew there was more, and I wanted to hear it.

"No, then. I wanted to kiss you for we are the same. We are alike, clever and full of mischief, and have been through the same things and will be through the same experiences. We have both lost everything yet lived on. And on. And because you are beautiful."

"Better." I struggled to my feet. I wanted him to kiss me again, but it was probably not fitting to allow him to kiss me on the ground, especially in those deserted woods.

He pulled me toward him. "But you must leave Salem, Kendra."

"Must I?" I stared at him. "First, you kiss me. Then, you say I must leave?"

"Yes. It is not safe. There are more murmurings. Your performance at the shop did not help. They are closing in."

I thought of Ann, Ann with the wolf. He was right, I knew. But still . . .

"I do not want to leave . . . not alone." I willed him to say he would go with me. "I have finally found a place where I am comfortable, with the Harwoods and . . ."

"And what?" Even in the darkness, I could tell that he was smiling, laughing at me.

"Do not make me say it." The wind chilled my bones. "With you."

"Would you leave with me?" He moved closer. "Would you?" He whispered it into my hair.

"Yes," I whispered back. "Yes."

"Then you must go tomorrow. Leave Salem. Go to Boston and find lodgings. I will follow."

Was he asking me to marry him? He must have been, because it would not be proper for us to travel together otherwise. I would say yes. Though we had known each other but a short time, such brief courtships were commonplace. We had forever to become acquainted. "Why can we not both go now?"

"For us both to leave in the night would excite suspicion, especially since suspicion has already been excited about you."

"What do you mean?"

"The Putnam girl is speaking of you."

I drew in a sharp breath. "How did you . . . ?"

He took my wrists in both his hands and pulled me toward him. "Wait in Boston but a few days, Kendra. I will say I have an urgent matter at home, and I will follow. I *will* follow, and we shall be married there."

It was all I wanted. "Yes, yes. I will."

"But now, the sun is about to rise. Fly only as far as the edge of the woods, then walk home and get into your bed before the Harwoods find you missing."

"Yes." I did as he said. We were to be married! I flew, happily as a lively sparrow, then fairly ran the rest of the way home. But when I reached the Harwoods, men were there, waiting for me. One had a warrant in his hand.

It was as James predicted. I was arrested as a witch within the day of seeing Ann Putnam and Betty Parris in town. I was taken to jail with another woman, an old woman named Martha Corey.

In jail, they stripped us naked and examined our bodies for witches' marks. I felt the jailers' hands groping at me, at my legs, my breasts, taking far too much time and too much pleasure at their task. They searched the pits of my arms, my nostrils, the undersides of my eyelids, every cavity of my body. Every cavity. When they found nothing, they examined me again. But, of course, they found no mark, no scar, no scab. My body was young, and it was perfect. I was a witch, so I made it so.

Martha Corey was not one, and she was old, her skin spotted with age, so the jailers found numerous marks upon her.

"What is this?" they asked her with each new discovery.

"'Tis a mole," she said each time. "You have one yourself. On your cheek. With a hair growing from it."

I wished there was some way I could have removed her marks, made her skin as clear and young as mine, but that in itself would be suspect. She was a tart old woman, though, and seemed little disturbed by what was happening.

Finally, they threw us back into the jail cell. I knew that elsewhere in the jail were others who had been arrested weeks earlier. It must have been near dawn, and we were very briefly alone, lying on a pallet of straw on the cold jailhouse floor.

"Are you frightened?" I asked Martha.

She laughed, a hard laugh. "Why would I be frightened? I am no witch."

I nodded, knowing that to be true.

"There is no such thing as witches," she said.

And I knew that not to be. "Do you think that is a good thing to say?" It seemed to me that that mocked the accusers' beliefs. Much as I enjoyed a good mocking, these people were very serious. To be a woman, and to express strong opinions, caused one to be called a witch. There will always be those who fear women with power, even if the power is merely in our tongues.

Still, it was best to hold mine, and I wished Martha would hold hers.

But she did not. "I do not care," she declared. "I am a pious woman, a God-fearing woman. Would they believe the rantings of children over the word of such a one as me?"

I sighed. "I do not know. Ann Putnam, she is the daughter of Thomas Putnam, a well-regarded citizen."

"A well-regarded fool." Again, she laughed.

I wondered what I would say if questioned. Could I mention seeing Ann speaking with the wolf? It seemed I could not, for she was Putnam's daughter and thus above reproach. Yet I knew that was why she accused me. I had no wish to harm her, none at all. I had no wish to harm anyone.

I looked to the window. It was dimly lit by the full moon, and I wondered if I could turn myself into a bird and fly out of it. But the crossed bars of the windows were close together, too close even for a crow.

The jailer came to the gate of the cell and poked Martha through it with a stick of some sort.

"Ouch!" she said. "What are you doing, young man?"

"Making sure you do not sleep," he said. "If you sleep, you can summon your familiars, and they can work their devil's work."

"Samuel, this is Martha Corey." The old woman's voice was steady, terrifying. "I knew your mother. Would she be proud of what you are doing, if she knew?"

It stopped the jailer for only a second. "Aye. She would be proud that I am doing the Lord's work."

But he left right away with a quickened step.

I stared, again, at the window until I heard Martha snoring. My body ached from the examination. Still, I struggled up on my hands and knees, then to my feet. I crossed toward the window, slowly, quietly, hoping not to alert anyone to my movement. I looked out.

I wanted so much to see James.

And then I heard footsteps behind me. I whirled, expecting a guard.

But it was James there, opening the door with a key. Had he just walked past the jailers? He was entering the cell.

Then I saw in the hallway outside, the jailer, Samuel, frozen in midstep. I knew, somehow, that Martha was frozen too, that everyone in the jailhouse, asleep or waking, was.

I collapsed into James's arms. "Oh, James! James! What should I do?"

"Does she know?" he asked, looking round despite the frozen state. "Do they know what you are?"

"I do not think so. I mean, they call me a witch, but they have no reason. They call Martha that too. They do not know I am different from the others. . . ." I was weeping, so frightened was I feeling. I knew it was improper to touch him so, but I felt like I might fall over if I did not, so I clung to him. "I saw the girl, Ann, in the forest. She was talking to a wolf."

"A wolf." His voice was steady.

"Yes. I think she accused me to make me be still."

"Perhaps. But now what?"

"Might I escape?" I looked out the bars.

"You might," James said, "but if you do, it would be confirmation that you are a witch, that there are witches. It might make things worse."

"Worse than what?" *And for whom?* For if I escaped, I would be gone. "Worse than it is now? Five women have been arrested in a few weeks, all on the hearsay of silly children."

"Oh, Kendra." He squeezed me tight. "I have seen so much worse."

I knew what he meant, the witch burnings in Europe, when hundreds of innocents were killed. And I remembered what he had said about his mother. I did not want that to happen to me. "I am frightened," I said.

"I will not let them burn you, Kendra." He kissed the top of my head. "I will not let them burn you."

"How can you—?"

"I will burn Salem to the ground before I allow that to happen. But you must be strong. You must be strong for me."

I had lived these decades alone, no family, traveling to a strange country. I had been strong for so long, but I was tired. So tired of being strong with no encouragement.

"What do I say when they question me?" I asked.

"Admit to nothing. Implicate no one, not even Ann Putnam. I must go, but I will be back tomorrow."

I nodded. I knew he must go, but I wanted him to stay.

For just an instant, his lips were on mine. They felt soft and warm, and all the terror evaporated from my mind. I was not alone.

When he pulled away, he repeated, "I will burn Salem to the ground before I allow them to harm you."

And then he was gone, but I saw that the jailer remained frozen in his tracks for a moment. Then he walked away in the opposite direction. The sun was soon to rise. I drifted off to sleep.

Ann Putnam
A Month Later

Since the night I made my accusation, my pains have worsened. I am told that Martha Corey and Kendra Hilferty are kept up all night in jail. Father says it is necessary, for all our protection. This means, however, that they are conscious at all times, to trick and torment me. That must be what it is.

Though it is April, there is no spring, only bitter cold. Yet I am up past midnight, sweating in my bed, wondering what new horror will befall me. Does Martha make Satan bring flames upon me? Does Kendra have him blow in a cold wind to chill me just as often? And what will Kendra say to them, when she is questioned? Will they believe her?

Father called me over to see him tonight after the evening meal.

"They will be trying Kendra Hilferty soon," he said. "And

Martha Corey and Rebecca Nurse after that."

"Oh." I nodded, unsure what response was expected.

"These women will not confess to the evils they have committed. They are not like Tituba. Mr. Hathorne and Mr. Corwin have spoken to them. They will insist upon their innocence despite what they have done to you."

Outside, I heard the wind whipping up, flinging the snow up to our window. My father was saying that he knew how tormented I was, that he believed me.

"Martha, especially, will lie. She will say you are a hysterical child—she already has. They will want you to give testimony."

"Give testimony."

"Tell them what these women are doing to you."

"I have to be in court . . . with them?" My mind was whirling, and I felt that they were tormenting me right then and there. My stomach hurt like daggers, and my head was pounding. At first, when I made my accusation, I was looked upon as a heroine, but now I saw the sidelong glances I received in church. Some did not believe me.

But they feared me, which was better.

"Aye. But as long as you say the good Lord's truth, that the women have tormented you, that they rip at your flesh, that you have seen them at your bedside with the devil himself, you will be believed. The other girls will be there too."

"Aye, Father." I did not recall having said anything about seeing the women at my bedside, or seeing the devil, but perhaps I had, when I was in the throes of pain.

"Run along to bed now," Father said.

Hours later, I was still lying there listening to the untroubled breathing of my sisters against the howling wind, the snow pounding at the window. The winter was trying to get in, to invade our house and freeze us all. Then I heard another kind of howling. A wolf.

Was it my wolf?

I stumbled over my sisters to the window and peered outside.

It took me a moment to make the shape out through the snow-covered window, but finally, I saw him. Against the whiteness of snow was a large, white wolf. My wolf, shadowed in the light of the full moon. He raised his head and howled again, as if calling to me.

Although I was barefoot, I grabbed at the first coat I could find, Elizabeth's red cape. I stumbled to the door and went outside.

"Why are you here?" I said. "If Father sees—"

"Your father sees little. It has been days since I have encountered you."

"I am ill. I seldom leave the house."

'Twas true. In the time since my first convulsion, I had been nearly always in bed, forgiven from my chores, for who would expect one as tormented as I to work? Through it all, Mary and Mercy had stayed at my side, feeding me cookies and laying a compress upon my brow. Mercy was charged with much of my work, also.

"Ill, are you?"

"Aye." A cold wind blew through me, and I clutched the cloak more tightly around me. "Father says I will have to give testimony against Martha and Kendra. I do not know what I will say."

"What did your father tell you?" the wolf asked.

"He said to tell the truth." I remembered what else he had said, about seeing them with the devil, but it was the same thing, I supposed. I shivered again, and then the wolf was at my side, rubbing against me, warming me.

"What is the truth?" the wolf asked.

"I have had . . . aches . . . chills. I feel hot and like I cannot breathe."

"And these women, they cause that?"

"Of course!" I said. "Kendra Hilferty, she hates me. She torments

52

me all the time now. I cannot sleep for it."

"And this only just started," the wolf asked. "Have these women not lived in Salem for many years?"

I thought about that, stroking the wolf's soft fur. I tried to think of when I first encountered Kendra Hilferty. She was not from a Salem family, but must have come here seeking work. Still, I had seen her for a year or more in church or in the store, as I had on the day I accused her.

Martha Corey had lived in Salem my entire life. Nay, longer. I had often looked over from gossiping with Mary or trying to discipline my younger siblings and seen her scowl. I tried to avoid her eyes, and I had always a sinking sensation in the pit of my stomach when I saw her. I had thought it to be merely nerves. Now I knew better.

"Martha Corey has long given me chills," I told the wolf.

"And Kendra?" the wolf encouraged. "What will you say about her?"

It was cold, so cold, and my fingers felt stiff with it. I dug them into the wolf's fur, and I remembered. The memory was on the tip of my mind, where it seemed like it had happened to someone else. Yet I knew it was me.

"Once, we were leaving church on a fine summer day. There was a bird singing in the oak tree. I looked up at it and saw that it was a mother mockingbird, sitting on her nest. I bent down to lift up Deliverance, that she could see it more clearly, see the eggs. She was only three then."

"You are a wonderful sister," the wolf said.

"Yes. But as I did this, the bird swooped down on Deliverance and me, squawking and angry, and it made as if to peck at our eyes. It was at this exact moment that I saw Kendra Hilferty, staring at us."

I remembered it now, as though it had just happened. Kendra

stood there, as if frozen when the bird swooped down on us. Then she saw me seeing her, and only then she ran toward me, swinging her arms and yelling at the bird to stop. At the time, I had thought her kind. Now I realized that it was she who had sent the bird to torment me. She had only chased it away to keep others from recognizing her trickery.

"She sent a bird to peck at my sister, to attack me. I know it was her."

"Indeed, she is evil," the wolf said, calmly. "Thank the Lord you were there to protect Deliverance."

"Yes." So many times, I had been impatient or annoyed with Deliverance. If only I had realized that she, like I, had been victimized by a witch. Who knew what she was suffering?

"Yes, you are such a good girl," the wolf said.

And then I remembered other instances, so many other instances, when I had tripped in town and twisted my ankle just as Kendra Hilferty turned the corner, or when I had a headache or heard a bump in the night and knew Martha Corey was behind it. Indeed, I was fortunate to be alive.

I told the wolf all of it, and he walked round and round me, his coat warming me until, finally, I was able to slip into untormented sleep for the first time in a week.

It was Mother who found me in the morning, alone and half frozen in our yard.

"What happened?" she asked, summoning my father to carry me in. "Why are you out here?"

As my father scooped me up in his arms and carried me inside, I whispered, "Witches."

Kendra

Every night since my arrest, I had been tormented, poked, and pecked at with questions, questions about why I tortured children, why I consorted with the devil, and whether I had seen anyone else while I was doing so. To all, I answered simply no. Or I did not know. Another woman had been arrested, added to our cell. Rebecca Nurse was old, at least seventy, an esteemed member of the church, a grandmother. She was not harsh, like Martha, but kind and dear, and when she saw me, she walked over and caressed my cheek, saying, "It will end. The Lord will keep us safe." She said that to me every day. She believed it, believed that if she was good, no evil would come to her. I hoped so. If a woman of such dignity and godliness could be found guilty, what chance was there for someone like me, someone who actually was a witch?

It had rained every night for a week, thunder and lightning, which bothered me even though I could not see the sun. My trial was in a week's time. James visited me every night telling me news of the town.

"It will end," he said last night, as every night. "I believe it will end."

"How can you be so certain after what happened in . . . with your mother?"

"It was . . . different. My mother, she was a good woman, good to me, but one who always lurked about the outskirts of society. The women accused here at first, they were the same, women like Tituba and . . ."

"Me?" The rain pounded upon the roof above.

"Yes. You are a stranger. You are no one's daughter, no one's grandmother. People know little of you. But now they are accusing women like Rebecca Nurse, fine, God-fearing women."

"I am not God-fearing?" I asked.

"Are you?" he asked back with a smile.

I considered it. I knew I was unlikely to die. Therefore, I never feared hell. There were other sorts of hells for me, but not one with a horned man with a pitchfork, not one with flames. Since my parents' deaths, I had not even been sure if God existed, but if he did, he had no dominion over me. That is what it was to have nothing to lose.

"No."

He nodded. "And there is something else," he said. "Mary Warren."

It took me a second to remember who Mary Warren was. There were so many Marys—several among the accused, at least two involved in the accusations, Mary Walcott, who was Ann's cousin, and Mary Warren, who was a servant at John and Elizabeth Proctor's home. She and I had been friends. Or, at least, friendly. And she had been there the day I had spoken to Ann, the day she accused me. "What of Mary Warren?"

"Silly girl. She posted a note at the church, asking for prayers of thanks, that her affliction had ended."

"Ended?"

"She had stopped having fits. She said it was not real."

"She did?" Mary Warren had never been the smartest creature. I was not sure if this statement rather confirmed or contradicted my thinking that.

"Not in so many words," James said.

"In what words then?"

"She said that her visions might have been her imagination. She all but accused the girls of lying."

I saw the flash of a lightning bolt, then after it, the echo of thunder.

All but? "And then what happened?" For I suspected I knew.

"Well . . . ah . . ."

"Tell me." I looked at Rebecca, frozen asleep. I had helped her with the pains of her arthritis that day. My healing powers were of some use here, though sleeping on a feather bed would have done her more good. This madness had to end! I did not care so much for myself. I had time, nothing but time. But I wanted her to be released, to be allowed to return to her family. And Martha too. Of course, Martha.

"The girls accused her of being a witch, and she changed her mind. She said that the Proctors had tricked her into saying that."

"Oh no." It was as I had feared.

"But it made people suspicious. Don't you see?"

"I see that everyone who becomes suspicious gets accused of being a witch themselves."

He sighed and stroked my arm. "Perhaps I should become suspicious then."

Alarmed, I said, "Why would you do that?"

"So I could be here. With you. So you would not have to go through this alone."

"No!" My mind was whirling, spinning in the light of the lightning and rain. I wanted him to be safe, but I knew I could not say that. He was a strong man, a man who would not stay safe at my command, nor at my expense. So, instead, I said, "I need you to be out there, to report back to me."

He nodded. "Just so you know I would do it."

"I know."

He took me in his arms. "I love you." He kissed my neck, my throat. "When this cruelty is over, I want to—"

"Shh." I put my hand to his lips, stopping his words. I knew what he was going to say, that he wanted to marry me. But I did not know if I would ever be free, or even if that was what I wanted. It seemed safer to be alone. There was no one to disappoint.

"I love you too," I said. "But we must not speak of the future. We must only concentrate on the present until this is past."

Still, he kissed me again before he left.

A week passed. Then it was the day of my trial before Judge Hathorne. The weather had gone from being bitterly cold to hot, and as they led me into the meetinghouse, which had been made into a courtroom, I was already sweating. The room was filled with what looked to be half Salem's population. Though it was a Monday and near summer, no one in Salem was planting beans or shoeing a horse or chopping lumber that day. They were all there to see. I was only the second to be tried, and the first had been convicted. I saw Goody Harwood with her daughter and son. She had a basket with her, and I wondered if it was a picnic lunch. In the front row sat Thomas Putnam and his wife, with their oldest boy and Ann. I wanted to wipe the sweat from my brow, but my hands were shackled. I could have done it with magic, but perhaps it was better for me to look as uncomfortable as the others.

The only sounds in the room were my footsteps and the jailer's and the clinking of my chains. All eyes were upon us. I scanned the room for James. I did not see him for a long while, and I thought perhaps he was not there, perhaps he did not wish to see me prosecuted. But then I found him in a corner in the back of the room. I looked away, lest he make some motion, some gesture, some look that would tell people he knew me, tell people that he did not believe I had done it. Any such indication might cause him to be suspected as a wizard.

I did not know what would happen, if I would be led up for questioning or if others would testify against me first. I did not know what I would say, except that I had never harmed Ann or anyone. But the jailer led me to a bench near the front of the room, away from where the Putnams sat. He shoved me down. "Sit!"

I sat. I found I was trembling, though it was so hot.

The jailer pushed me. "Be still, girl!"

I tried, but when I looked around, I realized that no one in the room, save James, was my friend. My friends were the women I rotted with in jail, Martha, who was suspected on Ann's word and because her husband had said she read too many books, and Rebecca. No one would believe me. No one would even care if I was convicted, except for the spectacle of a hanging. Goody Harwood had brought a picnic! I wanted to tremble more, but I summoned my magic to calm me. I breathed. How odd to think that fidgeting and sweating would make me look suspicious when, really, witchcraft was the cure.

In her seat, Ann was trembling too, I noticed.

The judge entered, and everyone stood. I wasn't sure if I was expected to stand, since I had just been ordered to sit. However, the jailer helpfully yanked me up.

"Hear ye! Hear ye!" a man I did not know called as the judge walked down the aisle. "By the will of God, this court is now in order!"

We stood while the judge said a prayer in a booming voice. I felt eyes upon me, perhaps to see if I flinched at the word of God. I did not. When Judge Hathorne finished, the jailer forced me down to sitting again.

"Who is here to witness against this woman?" Judge Hathorne asked.

Thomas Putnam stood. "My daughter, Ann."

"She must approach the bench, then," Judge Hathorne said. "And she must speak for herself."

Ann stood. She looked smaller than when last I had seen her, thinner and paler. I wondered if she had been ill. Or was it the weight of her lies that made her appear so sickly and trembling? I had seen her many times over the year I had lived in Salem, a boisterous girl, full of humor and mischief. I remembered one day when I had seen her lift her younger sister up to look at a bird's nest in a tree. The Ann who walked to the front of the room looked like she could barely have lifted a feather.

As if to confirm this impression, Ann fairly fell into the seat beside the judge. When he spoke, his voice was half as loud, as if he did not wish to frighten her.

"You are here to give testimony in this case?" he asked.

"Aye, sir." Her voice was barely a breath of wind.

"You must speak clearly, girl," he said.

"Aye." Ann said in a proper whisper.

The other man approached her. He carried a Bible and held it before her. He placed her hand upon it. "Do you swear to tell the truth in all matters, so help you, God?"

"Aye," Ann repeated.

The judge addressed her. "You are acquainted with Kendra Hilferty?"

Ann nodded. "Aye."

"You see her here?"

"Aye." She searched for me. I did not know where to look, whether to meet her eyes, try to make her understand I meant her no harm. I would tell no one what I had seen if she would just let me go. In truth, I had already determined to leave Salem if released. It would not be the first time I had fled a place, and it would likely not be the last. But what if, by looking at her, I made people think I had enchanted her? I decided to stare at my hands. They were startlingly light for not having seen sun in months. I stretched out my fingers in my lap. Out of the tops of my eyes, I noticed that Ann did the same.

"What have you to say about her?" the judge asked.

"Oh, your honor," Ann began. "It has been awful. Since Kendra came to this town, I have had so much pain, so much torment at her hands. I do not know why she torments me so."

I stole a glance up at her just as Judge Hathorne asked, "How does she torment you?"

"She clutches at my throat, so that I cannot breathe, and she causes me great pains in my stomach, and—ouch!" She clutched herself as if she felt a great pain. "She is doing it now! She is looking at me, and making me—ouch!" She gripped herself harder.

Judge Hathorne addressed me. "Why do you do this to her?"

"I am doing nothing!" I cried out, spreading my hands to indicate there was nothing there.

"I am doing nothing!" Ann cried out after me, also spreading her hands.

"Do not do that!" I cried, clenching my fists.

"Do not do that!" Ann cried, clenching hers.

Was she trying to pretend I controlled her movements? Truly? All eyes were upon me now, and I was near tears.

"Ann, please! I bear you no ill will."

"Ann, please! I bear you no ill will." As she said it, we both held out our hands, pleading.

"How are you controlling her?" Judge Hathorne asked. "What devilment are you using on her?"

"None! None!" I gasped. Sweat poured from my forehead and soaked through my dress.

"None! None!" Ann's voice was a pale echo of my own.

I was silent then, shaking, and so was Ann. I was not controlling her movements, but, I realized, I *could*, if she wished to play at that game.

I stared at her, suddenly feeling cool and calm.

She stared back.

My witchcraft was my friend, my only friend. I could summon it to help me. I would. I did.

Suddenly Ann burst out, saying, "I am a liar!"

I said nothing. I looked, as anyone in that situation would, surprised.

"What?" Judge Hathorne asked.

"I am a liar!" Ann repeated. "My accusations are lies. I am pretending at my affliction. I am a scared little girl who—"

She stopped, midsentence. I had meant to have her say that she consorted with familiars, that she ran with wolves, that she was afraid I would tell on her, but it was as if someone held an invisible hand over her mouth. I saw her lips trying to move, but they did not. She breathed frantically through her nostrils, loudly enough for me to hear in my seat.

"What is wrong with her?" Judge Hathorne asked everyone, the court at large, me.

I shook my head. "I am doing nothing." I knew someone else, someone not me, held her under an enchantment. I looked to James. By his shocked face, he let me know he had no hand in it. I believed him. My gaze darted around the courtroom, searching for another witch. They fell upon the Putnams in the front row of seats.

Goodwife Putnam bounced in her chair, as if she might run up to save her daughter at any moment. Thomas Putnam was silent, deep in concentration. His wife commenced to screaming, "She is ill! Your honor, she is ill! This woman, this witch, has made her so!"

Before the court, Ann was still struggling, tearing at her mouth.

"We must stop the trial!" Goodwife Putnam shrieked. "She cannot breathe! I beg you!"

Thomas Putnam said nothing. He shook his head.

At that moment, Ann passed out. Was it from loss of breath? Or a spell?

Thomas Putnam ran toward her only then. He shook his fist at me. "Why have you done this to her, Kendra Hilferty?"

His eyes met mine, and I found my voice. "I have done nothing to her. Why would I, when she was on the verge of admitting her deceit, that her affliction was merely a pretense? She is a scared child who should go home and work on her sewing. She should not be here at court."

"Order!" Judge Hathorne yelled. "Order!" He looked down at Ann, who lay as if dead on the floor. Goodwife Putnam knelt over her.

"Let me take her home," Goodwife Putnam pleaded.

Judge Hathorne nodded. "The witness cannot testify. We will reconvene on Wednesday." He nodded at the jailer. "Take the accused back to jail!"

What had I done?

Ann Putnam
Later That Day

My father brought his wagon from the farm to carry me home, for I could not walk from the shock of it. My brother, Tom, drove, while Father sat beside me and Mother cradled me in her arms. "Will this never end?" I moaned.

"It will end when they are hanged," my mother assured me, stroking my brow.

My head ached. All these weeks, I had thought Kendra was torturing me, thought Kendra controlled me. But today, today was something different. Today, something had made the words spring from my lips. That something was magic. Real magic.

"I cannot go back there," I said. "I cannot see her. I will surely die if I do."

Suddenly the wolf was there, I knew not how, sitting beside me in broad daylight. I glanced around, to see if the others saw him. But they did not seem to. My mother still fawned over me. Tom looked straight ahead, and my father, I could not see him at all. It was as if he was not there.

"You must go back," the wolf said. "Everyone will believe you a fraud if you do not."

"Perhaps I am a fraud." My head lolled on my mother's lap. "I only wanted to be a good girl, to have everyone know that I am a good girl. Is that vanity?"

"No." The wolf's white fur and silver eyes looked so strange against the summer trees. "It is nothing but the truth. You are a good girl."

"But I lied. I lied about Kendra. I did not want people to know of my sinful ways, that I spoke to you. And now I am caught. I said in front of everyone that I lied."

Could my family not hear me? Could they not see the wolf?

"That was her witchcraft that made you say that," the wolf said. "You would be able to testify . . . about the others? Martha and Rebecca?"

I thought about it, though my head ached from when I hit it in my fall. I was now certain Kendra was a witch, that she had been the one controlling my actions, making me confess to what I'd done. Yet it was her I did not want to confront, did not want to testify against. To see Martha or any of the others in court did not frighten me. They were silly old women. Kendra was the one who terrified me, for she, like the wolf, saw me for what I truly was. A liar.

"Yes," I said. "Yes."

"Then I will take care of Kendra," the wolf said.

I nodded, half closing my eyes. When I next opened them, the wolf was gone, and my father again sat in his place.

Our carriage trundled home. The woods were ahead, cold, dark, though it was June, the overhanging tree branches creating shadows that reached out to me, scratched at my arms, and tried to grab me. I cringed against my mother's skirts.

Kendra
That Night

"What did she say then?" Rebecca asked yet again in the darkness of our cell.

"She said that I tortured her, gave her pains in her stomach. And then she pretended that I controlled her actions, that she could only repeat what I said." I left out the fact of my actually controlling her actions. I had no idea what the impact of that stupidity on my part would be.

"The poor child," Rebecca said. "The poor child is ill."

Martha let out her breath in an annoyed scoff. "The poor child is evil. You know that she, of all of them, has reason to lie. The Parris girl is young and stupid, but she—"

"Martha . . ." Rebecca glanced at me.

"'Tis true. Her father has a quarrel with your family, and he has a quarrel with Giles."

I had heard this before. Giles Corey was Martha's husband, and he and Thomas Putnam apparently had a feud of long standing.

"That is why we are here on the accusation of his daughter," Martha said. "He has given her the idea, as surely as if he controlled her lips."

Rebecca sighed. "The good Lord will save us."

"He had better hurry," Martha said.

"If he does not save us in this life," Rebecca said, "He will save us in the next."

I envied her this certainty, this knowledge that she was good and would go to heaven. All the women here in jail seemed to have it, all except me.

They continued talking like this, as they did every night, until they drifted off to sleep.

I remained awake. It was strange that Samuel did not walk by to look in on us or to wake the women up, stranger still that James was not there. I had expected him to come, to talk of what had happened in court, to comfort me in my stupidity or to chastise me for not following his advice.

Then he was there in my cell with me. He held a brick in his hand. Before I could speak, he heaved it at the barred window. The bars smashed to pieces. With a wave of his hand, he was gone.

I looked down. No, not gone. Transformed into a crow. He flew up to the window and stared at me until I, too, became my bird self and flew up to the windowsill, then flew down to the ground.

Once there, we transformed back, and I followed James around the side of the jailhouse building. There was a carriage waiting. "Go!" James whispered.

"What do you mean, go?" I asked.

"You are escaping."

I peered inside the carriage. Two men were inside, John Alden and Phillip English. I knew they had also been accused. How had

67

they escaped? Were they also true wizards?

"I do not understand," I said. "Escaping? Just like that?"

"I had a thought you might be found innocent. But now . . . I do not think anyone will be." James nodded toward the men. "These men have been planning their escape. I found out about it. You must go with them."

"But I . . ." It was insane that I was protesting. I wanted to escape. But I wanted to escape with James, to flee with him, go back home to Europe, where we could be together and pretend there was no danger. Before, I had had no reason to stay in Salem. Now, with his nightly visits and his comfort, I had no reason to be anywhere else either.

"You must go," he repeated.

"But . . . will I see you again?" I wanted to know whether we would still meet as planned.

"Shh. We have eternity. Of course you will see me again. Of course you will, when this is over, when it is safe for me to leave, I will find you. But now they will only take you. Go. We will meet in a week and make our plans." He broke away from me and gestured toward the carriage.

I walked toward it. Mr. Alden beckoned to me to get in, quickly. With one look back at James, I did.

He shut the carriage door behind me. The carriage pulled away.

I stared at him out the window until I could no longer see him. As we reached the edge of town, I noticed an animal following the carriage, watching us. A wolf. A white wolf. Ann's wolf. I watched it through tear-filled eyes until I could barely see it. Then, perhaps it was the moon or maybe my eyes were playing tricks on me, I saw him transform into a man.

It was Thomas Putnam. He watched us drive away.

* * *

We escaped to Duxborough, where John Alden had friends who would shelter us. I waited for James for a week, then two. When he did not come, I booked passage to Europe, to a new life.

I did not see James again for over a hundred years.

Ann Putnam
August 26, 1706

Every one of Tituba's prophecies came true. In 1699, both my parents left me. Or, rather, my mother died. I was never certain what happened to my father. It was said he died. There are those who said he was too mean to die, though, and I believed this to be true. I believed he might still have continued to walk the earth somewhere. I took care of my younger siblings. I never married. I was an old maid, just as Tituba said I would be.

When I looked back on the events of 1692, I felt nothing but shame and regret. My pains subsided some—perhaps they were cramps from my first blood, perhaps a nervous condition, perhaps both, but I never fully got over them, even after so many were hanged. In all, twenty people were executed in Salem, many on my testimony. Rebecca Nurse and Martha Corey, good, churchgoing women whom my father disliked, were among the first. This may have been why no one ever married me. While most said they believed me, in truth, many did not. Or they were not sure. I frightened them.

I did not blame them. I was not certain if I believed myself. The deaths of those women haunted me, haunted me every night, and every winter after that, I saw the wolf, but I ignored him. He had led me astray. I believed the wolf was sent by Satan to beguile me. Maybe the wolf was Satan himself.

It was because of this that, yesterday, I went to church and read my confession. I apologized to the families of those who died, but I could not make it right. I could not make it right. I could not bring back the women who died because of me. And I could not bring back the goodness that was within me before I spoke to the wolf, before I lied.

May God have mercy upon my soul.

Kendra Speaks

After I left Salem, I journeyed back to England, the place of my birth. I had made some enemies in England, based upon a certain incident with a gingerbread house, but presumably, many of those people were dead. One of the grand things about being a witch is the ability to outlive one's enemies. Many decades—nay, centuries—hence, I would search the online Find a Grave site for members of the Nurse and Corey family, to pay my respects. But in the seventeenth century, I stayed in England a year, then moved next to France, taking a scenic, circuitous route and looking, always, for James.

I did not find him.

I later found out that, after I left, he was arrested in Salem. He was tried, and he was hanged. I know he did not die, though. I did not know where or how he went.

I tried not to wonder if he looked for me.

But, in Paris, I found Charles Perrault, a writer. I told him the story of Ann and the wolf, and he adapted it into a story of his own about *Le Petit Chaperon Rouge*, a young woman with a red cape. In his version, however, the saucy maid gets eaten alive!

In 1744, I was banished from France (an incident involving a princess and a pea—don't ask!) and moved again, to Germany. The Germans had finished hunting for witches by then, so it was a nice place to live at that point. I chose Bavaria, where I opened a bookstall at the Viktualienmarkt. I developed quite a following as a storyteller in my own right, so much so that by the nineteenth century, some brother professors came all the way from Göttingen to fanboy in my presence and hear my stories. Many of my exploits (including the one you are about to hear of, involving my assistant, a strange, short young man with rather specialized abilities) would serve as the inspiration for later works of the Brothers Grimm.

But I never did find James, though I searched for his face in every customer, every new fishmonger, every delivery boy. I never saw eyes as blue as his.

One day, late in the eighteenth century, I had walked into a stall in a far corner of the market. It was an odd stall, one I had not noticed before. While most of the sellers there sold something in particular, something people would want, this stall was called Krimskrams, or "Bits and Pieces," and was more likely to contain a broken doll's head, a stake said to have belonged to Vlad the Impaler, or a petrified mouse than ordinary household items like thimbles or bed warmers.

So, of course, it fascinated me. What need had I for the ordinary?

It was there, tucked beneath a bone saw, behind a working flea circus, that I found my mirror.

It was a grand mirror, sterling silver and larger than my head, with ornamental curlicues and sculpted flowers—roses and chrysan-themums. In its tarnished state, you could not detect it, but I knew that polished, it would be fit for a queen.

I found the shopkeeper, an old man with a sort of hump, and asked how much it was.

He quoted a price many times what I felt its value should be.

"Oh, that is too much," I said, nestling it back into place, think-ing that, now that I had seen it, I could conjure one of my own.

"What you do not understand, *Fräulein*, is that it is a magic mirror."

"Oh, a magic mirror! Well, that's different." I laughed, recalling the lad I knew who had sold his cow in exchange for some "magic" beans in a similar flea-market situation.

"It is true. With it, you can see whomever you wish, wherever he may be."

Oh, wait. The beans in Jack's story *had* been magic. I found myself bouncing, inadvertently, on the tips of my new shoes, which were made of black satin with Italian heels. If it was truly a magic mirror, perhaps I could use it to find James at last.

I pushed from my mind the idea that he might not be alive. He must be alive. I could see him, finally!

I drew in my breath, seeing my face in the glass. The girl there was smiling, appearing more excited than I had ever seen her before. "May I try it?" I asked.

The old man grinned, revealing a tooth of gold. "Certainly. Just ask for who you want."

I stared into it, hesitating before saying, "I want to see James Brandon."

And suddenly he was there. He was there! He was on a battle-field, I could not tell where, but it was hot, and he wiped the sweat from his brow.

74

But oh! He was so handsome, still. The style of his auburn hair had changed a bit, and he wore a blue uniform and carried a long rifle. He also had a cocked hat (what we later called a tricorne), all of which showed him off so much better than the dour black doublets and frilly collars in which I had seen him last. He had also grown a mustache, but I would have recognized him anywhere for his eyes, which were as blue as the Danube River.

I stared for too long, yet not long enough, before asking, "Is it . . . can I use it to find someone? Is there a way to know where the person is?"

The old man's gold tooth really got a thrill out of that one. "Ah, we are searching for a lost love?"

"Something like that." Exactly like that. I felt my throat tighten with the tears at seeing him again.

But the old man shook his head. "No way to tell, unless he says so in conversation."

"I . . . can hear him speak?"

"Yes," the peddler said, "if he is speaking. Ask to see someone else and check."

"I wish to see my assistant," I said, much as I hated not to see James.

Immediately, the picture switched to my assistant, who was helping a customer. "Yes, we have Goethe's poems right here," he was saying.

"I'll take it," I told the old man, knowing I would pay any price. "And do not wrap it up."

As soon as I left the stall, I told the mirror, "Let me see James." I stared at him all afternoon, but he did not reveal his whereabouts.

Every spare moment, I looked at James, overheard his conversations, which made me feel guilty for spying, but not *that* guilty, for I had to find him.

I felt even less guilty when I heard this conversation, in a barrack (the language James was speaking was English, so that narrowed his whereabouts down, at least somewhat).

"D'ya ever plan to marry, James?" a man, one of his friends, asked him.

James shook his head, sadly. "There was a girl a long time ago, so long it seems another lifetime."

His friend laughed. "Yes, another lifetime. What is your age—maybe twenty?"

"Well, it *seems* like a long time," James said. "Anyway, I loved her, and she went away. I told her we would find each other again, but I'm afraid I've lost her."

His friend slapped his shoulder and pretended to weep, but I knew he'd meant me. I had to find him.

I tried for years, but to no avail. I could see him, but I could not talk to him, and he was always on some battlefield somewhere. If only Google had existed, I could have narrowed down his whereabouts, researched his uniform. But no. It was no better than a photograph, but it was better than nothing.

In the meantime, I discovered some interesting things about that mirror, one of them being that I could reproduce it, make a second one with a sort of copying spell, and the duplicate had the same powers as the original. This realization made me a bit angry, for I realized the seller had charged a great deal for what might well have been a duplicate. Still, it was useful, for it meant I could give a mirror to someone I wished to be able to see me—while still keeping one for myself. In this way, we could communicate, like a sort of nineteenth-century smartphone.

I used it to help a girl, Cornelia, whose story is included below.

1

Wheels
Bavaria, 1812
Cornelia

For seventeen years, my life was like the Isar River, which flowed past our mill, beautiful but all too consistent, always the same, lapping gently against rocks worn down by time. My sisters told me of the ocean, which rolled and churned, changing by the second, sometimes leaping up to take them by surprise, but my life had no surprises. My life was like the river, dependable and dull. Until it wasn't. And then I wished it was.

There was once a girl with a very big problem. Well, two very big problems, only one of which was her inability to spin straw into gold.

Allow me to begin at the beginning, for I know this story far better than I would like to. It is the story of a poor miller's daughter who found love—or something like it—with a handsome student who was not what he seemed, and she was never the same again.

No, indeed, she was forever altered. I know it is so for that girl was me.

Is me, for I am still alive and I am still on the horns of a dilemma, which is appropriate because my name, Cornelia, means "horn."

I met him at the marketplace. It was a fine April day.

I generally took my time at shopping. I lived alone with my father. Mama was dead, and my older sisters and brother had long since married and moved out. I was seventeen, not yet a wife, so it was I who bore the brunt of all the housekeeping and chores, the cooking and baking, which I quite enjoyed, and the cleaning and laundry, which I did not. Monday, I washed the clothes. Tuesday, I baked bread and cookies and churned butter. Wednesday, I swept the house from top to bottom (or, rather, bottom to top, for I did not want to track dirt back in). But Thursday—oh, Thursday—I got to go to the marketplace. I went every Thursday unless it poured. It was one of the few opportunities for something approaching fun. So I dawdled, watching the children at the maypole in the entrance, smelling the aroma of strudel and the odor of fish, gazing at the flowers, trying on the lavish fabrics in the fabric seller's stall (it was on Fridays that I sewed), and imagining I had someplace to wear the peacock-blue satin that brought out my eyes or the royal purple velvet, imagining also that I might go to a grand ball at the palace, which I often walked past, just to look, or even a dance at church. But my favorite stall was the bookseller's, for though my late mother had taught me to read, my father viewed books as frivolous. We had few at home, and those we did have, I hid in the cupboards or under pillows to read after I finished my chores. At that stall the stories curled around me as surely as the satins and velvets, and I always stayed until the bookseller chased me off.

The bookseller was a strange lady, seeming at once young and old, dressed in costumes of black lace, periwinkle tulle, or once, green leather, like a fairy princess, a witch, and a dragon, all rolled into one. Sometimes, she allowed me to dawdle among the tables for an hour or more, reading the mythology of Greece, the plays of England, the history of the entire world, or the fairy tales of my own country. Other days, she asked me if I had any money and chased me away when I admitted I had none.

On the day I met Karl, she was nowhere to be found, and there were few customers. I was reading a book about European history, taking particular interest in the fall of the French monarchy, which had happened some twenty years earlier, when I felt eyes staring at me.

I looked up.

"Is that an interesting book?" someone asked.

It took me a moment to see the man. Even though I looked toward him, he was rather short, no taller than I was, so initially, I looked above his head. But finally, my eyes met another pair, close set and gray as cobblestones. I started, then recognized the bookseller's employee, a young man my own age, but, like the bookseller, with a countenance which seemed beyond his years. I had seen him before. I always smiled at him when I came in, and he hovered nearby, likely in an attempt to intimidate me so I would not tarry too long over the books (it worked!), but we had never before spoken.

I said, "I will put it away. I know I have stayed too long."

"No." He shook his head, his brow furrowed. He carried a broom and swept a bit of imaginary dirt out of the way. "I didn't mean that at all. I like to see you . . . I mean. . . I like to see *people* enjoy the books. I mean, so few young ladies read. I mean . . . I do not know what I mean." He stopped, flustered.

"It would be better if I could buy them but, alas, I have no money. I have been saving my pennies each week, but I haven't enough yet." I would not have enough for a year. "The bookseller is inclined to chase me off."

"Not today. She went off to run errands." He grinned. "She will not be back for half an hour, at least. *I* will not chase you off."

It was too much to hope for. I hugged the book to my chest, then held it out, lest I harm its spine. "You are so lucky to work here." I wished I was a boy and could have a job at the market.

He seemed surprised but then nodded. "Why, yes. I'm not used to thinking of myself as lucky, but I suppose I am. I have read most of these books." He flung his arm out, encompassing the little stall, and seemed very proud. "And hundreds more."

I nodded, wanting to get back to my own reading. "Lucky."

"Sometimes, when it rains and there are few customers, I read all day. Kendra—that's the proprietress—says it is good to be familiar with the merchandise. I mean to read them all, and I hope to have a stall of my own someday." He walked closer, adjusting his glasses, which had slipped to the tip of his nose. "Which book will you buy, when you have enough money?"

I nodded toward the one in my hand. "This one."

"Why do you like that book so much?"

"Because nothing ever happens in my life. It is the same, week after week. So I like to read about more interesting people." I inhaled the scent of the book. It smelled of other places.

He glanced at the title. "People like Marie Antoinette?" His teeth were a bit crooked. He pretend-swept again.

"Why, yes. Her life was so much more glamorous than mine."

"It didn't turn out so well."

I shrugged. "And that makes me feel better about my own life."

"Ah, schadenfreude! The best reason for reading!"

I laughed. "I like happy stories too. There just aren't very many in history."

He had a funny face, with a nose that turned first up, then down, and cheekbones that were high and sharp. "Well, you know what they say—history is written by the winners."

"That is why we have fairy tales as well."

He glanced over to the fairy-tale books across the way. "Which do you like better?"

"Histories," I admitted. "I like sad stories."

He squinted his eyes, as if trying to think of a way to extend the conversation. Now I rather hoped he would. No one was ever interested in what I had to say. But suddenly he looked down, finding an actual bit of dirt on the ground. "I should leave you to your reading. Will you . . . be here a while?"

I glanced outside. The sun was low in the sky, and I knew I needed to do my shopping. I wanted to stay, though, and regretted the time I had spent at the milliner's. I could not afford a new bonnet or a book, but at least I could read the book at the stall. "I have to go too. But I'll be back next week."

He smiled, and though his bottom teeth were crooked, it was a kind smile. "I will look forward to it. Perhaps . . ." He stopped, sweeping.

"What?"

"Perhaps you will let me talk to you again?"

"Perhaps I will." I handed him the book.

I left the store, grinning, then rushed through the market. I visited the butcher's and the fishmonger's stalls in rapid succession and was halfway through the greengrocer's when I heard a voice above my head.

"Excuse me, miss? Can you help me?"

At first, I did not realize he spoke to me. No one ever did, other than to tell me to move on. The conversation with the bookseller's assistant was the longest I had had in a year with anyone who wasn't Father. Even Father didn't talk much.

Only when the voice repeated itself did I look up.

"I am sorry. I didn't realize you were speaking to me."

"No, it is I who am sorry. Perhaps I was rude to interrupt you."

"Oh, no." I looked up.

Up was where I had to look to see this young man. He was very tall, and when I beheld his face, I almost had to suppress a gasp, for he was beautiful, the most beautiful man I had ever seen. He reminded me of nothing more than the sun, for his face, his smile, his eyes of blue, all framed by curls the color of chestnuts, warmed me, warmed my face, my body, my heart.

"Oh . . . no . . . ," I stammered again, unable to form any longer words. Did I know any words?

He looked away. "I know it is wrong to address a young lady without a proper introduction, but I cannot ask the greengrocer for any more help. I have asked him twenty times already, but I need aid in selecting these pears."

He pointed to a bin of pears. They were in season, large and golden green with barely a hint of red.

"Pears . . . you . . . my help?" I would have helped him with horse dung, had he asked, but it was strange that he asked for my help with pears.

"I am here shopping on my own," he explained, "and I do not know much about selecting fruit. These pears, for example. How do I choose some that will not turn to mush in a day?" As I looked closer, I realized he was not a man at all, or barely. He might have been my own age.

"It depends," I said when I could next breathe. I wished I had worn a newer dress. "Are you going to eat them right away, or is your wife making a pie?"

He smiled a bit ruefully. "Alas, there is no wife. It is only me, a poor student, buying them to eat in my lonely room."

I looked around, adjusting my blond curls as I did. The greengrocer did not appear busy, truth be told. In fact, he was examining the young man almost as closely as I was, very likely staring at his cloak, which was fine looking, for a poor student's cloak. In fact, I shivered as it brushed against me.

"Of course I can help you. I was just . . ." wondering if you had a wife. "Here."

I reached into the bin and seized one golden pear. "This one, for example, has a good color, but it has been picked too early." Never an authority on fruit, I waxed rhapsodic on the subject, trying to impress the handsome stranger.

"How can you tell?"

"It's hard like a rock. Poke it."

He reached out to touch it and, as he did, his hand brushed mine. His was soft, so soft, as if it had done not a bit of work. I folded my own fingers inward, that he would not notice the calluses from my Tuesday churnings. How could a man's hand be so soft?

"Do you feel how it has no give at all?" I asked him.

He nodded in earnest, as if he found the subject fascinating. "I do."

I groped around in the remaining pears until I found one perfect, red-gold one. "Now try this one."

He did and, again, his hand brushed mine. This time, I was ready for him, with the pear held in my softer left hand.

"Feel how it has just a bit of give?" I asked.

"Yes." His eyes met mine as he touched it. "Lovely."

I gazed at him. "Perfect." He had such long lashes I almost gasped.

The greengrocer came upon us. "Can I help you? Miss?" His eyes held a question, for I never talked to anyone.

"Oh no, I am fine. I was just helping this gentleman."

I placed the pear inside the basket he carried and looked at him. "Do you want more?"

"As many as you care to find me."

I could have stood there all day, but I did not believe he wanted a bushel, so I helped him—slowly—to select five more. "I always choose one that is fully ripe," I told him. "That is for the walk home."

He smiled at me, his blue eyes crinkling at the corners, and said, "Splendid idea. But select two of those."

I laughed. "You must be very hungry."

He laughed in return. "Something like that."

So I helped him select two pears that were a bit riper, that lightly caved in at my touch, and I tried not to notice how my heart caved in at his glance and at the thought of him leaving, going off in one direction while I traveled in another.

He stayed with me while I selected my own meager groceries. I had no money for treats like pears, but I bought beans and potatoes, boring things, and counted my coins to afford those. There would be no penny for my book fund today.

When we left the stall, again slowly, he pulled one pear, then another, from the bag. "For the walk home." He held out the larger one to me.

"Oh, I couldn't. I wouldn't."

"Nonsense. It is only a pear. Think of it as payment for the help you have given me."

I thought I had not helped him at all. Anyone could tell when a piece of fruit was ripe or rotten.

And that is when I realized, yes, anyone could. I looked up at his handsome, smiling face. Anyone could. He could. He had asked for help because he wanted to talk to me.

This was quite a turn of events.

"Of course." I plucked the fruit from his hand. "I was rude. I would very much enjoy a pear."

This was true. It had been a long time since I had had one, but the young man tempted me more. Where was he from? Why had I never seen him before? I knew all the young men around here. They were all dull. Someday, I would marry one of them and have dull babies who would grow to adulthood and have dull babies of their own. But I had not yet singled out the one—nor had one singled me out. I would have noticed this young man, had he been there. He was anything but dull.

"Thank you." I sniffed the pear's aroma. "For the pear."

His teeth were straight and white like the fence posts in front of the church. "Thank you again for your kind guidance. Might I walk you home?"

I hesitated just long enough to appear demure.

"It is darkening," he said, unnecessarily. "I have kept you too long. I would blame myself if you got lost or . . . worse."

I knew I would not get lost on the path I had taken hundreds of times. Still, it was not an effort to lie. This was not an instance where I wished to appear competent. No, I needed to be fragile like a delicate wildflower, ill suited to walking alone at dusk.

"All right," I said.

"Allow me to take your bags as well."

I handed over my satchel, and again, his skin touched mine. The moon was visible, a crescent moon like a frog's eye, peeking out of the murky water. At first, there were sounds of the closing market, merchants and boxes, children and chickens. Then they all faded into the distance and there were only our footsteps and the music of the twilight, a breeze, crickets, and nothing else save my own breath.

And his voice.

"I don't . . . I don't suppose you'll tell me your name."

"Cornelia," I said before I wondered if it was improper to introduce myself to a stranger. Probably no less proper than walking with one. I had waded into the river. I might as well swim.

"And you?"

It took him a second to answer, but finally, he said, "Karl," and at that moment, the moonlight streamed through the trees, and I saw his smile. "Do you come to town often?"

"Only on Thursdays, to market, and Sundays, for church. Other days, I'm too busy. My father runs the mill, and since I am the only daughter left at home, all the housework falls to me, the cooking and cleaning and caring for the animals."

I stopped. I was talking too much. I sounded like a drudge. Why did I think he would be interested in my work? What man would be? Certainly not a man as handsome as this one. Maybe someone seeking a good scullery maid.

Or a wife.

"I am sorry to be so dull."

He laughed. "You're not dull. I like to hear what other people do."

"Other people?" A breeze riffled across my arms, and I shivered.

"People who aren't me. What of your mother? Does she not help with the chores?"

"No. She died when I was little."

"Ah, that is something we have in common then. My mother is also gone. She died when I was a baby. I do not remember her."

I felt a stab of pity for him. I yearned to take his hand, not merely because he was so handsome (I told myself) but because I genuinely sympathized with the poor, motherless boy he had been. Instead, I said, "I am sorry. My mother and I, we were great friends. I cannot imagine growing up without her, even though I did not have her long."

"What was she like?" Karl paused in his walking and looked at me. I thought I should keep going, should get home, and yet I wanted to stop. It had been so long since I had talked to anyone, at least about anything, except to Father, about whether we needed more

86

chicken feed, or to my sister, asking if I could watch her baby for the day. Karl seemed actually interested in hearing me. But perhaps he was merely being polite.

But why would such a beautiful young man even be polite to me?

"Mama." I pictured her, in her bed, the feather pillow atop her face to block the noise and light. "She was always sickly. I never remember her being well. I suppose I should not complain about the work, for my sisters had all the work before me, and they had to care for me. And care for her."

"They are gone now, married?"

"Yes. Sometimes, when they were out at market, and Mama and I were alone, I would crawl into bed beside her, and she would sing to me. She also taught me how to read."

"You can read?" He sounded surprised.

"Yes. Can you not?"

"Of course I can. But I'm . . ." He hesitated, and I heard his unspoken words. *I'm a man. You're a girl.* But he said, "I'm a student. I do little other than read. I would think you would not have time to read."

"Father says I do not. But Mama taught me, for it was the one thing we shared, and now I read every night to remember her. I only own two books, but one of them is the Bible, so it takes a long while to read."

He smiled. "And what is the other?"

I felt my face get warm, and I looked away. "You will think it silly."

"Try me."

"It is called *Exciting Stories*, and it is a book of stories that are . . . well . . ."

"Exciting?"

"Exactly," I whispered. "I know it sounds like a waste of time, but nothing exciting has ever happened to me." *Until today.* "Each day has been exactly like the one before, except when Mama died, which was bad, or when my sisters married, which was good for them but merely a big party and a lot of work for me. And then more work when they left."

He nodded. "I understand. Nothing very exciting happens in my life either." He drew in a deep breath.

"But how is that possible? You're a student." I did not know what students did, exactly, having never been to school. But I had seen the group of buildings, the university, and I pictured young men, all learning from books and from one another, and then going out into the world to accomplish things and lead lives that had nothing to do with mine.

"Yes." He nodded. "I know I am lucky, but like you, I do the same things all day, and they are exactly what someone else—everyone else—expects of me. I have started to go to the market and talk to people, just so I can see how they live."

I nodded, understanding. I wanted so much to touch him but, of course, I didn't. Still, he was so near I could almost feel the warmth of him, anyway, could almost imagine how his hand would feel, clasped in mine.

I could not give in to it. In fact, I had to get home. It was dark, long past the time when Father would be expecting dinner. I had put soup on the fire. Still, he would wonder and disapprove.

"We should walk," I said.

"Of course. But I like talking to you. Can you keep talking? Maybe tell me one of the stories from that book. Is there one you know by heart?"

"Of course. I know all of them by heart." I began to walk, though slowly. "I have read them so many times."

"Then please?"

I thought about which one to tell, and finally, I settled on one about a sailor who fell in love with a mermaid.

"There once was a sailor who was very lonely out at sea. The other sailors had loves at home, but he didn't, so he would sing sad songs all his days. Then, one day, he saw a mermaid on the rocks. She also sang a sad song, and soon, they sang together. They fell in love, but of course, they could not be together, for she had to live underwater while he could only breathe air.

"The sailor was very sad, even sadder than he had been before. Now that he had known love, he could not live without it. So one night, he tied an anchor to his leg and plunged into the ocean. The mermaid saw him, and she rescued him. She dragged him down to her watery kingdom where they lived happily, under the sea."

We were close to home when I finished. I could hear the Isar, lovely and cold, a bit like the ocean with the mermaid. I looked down, afraid he would think my tale too simple. But he said, "That was lovely. It has been a long time since anyone has told me a story like that."

"But you read all day."

"Only boring history, stories of kings and queens."

"Kings and queens are fascinating. I would love to be a queen."

"You think you would, but kings and queens accomplish little. They are born to their position and have little power and less sense."

I did not think this true, but I said, "But you must read about military leaders too, people who accomplish a great deal. I was reading a book today at the bookseller's, a history book. It was so fascinating I wished I could have it."

"Yes. I like those books better. Most people don't." He looked down at me. "You are a very smart young woman."

"I love to read history, all the things that happened to other people, better people than myself."

"Did you think your story was happy, or sad?" he asked. "The one you told me?"

"Mama thought it was happy, but I was never sure. I didn't know if the sailor was magically able to breathe underwater, or if he died."

"Exactly. Perhaps that was why he could breathe, because he was in heaven."

"I have thought about it a great deal, and I think it is happy either way. If he lived, they were happily frolicking under the ocean, and if he died, he didn't know any better."

"A poet said ignorance is bliss." His hand brushed mine as he said it, his soft, soft hand.

We had reached the clearing by my house, and I stopped walking again. I could not take him closer. I didn't know the poet to whom he referred, but I knew what he meant, *ignorance is bliss.* It meant one could be happier not knowing the truth.

"Yes, bliss," I said. "You cannot come closer. My father can't know a man walked me home."

I held my breath. If I was quiet, I could almost hear the animals in the barn, awaiting their feeding. My father would be angry that I was so late.

Was it all a dream? Had I jumped into the ocean myself?

"Cornelia?" Karl touched my arm. It was just a brush, like a breeze through the autumn leaves, but it brought me back to reality.

"Yes?"

"Can I see you again?"

I so wanted to.

"Only on Thursday. That is the day I go out to market."

"What time do you go? Can we meet early so we can spend the day together?"

"Yes." The moment was so beautiful, the river in the distance and his handsome face before me. "I spend the day there. We could meet at the bookseller's stall."

"Cornelia!" The voice was unmistakably my father's. He said something else I couldn't make out, but he sounded annoyed.

"I have to go."

"I will be there at noon," Karl said.

"Cornelia! Is that you?" My father again.

"Coming, Father!" To Karl, I said, "I have to go." I started to walk away.

He grabbed my hand up in his. "Wait!"

And then he pressed it to his lips. They were so warm and even softer than his hands. He rubbed my fingers against them, warming them.

Finally, he released my hand.

I ran to the house, where my father scolded me for dawdling, scolded me for being a silly girl, scolded me for the stew that had gone dry and burned on the bottom. But I did not hear half of it nor did I care. I was going to see him again! He had kissed my hand! It was my first kiss, but I did not mean for it to be my last.

But the next morning, I woke wondering if I had imagined the whole thing. It was insane, someone finding me like that, someone so beautiful. There was no way to prove it had happened, either, no brand upon my skin where his lips had grazed it. I mended Father's pants, my Friday chore, and cleaned the chicken coop, all the while searching for evidence, but I had none, not even a pear, for I had eaten that. Love was invisible, intangible. Maybe it wasn't real.

Yet when I returned from the chickens, I found upon the doorstep a package, wrapped in brown paper, tied with a red ribbon. My name was written neatly in an unfamiliar hand.

I opened it. It was a book. *The* book, *The Complete History of Europe*. I ran outside to look for whoever had brought it. There was no one, only a light rustling in the trees and the continued rushing of the river.

As one might imagine, it was difficult to wait until Thursday—Thursday!—to see him again. The only thing that kept me from looking for Karl before then was the simple fact that I knew nothing about him. I knew not the name of the university at which he studied. I knew not where he slept at night, though imagining him in bed filled me with a sort of tingly feeling I had never felt before. I did not even know his last name.

It was for the best. Had I known any of it, I might have sought him out—and made a fool of myself. As it was, I did not do my work, at least not much of it. Our dinners that week were overcooked meats and potatoes, all forgotten as I fantasized about Karl or lost myself in the book, reading about the battles of Napoleon or the wives of Henry VIII. But at least I put forth the appearance of work.

Time passed slowly, but eventually, it did pass, as time always does. Finally, Thursday arrived! I left my house at daybreak and arrived at the bookseller's stall quite early. I walked past the lady bookseller brazenly. She could not kick me out, for I had someplace to go. But the little man ran up to me.

"Miss, you are well?"

"I have no money this week either," I said, heading him off. I did not need him following me around. "I am only meeting someone here. I will be gone soon."

"No, no." He shook his head. "It is all right. I know you love the books as I do. Being around them enriches the soul." He paused, awaiting my reply.

"What?" I looked around, searching for Karl, but it was too early.

"I only wondered if you had, perhaps, done any reading this week?" He looked over his shoulder, probably to see if the bookseller was watching him.

I smiled despite my annoyance, thinking of the book, the secret book which, even now, resided under my pillow. I knew it was none of this funny boy's business. Still, I could not resist the urge to say, "In fact, I have. I have a new book of history, and it is wonderful."

His grin was wide, revealing his crooked teeth. "Really? I would love to know more about this book you enjoyed so much. Where did you get it?"

Ah—I saw what he was about. He thought I had read their books for free, then purchased elsewhere. "Oh, oh, no, it was a gift . . . from a friend."

"I see." His gray eyes shone. "So tell me what you thought about it, please, for I so seldom meet a young lady who loves books as you do."

He was so strange. I was about to answer him, just to make him stop talking to me, when a long shadow appeared. I turned, then looked up. "Karl, it is you! You are here!"

"Indeed, I am." Karl reached out to me, then realized it would be inappropriate to take my hand in public. Instead, he shook the young man's hand. "You work here?"

The young man's countenance had changed entirely. His brows were knitted together. "Yes."

"A fine establishment," Karl said, "and one my Cornelia likes a great deal." Through a crack in the stall's curtains, a ray of sunlight streamed and glinted off Karl's beautiful hair.

"Yes," I said, noting how he said *my Cornelia*. "I was just telling this young man about the wonderful book I received this week."

"You have a new book?" Karl feigned surprise. "Then you will have to tell me about it—over the picnic lunch I brought." Karl swung his arm, and I saw that he held a hamper. Its contents were concealed by a blanket, but I could see a loaf of bread and the neck of a wine bottle.

"I have been waiting to tell you about it!" I said.

"Then let us go."

I had gone a few steps before I thought to bid the young clerk good-bye. But when I looked back, he had already trudged away.

Karl and I went to the little wood across from the market, and Karl spread out a red-and-black plaid blanket. I wished I had thought to bring a picnic, to show Karl my wifely skills, for I was an excellent baker. "I will bring the picnic next time. But let me help you unpack now."

I peered at the basket's contents and was rather amazed at their elegance. Besides the bread and wine, there was a clove-studded ham and a hunk of cheese wrapped in wax, some lovely cookies, and two of the most beautiful pears I had ever seen. But most incredible of all were the service plates, thin as eggshells, and forks and knives that gleamed silver, and glasses that sparkled like diamonds. It all seemed too fine for a poor student. Perhaps Karl was rich! I laid it all out prettily, but then I was too excited to eat. Or maybe too nervous. What if food fell from my mouth? What if crumbs sullied my dress? What if the cheese made my breath stink? I nibbled at the bread and the ham, sampled a bit of cookie, as daintily as I could, but mostly, I stared at Karl. His shoulders were so broad that they blocked the view of the market. To cover up what I was not eating, I talked of the book, proud that I could remember which of Henry's wives had been executed (Anne Boleyn and Catherine Howard) and which Catherine and Anne he had, fortunately, divorced (Catherine of Aragon and Anne of Cleves). Karl listened—and ate—with equally rapt attention, asking me questions that I happily answered. At one point, he said, "And where did you say you got this wonderful book, my lambkin? A week ago, you had only the Bible and a storybook. Now you are a wealth of information."

I giggled, perhaps because I thought him funny, calling me his lambkin, but more likely from the wine that Karl kept pouring and pouring. I feared to place it down upon the blanket, lest it spill, so I had to drink it. My head felt like a gas-powered balloon, soaring over the treetops. "Oh, I don't know." I brushed his arm with my hand. "It arrived on my doorstep Friday, likely from a secret admirer."

He laughed as well. "I am glad you enjoyed it. More wine?" He held out the bottle.

"I should not. I will have to stumble home somehow, and I still have my shopping to do."

He filled my glass. "I will walk you home. I will walk you anywhere you need to go. I will help you with your shopping, so you can afford one more glass. Please—it is sweet, like you."

His face was so handsome, his voice mellifluous, and the wine was the sweetest I had ever tasted. "Maybe half a glass."

But I did not protest when he filled the sparkling goblet all the way.

The rest of the afternoon was a happy blur. I lay upon the blanket with my head in Karl's lap, which may have been improper, but I felt slightly ill—and no one saw us anyway. As the sun sank lower in the sky, Karl helped me with my shopping and carried my groceries home. We paused a little farther from my house than we had the week before. My head was clearing a bit, but my stomach was empty, and I wished I had eaten more.

Above the rushing water, Karl said, "Will it really be a week before I can see you again?"

I sighed. I looked into his blue eyes, and my heart just broke. Why must I be a poor miller's daughter and not a rich girl with nothing to do but flirt? I placed one hand upon his arm. Then, boldly, I placed the other one there too.

"I know. It will be so long."

I looked up, willing him to come closer.

He did, placing both hands upon my elbows and drawing me near.

And, in that moment, I knew he was going to kiss me, and I was powerless to prevent it, powerless from the wine, but also from the wanting. I had not the will to stop him. I needed to feel his lips upon mine, his body crushed against me. I stood on tiptoe, smelling the wine on his breath, hearing the birds above me, the dove's mournful call, the chatter of the river, then only our breathing as he pulled me toward him and his tongue explored mine.

It seemed an eternity, and perhaps it was. Perhaps everything in my life would be measured as either before or after that kiss. It changed everything. I was no longer some dull miller's daughter, destined to bear children and milk cows. I was the girl Karl had chosen, and even as I went about my boring chores and read by candlelight, I would know that. I would remember it.

Finally, we broke apart, and he said, "Do you have to go?"

"I . . . I think so." The words were a gasp, my last breath.

Karl picked up my packages and handed them to me. "Same time next week?"

I nodded. "And same place."

He started to turn away. "We will pick up where we left off."

"I will bring the picnic."

He smiled. "And I will bring the wine."

Then he was gone.

I spent the week baking, rolls, *apfel* strudel with a crust light as air, and so many fancy cookies. I was a good baker and wanted to show off. Father ate well that week for, of course, I had to make duplicates of each item, so he would not know I was meeting an admirer. I did not know why I thought my father would disapprove of my meeting Karl. Yet I knew he would. Perhaps it was because of the joy I took in the meetings. I knew I would marry someday, but I would be expected to marry someone of my father's choosing, someone with a proper trade like a farrier or a wheelwright. Or perhaps I would simply stay here and take care of my father as he aged, then move in with one of my sisters, an old maid. That was not what I wanted, not anymore.

I knew, also, that Father would see that Karl was a rich man's son. He would question his interest in me.

I questioned it myself. I saw the question in others' eyes when we met the following week at the market. I saw it in the eyes of the bookseller's assistant, who did not ask about my reading, but rather fake-swept another part of the stall when I arrived. Karl wore a coat and waistcoat of deep-blue brocade, trimmed in gold braid, far too fine for a girl like me. Everyone could see that.

But when Karl looked at me, his eyes widened then narrowed, as if he had been exposed to too much sun. He rushed toward me, whispering, "My ladybird, it has been torture without you. A week might be a lifetime!"

I felt the same, but I was surprised that he did, and my cheeks spread into a smile so wide it almost hurt. "Shall we go?"

"We shall, my mouse." He offered his arm. I took it, and we walked—nay, promenaded—between the shelves of books. I thought I heard the young assistant cluck his tongue as we passed. Perhaps he was envious of the love we shared. Who would not be, after all? Especially one as homely as him?

Everywhere in the market, I felt the envious stares of the other young ladies at their shopping. Karl suggested that perhaps we should visit the stalls first, the better to take our time at lunch later on. I agreed, and Karl held the basket while I chose fish and vegetables. I did so as quickly as possible, and then we went to the woods.

We walked farther in this week than last. "It is such a wonderful afternoon for a walk," Karl said, and though I felt a bit warm, I did not disagree. It grew cooler as we journeyed farther into the woods, and though the birds sounded more distant as the trees grew taller, there was something so lovely about the whisper of the branches. I had never been so far off the path before, and I smelled exotic wildflowers and kicked at strange purple-and-orange mushrooms. Finally, we reached a clearing near the brook.

"Look!" Karl pointed to the other side of the water and touched my elbow. I felt my teeth chatter at his touch, and then my body went warm.

It was a mother red deer and her fawn, drinking at the stream. "They are so beautiful," he said.

"You are a city man," I said.

"What do you mean?"

"On my father's property, there is a herd of deer. They drink from the river, sixty or seventy of them sometimes. I see them when I walk out at twilight."

"It must be a very beautiful place."

I had not thought about it, but I supposed it was.

"It is. There is a waterfall that runs over the craggy land and a stand of apple trees behind it. It is most beautiful in autumn, when the leaves turn red and orange and you can see them reflected in the water. When I was a little girl, I used to collect the leaves and throw them into the river, then watch them float away like merry little boats."

"That is lovely. I wish I could go there." I felt him move closer, his arm against my elbow.

"Maybe you can. I can bring you to meet my father someday, and to visit."

His hand brushed my body. "Perhaps."

At that moment, the mother deer noticed us. I saw her eyes meet mine. Then she gave some secret signal to her baby, and they both ran away.

Karl moved closer and kissed me. He laid down the basket and spread the blanket on the ground. He held out his hand. "Shall we picnic here, milady?"

I took his hand and sank down to the ground, sitting beside him so our thighs touched. Being near him made my stomach feel like a trapdoor with the bottom dropping out of it. I wanted him to kiss me again, yet I knew I wasn't supposed to want that, much less act upon that desire.

I said, "Let me get out the dishes."

I unpacked the hamper, and he exclaimed at all the items, seeming amazed that I had made the bread, and the butter and cheese, marveling at the cookies I had decorated with frosting and dipped in chocolate.

He tore off a hunk of bread and found a knife to slather it with butter. Then he fed it to me, as if I was a baby bird. While I ate, he poured more wine the color of the black-red tulips that bordered our garden. He held up his own glass.

"To fresh-baked bread and the girl who bakes it."

I drank heartily, wondering if he would kiss me again.

"My father wants me to join the army," he said.

The change of subject was so abrupt that, at first, I thought I had misheard him. Then his words sank in, and I was first sad, then elated, sad that I might not see him for a while, but elated that here was an occupation my father would understand, respect even.

"My sister's husband is in the army," I said.

"Oh, he must be very brave. I fear I would be a coward. It is so much easier to read about wars than to fight them."

"But if you felt strongly about the cause . . ."

"That is the problem. I am not certain I do. Is that horrible?"

I thought about it, drinking the wine he poured. I knew I would never want to go to some open field and have people shoot at me. But that was not expected, because I was a girl. Was it wrong for a man to feel the same way?

"No," I said. "Some people are just meant to be readers. Does your father not understand that?"

He chuckled. "Sadly, no. And I cannot explain it to him."

We were silent for a time, drinking wine and listening to the brook. "I wish we could stay like this forever."

"Me too," he said.

I reached for the hamper to take out the strudel I had baked, that he might admire that too, but Karl caught my hand. "Would you . . . wait for me, if I went off?"

"Wait for you?" Did he mean what I thought he meant?

"I love you, Cornelia. I have never met another girl like you."

And though part of me said there were hundreds, thousands of girls just like me, I said, "I love you too." I did. I had since I'd first beheld him.

He kissed me hard upon the lips, his tongue exploring mine.

"Should I . . . ?" But now he was kissing my neck, and my hands found his hair, his chest, and there was no one there to see, and we were entangled in each other, and I was like the river crashing through our mill, nowhere to go but where the forces took me, predictable yet beyond my control. I was the river, carried over the hard rocks below.

Finally, gasping, it ended. Karl poured me another glass of wine to replace the one spilled in our tussle. I could not even blame the wine for what we had done. I hadn't had that much. I had wanted him.

That night, Karl walked me home, and we planned to meet again.

We met the next week and the week after, and it was always the same. The picnic lunches, our embrace. Karl never again mentioned his father's plans for him, or his wish that I would wait for him. I wanted to ask him, but my happiness was such a new and fragile thing that I didn't want to blow upon it, lest it break. I hoped—I did not know what I hoped would happen, something that would allow us to marry soon. I began to hope that even more fervently when my monthly flow did not come. I knew from my sisters' whisperings that this meant I was going to have a baby.

How I longed for the time when my life had moved slowly, like the river, always the same, always the same.

When I told Karl, he was stunned.

"You cannot be," he said.

"Of course I can." I picked at the blanket beneath me. It was my week to bring the picnic, but I had felt nervous and a bit sick that morning and had burned the bread, dropped the butter. Still, I had not expected his denial. "What we have done is known to result in . . . babies." Even a poor miller's daughter knew that. A smart student like him should.

It occurred to me, not for the first time, that I had been stupid, that I knew nothing of this man, other than that he had a handsome face, charming manners, and that he loved me, said he loved me. If he chose to abandon me in my condition, what recourse would I have? I could follow him, perhaps, but once there, what would I do? If he left me, I would be like one of the leaves I tossed into the river, floating untethered, bobbing for a while until I would eventually sink.

I might as well throw myself into the river.

I did not want to believe that he would abandon me. Karl was good. Karl was kind. He had told me his own fears. He couldn't belittle mine.

"Are you not going to marry me? You said you loved me." I tried not to cry, but the effort made my face feel swollen, like a bee sting. "I thought you were honorable."

I knew I had no reason to believe that.

"I do." He rose. "I am."

But he did not say, *I will*.

He began to pace, like a chicken trapped in a coop. He had no reason to stay, and I knew that if he left, it would be forever. In the distance, I saw a mother deer and her fawn, perhaps the same ones we had seen that day. I wished I could go back to when I first saw them and do everything differently.

"I do love you." His eyes were those of a frightened child. His face was almost unrecognizable to me. This was not the man I thought I loved. He was not a man at all, just a terrified boy. "I just . . . my family will never approve. I shall be in so much trouble."

And he began to weep, still pacing, mumbling incoherently until I wanted nothing more than to run away, forget I ever knew him.

At least he did not seem to realize the delicate position I was in, that he could simply leave and be gone. At least he was taking his responsibility seriously.

But then he said, "I must go."

"You can't. You cannot just leave me."

"I need time. I will come back next week."

He began to walk again, but now he walked away, down the path and through the forest, out to the marketplace, answering my cries only with, "Next week!" I followed him, but when we reached the marketplace, he continued walking.

I knew I would never see him again.

I stumbled toward, then away from, the lively stalls. I could not go crying through the market. People would see me, people who knew my family. And I had left the blanket, the basket, the items I had purchased, everything. I stumbled back to the woods to retrieve them. Habit steered me like a horse heading home, for surely, it did not matter if I had the vegetables or the fish when the world had ended and the stars had exploded. Still, I went, for I had nowhere else to go.

When I finally walked through the market, I felt no calmer. But I had a plan. I would live the next week as if Karl were honorable, as if he had not run from me, as if he were going to come next week and pledge to marry me.

And, if he did not, there would still be time to throw myself into the river.

With this grim thought, I headed home.

The road was lonely, and though it was not yet night, the sky was dark with threatening clouds. I felt a sudden chill across my arms like rain about to fall. I shivered and walked faster, though I had no wish to return home.

"What is the matter, my child?" The voice came from nowhere. I looked around and saw nothing. There was no one there.

But then suddenly there was a woman where I was sure no one had been. She was dressed in a black lace gown with a severe collar. Still, above it, her face was kind.

I recognized her. The lady bookseller. Kendra. I had never seen her on this road before. Had she followed me? Had she seen me crying?

"N—nothing. Nothing is wrong." But I could not keep the ripples of tears from my voice, and without thinking, I wiped my eyes.

"I may be able to help." She came closer, and in the strained moonlight, she seemed almost birdlike in her movements.

"No, you can't," I said, shivering again.

She held up a cloak that I had not seen before. She enveloped me in it, draping it around my shoulders, then smoothed it with firm hands. She had barely spoken to me before, yet her touch felt so warm, so like my mother's that I began to sob. She took me in her arms, enveloping both of us in the cloak, which seemed to grow to our size.

"Is this about your young man?" she asked.

And, all at once, I was pouring out the whole story, my dull life, my romance with Karl, my plight. All the time, she held and rocked me like a mother, like my mother.

"I am so foolish. I do not even know where he is, who he is, where he lives. I do not know if he will come next week. I do not know anything about him!"

Kendra did not answer for a moment, but then she said, "I can help you with that."

"How?" I sniffled.

She backed away, allowing the cloak to fall around my shoulders. From somewhere within the folds of her dress—I knew not where—she extracted a mirror, silver and larger than my head, trimmed with ornate scrollwork like something from a museum. She held it out to me. "Take it."

I did. It felt cold and heavy, like a block of ice. I sniffled and looked my question. Why a mirror? Even in the darkness, I could see that my face was red and blotched with none of the beauty that women expecting babies are said to have, beauty which, no doubt, came from their husbands' love. I made to hand the mirror back.

But she said, "No, keep it. This is a magical object you hold in your hand."

"Magical how?"

"With it, you can see anyone you wish, merely by asking."

This seemed insane. "But what good will that do me? I need Karl to come back. I need him to . . ." *Love me. Want me.*

"With this mirror, you can observe him, see where he is, *who* he is."

The mirror suddenly felt heavier. My hand trembled with its weight.

Kendra reached out to steady my arm. "Just ask the mirror to see him."

Her hands gripped me like pincers. This was impossible. Still, if I did what she asked, she would let me leave, so I said, "Can I please . . . I have to see Karl."

I expected nothing. Yet suddenly my face disappeared, replaced by a scene that looked like one from a book, a room with floors that shone like the river in sunshine and lights that hung from the ceiling, surrounded by showers of diamonds. A palace! Through it all walked a young man I did not recognize at first. He was dressed in the blue uniform of a Prussian army officer. As he drew close, I realized it was Karl.

He passed another man. The man bowed down.

"Your Highness," the man said.

Only then did I realize where he was, what I was looking at. I had seen it before on walks with my mother as a little girl. We had stared in admiration, though of course I had never been inside. The palace!

Karl was the son of our king! A prince!

The mirror fell from my hand. I heard it shatter before I hit the ground.

"Young woman! Young woman! I am sorry, but I do not know your name, though we have met so many times, I feel I know you."

I cracked open my eyes. The dark sky swam up toward me, and I closed them again.

"Oh no," I said, for I knew Karl, a prince, would never marry a miller's daughter. My life was over! But it wasn't true. The mirror couldn't really have shown me Karl. It was some sort of trick.

The bookseller held out the mirror. Miraculously, it was unbroken. I gaped at her.

"I can't . . . I don't understand." But I seized the mirror. I did not understand its magic. Perhaps it was a trick. Maybe it wasn't really Karl I had seen.

"I need to see Karl!" I hoped that the mirror would show me something different.

Another room took shape in the mirror's mists, another beautiful room with walls of gold. But the face was the same. Karl. My Karl. He was talking to someone, likely a servant.

Karl looked down, perturbed. "I require a moment alone."

"Yes, Your Highness. But dinner is soon to be served."

"Alone," Karl repeated.

The servant left and closed the door. Karl paced upon the crimson carpet and, for a moment, it felt wrong to spy on him, But we had been lovers. He had loved me.

Had he not?

As if in reply, Karl settled onto a large chair and buried his head in his hands.

He sat a few minutes. Then he straightened up his shoulders and called for his servant to dress him for dinner.

"You must go there," the bookseller said. "Go to him."

"How can I? What can I say?" Yet I was already planning it. I would wait to see if he came next week. But if he didn't, I would go to him, storm the palace, demand that he be with me, with our child.

But how could I? I was only a girl.

As if reading my thoughts, the bookseller said, "If he does not come next week, come to me. I will help you." At my questioning look, she said, "In case you haven't realized, I know a bit of witchcraft."

I nodded. At least she was an ally, though a bizarre one.

She held out the mirror. "And borrow this, to talk to me. If you get lonely or confused, ask to see me. Kendra."

I took it from her. It was dark, and I needed to go home. Father would be angry at my lateness, angrier still if he knew the truth. If Karl forsook me, I might not have a home to which to return.

I did not see Kendra when I walked into the bookseller's stall. The male clerk was there, as usual. His eyes brightened when he saw me, and he picked up a book.

"It is new!" he said. "It just came in yesterday, and I thought you might like it."

It had a green cover with gold lettering. The title was *Faust: A Tragedy*.

My life was a tragedy. I remembered that I had spoken to him the very day I had met Karl. If only I had tarried, read another book that day instead. If only I could turn back time.

I had barely survived the week, doing chores, though I was sick each morning and terrified what Father would do if he found out. All day long, the river called to me, asking me to become one with it, like the sailor in the story. I was already of the river. We had grown up together, like siblings. It would be easy, so easy, the ripples overtaking me, sparkling like diamonds, turning me into a diamond, bright and dead.

I waved the clerk off.

The young man's face fell, and he pretended that he had merely been shelving the book. He dusted it off, even blew on it. I did not see what he did next, for I turned away. I was looking for Karl.

He did not come. He did not come. I searched from one side of the stall to the other. I walked outside and all around. The brightly colored wares hurt my eyes, and the merchants' chatter assaulted my ears. He did not come. He would not come. My life was more tragic than Faust's, whoever he was.

Suddenly I felt something touch my shoulder, light as a butterfly. Kendra.

"He did not come." It was a statement, not a question.

I shook my head, more of a twitch, really. I did not want to think about it, much less admit it.

"Then you must go to him."

"How?"

"I will help you."

She told me she had heard (she omitted how) of a large party of dignitaries and their servants who would be visiting the palace in the coming days. Kendra would use magic (the mirror was just the beginning of her powers, apparently!) to help me gain entry as one of this party. Once I did, I could confront Karl.

Or, rather, his father, the king.

"But what will I say to them?"

A drop of rain fell onto my cheek with a splat. Then another on my shoulder. I didn't care. I was like the rubbish left out, rubbish to be rained upon.

Kendra ushered me inside the stall, waving off the young assistant's curious glance.

"Tell the truth, plain and strong. They will surely listen. What parent could ignore his own grandchild?"

"He is a prince." I was weeping. "They will want him to marry a princess, someone . . . special."

Kendra stroked my hair and said, "They will love you. And, if all else fails, tell them you can spin straw into gold."

"What?" I looked up at her, certain I had misheard. She had turned away, looking at the young assistant. When she saw me, she looked back.

"Nothing, dear, nothing." She produced a handkerchief, seemingly from nowhere. "Nothing. I am certain they will love you on sight."

The party was to arrive on Saturday afternoon. Early Saturday morning, I snuck out before Father even woke and met Kendra outside her stall. There, she used magic to outfit me as a grand lady, much like in Mr. Perrault's story of Cinderella. She handed me a small satchel with a change of clothing and the mirror. "If you have any trouble, contact me."

She led me to the town, to the castle, where the crowds stared, where I once had stared, hoping for a glimpse inside. I felt ill.

"How will I get inside?"

Kendra gestured toward the gates, and, as she did, the crowds parted, allowing me through. At the front of the crowd, there was a party, wealthy and grand.

I surveyed the group of travelers. The gentlemen wore wigs and coats embellished with gold braid. The ladies were all fashionable, with low-necked gowns displaying their pearls and jewels. I glanced at my own chest. Though Kendra had outfitted me as a wealthy woman in green velvet, my only jewelry was a cross from Father and a small ring that had been my mother's. They would know I was not one of them. They would know their own party, of course.

I glanced at Kendra to tell her this.

She was gone.

I wanted to run, and I was going to, but my feet felt as if cast in plaster, and I could not move.

At that moment I felt a light touch on my shoulder. I turned, expecting Kendra.

It was not Kendra but a young woman my own age, tall and gawky, with carroty hair and freckles dotting a bumpy nose.

"There you are, Sophie." She looked right into my eyes.

I started a bit, still unable to move, to speak even.

"Sophieeee . . ." She tugged upon my arm. "Come. They are going inside. We need to hurry, the better to procure adjoining rooms."

"Adjoining . . . ?"

"Silly! If our rooms are too far apart, it will be much more difficult to sneak around and gossip about *him*."

"Him?"

"The prince!" She giggled. Did she think I was her friend?

I felt myself giggle too, and somehow, I knew this strange girl's name. Dared I to say it? What if I was wrong?

Yet I knew I was not wrong. Kendra's magic made it so, made this strange girl believe I was her dear friend . . . Magic!

"Sophie!" She grabbed my hand. "Did you not hear me?"

"Oh, Agathe!" I said, using the strange girl's name. "I am sorry. I was just thinking about meeting Prince Karl!"

Her reaction let me know I was correct. I squeezed Agathe's hand, and together, we fairly vibrated with excitement. Or rather, she vibrated with excitement. I trembled with fear. I could not help but wonder about Sophie. Was there a real Sophie? What had happened to her? Was she trapped in a cupboard somewhere? Or did Agathe merely believe she existed? Was I an illusion? Did I still look like me? And, when Karl saw me, would he recognize me?

I wanted to take the mirror from my satchel, both to examine my face and to ask Kendra all these questions. That's when I realized I did not have the satchel anymore. I glanced around. A servant in a black uniform had my bags.

Agathe said, "I know. I cannot wait to meet the man I am to marry!"

My mouth fell open, and I dropped her hand. I felt cold, as if I might freeze into a block of ice and fall over. To marry Karl? I stared at the girl. She was not pretty, not really, but she had a neat figure, and she was rich. She was smiling, for she was to marry Karl!

I wanted to scream out everything, but she would not believe me. She thought I was her dear friend Sophie.

I had to be alone, to speak to Kendra. This could only be accomplished if I unfroze myself, placed one foot in front of the other, and walked into the castle.

I smiled, though I felt as if my face would crack when I did.

"Of course." My voice shook, but I steadied it. Perhaps she merely meant she *wished* to marry Karl. I held out my arm to the lovely, rich Agathe. "Let us go."

And we linked arms and walked into the palace.

This too was dizzying, for it had pillars as large as the hundred-year-old chestnut trees that grew near our mill. When we entered, I nearly gasped. The gold on the ceiling and walls was blinding.

Agathe gave me a sharp look. "What is wrong with you?"

"It is so beautiful!"

She shrugged. "No more beautiful than our palace at home, and you have been there hundreds of times."

I recovered myself. I was a young lady accustomed to entering palaces, apparently.

"Well, that is beautiful too. This is just different." I assumed all castles did not look alike.

"True. Our castle is much older. This one is more modern." She nodded happily, surveying the room like one who expected to live there.

There was an elaborate luncheon, but I ate little of it. I searched for Karl. He was out, hunting, they said. We would meet him at dinner tonight. And a ball. Agathe grabbed my hand when this was announced. I felt the tiny bit of venison I had consumed threaten to come up. I stood, attempting to breathe.

Finally, finally, I was alone in my bedroom. I peered into the mirror. I looked like myself, but a heightened version of myself, dressed beautifully, with hair that had been curled with great care. I could be a princess.

Except I was not a princess.

"Show me Kendra." I wondered if the tremble in my voice had become a permanent condition.

She appeared in the mirror.

I burst into tears.

"What is it, dear?"

"He is to marry that Agathe! He was never going to marry me!"

"You do not know that."

"I do." Now I saw it clearly. "He went to the market dressed as a peasant, to meet some peasant girl to . . . to . . ." I could not form the words. "I was nothing to him but a bit of fun before his marriage to a noblewoman. And he was everything to me!"

I thought of the book Karl had sent me. I had loved it but, more than that, I had loved the idea of it, the fact that Karl had understood me so well that he had picked the perfect book, the very book I had wanted. He did not believe me a stupid peasant, or at least, he did not seem to. He found me a smart and accomplished young woman! It had been the book that had made me certain of him, the book that had made me love him. That and his face.

"It was all a lie," I said, sobbing. "If only he had not sent that book."

"Book? What book?"

"He sent me a book of history. It was that which made me fall in love with him."

A shadow crossed her eyes. "A book of history?" She frowned, then seemed to recover and reached her hand forward as if trying to touch me through the mirror. "It will be fine."

"What shall I do?"

"I will tell you, but you must be calm. Be calm."

Her voice was soothing like wind in autumn leaves, and I felt myself relax. My neck began to droop, and even my feet felt heavy, the way they felt at night before sleep overtook me.

"Mmm . . ." It was the only reply I could manage.

"All right then. Tonight at dinner, you will see him. He will pretend not to recognize you. Perhaps he will even hope he is mistaken, but you must remain calm. Understand?"

"Calm." I nodded and took a shaky breath.

"As you file in, you will be introduced to the king. You will curtsy, and you will be called upon to make some small talk. When dinner ends, you will play your hand."

I must have misheard her. There must be more. But no, Kendra was nodding as if it was decided.

"That is your plan?" I asked. "That is your magic? Sneak me into the palace only to reveal myself over dinner? They will throw me out."

Kendra frowned. "The king may be sympathetic. After all, it is his grandchild you are carrying."

Again, her voice soothed me like a glass of Riesling. "Of course."

"But if it does not work, you have still your secret weapon."

"Secret weapon?" My voice was like a clock's pendulum, regular, false. I did not know I had a secret weapon.

"If all else fails, tell him you can spin straw into gold."

"But I can't spin straw into gold. Why would I say that?"

"Just tell him you can," Kendra said, as if it made perfect sense.

And I agreed, because I wanted it to.

Kendra Speaks

Poor Cornelia! Poor little fool! For a miller's daughter to fall in love with a prince was dumb. And for a miller's daughter to sneak off to the woods with a man she barely knew was sheer idiocy. This was how the foundling homes got filled, and how young women were cast out by their families. And yet my heart went out to her. Life was hard for a young woman of limited means. The men had all the power.

Cornelia might have thought I didn't know her, but I did. She had been coming into my stall for some time, first with her mother, then with her sisters, and finally, by herself. She loved the books there. And my plain, dour assistant fancied himself in love with her. For hours each day, I listened to him wax rhapsodic about her beauty! Her brains! The talents he was certain she possessed, though we had seen no evidence of them at all! Every Thursday morning, he came in smelling of cologne—men's cologne was a new invention, and he bought it by the bottle! If she came, he followed her like a pup, and if it rained and she did not come, he moped for the next week.

In fact, I knew that it had not been Karl who had sent her the history book. Perhaps you, dear reader, had guessed it too, but I knew for a fact. Indeed, I had been the one to sell it to my lovestruck boy!

And it was because of this lovestruck boy that I told Cornelia to say she could spin straw into gold. I have mentioned that my assistant possessed a rather rare ability. With it, he would help Cornelia—one way or another.

Well, back to her!

Cornelia

So that is how I, a mere miller's daughter, ended up in a barn, far from the castle, with the chickens, expected to spin straw into gold.

I would much prefer not to narrate the dinner. Perhaps you think you can imagine the horror? You cannot. I wish I could rip it from my own memory as well, but I am afraid it will haunt me forever.

Once, when I was little, my mother took my sisters and me to a play. It was a wonderful entertainment about a clever girl named Finette who outsmarted an ogre, gained a magical chest of clothing, and married a prince. I loved the story so, and for weeks, even months after, I could close my eyes and see it before me, Finette chopping off the ogre's head, the king offering his son's hand in marriage, Finette in all the finery from the magic trunk, as if it were still happening. It was a wonderful thing!

This story is less wonderful by far. Yet here, too, I live it over and over and over in my head.

An hour before dinner was to begin, a woman knocked upon the door. She was, it seemed, my maid. Sophie's maid. And she had come to dress Sophie and do Sophie's hair, even though my dress and hair were already more wonderful than they had ever been, better than I had looked at my sisters' weddings.

Thankfully, I was too dumbstruck to say any of this. Rather, I accepted her ministerings as if they were my due. It reminded me of when I was a little girl and my mother used to braid my hair. In an hour's time, the perfectly perfect pink silk dress I wore was traded for an even more elegant blue one, and my blond hair was brushed and fussed with until it shone like straw spun into gold. I looked in the mirror and knew that, when Karl saw me, he would love me, even if he never really had before.

Finally, my maid said, "The time, milady," and I emerged from my room.

Agathe was in the hallway, fairly swaying under the weight of a satin gown the color of wine. She turned to me, and her face was white as milk, which made her freckles stand out like measles. "Oh, Sophie! Do you think he will like me?"

No. Of course not. Or, if he does, it will merely be because you are rich. I took her hands in mine, noting the blue vein that pulsed in her high forehead. Indeed, the vein was bluer than her eyes.

I wanted to tear at it. Silly thing! Why should she have Karl?

Yet she stared down at me so pitifully, and I had to say, "Of course he will, my dear. You look perfect."

And then, still holding hands, supporting each other, as we were both too nervous to walk, we went for dinner.

"I am so glad you are here," she said, as we descended a grand marble staircase into a room so large I felt like I was jumping into the ocean in all my elegant clothing. As the stairway curved, Agathe slipped and grabbed onto me. For a moment, I thought we might both pitch forward, rolling over and over each other, down the staircase and into the roomful of people, a pile of torn finery. Fortunately, I had the presence of mind to grab the banister and steady myself until I was able to drag up the dead weight of Agathe. "Hold on," I whispered.

And then I saw him.

Karl.

Prince Karl.

He was dressed more elegantly than I had ever seen him. Far from playing peasant, now he was dressed impressively. He wore a red-and-blue coat trimmed in gold, so much gold it hurt my eyes. I gazed in wonder at the ornamentation, with flowers and even little frightened faces incorporated into the stitching. Finally, I looked down. My eyes were watering.

"Go!" Agathe tugged at my gown, and I realized I was to curtsy. I did, winking back the tears. When I rose, Karl bowed low. "Ladies."

He did not look at me. At least, he did not *see* me. I felt as if I had descended into the river, and now my skirts were waterlogged, tugging me down into the depths like the young child who once had drowned near my father's property, dragged down by the force of our mill. I was sinking.

Karl offered his arm to Agathe, who took it, giggling like the ninny she was. From somewhere, another gentleman materialized, offering his own arm to me. I took it. The gentleman told me his name, which I did not even hear, and I must have told him mine. He led me to the dining room.

The table was the size of my father's barn. Laid for thirty or more with lit candles reflected in gleaming silver and sparkling glass, it was piled with tureens of soup, towering plates of vegetables, and platters of fish and meats, one wrapped in a sort of crust like a strudel. I felt that if I ate any of it, I might explode like an unmilked cow.

I fell into my seat. Karl was on my other side, and I tried to catch his eye, but he looked only at his own companion, Agathe. My escort, the nameless, faceless young man to my left, tried to converse with me as I decided which of the seven forks and three knives were for the fish.

"You had a long journey," he asked.

"Yes," I barely whispered. "Three days." I did not know how I knew this, but I did. Kendra's magic at work, I supposed.

A silence. I had nothing to say, I knew nothing of this man. I suppose, if I had thought about it, I could have told him of the books I had read, the history Karl had sent me, but instead, I sat there, dumb, as the hall filled with more and more people. The cooked fish with its head still on stared at me with disapproval. I glanced to my right, at Karl. He still did not notice, did not see me.

"And was your journey a pleasant one?" The young man attempted again to engage me.

"Yes. I mean, it rained." I tried to look at him. He was dressed similarly to Karl and was tall and looked strong.

Would you rescue me if I began to drown?

"Ah, that is unfortunate," he said, "though I suppose the peasants will be glad of it. Rain, I am told, is good for the crops. Peasants are always worried about the crops."

"Yes," I said. "Silly peasants."

Peasants like me.

"Of course, a young lady like yourself need not worry about such things," he said. "You are only concerned about how the weather affects your complexion."

I took a bite of the fish. I had decided to begin with the fork closest to me only to realize that others had done the exact opposite.

I wiped it off upon the tablecloth and started again. I took another bite. And another. And another. And then servants materialized to take away the largely unconsumed food. They brought more, and my escort said, "Oh, it is time to turn the conversation." He seemed relieved.

And, at that, he swiveled his body toward the lady on his other side. I realized that the entire table had done the same, and I was looking at the back of the gentleman's head.

I turned too and found myself face-to-face with Karl.

"Did you have a good journey?"

He spoke as if he did not know who I was. But I looked the same. Had he never seen me? Or was he pretending not to know me?

"I imagine the rain must have slowed your pace."

A servant set down a giant pig with an apple in its mouth. Its eyes met mine and rolled heavenward. Then it spit the apple right out. The fruit banked off the king's chair and into Agathe, knocking her over. The animal stood, squatted down, and sprang onto Karl's head. It began to urinate.

Karl said, "Was your journey a slow one?"

I blinked at the platter. The pig was still upon it, setting on a bed of greens, the apple still in its mouth.

"Do you not know me, Karl?" My voice was a whisper. I no longer knew what was true or false.

I did. This child in my belly was true.

Karl laughed. "Know you? Of course. You are my dear Agathe's friend, Sophie."

I reached out my hand and grabbed his chin. Beside me, I heard Agathe gasp.

I said, "Look at me, Karl. Look at me."

Out of the corner of my eye, I saw one of the servants—or perhaps a guard—advancing upon me. I needed to speak, and quickly.

I stood. "Karl, I am more to you than Agathe's friend." My voice quavered, but it was loud. "You know I am Cornelia from the market. We have been . . . lovers."

"Oh!" A gasp rose from the assembled guests, and a moan from Agathe. I faced the king, a corpulent man with a long, curled beard. This was my one chance.

"You must believe me, Your Majesty."

"I do not know this woman, Father. I swear it."

"He knows me well, and I know him. I know that his favorite story as a child was about the animal musicians who scared the robbers. I know that he hates turnips but loves strudel, especially when I make it. I know he has a birthmark like port wine on his stomach. I have seen it, touched it, when we—"

"No! Sophie!" Agathe yelled, and the king buried his face in his hand.

"You must help me. I am going to have a baby."

The king stared at me. Around the table, all was silent except for Agathe's soft whimpers and Karl's whispered "No, no . . ."

The king rose. He was a tall man, and he walked around the table to meet my eyes.

"What did you say?"

My throat felt closed from the inside as if I could neither swallow, breathe, nor cough.

I finally managed the latter. Then I whispered, "I am having a baby. Your grandchild."

The king nodded, but not at me.

A pair of strong hands grabbed me from behind. The guard. He must have moved in when the king rose from his chair, and now he was lifting me, pulling me toward the door. This could not be happening. Kendra's magic could not have failed me so spectacularly.

Failed.

"Wait!" I yelled. "Wait! You must listen to me!"

"I must listen to nothing!" bellowed the king. "You are a fortune hunter out to trap my son."

I remembered the bookseller's instructions and straightened my shoulders. The guard pulled me back, but I yelled for all to hear.

"I have no need of fortune-hunting. I can spin straw into gold!"

Why had I said it? In years to come, when people hear this story (and I have little doubt that they will), they will marvel at my stupidity. I suppose it was the lack of other choices.

And now I am in a barn. A lovely, large barn one would expect from a castle, but still a barn, surrounded by straw, straw, straw! The animals, which could have been a comfort to me, have been removed from the barn to make room for more straw and, presumably, because it would not do to have them eat the straw. Still, I can tell from the stink that there were once goats here. In the dim light from the moon coming through a high window, I can make out the shape of chickens, asleep in their coops. Chickens, of course, do not eat straw. Perhaps I can get an egg from them in the morning. I do not know if my captors intend to feed me. I do not know what will happen when they realize my lie. I do not know what I was supposed to do *after* I told them I could spin straw into gold. Kendra did not tell me.

I must speak to Kendra. But how?

I stand, feeling the straw crackling under my feet. I am mentioning straw quite a bit, but really, it is my entire life. I need the mirror. I begin to pace back and forth. In the darkness, the straw feels unstable, slippery beneath my worthless dressy slippers. I steady myself on an object, then realize it is a spinning wheel. They have left me a spinning wheel with which to spin my lies. No, to spin my straw.

Because my life was not hideous enough before now.

I hear a rustling. Then the door creaks open. Have they sent someone to check on me? What will I tell them?

"Darling!"

"What?"

"Cornelia? Are you here? It is so dark. They must bring you a light."

It is him. Him. Karl. Has he come to rebuke me? Or to save me? I rush toward him.

"I have not yet been able to spin straw," I tell him. "It is dark, and I need my satchel. I will do it, though. I will do it if you bring it to me. I promise." It is a rush of words cut off only by his mouth upon mine, his arms around me. I do not want to want him, to succumb to him, but I do. I melt into his body.

"Darling." He kisses me, kisses my mouth and my cheeks, his hands groping his way down my back.

I pull away. "You abandoned me! You threw me away! Am I nothing to you? You did not even recognize me when I was in front of you!"

"You surprised me. And I could not, anyway, not in front of my family."

"You could have if you loved me."

"I do love you, darling." Again, he embraces me, and I want for

126

all the world to give in, to relent, like the water rolling through the mill, even if it means I will drown.

I hold his head in my hands and kiss him.

Drowning.

"You did not come on Thursday. You did not come, and I waited."

"I could not. I was detained. And I did not know how to send word to you. I did not even know your full name."

"I did not know yours, apparently." I gasp as he kisses me, as his hands, his lips rove over me, pulling me closer, closer to the abyss.

"You want a princess, not a peasant," I say.

"I want you," he whispers. "Do you not see? I went to the market dressed as a peasant to meet a girl just like you."

To take advantage of, whispers a horrible voice inside me. *To have before you have your proper princess. Who knows how many other girls there have been.*

But I only say, "Why?"

"To find someone who would love me for myself, as Karl, not Prince Karl Theodor of Bavaria. I am tired of these noblewomen who only wish to be princesses. I had to meet someone who did not know who I was."

"And . . . ?" My eyes have adjusted to the light, and I stare up at him, at his beautiful face. I cannot make out the color of his eyes, only his long eyelashes, his brows knit together.

"And I found you, my darling. The sweetest, kindest . . ." He begins to kiss me again, my eyes, my cheeks. "The most wonderful girl in the world. Cornelia! We *will* be together."

"Yes." It is what I want, the reason I came here. Kendra's magic worked. I do not know how, but it worked after all!

"So you spoke to your father?" I hold him at arm's length to gaze at him.

"Yes, my love. Yes!"

"And he knows I am not a fortune hunter?" I lay my head against my darling Karl's chest. It will be all right.

"Of course not. Once he heard of your talent, he knew you could not be."

"My . . . talent."

"Yes. Why would a girl who could spin straw into gold need to marry for fortune?"

"What?"

"Yes, 'tis true. Father said that once you spin straw into gold, he will know you are not a fortune hunter. Then we can be married. We will be together, my love!"

He gazes down at me, and even in the near-darkness, I see the light of happiness in his eyes.

"Are you not overjoyed?"

I lay my head upon his chest, again feeling sick, more than a bit sick. Part of me whispers that if Karl only wants me contingent upon my being able to spin straw into gold, he is not worth having. But of course he is! He is a prince! If I marry him, I will be a princess. And if I do not . . . if I do not . . . I will be a wretched, abandoned miller's daughter, disgraced with a prince's bastard, a piece of garbage who may as well throw herself into the river.

"Oh, yes, Karl, I am so happy. I just need my satchel."

He backs away. "Of course, my love. I will send for it. You must work through the night, so we can be together."

"I will, my darling. I will."

He leaves then. I settle into the straw to wait. I can only hope that Kendra will be able to fix it.

But Karl does not return with my belongings. He does not bring the mirror. He does not bring anything. The moonlight rolls across the window, and I listen to the night noises of the barn, the movement of the chickens. What if he never returns? The straw feels scratchy

128

against my arms. No. Of course he will return. He loves me. He said he would. In the corner, I see the shadow of the spinning wheel like a smaller version of our mill. Oh, if only I was home. No, I do not want, I cannot go back home. I have to stay, to do this. Sometimes, people have to do things they do not wish to do, in order to be rewarded. I came here to change my life. It will change. It must.

An hour or more passes, and my arms feel scratchy, as if hundreds of insects are crawling upon them. Where is Karl? Where is the mirror? I rise and walk to the window. There is no one there, nothing. I run to the door. It is locked from the outside. I am trapped, a prisoner. I knew Karl would not return, I knew it. What will happen tomorrow morning when they find me, asleep in the straw that is still straw, not gold? When they see I am a liar? Will I be executed?

Perhaps it is for the best.

In the darkness, I hear a mournful sound. A cow, mooing. I walk over to the corner whence the sound came. A cow! One cow. My hand meets her smooth back, and I slide my arm along it, stroking it. We have a cow at home, Brunhilde. Soon, she will wake, and there will be no one to milk her, and Father will know I have been gone all night.

I lay my head upon the cow's back. She feels warm and familiar, and I begin to sob.

A streak of light shoots through the barn. Is it him? Karl? With my mirror?

"Young lady?"

It is not. It is a man's voice, strangely familiar, but not Karl's.

"Young lady, are you here?"

I raise my head from the cow's back. I see a shape, only a shape in the darkness. A man, walking toward me. He holds a lantern, but low, so I cannot see his face. As he comes close, I see that he is a small man, short and slight, with curly hair and a crooked, wrong-turned nose. The young man from the bookseller's stall!

"You! Why are you here?" I fairly gasp.

He walks closer. His eyes are the color of the steel poker I use for the fire. He does not smile but says, "I have come to help you."

"Help me escape?" For I note that the door is still closed, must have closed behind him. Stupid! Can he open it again?

Now he laughs. "No, my fine lady. I have come to help you spin straw into gold."

"But that is impossible."

He smiles, a queer smile, as if he possesses a wisdom I cannot see. "Not for me. We all have our talents. That is mine, though I may not be a handsome prince." He rather spits the words *handsome prince*, and I wonder if he knows what Karl did to me, if Kendra told him. "I am here to help."

"But how did you know I needed help?"

"Kendra has ways of knowing." He gestures broadly around with one arm, and as he does, the barn is bathed in light. "Do you wish me to leave?"

"No. No! I just didn't know why you were here, why you would do such a kind, generous thing for me." I do not believe he can do it.

He winks a bit at that. "Oh, I am not kind or generous. I require payment for my efforts." He walks closer and lays his hand upon my arm, staring directly into my eyes. His smile is crooked. His eyelashes are long, and when he blinks, they brush his cheeks.

"Payment?" He does know about Karl and me.

"People only value that which has a price. Remember that in all things, my dear."

I know not what he means by a price, but I nod. He keeps gazing at me, and I relax under his gaze. He will help me. I know it now. But that is silly. I do not know this man. I know nothing about him except that he likes to read books.

130

Still, the fact that a person likes to read books makes him rather more likely to be worth knowing than not.

But what if he wants something that I do not wish to give?

"What sort of payment?" I ask, not moving from his hypnotic gaze.

It is he who backs away now. He looks me up and down, down and up, before his strange gray eyes settle upon my hand. He smiles.

"Your ring."

The ring is nothing special, a fede ring with a symbol of joined hands. It was my mother's. I love that little ring. It reminds me of happier times. It belonged to each of my sisters first, but they gave it up once they had wedding rings to wear. It is mine now, and I meant it to be my daughter's.

"Why do you need it, if you can make gold?"

"I told you. People only value that which has a price." That makes me think of Karl. I gave myself too cheaply.

I slip the ring from my finger. He reaches toward me with a hand long and bony and nothing like Karl's powerful ones. I drop the ring into his outstretched palm. He pockets it and then rummages in a bag he carried on his back. He pulls out a book that is barely a book, more a collection of old pages, held to its broken spine by a bit of ribbon. He holds it out to me. I fear to take it, for it crackles so much in his hands that I worry it will fall to dust in mine.

He says, "You will sit with me and read as I spin. You will keep me company."

At the very sight of the book, my eyes start to close. I would much rather sleep than talk or read. But I can hardly deny his small request when he is about to do so much for me.

Having relieved himself of his burden, the man drags the spinning wheel over to several large bales of straw. He sits upon one, and it crunches. He gestures to me to sit upon another.

I want to watch, to see him spin straw into gold, but when I look at him, he points to the book. "Read," he says. "You do your work and I mine. You spin stories as I spin straw."

So I open the book and begin the story of Kriemhild, the prince's sister, who has a dream of a falcon killed by eagles. Her mother says this means that Kriemhild's husband will be killed. So Kriemhild vows not to marry.

How incredible to be able to make such a choice! Oh, I just *choose* not to marry! Of course, Kriemhild is obviously a rich woman, and rich women have more choices.

As I read, I can hear the whir of the spinning wheel, the crinkle of the straw. But any time I hazard a glance up, the little man stops working and points at the book. I notice that the lights have gone dim again, with only a circle near me from the lantern he brought, so I can read, listening to the whir of the wheel as I tell about the childhood of the hero, Siegfried. But just as I begin chapter three, the lantern goes out entirely. I sit silent, listening to the whirring, whirring, whirring of the wheel.

"Why did you stop reading?" the man asks. His voice sounds different in the darkness, or perhaps it is only because I cannot see how small and slight he is. It is a manly voice, low and musical and bigger than he appears.

"The light went out, and I was very sorry, for I wished to know if Kriemhild made good her vow, or if she grew up to marry Siegfried."

He chuckles. "What do you think?"

I lower the book down to the ground. I have no need of it anymore. I lean against the scratchy straw. "I think . . . why would the writer tell us about Kriemhild's prophecy if she were not going to marry?"

"Clever girl. Do you want Siegfried to marry Kriemhild even if it means he will die?"

I think about it, but not for long. "We will all die someday."

"That is true enough." The machine never stops whirring as he speaks.

"To die without true love is a great tragedy."

A sigh. "That is true as well." The wheel continued to whir. After a time, he says, "Do you want to know what happens in the rest of the story?"

"Do you know?" I ask, surprised.

"Indeed. It is my favorite story, a story that helped me in many a lonely time. And it is an old legend. Some believe it to be partly true."

"Then do tell me."

So, as he spins and spins, the bookseller also spins the story of Kriemhild bathing in dragon's blood to make herself invincible, then helping the king, Gunther, to win the hand of the warrior, Brunhilde (like our cow, I think). Siegfried does marry Kriemhild, and so, of course, he dies. About an hour before dawn, the man asks me to rise from the bale of straw upon which I sit. I do, and I sink down in the corner, but I cannot find a comfortable spot, as the entire barn floor is covered in something hard as stone. The bookseller's assistant continues, and as Kriemhild learns of Siegfried's murder, the sun begins to rise, and I behold a room full not of straw but of gold, sparkling all around me. In the middle of it, the little man stands, spinning the last of it, smiling.

"Do you like it?" he asks.

I nod. I do, of course, and yet I feel a twinge of something, some emptiness, some regret. I do not know why. I am going to marry the prince! I am going to be a princess! To have everything I ever wanted!

And yet, like Kriemhild, my story is tinged in tragedy.

I say, "Yes. Thank you. But I am sorry too."

"Sorry?"

I nod, slowly realizing the reason for it, what must be the reason. Karl does not really love me. I will never have true love. I see that now. No one will ever love me.

I think of the baby growing inside me. Perhaps he will.

"I do not . . . I will not know how the story ends. Can you leave me the book when you go?"

In truth, I am not ready for him to leave. I am scared to see the king again. What will he say to me? What if he asks me how I spun the straw?

But he laughs, a rather cruel laugh. "Silly girl! I have given you riches, a barnful of gold, and you want more. You want my book?"

The light glinting off the transformed straw hurts my eyes, and I shut them. "Sometimes, a story is worth more than gold. Sometimes a story is everything."

"I agree," the man says, his face growing solemn. "And some of us have only stories to keep us company. Books allow us to be what we will never be in reality, have what we will never have. I am afraid I must take my book with me."

I nod. "You have done much for me."

He takes the book from my hand. "You can always read the other book with your beloved." His voice, when he says, *beloved*, is caustic, just as it was when he said *handsome prince*, like someone spitting out a bad flavor.

I stare at him. "What book is that?"

He gathers up the pages of the book, fumbling with the ribbon that had held them together. "The history book."

"How did you know about the book Karl sent me?"

His eyes meet mine, gray and strange with a hint of surprise, like a cat startled at ferreting out a mouse. "How did I . . . ?" He looks down, tying the ribbon not very well. "Why . . . Kendra told me, of course."

134

Having gathered the pages, he bows. "I must go. Best of luck to you . . . princess."

Princess. I will be a princess. I smile at the thought.

And he is gone as suddenly as he appeared. I cannot even see where he went. I run to the window to try to find him, but I only see the orange sun, hurting my eyes. When I turn back, they burn so much that they fill with tears.

I sink onto the golden floor. It is so hard, and I remember the story of King Midas, who turned everything he touched into gold only to find it gave him no happiness. The barn floor is cold and hard, uninviting. Still, I curl up on it and fall asleep.

7

"What is this?" A voice wakes me. "She's done it? Is it true? Go and tell His Highness and the king."

I do not, cannot stir. Too tired. Also, the voice is not the one I want. Not Karl! I barely hear the barn door slam before I go back to sleep.

"My darling! Wake up!"

It's him! This time, it is him. My eyes flutter open. Is my hair neat enough? I feel a bit sick, as it is morning, but it is Karl! Karl, leaning over me!

"I did not believe it possible," he says. "Why did you not tell me of your wonderful talent before?"

"Are you the only one who can have secrets?" But the golden light assaults my eyes, and again, they well with tears. I turn away and see men, burly men with wheeled carts, already hauling the gold away.

"Father is so happy, my darling!" Karl's hand is upon my shoulder, and I try again to look at him. Again, my eyes ache. I reach up and draw him toward me.

"Are you happy, my love?" Over Karl's shoulder, I notice more men, this time bringing something in. Straw. More straw for the animals, of course.

"Of course I am happy, my love." He kisses me and holds me so tight I can feel his heartbeat. "There is only one thing."

I twist away from him. I do not want one thing. I have had enough of things. When someone says, *only one thing*, it is never a pleasant thing!

"Well, uh, Father wondered if, perhaps, you could do it again."

Behind him, the four bearlike men are still hauling away the gold while the other men bring in straw, more straw, mountains of straw.

"Again?" The dust from the straw—or possibly the gold—sticks in my windpipe, making it impossible to swallow, nearly impossible to speak. Finally, I choke out, "Why?"

He smiles his glorious smile and squeezes my hand in his. "It is just . . . I am so proud of you, darling. Your ability is so wonderful, so astounding, not at all what is expected from . . ." He stops speaking.

"From a commoner? From a miller's daughter?"

"No!" He shakes his head. "No, not that. From anybody. To have such an ability, it boggles the mind. Father has told all our guests about it, and they do not believe him. So he thought to have you do it again, show our guests the straw and then, in the morning, the gold."

"That makes sense . . . I suppose." But I have no abilities, none at all. What if his father's request is merely a trick to reveal that? And what if the little man does not come back?

"Of course it makes sense."

"Of course." I want to run away, to go home even to face my father's wrath. I say to Karl, "Of course. But since I have done your father's bidding, must I be a prisoner here?" It is bold, but I have no choice.

Karl raises his eyebrows and furrows his fine, high brow. "You have never been a prisoner, my love."

"I have. I am. Your father did not believe me. He threw me into this barn to trap me into it."

"No, my darling. No."

I continue. I need to get my belongings and the mirror. After all, I cannot spin straw into gold, and what if Kendra forgets me this night?

"Please, may I return to my room and tidy myself? I want to look pretty for you. And I need my belongings. Perhaps we can read the book you sent me. I brought it with me."

Behind me, a rope of gold drops with a thud, and Karl's fine face is blank with confusion. "Book? What book?"

"The history book, of course. The one you sent me when first we met." Is it possible he does not remember? Has he been sending presents to milkmaids and shepherdesses and miller's daughters across the land, to such a degree that he does not recall them all?

But no, there is light in his eyes. "Oh, of course. The *history* book. It is in your bedroom, you say? Of course I can retrieve it for you."

"Can I not go outside then?" I feel, again, as though the dust from the straw is choking me. "I am your beloved, am I not?"

"Yes, my love." Karl leans over to kiss my forehead. "Try to get some sleep. You look frightfully tired."

"I am. And hungry. I need to eat and drink, but especially, I need my belongings."

"I will get them."

And then he is gone. I walk over to the side of the barn that is already filled with straw, more straw than the previous night, away from the workers who are hauling away the gold. I wonder what it would be like to be a worker, a man, free to do what he pleases, instead of a woman trapped—literally trapped—in a barn and in my life, trapped with a baby, my only hope to be made a wife.

Even if Karl is not my true love, he is the father of my baby. He must marry me.

I sink into the straw. Ordinarily, my worries would prevent me from sleeping, but I am still so weary, so exhausted, and my weariness pulls me downward, sends me plummeting into sleep as I dream of the river running through the mill, turning, turning, turning it into oblivion.

I wake to a shaking. My eyes flutter open. "Karl?"

But he is not there. Instead, it is a woman, a maid, judging from her crisp black gown, though it is finer than my everyday clothes.

"Oh, no, miss. His Highness is not here, but he asked that these items be sent to you." She shakes me yet again, and the sour expression upon her face lets me know she is well aware of my situation. I am still blinking, blinking at the shame of it, not from the light shed by the gold. The gold, indeed, is gone. Instead, I am surrounded on three sides by walls of straw. My dress is covered in dust.

I look at the items the woman is gesturing at. My satchel, which I trust contains the book and mirror, is on the right. On the left sits a picnic basket, the very same one Karl brought to our meetings.

I realize I am starving. I fall upon the picnic basket, fumbling at its contents, hoping there will be some note, some explanation from Karl. There is none, only a loaf of bread, a roasted chicken, and some fruit. I fall upon it, ravenously, but I leave half of each item and all of a chocolate cake. If my helper comes tonight (pray to God he does), I should feed him in exchange for his kindness.

Only after I consume the feast do I go for my satchel. I should pick up the mirror immediately, but instead, I snatch up the book. The book from Karl. I stroke its gold-edged pages. I open it, randomly, to an illustrated plate of a great battle with armored horses and men carrying spears. The pages feel cool, smooth. I inhale deeply, remembering exactly where I had been when I first breathed in the book's clean scent.

But the book reminds me of someplace else. Not my home. Not Karl. But the bookstore. I had talked about it to the little man that day.

I seize up the mirror. "Show me Kendra!"

She appears, clad in purple brocade and holding a large black volume in her hand. Is it a book of spells?

When she sees me, she laughs. "Haha! Did I not tell you that you would be able to spin straw into gold?"

"But I can't. And now Karl's father believes I can. He has boasted about it to his guests and will be humiliated if I cannot do it again."

"Again? Humph! Sounds a bit greedy."

I think so too, but I say, "I must do it if I am to marry Karl."

Kendra shrugs. "Is he even worth it?"

"Worth it . . . what does that have to do with anything? I must marry him or what else will I do?" My choices, narrow before, have constricted to only one: marry, or die?

Kendra shrugs again, as if the situation does not seem dire to her. "All right. I will help you. Be ready at sunset."

And that is it. After she disappears, I sit and read the book some more until the barn grows gray and the words compress to nothing.

"Are you waiting for me, milady?"

I start. It is him! The gold spinner, standing before me. I feel an urge to run toward him, to embrace the only familiar, good thing. Instead, I say, "I do not know your name."

"It is of no importance, is it?"

"It is your name. I want to have something to call you, as you are being so kind to me." In truth, I wanted something to call him when I asked Kendra to send him. It was odd to admit I had never asked his name. But we had met numerous times, and at some point, it seems like the opportunity is missed.

He smiles, a little grin that twists to one side. "Is that what I'm being, kind?"

"More than kind. Wonderful. You are saving my life."

He opens his mouth as if to reply, then shuts it. He looks around, his gray eyes taking in the bales and bales of straw.

"Really, I have no time for pleasantries right now, do I? If you still care about my name after you have married your prince, I will tell it to you, certainly."

I try to protest, but he says, "What payment do you have for me, for this wonderful kindness I am about to do?"

"A necklace?" It seems at once too little and too much, too little because he is doing me so great a favor. Too much because the necklace is all I have in the world, all I have of my father, my family, the home to which I might never return.

His stare is greedy. "You are certain?"

"I have no choice."

"One always has choices. But, if you want to marry a prince, I suppose you are correct."

I don't know if that's what I want. A week, even a day ago, it was. Like most young women, most people, I suppose, what I *want* is something I barely consider. My life has been ruled by what is expected of me. I am expected to be a good daughter, expected to help, expected to marry, have babies, expected to die. Perhaps it is the same for Agathe or even Karl. Unless you are king, someone else makes the decisions for you.

I quickly unclasp the necklace and hold it out. For a second, it dangles between us, catching the waning light, and I remember my mother putting it on me when we went to church.

He hesitates, and in that instant, our hands meet beneath it. I don't know if I want him to take it. I don't know what I want at all. But finally, he snatches it from my hand and pockets it.

"To work, then! I brought you this to read." He hands me a book with a title in gilt script I can barely make out, *Faust: A Tragedy*. "I showed it to you last week, and I am longing to devour it. It is what I had planned for this evening before I heard of your plight."

"The proprietress allows you to read any book you desire then?" I take it from him. "Even the new ones?"

"As long as I do not crack the spines or muss the pages. You must be careful about that too. She thinks I can better sell a book to customers if I have read it myself."

"You are the luckiest creature in the world!" I rub the book's embossed cover, then hold it to my nose to sniff. Someday, when I marry Karl, I will own dozens, even hundreds of books, and when I smell them, I will always remember this day, this place, this man.

It will not be a happy memory.

"Lucky? Because I can read a book?" He laughs, and his eyes sparkle as he does, and for an instant, he seems less plain.

"You can read any book and come and go as you please and stay out late without anyone caring and up late without someone telling you that you had best get to bed because there is work to be done in the morning. Your life is your own."

He looks away, feeding the straw into the wheel and beginning to spin. He does not tell me to keep my eyes on the book this time, I notice.

"You are right. Sometimes, I stay up all night reading book after book, for I have no family to object, and when I wake in the morning, slumped over a table or fallen off a chair, back aching, cold because no one thought to cover me with a blanket or tell me to come to bed, I feel very fortunate."

Silence except for the whirring of the wheel, the tap of his foot upon the treadle.

"You have no family?" I start to open the book.

"I grew up in a foundling home. There is one in town where women can leave their babies if they do not want them."

I feel his eyes upon me, but when I look up, he is staring at the wheel again, concentrating.

"They . . . leave them there?"

"It is a sort of contraption, a wheel. There is a door on the outside, and the woman, the mother, opens it and places the baby in a sort of bed on a shelf. Then she closes the door and turns a crank and—no more baby."

"Where does it go?" I feel breathless. Are there many women, women like me, women in my situation? I have never known such a girl, but maybe I did and just didn't realize it.

"Inside, where someone finds it. Hence the term *foundling*, I suppose."

"And they care for it? They . . . ?" Someone had raised him. It must, therefore, be a safe place. Better than the alternative, for both of us to die in the river.

"Many of the babies die soon after." At my intake of breath, he adds, "But for those who live, I suppose it is not a bad existence. It was there that I learned to read, after all. Had I grown up on a farm with plenty of area to run and play, I might have been illiterate."

He is trying to cast a good light on it but not doing a very good job. "Did you have many friends among the boys there?"

He laughs, a rueful little laugh. "What? Oh, no. I was always an odd one, I suppose, not fast or good at the games. But there were brothers who taught us, and since I was not interested in playing with a ball or running about like a fool, I got the lion's share of the teaching. One day, when a lady came around looking for an assistant for her shop, I was hired. I was very lucky that day. Kendra allowed me to sleep in the back of the store until I found a place, and she let me read to my heart's content."

I wonder if it was she who taught him his talent for spinning. It seems an impertinent question, though, so I do not ask.

I remember the food I had saved from dinner. "I have something for you." I walk over and set the basket before him, careful to put down the book before I do.

He looks at it and smiles, though his smile does not reach his eyes. "You are kind." He stops spinning, lifts the fork, and takes a bite of the cake. But I can tell he is only being polite.

This is confirmed when, after only the one bite, he says, "I must work. There is so much more straw than yesterday."

I sigh. I know. And I know not why Karl failed to visit me.

He sets the wheel to spinning again. "Read."

I pick up the book. *Faust: A Tragedy* does not sound like an enjoyable story but, at first, it is, and a very imaginative one. The elderly scholar, Faust, realizing he has wasted his life, makes a bargain with the devil (signed in blood!) to enable him to once again be young and handsome and seduce the lovely maiden, Gretchen, who falls into his evil clutches.

Oh, how I sympathize with Gretchen! Especially in scene fifteen when, alone after her encounter with Faust, Gretchen spins upon her spinning wheel, sighing that she will never find peace without him. As the man's spinning wheel clacks in the background, so does Gretchen's spinning wheel clack in my mind. I read her words:

Only to see him do I look out the window.
Only to find him do I leave the house.

144

I remember those days when I wanted to run away, to find Karl no matter what, for my life was otherwise worthless.

His tall carriage;
His noble figure;
His smile;
The power of his glance.

I stare at the page. Karl's eyes meet mine through the lines. The spinning wheel clacks and clacks, turning and turning. Did he really love me? Ever? Or was he merely a seducer, sent by the devil to ruin me, as Faust had ruined Gretchen?

His magical voice!

My own voice breaks into a thousand pieces.

The clasp of his hand!
And, oh! His kiss!

The book falls from my hand as I imagine it. Karl's face, coming toward me. His beautiful face. Was it ever real?

I do not want to know the answer, and as I think upon it, collapsed upon myself, unable to go on, I hear the clacks of the wheel, endless and desperate as the river, exhorting me to its waters just as the clacks of Gretchen's spinning wheel exhorted her, just like the whirring of Gretchen's mind as she considered, as she thought, as she *knew* that Faust would not return.

But the clacks become irregular now. They slow. They stop.

"Is it too dark to read then?" a gentle voice whispers beside me.

I look at him, for it is not too dark, not quite. I can see his face. I had thought it so ugly, but in the dimness, his eyes are gentle and kind. He had thought to spare me embarrassment by pretending my failure was due to outside influences. My failure was my own, only my own.

I draw in a breath, a shaky one, but at least it is not a sob. I let it out, then draw in another before speaking.

"It is . . . a bit dark . . . I suppose . . . and . . ." I stop again.

In the grayness, I see him nod. "You do not like tragedies, I think." Before I can answer, he says, "Perhaps, then, you can sit beside me and feed straw into the spinning wheel. And since it is too dark to read, you can tell me a story you do like."

"I do not know very many stories." A lie. I want him to tell me one, a happier one, for he knows so many more. But I move off my seat and gather a quantity of straw. The scratchy feel of it takes my mind from other things.

"How about that history book? The one you say your beloved sent you?"

The one you say your beloved sent you. There is a tartness in his voice as he says it, and I know he does not think much of Karl. Nor should he.

"Have you read it?" he asks. "If 'tis too dark to read, perhaps we can discuss. What is your favorite part?"

I am still pondering his words, but finally, I say, "I do not have a favorite part."

I think I hear him sigh in the darkness.

"I mean," I say, "I read all of it. It was as if I had been starving, and someone placed a feast before me. I devoured it. I like knowing about things, people I'll never meet, things other people don't care about, like Queen Elizabeth or Charlemagne, great rulers or terrible ones. They just seem so . . . real, more real than people I actually know."

As I say the last, he says at the same moment, "Exactly. More real than people you actually know."

The spinning wheel vibrates beside me. I reach over and, careful not to upset the lantern, lest the entire barn go up in flames, I pick up some more straw. I give it to the wheel.

"I do not know many people," I say. "Just Father and a few of his friends. Karl was . . ."

"Me either." His voice is rhythmic with the clacking. "Books and the people in them are the only friends I have. I always wanted someone to discuss them with. That is why . . ." He broke off.

"What?"

"Nothing. You are very lucky to have your Karl to talk with."

I nod, not feeling very lucky to have Karl, if I have Karl. I wonder where Karl has been all day, who he was with. I can see him if I use Kendra's mirror. Yet I do not want to know. I fear to know.

He says, "When I read that book, I pictured the War of the Roses taking place in the wheat field near where I once lived."

I laugh, for I did the same thing. Unable to visualize places I had never seen, I pictured Joan of Arc in our little church and Queen Elizabeth at the mill. Probably, she lived in a palace like this palace, but I had never been inside one before.

"You have read the book I have?" I ask the man.

"Of course. It was at our shop. You saw it there."

"So did you sell it to Karl then?"

He does not answer for a moment, but when he does, he says, "I do not remember. Perhaps Kendra sold it to him." He rises and picks up the lantern, placing it closer to me. "I do not need the light to see. Perhaps if I put it here, you will be able to read."

So I do. I find the book in my satchel and open it to where it will fall, reading about the Thirty Years War and Martin Luther and witch persecutions while the spinning continues.

It is the last that makes me ask, "How is it you can do this, that you can spin straw into gold?"

He stops what he is doing and stares ahead, as if dreaming. Finally, he shrugs.

"I suppose we each have our gifts and abilities. Some people get to be princes or great artists or lead armies. Others get this."

"But how did you realize it?"

"That is an interesting story. When I lived at the foundling home, people would come occasionally looking to adopt an orphan. Typically, they wanted a baby. If they chose an older child, it was because they needed a robust lad to help on their farm, or their business, or a girl for the washing. I lived there for many years, and I was never chosen, but one day, a man came in, a farmer. He was looking for a boy, someone to help him. He had three daughters, but he wanted a son."

"And he chose you?" As soon as I say it, I slap my hand to my mouth, to push back the incredulous, insulting words.

But he laughs. "Oh, I know. All the bigger, stronger boys had been taken by the smart farmers who had arrived earlier. But my farmer was stupid, so all he got was me. Also, they told him I was nine when I was twelve, so he thought I would grow more. I did not, as you might guess, excel at farmwork. I was too weak to push a plow, too slow at picking, useless even at milking the cows, a chore his daughter, a girl of only eight, could do."

"It requires a great deal of strength in the lower arms," I say, still trying to make up for my prior comment.

"I was afraid of cows. With each failure, the farmer beat me, and then he assigned me what he believed to be an easier task. The last of these was merely to care for the chickens, a task which, he said, his six-year-old daughter could do."

"You could not have been afraid of the chickens," I say, trying to lighten up the mood, and as I do, one of the chickens clucks loudly, as if she has heard. I can well imagine his disappointment in his failures. I felt it myself, trying to keep up with my older sisters. But I was not beaten.

"I could well have been afraid of the chickens," he says. "They were quite threatening, I assure you. But no. For the first days, I was all right. I fed the chickens and gathered the eggs and cleaned the coop, all just as well as the six-year-old did. But, on the third day, the farmer's wife instructed me that I should spend the night in the barn, watching the chickens. The boy who used to do it had been let go, and this would be my new chore. 'Surely,' she said, 'even one as stupid as you can sit and watch sleeping chickens so they do not get eaten by a fox.'"

I know what is coming. "You could not?"

He shakes his head sadly, his foot moving the treadle more quickly. "The problem was I had been up all day. So though, in the farmer's eyes, I had accomplished nothing, after a full day in the summer sun, I was tired. I struggled to stay awake, but I eventually succumbed to the sandman's sprinklings. When I woke, two of the chickens were gone. I knew a fox had gotten them.

"It was the farmer's wife who discovered me crying in the barn, crying because I loved the chickens. I had never owned a pet. But I was also crying because I had failed again, and I knew what that meant. The farmer's wife said, 'When my husband returns, he will give you the beating of your life and send you back to where you came from.'"

"But it was not your fault!" I say, feeling my stomach clench at the injustice of it.

He laughs and, for a second, with his eyes crinkling and his mouth upturned, he is almost—almost—handsome. Not handsome like Karl, but pleasant-looking. I look at his face a moment longer than I need to, for I quite like it.

"Fault is a relative concept. Do you suppose people often care whether scrawny foundling boys are at fault for their transgressions?" When I shake my head no, he says, "I did not mind being sent back to the foundling home. The food was poor, and I was not loved. But these things could be said of the farm as well. It was merely the beating I wished to avoid. So, when the farmer's wife locked the barn door, I hoped to escape through the window high above me. But how could I reach it? First, I tried to pile up the straw to climb upon it. But it was too thin. I fell through it, and there was not enough to reach the window anyway. I was sad and tired and hungry. I tried to eat eggs from the chickens that clucked around me—the ones I had not carelessly allowed to die. And, in so doing, I spied a spinning wheel in the corner.

"Spinning was something I actually could do. There had been a spinning wheel at the foundling home, and one of the women had taught me to use it. I often helped them. I had not thought to tell the farmer of this ability, for I knew it to be women's work. But now I thought if I could weave a rope of the straw, perhaps I could pull myself up on it and escape."

I sigh at this. I know enough about straw to know this would never work. Such a rope would be flimsy and fall apart much like the daisy chains I made with my sisters. It would not lift even his slight weight.

"Of course it did not work, and as I saw the sun grow high in the sky and then sink again, I knew the farmer would be back soon. I spun furiously and wished and concentrated and wanted the chain to be made of a stronger material, and suddenly a rope of gold began to fall from the spinning wheel and onto the floor. I did not know what I had done other than wanting it—desperately—but I put in straw and out came gold! Gold!"

"Had anything like this happened to you before?"

"No. Maybe. Little things like wanting a pfennig to buy a sweet, then finding one."

"Then can you get everything you want that way, just by wishing?"

He stops spinning then and turns toward me. His gray eyes sweep from my face to my toe, then back again. Finally, he says, "No. No, I cannot get everything I want by wishing."

He begins to spin again, faster than before, and I think I hear him say something under his breath.

"What?"

"Nothing." The wheel turns furiously. "To finish my story, I climbed the golden rope to the window by swinging it over a nail I saw. That I was able to climb it was as miraculous as being able to spin straw into gold, for I was quite weak at such pursuits. When I reached the window, I could see the farmer, coming in from the fields, so I knew I had no time. I swung down upon it, then I gathered it to take with me. It proved too heavy, though, and I left it in the wheat field, a good surprise for whoever found it. I ran back to town, fast as I could. I likely need not have bothered. No one there wanted me. I made my way back to the foundling home, where they were none too delighted to see me either. So that is how I happened to be there when Kendra came in a few months later.

"'I seek a child with special abilities to work in my shop,' she said. 'Do you know such a child?'

"She looked at me when she said it, and I thought I knew what she meant.

"'I can read,' I said. 'I mean, I enjoy reading.' This could be said for few boys I knew.

"'Reading is a marvelous ability,' she said with a smile, 'but it is not the one I seek, not the only one. Has, perhaps, anything unusual happened in your life, in any of your lives?' She looked at all of us, but she started and ended with me. Some of the others raised their hands, volunteering their skills: They were hard workers. They were the fastest runners. One of the boys said he was an expert pickpocket, so he could catch thieves in her store. Kendra smiled pleasantly at each, but finally, she turned to leave.

"I could not believe it! The opportunity to work in a bookseller's stall, gone forever. Squandered! I had to say something, do something to make her stay, to make her choose me.

"As her hand reached for the doorknob, I jolted up and barreled toward her. When I say I barreled, I mean I literally went as fast as a rolling beer barrel, knocking against two other boys in the process. I arrived at her side, breathless.

"'I . . . I . . . ,' I stammered.

"'What is it, young man? You have already told me your accomplishments, that you can *read*. Have you any other, less tiresome abilities?' But, despite the cruelty in her voice, the gleam in her eyes said she knew I had. 'You can whisper it in my ear.'

"With my hand, I beckoned to her to lean down. Then, I whispered, 'I can spin straw into gold!'

"A boy who had been standing nearby heard and repeated it loudly. This caused all the assembled boys to roar with laughter. I started to slink away. But I felt Kendra's hand upon my shoulder, turning me back toward her.

"'You have done this?' she whispered, and when I nodded, to the boys' further laughter and the disapproving sneers of the other adults, she pulled me away, out the door into an alley, where she said, 'Where? Under what circumstances?'

"So I told her about the farmer and the barn and the chickens and my marvelous escape. And when I finished, she appeared interested. Not only interested but smiling.

"'And you believe you could do this again?' she asked.

"Away from my taunting peers, I said, 'I think so. If I needed to enough.'

"She nodded and took my hand in hers. 'You need to.' She took me back in to the matron in charge and said, 'I will take this boy on trial.' She squeezed my hand, then took me away, and from that moment on, I was no longer a foundling but an employee. I was special."

I smile at this, then frown. "But if you can spin straw into gold, why work at a bookseller's stall or anywhere else? Why not travel, see the world?"

"I did, a bit, but then I came back. After a while, a man wants a home. I have that, a little flat and lonely, but still a home. A man wants to feel useful to someone. A man wants . . ." He looks down at his shoes. "I may travel again someday."

I wish I had such choices. But perhaps I am better off not having them, for when I do have choices, I invariably make the wrong ones.

"Are you angry at your mother for leaving you?" I ask him. "You are so . . . remarkable. If she knew, she would wish to know you."

A bit of something darts behind his eyes, and he looks down toward the spinning wheel. "I doubt that. I am not angry. I am sure she felt she was doing the right thing, that she had no other choice. But . . ." Again, his voice trails off.

"What?"

"Sometimes, people think they have no choice, when really, they have not thought it through. Perhaps they do not know that others might help them." He glances up. "I have talked enough about my dull life. Either read to me from that book or tell me a story of your own."

So I pick up the book and turn it to the next chapter. But, even as I read, I wonder. Do I have choices? Is there something I have not considered?

The wheel spins and spins like Gretchen's mind, and the room fills with gold, gold, and more gold.

At some point, I fall asleep, for when I wake, my visitor is gone and I am lying in a corner with a blanket bunched around me. I remember what the man said about no one covering him when he fell asleep. Had he carried me? The rest of the room is filled with gold, more gleaming gold, overwhelming me with its richness. I feel first gratitude, then guilt wash over me, like the rapids of the river. I did not thank him. I did not thank him, and he has done so much for me.

I still do not know his name. What is his name?

I will never see him again.

Nonsense. After I marry Karl, I will seek him out. I will find him and thank him.

After I marry Karl.

Where is Karl? The palace is awake, for the men are taking away the gold. Also, they are bringing more straw, so much more straw.

It is more than an hour before I see Karl, and in that time, the stable turns from golden to the dull yellow of straw. Outside, it is raining, so there is barely any light.

Finally, he comes. He seems out of breath, as if he had run. He says, "My ladybird, I have heard what you have done. You are a marvel!"

"So can we be married then? Today?" Even as I say the words, I know what his answer will be.

"Well . . . ah . . . my father would like you to stay one more night."

I look around at the straw that fills every corner, piled to the ceiling. I realize that it is dark not only because it is raining but also because the windows are blocked. It is amazing that they have such a limitless supply of straw at the ready. But, then again, he is the king.

"Stay another night, or stay another night and spin straw into gold?"

He winces a bit. At least he is ashamed. "Thing is, we have some expenses. A barnful of gold could help with them. Just one more night."

I start to say that I can still spin straw to gold after we are married. But I stop myself. I cannot spin straw into gold. And something tells me I will see the man no more if—when—I marry Karl.

The thought makes my eyes sting, and I feel like I have lost something precious. I want to see him again.

"Just one more?" I ask.

"I promise, my love, and today, I will come back and have lunch with you and take you for a walk on the grounds. The servants have brought you breakfast too."

They have, meat, likely left over from yesterday's dinner, and soup. It is delicious, and Karl does come back to see me later on. It is a lovely walk, and I hate to complain, but my entire body aches from sleeping on the hard floor, and my arms itch from bugs in the straw. And I need to speak to Kendra.

The grounds are beautiful, with tall trees and a fountain, and Karl weaves flowers in my hair, though my condition causes their scent to make me ill. We talk of the day when we will have a family.

On our way back, I remember the question the man asked me. "Karl, what was your favorite part of the book you sent me?"

"The book?" Then he understands. "Oh, the book I gave you. I am not certain, for I liked all of it so much. What was your favorite part, my darling?"

I smile and say I liked all of it too.

"That's my girl. When we are married, you can—"

"I know! I intend to read every book in the palace's library and discuss them with you over dinners! I am so looking forward to it!"

He laughs and pushes a curl from my shoulder. His hand lingers, then travels down to graze my breast. "I was going to say you could put such things behind you."

I nod. "But, at least, I will read bedtime stories to our children."

I watch to see his reaction to the words. I hoped he would be excited, but he does not react at all, as if it had nothing to do with them.

"Of course, mouse. Whatever you want." He kisses me.

I kiss him back, but when his hands roam, I twist away.

"Someone will see us."

"So what if they do? They are only servants."

His hand is hot upon me, and suddenly I know I do not want him to touch me. He did not give me the book. I am certain of it. It was a lie, all a lie I had perhaps told myself because I wanted it to be true. His love is a lie. I want to ask him if he ever intended to marry me, but I do not. I do not wish to know the answer. I want to hold just a bit longer to the possibility that everything is as I dreamed.

But is it what I want?

I remember what the man had told me about the foundling home and the baby wheel. I can find that home—he can tell me where it is when I visit him at the market. I can take my baby there. I can open the door and turn the wheel. Things can go back to the way they were.

But I do not want that either.

Before, I had dreams, hopes, expectations, the possibility of love. Now I know they aren't real, for no man will want me if he knows I had another man's baby. Yet if I hide it, would my life not be a lie?

All I want is a man who will stay up with me throughout the night, talking of books we have read. That is what I want. Someone who understands the loneliness I have felt, someone who, like me, has thought of books as his only friends.

I don't want Karl. I know who I want, but he will not want me.

I jerk away from Karl. "I feel ill. The baby. And I should sleep if I am to be awake all night, spinning." The word, *spinning*, is a hiss, and in that moment, I make a decision. I do not want to be with Karl, not if I must do everything he asks and hope that he will love me.

He nods. "You are not well. I will take you back."

"Back to the barn?"

"It is only one more night, my lambkin."

I do not answer but follow him back to the barn, which is now filled with so much straw that it is nearly impossible to walk.

As soon as Karl leaves, I search for the mirror, finally finding it under a bale of straw. "I need him to come back," I tell Kendra.

"Again? You are using him sorely."

"Just once more."

She shrugs. "Very well." She squints, as if trying to see something at great distance. "I wonder what your Karl is doing now."

And then she is gone, leaving me with her question. I do not take the bait. I try to sleep, but that question and so many others make my head burst like an egg left on the stove after the water has boiled out. Several times, I am tempted to check the mirror, to ask to see Karl, to know if I will see what I dread—him and Agathe, or maybe Karl making love to a servant girl, or another girl he met at the market. Yet I do not. It should not matter what Karl is doing. My decision should not be based upon him but upon me.

Finally, I give up on sleep and pace the floors as best I can, waiting for him. The one I truly want to see.

Just at nightfall, he appears. "Kendra said you needed me. Just once more." He surveys the roomful of straw.

"Yes." I sigh. I realize I have no means to pay him. The ring and the necklace were all I had except for the book, and why would someone who works at a bookseller's stall want that?

He is walking through the bales of straw, but he turns to look at me.

"About my payment for my labors tonight." He meets my eyes, and his own seem so falsely stern that he resembles a child trying to imitate a parent. I hope to reach through to the kindness I know is behind, to the little boy who cried over the chickens.

"I have nothing left to give you, nothing you would want."

He steps closer. "I think you do. You wish me to spin the straw so that you may marry your Karl." He says *your Karl* not with a sneer this time, but with an air of disappointment. "If he marries you, you could promise to intercede, to have me appointed as a sort of palace librarian."

I smile at this. "So you can read all the books?"

He looks down, his bravado gone, and his voice is barely a whisper. "So I can still see you every day."

I catch my breath, then exhale just as quickly, feeling a bit light-headed. He does not know about the baby, I remind myself. If

158

he did, he would not say such things.

He sees my silence and walks away through the maze of straw, looking for the spinning wheel. He slaps his hands together as he walks. "So we have a deal, then? A barnful of gold to impress your Karl in exchange for a royal appointment?"

I know I have to ask him the question that has been on my mind. I follow behind him, and I place my hand upon his shoulder. He starts when I do.

I say, "I believe you know something about the book I have."

"The history book?" He does not look at me.

"Yes."

"I might know something about it."

"I was hoping you might have remembered who purchased the book I have? Are you sure you don't know?"

He finds the spinning wheel and begins to drag it back, but I am in his way. He turns and faces me.

"What do you want me to tell you?" he asks.

"Only the truth."

"You know the truth, though you may prefer the lie."

I do know the truth. I've known from the moment I entered the palace, maybe before. I knew the truth, but I wanted to believe Karl cared about me, did not just view me as a plaything. I nod.

He laughs. "Poor fool I was! Ugly fool. For months, I saw you at the market reading the books. Every Thursday, you came, every Thursday for months, and I waited for you. It was the high point of my week. I wanted to speak to you. Of course I was an idiot. One as lovely as you would never look at one like me, a nobody with no family, no name. I know I am not handsome. I know that. But I thought, perhaps, if I brought the book, we could talk about that, at least. I imagined you would know I sent it. After all, we had discussed it. I asked after you until I learned who you were, where you lived. I hoped we could be friends—a fool's fantasy. I left the book upon your doorstep and hid behind some trees to watch you find it. You did, on the way back from the chicken house."

I nod, imagining him doing this, remembering. "It was I who was a fool," I whisper.

He goes on as if he has not heard me. "And all the next week, I waited for the day that you would come. I waited for Thursday, for you."

"You wanted merely to be friends?" I ask.

"I did not hope for anything more. I wanted someone with whom to discuss books."

"Then why not Kendra? Or any one of the men who walked into the stall? You could not discuss books with them?"

A sad smile. "Maybe I hoped for more."

And I had ignored him that Thursday like all the others, intent only upon finding Karl. "I wish I had known it was you." I feel tears in my eyes, for I suspect it would have made little difference, had I known. I would likely still have been enchanted by Karl, the liar. I would still have overlooked this kind, clever, shy man. Nothing would have been different.

I say, "I don't think I can accept your offer, your offer to spin the straw in exchange for a favor by my husband. It wouldn't be right, because I do not think I will be marrying Karl."

He smiles. "Really?"

"Really. He does not love me. He put me here in a barn on the hard floor overnight, with barely enough food, to spin straw to please his father. I cannot imagine he really wants me."

He hunches his shoulders as if trying to retreat into a shell. But he cannot make himself any smaller than he already is. I think I hear him murmur something, but I cannot make it out.

Finally, he says, "I want you."

"You would not if you knew the entirety of my situation." I turn away from him, surveying the room. If only there was a way out. If only I did not have to face him in the morning without the work done.

"You asked me if I was angry at my mother for leaving me."

I turn to him, surprised by the change of subject.

"I am not angry at her. I am angry at my father, the man who left her in a situation where she felt she had no choice but to abandon her baby."

I turn toward him. He knows.

I say, "I want to have choices. I want to go home, but I do not know how to leave or what I will do if I go, what I will tell my father. Father does not even know where I am at this moment. I have no choices—persuade Karl to marry me or throw myself in the river. Those are my choices."

"You want choices. Here is one: The lady I work for, Kendra, is a kind lady, but lonely. She could adopt your baby, say she got it from her sister who died. Then you could go back to your life as it was."

That is a choice, but not one I like very much. I hated my life as it was.

"Or, on the other hand, you could marry me." He takes my hand and draws me toward him. "You could move into my flat and read all day and play with the baby, and other babies when we have them. And, when I come home, we could talk of books. Someday, I will have my own stall at the market. Not a bookseller, for Kendra has that, but something else. I am learning to be a businessman. You could help me." He holds out his hand as if pointing it out, and his eyes are shining as he says this.

"Could it be a bakery?" I say, caught up in his fantasy. "I am very good at baking cookies and cakes and bread. And you should taste my apple cake."

"A bakery!" He laughs, a great laugh, larger than he is. "Of course it can be a bakery. Do you want that?"

He is still holding my hand. I squeeze his. "I wanted the man who sent me the book, for he is the man who understands me, who knows what is important to me."

"What do you want now?"

"I want you to take me home, but I don't know how to leave. I cannot spin a golden rope to escape."

"I can take you home." His grip upon my fingers loosens. "But will I be able to see you again?"

Once again, I am on the horns of a dilemma. I want to tell him yes, of course, to bring him home to my father as my future husband. But was it too much to ask him to raise another man's baby?

I look at him and see he is holding his breath, anticipating my answer. I know the answer to my question as well. Yes, it is too much to ask. But if I ask, he will say yes.

"Yes," I say. "I want to see you, not merely on Thursdays, but every day."

"Really?"

"Really. And you would take care of me, and the baby?"

"Yes. I may be only a poor clerk at a bookseller's, but I can spin straw into gold."

"I would be happy even if you could not." With that, I hug him, and then his lips are on mine. It is a different kiss from the ones I shared with Karl. Karl's kisses were demanding, insistent. This kiss is soft, something he is giving to me, rather than something he is taking away. He whispers, "Can it really be true?"

"It is true," I say, thinking how fortunate it is sometimes, not to get what I want.

With that, he releases my hand and walks to the spinning wheel. In no time, he has made a long rope out of the straw, like the one he told me about. He places it upon the ground, then picks up a small, thin strand of straw.

"What are you doing?" I ask.

"You will see." He feeds the wisp into the wheel. It is so small I can barely see it, but when he finishes, he takes it out and holds up the perfect little ribbon of gold. Then he stares at it until it moves. It breaks in half, then forms two unbroken gold rings. He holds one out to me to see, but before I can take it, he slips it into his pocket.

"Soon, my sweet Cornelia."

He starts to pick up the rope, but first, he takes me into his arms once again. I feel him shivering, or maybe it is me.

"I do not even know your name," I say.

"It is an ugly name, I'm afraid. At the foundling home, they had to name so many, so many who did not survive, that they ran out of names. They couldn't name us all Hans. So it is the silliest—"

I place my fingers upon his lips. "I have to know what to call my husband."

I remove my fingers, and he says, "Rumpelstiltskin," looking down.

"It is a lovely name," I say, and I kiss him again. At that moment, I think it the most beautiful name I have ever heard, if a bit long.

Finally, we break apart, for time is passing, and it is best not to stick around when a king will be angry. My reading of history taught me that. We pick up the rope Rumpelstiltskin spun. It is slim, but heavy and strong. He hoists himself up to the high window ledge, then helps me up. We leap down into the courtyard, hand in hand, and disappear into the night.

Kendra Speaks

At the very moment my clerk, Rumpelstiltskin, was sneaking the miller's daughter out of the king's barn, I finally saw something I recognized in the mirror when I looked for James. Finally, he was not in battle. Instead, he was walking by himself along the riverbank, and I saw in the background a majestic building, made of brick, with four large turrets visible. It flew the British flag.

The Tower of London!

James was in London!

It had been many years, more than a century, since I had been there. A great deal had changed. But the Tower of London had been there since before I was born, and so had the river, the Thames.

James was in London, and now I would be there too. I would find him!

Cornelia
Seven Months Later

For seventeen years, my life was like the Isar River, which flows past our mill, beautiful but all too consistent, always the same.

Then I had a grand adventure. In hindsight, it is possible to see it that way. I met a man I thought I loved. And I met a man I do love.

Rum, for that is what I have decided to call him, takes me back to my father's mill. He says he came upon me, lost and alone. This is not quite a lie, as I was lost when he found me.

"Was anyone with her?" my father asks.

"No, she was quite alone," Rum says. This is true also.

My father peers at me. "What happened, Cornelia? Were you harmed?"

I know what he means, and I do not know how to answer.

Rum says, "I believe she is unharmed, sir, but her ring and her necklace were stolen from her."

I forgive him this lie, for it makes the story more believable. And he will give me a new ring, soon enough.

Once he ascertains that I am unharmed, my father is so grateful that he invites Rum for dinner the following night. I will cook, of course. And the night after. And the night after that. Each day, Rum brings a book with him. We read it aloud and discuss it. My father does not say that he thinks books are silly, for that would be rude to our guest. In truth, I think he comes to enjoy the stories as much as I do.

Within the month, we are married, and seven months later, I bring into the world a lovely baby girl, a bit early but very healthy. As soon as she finishes nursing, my husband (who is now the proprietor of the bookseller's stall, because the previous proprietress, Kendra, had a family emergency which, she said, compelled her to leave Bavaria, possibly never to return) plucks her from me. He holds her close, bouncing upon the balls of his feet to calm her. "Dear baby girl," he says, "dear baby girl."

"You are good with babies," I say, a bit surprised. We are living at my father's house, for he is old and would be lonely if I left. So I have to raise my voice to be heard over the rushing water from outside.

He grins, and though the baby, whom we named Gretchen, is still asleep, he continues to rock and bounce her. "Yes, at the foundling home, I often took care of the babies. It was the closest I came to having a brother or sister." He pulls Gretchen close and kisses the top of her head.

"My darling," I say, "I am so sorry she—"

"Do not say it." He clasps his hand around Gretchen's head as if covering her little ears. "Gretchen is mine, mine and yours, the first family I have ever had."

I smile. "I was going to say I am sorry you had to be up all night, waiting for her to arrive."

We both know that is not what I had planned to say, but he nods, accepting it.

"Father and I are your family too."

"You are." He places the baby on the bed beside me, then lies down with her between us. "This is what happiness feels like, I suppose."

Outside, the water races toward the mill. I know that, a few miles down the river, there lives a prince. I wonder if he thinks about us or is curious about my disappearance.

But I don't wonder for long.

"Yes, darling," I say. "This is it."

And we fall asleep listening to the water, steady and unchanging, going on forever.

Kendra Speaks

I traveled by train, then by ship, to London. Every day of that voyage, I searched for more clues as to James's whereabouts. My plan, if I found nothing else before I arrived, no street, no flat, was simply to sit on a bench on the banks of the Thames, staring at the Tower of London, hoping he would walk by. And then we would take a walk along the Thames together. It would be so romantic, the romance I had dreamed about all the time we were apart. The romance I had never had, never in so many years.

I was rather girlish in my naïveté. I realize it now. But I was so excited to see him!

But I did find something else, one night as I lay in my bunk, staring into the mirror. I saw him with a woman. They were walking in a park, or perhaps it was her garden. She was a prettyish thing, perhaps twenty, with bright blond hair, and he presented her with a bouquet of flowers he'd gathered. She held it out in front of her, like a bride. He laughed and kissed her.

"It won't be long," he said. "Next week."

"Thank goodness," she said. "So no one will know." She looked down at her stomach.

"I would have married you anyway. I did not think I would ever again meet someone I wished to marry."

"After your lost love." She pronounced *lost love* in an annoying, singsong way, as if she ridiculed the idea of it. Of me! "I know." She giggled a bit. Annoying creature.

He kissed her again. "You have finally made me forget her."

Forget me? I could watch no longer. I hated her. But, really, I had no reason to hate her. She'd done nothing wrong. It was James. He had said he would wait for me. He'd said that. But he'd lied. Or he'd given up, which was even worse. To wait all this time only to give up on the very eve of our reunion!

I wanted to throw the mirror into the North Sea. I waited for you, James! I waited ever so long! Was I not worth waiting for? It had only been a hundred and twenty years!

What if I was not the one he was waiting for at all? What if it was this woman, whose name I found was Lucy, all along? He certainly married her quickly enough. I had been staring at him for years, and I had seen no such Lucy in all that time!

But, instead of sitting in London with my broken heart, I decided to see the world. I spent a great deal of my time at sea, on the *Birkenhead*, the *Lusitania*, the *Titanic*, the *Morro Castle*. Ships I boarded tended to fare poorly. But I was not on the *Lancastria*, one of the greatest naval tragedies in history. I knew someone who was, though. I met him when I was in London, a hundred years after I lost James for the second time.

In the Darkness
London, 1941

"Shake a leg, Ethel. We don't want to be late."

"I don't want to go at all," my older sister Ethel said, staring at the wadded-up stocking in her hand.

"Oh, Esther!" I looked at my other sister, Ethel's twin. "Do something about her! We can't go as the Andrews Sisters with only two of us."

The party, a fancy-dress ball held at one in the afternoon in the basement of the primary school, was the first we'd attended in the half year since my seventeenth birthday, since the bombings had begun. Esther had heard about it, a fundraiser for the war effort, and it had been my idea to go as the Andrews Sisters, American recording artists who looked just like my sisters and me, two brunettes and one prettier blonde. We had spent the past week making over our dresses to look like their costumes. Since we didn't have three that matched, we'd decided that Ethel and Esther would wear their matching blue dresses from last Easter, while I'd wear a similar dress in pink. But Ethel was the best at styling hair, and so we needed her to perfect our victory rolls, a hairstyle created by sweeping the hair up into a V shape above the forehead, the way Patty, Maxene, and LaVerne Andrews wore it.

"Please, Ethel," Esther said. "Let's have a bit of fun for once."

"It isn't safe," Ethel said. "What if something happens? I still say it's wrong to go out and frolic when so much is happening. You never think of such things, Grace."

I thought about such things all the time. I wished my brother Jack were there, and my older brother, George. But Jack was my closest companion. We'd played together while Esther and Ethel huddled in the corners, giggling. He'd been at war these six months.

If Jack were there, even sitting inside would have been fun.

"Don't be a twit," I said. "That's why they're having it at one o'clock, to be safer. And it's in a basement." At night, the street lights were out, so that the Germans wouldn't be able to see us, and we had black drapes over the windows to keep any light from seeping through. The blackout had been going on for well over a year.

Ethel sighed. "And my stocking is ripped."

"Oh, well, if that's all . . ." I held up my eyebrow pencil. "I can fix that. You do Essie's hair."

"What are you going to do?" Ethel asked in that high, nervous tone I hated.

"You'll see."

So, while Ethel rolled and pinned Esther's hair, I used a ruler and my brown eyebrow pencil to draw a line up the back of Ethel's left leg, to look like the seam of a stocking. It would have been quite horrifying had anyone noticed, but no one would, and necessity is the mother of invention, especially in wartime. Then Esther crouched and drew a line up Ethel's right leg (we decide it would be better to have both legs match, even though only one stocking was ripped) while Ethel styled my hair. Finally, we waited for Ethel to do her own hair.

It was almost one before we were finished. Now, the true test. Our mother.

"Whatcha think, Mum?" I asked as we posed to be the very picture of the Andrews Sisters, me in the center, with Ethel and Esther leaning in toward me.

"You look very nice," she said, quietly.

If only she could have mustered up some enthusiasm, but she too felt my brothers' absence. I supposed she wouldn't be the same until they came back.

At least she hadn't noticed Ethel's stocking. If she didn't, no one would. Mum had eyes like an eagle.

It was strange going out in costumes in broad daylight. I had no idea who would be there, even. I supposed there would be some chaps my own age, who were still in school, but no one for my sisters, who were three years older. All the able young men their age were gone to the war.

Poor Ethel. Poor Esther. Lucky me. I fairly skipped to the party until Ethel scolded me.

"Remember your dignity, Grace," she said. "And if you can't do that, remember that those hairpins might not hold if you skip."

"Fine." I slowed down and walked just as I imagined Princesses Elizabeth and Margaret might walk, slowly and boringly. "But we'll be out of harm's way more quickly if we step lively."

So we did, and we got there soon after one.

They'd tried to make the room look swanky, with streamers hanging from the ceiling and some old balls made of blue and red

172

tissue paper, which I think they must have had from when I attended the school.

"It still looks like the basement of a primary school," Ethel said.

"Well of course it does," I snapped. "That's what it is. Doesn't mean we should stay home every day." I tried not to roll my eyes.

"Remember when we went to that dance at the church hall?" Esther asked, likely trying to distract me.

I nodded. It had been my first dance. I'd been thirteen and was wearing an old dress of Ethel's, but Mum had gotten a new sash for it.

"None of the boys my age wanted to dance with any of the girls," I said. "But when Jack asked me, I was embarrassed because he was my brother."

"But then another boy cut in," Esther reminded me.

"Ralph Martin," I said, remembering his hair, combed so neatly. "And then everyone was dancing. Jack saved the day!"

"Indeed he did," Ethel said, and even she had a little smile.

We walked around a bit, looking like the Andrews Sisters and admiring other people's costumes too, though most people had boring costumes like scarecrows and witches. A few people were dancing, but I didn't know any of the chaps there. But then I saw Dora and Helen, whom I hadn't seen since they'd finished school the year before, and my sisters saw some friends from the factory where they worked and our neighbor, a girl named Kendra. So we separated. Our costumes didn't make sense that way, but I didn't really care. I ran up to my friends.

"Girls, what's new?" They wore matching costumes, as a black and a white cat, which just involved wearing cat ears with a black and a white dress.

"Um, nothing much for me," Helen said, "just work, work, work. But I think Dora has some news."

That was the cue for Dora to remove her hand from behind her back and hold it up, showing off a ring with a speck of a blue stone.

"Ned?" I asked her.

"Of course Ned!" She beamed.

"Is he here?"

"No, he's enlisted," she said proudly, "but he's getting leave for the wedding."

"Oh, that's nice . . . but how hard for you to have him leave straightaway."

"I know. But at least we'll be married."

We went on like this for a few minutes, and then I noticed someone at my elbow.

I beheld a man who was tall, broad-shouldered, and graceful, with blond hair. He wore a red satin jacket and a white ruffled shirt. I looked up at his face and gasped. It was hidden by a mask.

"I see you've become separated from your sisters, Miss Andrews." His voice was soft and cultured. "May I have this dance?" He held out his hand, which jutted from a ruffled sleeve.

"I . . . I don't know. I don't know you." I noticed his hand shook a bit. Was he nervous to speak to me?

"I'm sorry. It was wrong of me to approach you. It's only . . . I just came back from overseas, from France, and I have no friends here who might introduce me. I saw you come in with your sisters. When I was in hospital, I listened to the Andrews Sisters day and night, and Patty was my favorite." He stuck his hand in his pocket, as if to stop it shaking. "You look like her."

"You were in hospital?" I said. "From the war? You were injured?"

"Yes."

Suddenly I recognized his costume. He was the Scarlet Pimpernel, after the film with Leslie Howard, and the books too. Had the Scarlet Pimpernel worn a mask? I couldn't remember. I didn't think so.

"My apologies. I would be happy to dance with one of our heroes," I said. "My name is Grace."

"Phillip." He offered me his hand. I worried that his palm would be warm or clammy, but it wasn't. It was cool and dry, and his grip upon mine was firm. He was a gentleman.

He led me out onto the dance floor. A new song was starting, "You and I," which was slow, but with a lovely, lilting beat. He put his other hand on my waist. He was tall, and I wondered what his face looked like behind the mask, but the rest of him was so handsome, and the hint of eyes I could make out were vivid blue.

"I love this song," I said.

"Me too." He turned me around. "I can play it on the piano."

"Lucky! I took piano lessons as a girl, but I gave it up. My mother said I'd regret it."

"Do you?"

"Yes. But I can sing."

He was very light on his feet, and since I was the best dancer in my class, we made a good pair. Only a few people were dancing, and some of the ones who did stopped to watch us. His elegant costume likely made us a handsome couple.

"Are you supposed to be the Scarlet Pimpernel?" I asked him.

"You're the first to recognize me!" he said.

"I saw the movie, years ago, with my family. My brothers, they're at war now. Your costume reminded me of happier times."

He smiled. "If I had a drink, I would drink a toast. To happier times." He raised my hand as if it was a glass. "And happier times to come also, I hope."

"Yes. When this is all over and they come back. I loved that movie."

"A nobleman going out in secret, fighting injustice," he said. "Sir Percy Blakeney. I wish I could be more like him."

"Exactly." I swayed in his arms. He was tall and made me feel tiny and light, like Ginger Rogers, the dancer. "But you did that. You're a hero like Sir Percy. You said you were in the war."

"I was."

"I'm surprised you didn't wear your uniform." Several boys had done just that.

He shrugged. "Well . . . it was fancy dress. And sometimes one likes to forget."

I nodded. I wondered what had happened to bring him back. Something horrible, maybe. I dared not ask what.

I felt his arms around me, guiding me. Nothing wrong with them. Or his legs either, judging from his dancing.

As if reading my mind, Phillip said, "I was on a ship. It sank off the coast of France."

"How awful!" I had not heard about a British ship that had sunk. I would have to ask Father. "And you were in hospital all this time?"

"Yes." Phillip smiled. "And while I was there, I was able to read all the books about the Scarlet Pimpernel. I've grown quite attached to the chap. He helped me forget that awful night."

On the record, the singer sang.

So to sweet romance,
There is just one answer.
You and I.

I sang along with it.

"You have a lovely voice," he said.

"Thank you. I sing at night, when we're stuck in the house. That's how my sisters and I decided to be the Andrews Sisters. We sing their songs together."

He was smiling. He had such straight, white teeth, and he said,

"How lovely. I wish I had someone to sing to me."

But then I felt self-conscious, and I didn't sing anymore, not even when the next song was "He Wears a Pair of Silver Wings," which was my favorite. Still, the evening felt like a dream.

"I read aloud sometimes too," I said finally. "I've read the Pimpernel books. Only I haven't read *Mam'zelle Guillotine* yet. I haven't got a copy. It's so hard to find things now."

"I have it. I could loan it to you . . . if I can see you again?"

I recognized the question he was asking, and I knew my answer. "I'd like that." I smiled up at him, then tried to suppress it. I didn't want to look like a fool. My sisters said I looked like a twit when I smiled too much, but I was so happy. I'd come to the party expecting nothing except to see some old friends, but instead, it was like a grown-up dance, and everyone was looking at me dancing with this man, a war hero, who wanted to see me again. "Do you read much then too?"

"Ever so much. There's an American author, Ernest Hemingway. He writes about war."

"I loved *A Farewell to Arms*. It was so sad, though."

"It was sad. That's what I liked about it." He held me a bit closer. "You're a beautiful dancer."

"Thank you."

"I mean it. I love to dance. And dancing with you, it makes me feel like I'm somewhere else, not a basement of a school in the middle of the afternoon."

"Where would you want to be," I asked, "if you could be anywhere at all?"

"Not so much where, but *when*. I'd like to be in Paris, before the war, or maybe after. I'd show you the Arc de Triomphe, and then we'd take a boat ride on the Seine."

"In the moonlight." I nodded. "It sounds so beautiful."

"And how about you?" he asked.

For a moment, I couldn't think of anything. I liked his idea so well that I almost said I'd like to go there. But that would be boring. "I've never been anywhere, really. I'd love to see Paris. But I'd be happy just to go to Regent's Park, to the Rose Garden."

"The way it smells in June!" he said. "Like springtime in an atomizer."

"Exactly! My mother used to take us all the time when we were little, and whenever I smell roses, I remember."

"We should go sometime. I know it won't be the same as before, but still."

"I'd like that." Did he mean he would take me?

Now they were playing "Stardust." We danced and talked about music and our lives. He was so easy to talk to about everything, and his arms were so strong, his presence commanding. I felt safe for the first time in maybe months.

The song switched again, this time to "Boogie Woogie Bugle Boy," which was the Andrews Sisters' latest and a fast song. Phillip and I stood there a moment. "They're playing your song, Patty," he said. "Swing dance time." He moved away from me a bit, to accomplish the faster steps.

But just then, Ethel ran up behind me.

"Hey, it's us!" she said. "Let's dance."

I didn't want to go, but Esther was right behind her. They pulled me toward the front of the room, where the record player was, to dance with them and pretend to be the Andrews Sisters. "I'll be right back," I told Phillip.

"I'll wait for you," he said.

Which he did, watching with amusement as we acted out "Boogie Woogie Bugle Boy" and "Hold Tight, Hold Tight," and just as we were finishing that, someone ran up to Ethel and whispered to her. I saw her face go white. She stopped dancing.

"We have to go," she said, and her eyes were full of tears.

"What is it?" I said.

"We have to go!" Ethel repeated.

"But what—? What is it, Ethel?"

She pulled me toward the door, Esther following. "There's been a telegram."

I felt the air leave my body. A telegram. It could only mean one thing. One of our brothers had been killed.

All thought of seeing Phillip fell from my mind, like a paratrooper crashing.

When we reached home, it was worse than expected. There were two telegrams, two on the same day. George was confirmed dead. Jack was missing.

"Maybe he's a prisoner," I said. I had to hold on to hope of seeing Jack again, dear Jack, who had held by hand and taken me to the zoo. Jack, who had helped me with my spelling, Jack, who'd been my ally in the war against my sisters.

"Missing just means they haven't found a body," Ethel said.

"Don't say *body*. I can't think of Jack like that." But I thought of Phillip's sunken ship, all men on board. They were likely "missing." Ethel was right.

In the weeks that followed, I had nothing to think of but grief. We had a small funeral for George. Then we wore black and went about our lives as if we weren't wondering how anything could ever be the same again. We shuffled about our lives by day, and at night, we sat in the dark, remembering what would never be, the good times that wouldn't be had, the weddings, the nieces and nephews never born. There was nothing even to look forward to. I cried every night for George and Jack, but especially for Jack, whose body lay God knew where in France. And the bombs continued to fall, one, two, even three nights in a week, without warning, so we never knew what was coming.

Only when the weeks became a month did I admit I was still thinking about Phillip, the man from the party. I thought about him all the time, about that day, the first time I'd felt like a grown-up. I wondered if he wondered about me. Probably not. Still, I looked for him on the street, at the grocer's, everywhere, but I didn't even know what he looked like, other than tall with blond hair. I asked people who had been to the party, people like Helen and Dora, who was now Mrs. Private Ned Stone, but they didn't know who he was. No one did. I hoped maybe he was searching for me, and I went to the only places I thought I might find him, near the elementary school. And Regent's Park, where it smelled nothing like spring-time in an atomizer. All of London stank of smoke and sulfur and motor oil and death. It was gray and hazy and cold as ice. I would never find him.

Over dinner one night, we were discussing, as usual, the possibility of leaving London.

"A bomb hit the Bank of England yesterday," my father said over a dull dinner of mostly vegetables and rice. "I think you should go and stay with my aunt Lydia. It would be safer."

"But we'd be leaving you," my mother said. "We could all stay in a shelter."

"That bomb gutted the Underground station. I want you to leave. If you left, I wouldn't always have to worry about you if there's a bombing."

I knew he didn't mean he wanted us to go away, just wanted to make us safe. Still, it sort of hurt to be sent away.

Mum started protesting. We all did. But then there was a knock on the door.

When we opened it, it was Kendra, the girl from our building. I didn't know her very well, but we nodded hello sometimes, and once she'd brought us a cherry pie with a cutout of a crow in the crust. Now she brought with her a tall man with piercing blue eyes, eyes that looked somehow familiar.

"This is John Harding. He has something to ask you."

My mother invited him in. "I apologize, sir, for not being on dress parade." She gestured around to the dusty tables, the wilted plants. "My two sons, we lost them in the war."

"Two sons?" the gentleman said. "It was my impression that only one was killed."

Mum winced, and my father said, "Well, yes, that is true. It is George we buried. Jack is only missing. It's hard to hold out hope, though."

"Oh, but you must," the man—Mr. Harding—said, sitting down on our father's favorite wing chair. "That's why I'm here. I had something, ah, to ask you." He looked at Kendra.

Kendra picked up on it. "What Mr. Harding is trying to say is, he has a proposal, that is to say, a favor to ask you."

"What?" Father said.

"What I mean to say is, we have reason to believe that your son Jack is alive."

A sharp intake of breath from Mum. "Reason? What reason?" She was shaking, and there were tears in her eyes.

"I am a woman of certain . . . powers," Kendra continued.

We looked at her strangely. The room went as silent as the nighttime, when we waited for the bombs to fall. Finally, Ethel said what we were all thinking.

"What does that mean? Powers?"

182

"Witchcraft," Kendra barely whispered. "I can bring you back your son Jack."

"Back from the dead?" Mum's voice caught.

"No, no, he isn't dead," Kendra said. "Not at all! I can find him. I can help him."

"Leave this house!" My father was screaming. "How dare you torment her like this?"

"John." Mum was clutching at my father's elbow. "What if it's true? What if she knows something?"

"Knows witchcraft? Knows something the British military doesn't? How is that possible?" He turned to Kendra again. "I want you to leave! And you also!" Father gave Mr. Harding a shove.

"Please!" Mr. Harding said, and his eyes seemed desperate. "Please listen!"

Kendra walked to the door, but as she did, she withdrew an object from the carpetbag she carried. A mirror. When she reached the door, she turned it toward my mother. "It's magical. Ask to see whomever you wish."

Mum recoiled from the mirror. "I can't. What if I ask to see Jack and he's . . . dead?"

"What if it's utter bollocks?" Father yelled.

Kendra looked at each of us, and Ethel and Esther repeated Mum's protestations. Only when she got to me did I seize the mirror. "It probably doesn't work anyway. There's no such thing as witches. So I'll look, and we'll get on with it."

"What if it's true?" Esther said.

"It's not true!" Ethel said. "There's no such thing, and she's tormenting Mum."

"If it's true, then we'll know," I said, and I felt hope for the first time in weeks. I wanted it to be true. I wanted Jack!

I held the mirror. My hands were like ice, and it was almost as if I could feel Jack staring into it from the other side. I so wanted to see his gray eyes, still with the light of life in them, once more. I peered into the glass. I saw a girl, pale and drawn, a girl Jack wouldn't recognize even if he did see me. "What do I say?" I asked Kendra. I knew it was stupid, but I wanted it to work.

She said, "Just tell it to show you your brother."

I looked at the girl in the mirror. Her eyes were full of tears. I took a deep breath and whispered, "Show me Jack. Oh, please, show me Jack!"

And the mirror did. It was like a movie. Jack was somewhere cold, crouched on a cot, and he was skinny, so skinny that his ears and his feet seemed out of proportion to his body.

But it was Jack. And he was alive. Clearly alive. He was shivering.

My hand was shaking too, so that it was hard to hold on to the mirror. I thrust it back at Kendra. "Is this real?"

"It's real," she said, taking the mirror from my hand.

"What is it?" My mother rushed over to Kendra, and when she saw the mirror, she gasped. "Look! Look!" My father and sisters were soon at her side. Esther and Ethel stepped back, but Mum was staring at the mirror, shaking.

"How can we get him back?" I felt as though I had seen something wrong, something frightening, like a ghost. Like Jack was back from the dead.

"That's why I've come," Kendra said.

She gestured to Mr. Harding and explained that he had a son who was injured in the war. He escaped death only by accepting a terrible curse. To break it, he had to marry. "If one of your daughters will promise to marry him, and to stay with him for one year as man and wife, his curse will be broken. And if you do this, I will bring your son back." She said it to my parents, but she looked at us girls, first Ethel and Esther, then me. Her eyes seemed to linger longest on me.

"What?" Ethel said. "But that's insane. It can't be true. There's no such thing as magic."

Esther chimed in. "You're just trying to trick us into marrying someone who may be awful. A masher or . . . worse."

Ethel appealed to our mother. "It's not like she can really bring Jack back. Even him in that mirror, it's some sort of illusion, a trick."

"If he's alive," Esther said, "he'll come back. If not . . ." She let her words trail off, but I knew what she'd been about to say. If Jack was dead, he was dead.

"Please." Mr. Harding spoke. "I know it sounds insane, but Kendra, she found my son in the hospital. She heard of the curse, and she helped him. She helped my son, and she will help yours. But we need your help."

I took the mirror from Kendra's hand again and stared into it a long time. Then, again, I whispered, "Show me Jack."

And Jack was there. It was him. I had no question. There was no way to make that up, his face, his eyes. Kendra didn't even know Jack.

I looked around at my parents, my sisters. My father's face was dour, but Mum's betrayed some hope. I knew why Ethel and Esther didn't want to marry this stranger. They thought they would meet someone else, someone who would love them. I had only briefly experienced that, with the man at the party, with Phillip. But perhaps I could love someone else.

I wanted Jack. I wanted to bring my brother back.

I said, "I'll do it. I'll marry him."

"But you can't," Ethel said, "You're only seventeen."

I narrowed my eyes at her. I knew what she was about. She didn't want me to volunteer because it would make her look bad. That was how she thought. I said, "I can, and I will. I want Jack to come home, no matter what it takes. If there's even a chance."

I looked at my mother. She nodded. Father too.

Kendra reached for my hand and squeezed it. "There is a chance. Jack will be back."

And it was done. Mum and Father tried to argue, half-heartedly, but once Kendra showed Father the mirror, the mirror with my brother in it, there was nothing to say. We had to try everything.

I didn't even think to ask about Mr. Harding's son, the man I was marrying. What sort of curse was he under? One that made him hideous? Or insane? It didn't matter. It didn't matter. I needn't ask, for it didn't matter. I would marry him no matter who or what he was. I would marry Mr. Harding himself, if need be. At least the son promised to be near my age.

We discussed details. We would be married the following Saturday, after dark. I didn't even know if it was legal, but Kendra said she was registered as a celebrant. Many people, like my friend Dora, were getting married quickly during the war. I could do it too.

In the days leading up to the wedding, I thought even more about Phillip. I searched for him in every shop window, every doorway, every street corner. I saw his shape in the corner of my eye as I walked to the grocer or waited on the long queue at the butcher's. He wasn't there. I couldn't bring myself to cry over him. We had only met once. I didn't even know what I'd do if I found him. Would I give up my brother for a man I barely knew, whose face I had never seen? No. No. I wanted Jack, who had held my hand when I was frightened, Jack who had danced with me. Still, I felt as if I had lost something I would never again find. In a way, I just wanted to tell him, to say good-bye.

Finally, the day of my marriage was at hand. Kendra arrived after dark with Mr. Harding and the man. It was all done in secret. Only our families were there. My sisters were saying all the appropriate things about "poor sweet Grace" and my "sacrifice," that they would have done it, but wasn't I sweet. I wanted to go into my room and hide, but I couldn't. I was the bride.

"Can I see Jack again?" I asked Kendra.

She nodded and handed me the mirror. I looked in the darkness. He was there. Seeing him strengthened me. He was cold, maybe sick. I had to help him. "All right."

I felt like I was going to my own funeral. I wore my pink Patty Andrews dress, as there was no time to get anything else. All the silk was being used for parachutes anyway. It didn't matter. The dress was my finest, for a wedding or a burial.

When the man entered, I held my breath. I couldn't see him. We were to be married by candlelight. Mr. Harding had specified it. I could only make out bits of him, that he was tall, with broad shoulders. I hoped he was, at least, kind. I knew nothing of this man. He might kill me in my sleep.

I was doing this for Jack.

As we were standing, waiting to pronounce the words of our vows, I said shyly to the man who would be my husband, "Hello . . . I'm Grace."

He said, "I know, Grace. I've been looking for so long . . . and now I've found you. I've finally found you."

His voice sounded so familiar. I gasped. It couldn't be.

In the darkness, he took my hand. "What's the matter, Patty Andrews? Don't you recognize me?"

"What?" It couldn't be.

"Sir Percy Blakeney? The Scarlet Pimpernel?"

I must have fainted, for when I awakened, I was in my Phillip's arms.

I still couldn't make out his face in the shadows, but his sweet voice was whispering, "Grace? Grace? Are you all right, Grace? Will you . . . do you want to marry me?"

"Yes." I felt tears spring to my eyes, tears of relief. "Yes, I want to marry you. But . . . you were looking for me? To break the curse?"

He shook his head, a shadow in the darkness. "Anyone could break the curse. I just thought . . . I wanted it to be you."

And so we were married, and afterward, we tripped down the dark streets across town. It wasn't safe, and we weren't supposed to be out, but it was my wedding night. "My darling," Phillip said, "I want to bring you to our home."

When we reached the flat, it was dark, of course. Phillip picked me up in his strong arms and carried me across the threshold to our bedroom.

My mother had spoken to me that day about what would be expected of me as a wife. I'd been nervous, of course. I didn't know this man! But, as he laid me down on the soft, cool feather bed, he said, "My darling . . . my lovely Grace. I don't expect . . . I know you don't know me, but can I kiss you? I have so longed to kiss you."

I sighed. "Yes. Yes."

He laid his lips against mine, finding them in the darkness. His mouth was soft and strong, and his hands were tender. He kissed my lips, my cheeks, even my hair. Then he enveloped me in his arms, and we fell asleep, entangled in each other's embrace.

I still had not seen my beloved's face. I didn't mind. I didn't care what he looked like.

I awoke in darkness. "No! No!" Someone was screaming.

"I can't find them! I can't find them!"

It was Phillip. He was flailing about like a frightened child.

"What's wrong, my darling? Is there a bombing?" I listened for a second, for the telltale sound of air raid sirens in the distance, but all was silent except my husband, whose breath came in great gulps.

"No! Please! I have to save them!"

He must have been having a nightmare. I put my hands on his shoulders and shook him awake. "Phillip! Phillip, wake up!"

"What?"

"It's only a dream. My darling, it's only a dream." The words *my darling* sprang so naturally to my lips. I realized I had been thinking of him this way since the party when we met. That he was so frightened only made me think it more.

"Oh no," he said when he finally realized what I was saying. "I'm so sorry. Some nights . . . it seems so real, like I'm there again. The water was on fire, the bombs dropping. We were covered in oil that might go up in flames, and I heard the shrieks around me, men dying, too many of them, and so many more below who never had a chance."

I held him close. He was sweating. "There, there," I said.

"They all wanted help. I tried to help them, but I couldn't. There were so many, and . . . so many. I couldn't help them all. I couldn't do anything."

"Of course you couldn't. Of course you couldn't."

"I wanted to." He was sobbing now.

"It's all right." I stroked his hair.

"You don't understand," he said.

"I don't. I know, I don't." I held him and rocked him from side to side. "But I know you're a good man. You did all you could."

"Did I?" he asked.

"I know you did."

I held him and kissed him until he fell asleep in my arms. When I woke in the morning, he wasn't there.

"Phillip?" I called. There was no answer. I looked around for him. When I walked over to the dresser, I saw he had left me a note. It said, "My darling, I had to go to work. Please make yourself comfortable in our home. The servants will help you find anything you need. I am especially proud of the music room and library. Love, Phillip."

Servants?

At that moment, there was a knock on the door.

"Madam?" a voice said.

Madam? I was *madam*. Yesterday, I had been *miss*, if anything, but of course, I was generally just Grace.

"Come in," I called.

The door opened, and a woman about my mother's age was standing there. She wore a black uniform, and she curtsied. "Madam, I am Mary. Would you like me to bring up a tray, or do you wish to come to the dining room for breakfast?"

I realized I wanted to look around at what my husband had called "our home."

"Oh, I'll come down."

But then, having said that, I didn't know how to behave. We had never had servants before. Could I come to breakfast in my bathrobe, as I might have at my parents' house? Or did I need to get dressed? And what should I wear?

"Shall I lay out something for you to wear, madam?" Mary was asking. "Or do you wish to have breakfast in your robe?"

I knew I was making a decision for the rest of my life. And yet I wanted a few moments alone, so I said, "Oh, I can get dressed, thank you. If you can bring me my suitcase."

Where was Phillip? Why had he gone so early?

I dressed in a sensible skirt and jumper and left the bedroom. The sight that greeted me was shocking to my eyes.

I stood at the end of a hallway with gleaming marble floors. It led to an elegant living room with a grand piano. A music room! Oh, Esther would love that! I looked inside and saw a phonograph with stacks of records. The Andrews Sisters were on top. I flipped through them. Next was "You and I" and "He Wears a Pair of Silver Wings." All the songs from the night we'd met. To the side, I saw another room with a tall door of shining dark wood. I opened it.

It was the library. On shelves of walnut that reached to the ceiling, there were hundreds, maybe thousands of books, almost like the lending library in town, except that here, every book I saw was something of interest to me.

On a table near the door was, *Mam'zelle Guillotine*, by Baroness Orczy, the latest of the Scarlet Pimpernel series. I picked it up, curled up on the sofa, and immediately became engrossed in the tale of Gabrielle, a girl near my own age whose father was to be hanged for a crime he didn't commit. Every little minute or so, I looked around the room. So many books! I could read all of them. I couldn't wait for Phillip to come home to discuss them. And maybe he would play the piano, and I would sing.

Phillip! I had found him without even trying. I had fallen asleep not in some stranger's arms, but in Phillip's. A day I'd thought would be a nightmare had become a dream.

Nightmare. Poor, dear man, to be so tormented. It must be because of what he'd suffered in the war. But now I would be there to comfort him, as his wife. I'd gone from being a girl to being a wife in minutes.

I didn't even know what wives did, what they were expected to do. I knew what my mother did; she took care of the children. Someday, I would have children, little boys and girls with piercing blue eyes like their father's. But, for now, I had little to do but read and listen to so many records!

I went back to Gabrielle's story until Mary came to the library door to tell me that breakfast was ready.

I considered bringing the book with me, but I didn't know if that would be rude, so I left it there and walked across the elegant room to the breakfast nook, where Mary was serving eggs and toast on fine china with sprays of roses on it.

"Thank you," I said. "This is lovely." I could not believe I had servants! I was a mistress! At seventeen! Should I offer to clear the table?

"Did you sleep well, madam?"

"Oh yes," I said, pushing back thoughts of being awakened. "You can call me Grace, though."

"Perhaps I can call you Mrs. Harding."

"Okay." I wanted to ask her about Phillip, my husband, but I couldn't think of a way to bring up the subject without it seeming awkward. Did she know we barely knew each other?

"Mr. Harding—your husband, that is—is a lovely man," she said, offering me tea.

"Oh, thank you. Yes, he is. Isn't he?"

"He works so hard, though. I barely see him anymore. He's only home at night."

"Oh." I wondered if she'd seen his face. Silly! Of course she had. "Have you known him long?"

"Oh yes, ma'am. His whole life. I was employed by his father when he was growing up. He was such a sweet boy, always offering to help me around the house or bringing home an injured baby bird. And he's a kind man. He even gave my dear son Albert money to continue his schooling."

"That's lovely." I wanted to ask her what he looked like, but that would seem odd. I would see him soon enough, in any case. Still, I looked around to see if there were any photographs. There were, but all of other people, including a woman who must have been his mother. There was one of a family. I walked over to it. I recognized the man in it. Mr. Harding, Phillip's father.

"Ah, you want to see what Phillip was like as a lad," Mary said.

"Yes. Is that him?" He was a handsome boy who resembled his father.

"Yes, and his sister." She picked up the plates and went to the kitchen.

I wanted to call her back, ask more questions. But, of course, it would be awkward.

After breakfast, I met the other servants, a manservant named Bryson and the cook, an Irish lady named Maeve. Then I fairly ran around the house, examining artwork on the walls, fine moldings on high ceilings! I had gone from nothing to such affluence! In the study, I threw myself onto a thick rug and just rolled on it! Then I ran to the music room and played all the records. I tried to play the piano. I remembered Minuet in G, and it sounded so elegant on the beautiful grand. Finally, I went back to the library and read my book, stopping only when Mary brought in tea. I wanted to finish reading so I could tell Phillip about it. At five, I went to my bedroom and changed into my second-best dress, after the one I'd worn for the wedding. I wanted to look beautiful for my husband. I would finally see his face!

But, alas, the sun set and he was not home. It was winter, after all, and the sun set so early. When he finally came home, I fairly flew to the door, wanting to see him. But the light was dim, and he was merely a tall, elegant shadow, a shadow that took me in his arms and kissed me.

"I'm sorry I'm so late, my darling."

"Can we not turn on the lights?" I asked. "There are curtains over the windows."

"I know." His voice sounded nervous in the darkness. "I . . . I can't. It's part of the curse that I cannot show myself to you."

"Oh." He had not told me.

"I was afraid to tell you. And now I know you must be frightened, believing me to be hideous."

"Oh. No." Was he?

And suddenly I remembered Phillip, Phillip in the darkness, in my arms, Phillip the hero. I didn't care. I didn't care what he looked like. "It's all right," I said. "Come. Maeve made dinner. It's on the table."

Over dinner, in the pitch-darkness, I told him, "I finished *Mam'zelle Guillotine.* Thank you for leaving it out for me."

I could almost see the outline of his smile, I thought. "You liked it then?"

"Yes. I loved it."

He laughed. "Tell me about it. What did you think of Gabrielle?"

"Oh, she was fascinating. To go from being an innocent young girl to a master executioner! I loved it!" It was so wonderful to have someone to talk to. At home, Mum was sullen and silent. My sisters spoke mostly to one another, and Father only wanted to talk about the war, the war all the time. I knew it was important, but sometimes, I wanted to forget.

After dinner, we went to the music room, and in the darkness,

Phillip played the piano, and I sang. I asked him if he knew "A Nightingale Sang in Berkeley Square," and he happily obliged. I sang along.

"I wish I could hear that nightingale," I said when it was over.

"I heard it," he said. "You sing like one." He pulled me toward him in the darkness and kissed me. I kissed him back.

"I love . . . your piano playing," I said.

"After the curse is over, I'll teach you to play. In the light."

I nodded eagerly, and I kissed him again. With my hand, I felt a roughness on his cheek. What was it? Phillip flinched, but he did not try to move my hand away. I touched the rest of his face, and it was smooth.

Finally, we retired to the bedroom.

Phillip slept through the night.

It went like that for the first week. My life by day was beautiful and tranquil, and at night, it was romantic and exciting. Phillip brought me flowers or presents, including records of every song I wanted. Most nights, Phillip slept peacefully in my arms, but sometimes, he was awakened by nightmares and told tales of men screaming, of holding on to a piece of the bombed-out ship for dear life. "A man was pleading with me. I helped him onto a beam from the ship, but I couldn't hold him. My arms . . . they felt like they were being ripped off. I saw him sink below the water! I could do nothing. Nothing."

"How awful," I said, remembering how helpful Mary had said Phillip was.

"It was. And all night, as we waited to be rescued, people were singing 'There Will Always Be an England' and 'Beer Barrel Polka' over and over, as more people gave up and drowned. I wish I never had to hear those two songs again."

"Why does no one know about this, the tragedy?" I asked him.

"They told us not to tell anyone. Not the press, no one. They threatened us with court martial if we told. If people knew of such a disaster, it would make them lose hope."

I thought about those long nights sitting in our homes, the continued threat of bombings, rationing, and gloom. It was worth it because we were going to win. We were going to defeat the evil Axis powers. To know that thousands had been killed in one night would make people lose hope.

But what if hope *was* lost? What if England were to lose?

"But this way," I said, "it seems like it never happened, like it was all a nightmare."

"A nightmare that just keeps happening," he said, and I could hear his voice shaking.

"Oh, my poor love," I said, taking him in my arms.

When I touched his face, I felt the roughness of the skin on one cheek. I had felt it before. I knew he had injuries. I didn't care. I was falling more and more in love with him.

After a week of this, I asked him, "Would it be all right if I visited my mother and my sisters? I'm so lonely during the day."

"Of course, my love. Or bring them over here so they can see where we live."

I *loved* that idea, showing off my beautiful flat to Esther and Ethel, who had always been so great compared to me, because there were two of them, and they were older. They'd be so impressed now! Perhaps they would even want to stay over. So on Tuesday, I had them over for tea. Although we were rationing, we brought out the jam, and Mary even made a cake for my family. We set out the good china, and the silver was polished until it sparkled. Phillip brought roses, and the house smelled like Regent's Park. I wondered what had happened to his plan of us visiting there.

When my family came in, they gasped. All of them, collectively.

"You look . . . lovely." I saw Ethel's eyes fix upon my pearls, an elegant double strand that had been Phillip's mother's. She seized them. "Are those real?"

"I think so," I said. They were.

"You can tell by running your teeth over them," Ethel said, tugging at them.

"Maybe later," I said.

"And your dress." Esther touched the green wool of the dress I had bought the day before, and I saw her noticing the emerald earrings Phillip left on the nightstand that very morning. "So lovely. I never have nice things anymore."

"At least we won't have to sit in the dark anymore," Ethel said.

"What do you mean?" I asked. I led them to the dining room, where again I saw their eyes fixing upon the elegant wallpaper, the expensive sconces. Even Mum ran her hands across the back of a chair.

"We're moving to the country to stay with Aunt Lydia," Mum said. "You could come with us."

"Oh no," I said. "I wouldn't want to leave, to leave Phillip."

"But you've only known him a week," Esther said. "You had to marry him, not stay with him."

"I do have to stay, because . . ." I thought of the nights spent in Phillip's arms. "I love him. He's so kind, and so intelligent. We stay up late and listen to music, and talk of . . . our dreams. Phillip plays the piano."

"He plays the piano?" Esther asked.

"Beautifully. He says he'll teach me too. I've never been so happy."

Ethel looked down. "And what does he look like?" she asked. "He must be very handsome."

"I suppose he is," I said.

"What do you mean, you suppose?" Esther asked.

"Well, I don't exactly . . . I haven't seen him." I looked around, wishing Mary would come in with the tea. "Let me go see what's taking the tea." I stood and started out of the room.

Ethel grabbed my arm. "What do you mean, you haven't seen him?"

"It's only been a week since we've been married. He's only been here at night."

"So late at night?" Esther asked.

"He works so hard. He has an important job, and he's away from dawn to dusk. But we have the most wonderful talks and—"

"He's a monster!" Ethel said. "That's the only possible explanation."

Esther was nodding, but she said, "I don't know about a monster, Ethel. He could just—"

"A monster!" Ethel repeated. "Why else would he need to force someone to marry him, then hide himself?"

"He didn't force me," I protested. "I met him at the party. I fell in love with him then. I would have married him anyway."

"Nonsense," Ethel said. "He was wearing a mask then too. If anything, that confirms it."

"It was a fancy-dress party," I said, though I knew they were right. I had thought of it myself.

"Here we go, madam!" Mary was coming in with the tea things.

"Oh, this all looks lovely, Mary," I said, willing my sisters to be still, to change the subject. "Thank you so much for preparing this special, special treat!"

"Of course. I would do anything for Phillip's wife." She nodded rather curtly at Ethel and Esther, so I knew she'd heard. "And her family."

I wanted to beg Mary to tell them Phillip was handsome, to tell *me* that. But it would have looked like a betrayal of Phillip. I couldn't ask.

"Biscuit, Mum?" I passed them to her as Mary poured the tea.

For five blessed minutes, they were silent.

As soon as Mary left, they were back to the same subject.

"You have to leave him," Ethel said.

"She can't leave him," Mum said.

"Well, find out what he looks like, then? Use a candle. Assure that he isn't a . . . freak."

"He isn't a freak," I said. "He's wonderful. He's a war hero."

"Yes," Ethel said. "He was injured in the war. How do you know he even has all his parts—his eyes, his nose, his—?"

"I've been close enough to know he has a nose. Even in the dark. I've . . . touched him."

"Have you kissed him?" Esther asked. "Or . . . more?"

"Yes," I said. "I know."

"You know . . . nothing," Ethel said. "If there can be magic, there can be monsters. Perhaps he's been able to deceive you . . . in the dark. But what of in the light?"

I looked at Esther, always the nicer of my sisters. She was nodding too. "I fear you must find out," she said.

We ate our tea and toast in silence. All the joy of seeing them was gone. I didn't even show them the music room before they left, though I had so wanted Esther to see the beautiful piano.

I knew they were merely jealous of me. They'd had their chance to marry Phillip, but they had refused. Now, seeing me here in an elegant house with jewels and all my heart desired, they were sorry. Still, it grated on me, and as I shut the door behind them, I thought about what I could do.

I wanted to be able to tell my sisters what I knew to be true, that Phillip was beautiful, inside and out. If I could look at him but once, I could say that forever. I would look that night. He had said he couldn't show himself to me, but if I snuck a glance, that would be different. He wouldn't be involved. I could pretend it was an accident.

I looked at the table. Mary had cleared away the tea things, and the table was empty, save two elegant candelabra with red tapers left over from the Christmas holiday.

I took one of the tapers and hid it in my dress.

Then I went into the kitchen, where Maeve was cooking dinner.

"I wanted to thank you for the wonderful tea," I said. "My sisters loved the cookies." I searched the room for the matches I knew were there. I saw them by the stove and walked sideways over there.

"Thank you, Ma'am," Maeve said.

"And what lovelies are you preparing tonight?"

"Oh, don't know about lovelies, with the rationing, but we're having chicken and potatoes and green beans."

Backed against the stove, I snatched up the matches and stuffed them up my sleeve.

"You always do so well with so little. Green beans are my favorites," I said, and took the matches.

"I'll remember that, ma'am." She smiled. "I can make them as often as you like."

I left the room and went upstairs. I secreted the candle and matches in the nightstand.

That night, after a dinner during which I told Phillip that everything had gone well with my sisters, we went to bed. But I lay awake until I heard Phillip's breathing become even with sleep, and then an hour more, until the clock downstairs struck one. Finally, I went to the nightstand and took out the forbidden candle.

I lit it with great effort. It was difficult in the dark, and I hadn't much experience of late with lighting candles. When it was finally done, I held it close and shone it upon my beloved.

In the light, I could tell that Phillip was not a monster. Far from it. Instead, he was the most beautiful man I had ever beheld. He could have been a movie star like Leslie Howard or Laurence Olivier. Tall and elegant, as I had seen at the party, with a shock of blond hair, Phillip had the features of a Greek god in a statue. I remembered, in school, reading of Cupid, the most beautiful god, whose wife, Psyche, could not look upon him. Phillip was like Cupid! The blanket didn't cover him, so I could see that his body was lean and muscular. My sisters would be even more jealous if they could see him! I stared, wanting to touch him but afraid. He stirred a bit in his sleep, moving his head to one side, and then I could see why he had worn the mask, for on the other side of his face, the flesh was seared away from his mouth to the top of his cheek and around his eye so the skin was puckered, shiny, and angry red. One brow was half burned off. I remembered him telling me about the water on fire. Had this happened then?

It didn't matter. He was still beautiful, so beautiful. If anything, the flaw only made him more so, for he appeared more real.

As I stood gaping at him, my hand moved, and a bit of hot wax fell from the candle and onto Phillip's hand.

He started awake.

"What? What is it?" he yelled.

"Oh, darling, I'm sorry! I was—"

"I know what you were doing. You were trying to see me."

I nodded, unable to conceal the truth of it. "I'm sorry," I whispered. "I'm sorry."

"Why?" he demanded.

"My sisters . . ." I was sobbing. "They said . . . I didn't think it would matter if you didn't know."

He turned his face so that the scalded skin was faced toward me. "Well, now you know."

"I don't care about that, this little scar." That must have been why he was hiding in the dark. "It is nothing, inconsequential. You have no need to hide it from me."

He shook his head. "I had every need to hide it from you. I told you it was part of the curse, or rather, part of the cure. I had to find a woman who would marry me, both marry me and trust me for a year. I tried to win your trust. I was kind to you. I gave you no reason to believe—"

"I only wanted to see what my husband looked like." The wax from the candle fell on my hand, and I jumped, then blew it out.

"Well, now you know. But I cannot be your husband any longer, I fear. I am sorry, for I love you, my Grace."

"What do you mean?" I felt the wax searing my hand, over and over.

Now we were in darkness again, and his voice came out of it, so soft against the nothingness of the night.

"On the day the *Lancastria* sank, I watched the men around me die. Many, so many, died even before the ship sank, when the bombs hit and tore it to shreds. The lucky ones, I among them, had a small chance to swim away, but there were many of us and few lifeboats, only little bits of flotsam to hold on to. I was injured, burned, and as I swam for my life, I thought I saw a woman. In the dim light, she looked like a fairy with long white hair and skin the color of seafoam. She looked like one of the *Dames Blanches*."

Had this fairy been the one who had cursed him?

"I begged her to help me. With all the dying men around me, I became a coward, and I pleaded with her to save me. I said that if I lived, I would do anything. Anything. So she reached out her hand where I could almost touch it. She said, 'I will save you if you promise to marry my daughter.'

203

"'Anything, anything,' I said, imagining my poor father receiving news of my death. I am his only son, and my sister died as a young girl. He would have nothing without me.

"So I took her hand, and she pulled me out of the melee to a waiting lifeboat. But, when I went to shore, in Saint Nazaire, covered in oil, I learned that the daughter was not a fairy as I assumed she would be, but a troll princess who would surely kill me in my sleep. I begged the one who had saved me to relieve me of the burden, but she said no. I could go home to bid my *adieux* to my family, but I must come back.

"I went with heavy heart, but on the way here, I met Kendra, who has an odd interest in shipwrecks. And witchcraft. I told her of my situation, and with her mirror, she helped me bargain with this woman, this fairy, this whatever she was . . . until finally she agreed that she would free me under the condition that I found a young woman to marry me, sight unseen, and that she would not look at my face for one year from our marriage."

"Why that? Why that condition?" But I knew. It was because she wanted to give him an impossible task. Any woman would want to look upon her husband's face.

Any woman, or just me?

"When I met you, my darling, I knew you were the only girl I wanted, and since you had not seen my face, you would be suitable. I enlisted Kendra's help to persuade you to marry me. She knew you would do anything to save your brother."

"Jack? Will Jack still be all right?" In all that had happened, I had almost forgotten about poor Jack! How had Kendra known about Jack? "Did Kendra kidnap him?"

"No. He is all right, but imprisoned by the Nazis. Kendra found out about him from your sisters. She used her mirror to locate him and has been protecting him with her spells. Perhaps it was wrong of me to use your brother as bait, but I was desperate. I will ask Kendra to help you find him."

"But you?" Now that I knew Jack was safe, my thoughts returned to my husband. I wanted him to stay my husband! It was as if, in that short amount of time, I had lived a lifetime, a lifetime of standing by the piano with Phillip each evening, of falling asleep in his strong arms. I could not live without him.

"I must carry out my bargain."

"By marrying a troll?" I knew little of trolls, except that they were said to lurk under bridges in children's stories. It seemed impossible that trolls even existed, but still more impossible that he would not be here, always, with me. That I had doomed him. I wanted to do anything to keep him from leaving, even if I had to burn the whole house down and turn us both to ash. "Oh, how could I have done this to you?"

"It wasn't your fault. I should have known it would be impossible. Don't blame yourself."

"But how can I not?" I began to sob. "And how can she punish you for *my* mistake?"

"Please don't cry, Grace." He touched my wrist, then pulled me toward him in an embrace.

"Can you stay?" I asked. "Stay with me?"

"I want to. I so want to, even more now that I know you, now that I have loved you." His embrace tightened.

"Then stay! What can she do?"

"I am supposed to go to a castle, east of the sun, west of the moon. There I will find my bride."

"Please! Please!" It was like the moment after hearing about George's death, when it felt like there was still something that could be done to reverse it, though of course there wasn't. At such moments, time seemed like a map with one event on one side of some chasm and the present on the other side. It seemed like it should be easy to traverse the pit, but in fact it was impossible.

"It was only a tiny mistake. Please don't leave me," I begged him.

He held me and stroked my hair. "I'll try not to," he said.

And yet, even as I fell asleep in his arms, I knew he would be gone when I awoke.

In the morning, he was nowhere to be found. In the evening, he did not come home for dinner.

Phillip was gone.

That night, I lay alone in the silent darkness. In the time we had been married, our sleep had not been interrupted by air raid sirens, but now I wondered what happened if there was a wailing in the night. Would I flee to the building's cellar? Would I cower there alone? Or should I return to my family's home? I didn't know if I should wait for my husband. I didn't know if I was even a wife anymore.

As I waited for morning to come, I decided. I had to find Phillip. I didn't know where he was, but I knew he would only be happy and safe in my arms—and I would only be happy and safe with him. Plus, I couldn't face my sisters. I couldn't let them know my husband had abandoned me. And I especially couldn't let them know it was because I had listened to their nonsense—though, really, it was their fault.

I slept for about an hour. The next morning, when I knew my sisters would be at work, I went to find Kendra.

She let me in cheerily, as if she'd been expecting me. "Grace! How are you? And how is dear Phillip?"

The way she said it, I suspected she knew that too. "He's missing. I must find him."

She invited me into her flat. It was much larger than our flat, larger, in fact, than I would have believed possible from the outside, and decorated much like I imagined Buckingham Palace would be. I sat on an antique chair and poured out the whole story.

When I finished, she smiled the sad smile of one who is sorry to be right. "I told him it would be impossible to expect a young woman not to see the face of her husband."

"But I love him. I love him despite his scars, despite his nightmares, despite the curse that is upon him. I love him. I want him back. You must help me."

"I will help you find your brother."

"I want that too—but I can't allow Phillip to marry a troll. Please!"

She picked up a mirror—*the* mirror—from a small table. She spoke into it. "Show me Phillip."

I saw Phillip. He was alive! But he appeared to be in a small room, very dark, and I could see nothing else.

"Where is he?" I asked.

"I cannot tell," she said. "I can't always tell. Even with my beloved . . ." She stopped.

"Then how will—?"

"If we can't use the mirror, we must use our wits. Where would the troll wife be?"

I hesitated. Trolls were known to populate Norway. But Phillip had not been to Norway, and I really didn't want to go there

208

unnecessarily. I said, "Where the ship sank? Off the coast of France? He said he had to go east of the sun, west of the moon, but that makes no sense."

"Where in France was the shipwreck?"

"I don't know. He said France." I remembered vividly Phillip's screams, the horrific stories he told of that awful night, but I didn't remember the name of the town. "Saint . . . something."

"Do you remember the name of the ship?"

I could hear Phillip's dear voice saying it, *The day the* Lancastria *sank* . . . "Yes," I said, "the *Lancastria*."

"You need to visit the War Office. Find out what happened to that ship."

"How can I?"

Kendra and I discussed a plan.

The next morning, early, I traveled to Horse Guard's Avenue to the giant War Office building. It looked like a temple, a neoclassical building with statues of horses on the front, and I was scared to approach it. Yet what choice did I have? I was not even sure if I was Phillip's wife. How much longer could I stay here, if he was off to marry another? And what would happen to Phillip?

I walked between the giant stone columns and into the building.

At the first desk, I spoke to a woman who was working. "I need to talk to someone about my brother. He was on a ship. I think it sank."

She pointed to another office. Once inside, I waited in a long line of women, widows, mothers. When I reached the front, I said, "I'm looking for information about the HMT *Lancastria*. My brother was on it. He's missing in action." I knew it was a lie, but Kendra and I had decided it sounded plausible enough. I could not, of course, ask after Phillip, for they would know he had lived.

"Down that hallway," the clerk said.

I went down that hallway, then up a staircase, then down to the basement. In each place, I repeated my query, and in each place, I was sent somewhere else. Finally, I was sent to an office in the top-floor cupola. The elevator was broken, so I had to take the stairs. When I reached the very top, the door was locked. I looked around, helpless, then banged on the door.

Someone opened it, and a woman bade me come in.

I was in a tiny room, so tiny as to fit only one desk. A very old woman sat at the desk. I couldn't see how she had opened the door, for she was nowhere near it and sat at her desk, about to cut up a yellow apple with a red-handled knife.

"What can I do for you, my child?"

"I'm looking for my brother. He was on the ship *Lancastria*. It sank, and he is missing."

"Your brother, is it?" The old woman set the knife down and passed the apple from one hand to the other. "Are you quite certain it is your brother?"

She looked at me sharply. Her eyes were blue, as blue as Phillip's, and I knew that she knew the truth. I could not lie.

"No, it's not my brother at all. I mean, my brother George is dead, and my brother Jack is missing, but they weren't on the *Lancastria*. At least, I don't think they were. It's my husband. He was on the ship the night it sank, and he is tormented by nightmares. I believe he may have gone back to pay his respects. I have to find him, but I don't know where the ship sank, or where he is."

The old woman stared at the apple with great concentration, then rolled it from one side of her desk to the other. It made a dull, deep sound like a kettledrum.

"Please," I said, "you must help me. I don't want to tell anyone about the . . . the tragedy. I just have to find Phillip."

"Did he say anything else?" she asked.

"He said he needed to go to a castle, east of the sun, west of the moon."

She set the apple down on the front of the desk in such a way that it would not roll. Once it was there, I could see that it wasn't a real apple. Rather, it was made of metal that gleamed like pure gold.

She said, "I don't know where Phillip is, but as reward for telling the truth, I will give you travel documents to get to Saint Nazaire, France. That is where you must pay your respects to the dead of the *Lancastria*. Perhaps you can find him there."

She reached into her desk drawer and took out official-looking travel documents, already filled out with my name, Grace Harding, which I hadn't given her. She handed them to me.

How had she known? Was she a witch? How many witches were there in London?

But I said, "Thank you."

"And take this." She held out the apple.

"Oh, I couldn't."

"I insist." With great effort, she pushed it toward me. "I lost my boys in the war as well. Take it for your brother George."

I took it from her. It was heavier than I'd imagined, as heavy as all the silverware in my new home. Still, I put it inside my purse with the papers.

"Thank you," I said.

But when I looked back up, there was no one there.

The next day, I boarded a train, then a ship to the port of Saint Nazaire. I took Kendra's mirror so I could communicate with her. I didn't want to upset my parents. I didn't want to admit my troubles.

When I finally reached the port of Saint Nazaire, everything was bustling. I saw a group of soldiers and thought perhaps they could help me. Then I saw the swastika emblem on their arms. They were

German soldiers! I remembered that Father had said France was occupied by Germany now! I held tight with one hand to the travel papers the old woman had given me, the apple with the other, though I was careful to keep the apple hidden.

To my surprise, they ignored me and let me pass without question.

I passed more soldiers as I walked into town. I tried to avoid their gaze. The town was gray and plain, with little sun and patches of dirt peeping through the dirty snow. There were few civilians outside, but in front of a grocery store, I saw an old woman sitting in a straight-backed chair, holding a carding comb that she was using to separate a small amount of sheep's wool.

Fortunately, I had studied French, so I approached her and said, "Excuse me, madame. I am looking for a castle."

She seemed not to understand me for a moment, which made me wonder if I had mispronounced something, or if she was merely being unfriendly. But finally, she said, "No. There is no castle."

"I am looking for a castle, east of the sun, west of the moon. My husband was on a . . ." I didn't know the French word for ship. "A boat. Under the water." I mimed a sinking ship.

"Ah!" she said, "*navire de transport!* British." She pointed to a house by the sea and said, "She is the one who takes in all the soldiers' bodies. Maybe if you help her, she will help you."

"Help her?" I asked.

"With the memorial," she said.

I remembered what the old lady at the War Office had said about paying my respects. Perhaps that was what she meant.

"Have you lost someone in this war?" I asked.

The woman nodded. "Yes. My son." She began to cry.

"I am sorry about your son," I said, but she kept sobbing and I took her in my arms, dried her tears, thinking of my own mother,

212

distracted with grief over George.

After a long time, her shaking shoulders went still. She sniffled. "I must get back to my work."

I understood that she was embarrassed to have been so emotional. "*Merci*," I told the woman and started toward the house.

"*Attendez!*" the woman said. She handed me the carding comb, meeting my gaze. I noticed that her eyes were blue as the ocean on a cloudless day, and the comb, which I had thought a dull metal, was pure gold. "For your kindness in comforting me. I hope you find your husband. I hope this will help you."

I took it from her with another "*Merci*" and went on.

The house was up a small hill, on a bluff. I climbed it. It was difficult, for it was rocky and blustery. From the top, I could see the cold, gray ocean, and I wondered if the house's occupants had seen the ship sinking, heard the men screaming on that fateful night.

I wondered if they still heard them, in their dreams, on dark nights when my family heard sirens and dropping bombs, or in their nightmares, as Phillip did.

When I reached the house, there was an old woman on the porch. This surprised me because it was quite cold, and she wore no coat. She held a spindle in her hand and was simply twirling it.

I spoke to her in French. "Hello. I'm looking for a castle."

She ignored me, still fiddling with the spindle.

"My husband was on the ship that sank. He has been tormented by nightmares of it, and now he has disappeared. I'm here to find him."

When I said "the ship," I saw her eyes look up to me. She kept looking at me as I said I was there to find him. Then she spoke to me in English.

"The ship, it sank in June. I did not see it, for it was too far away, but I heard the bombs that hit it. For weeks, even months after, the bodies, the bodies, they washed ashore, bloated, ripped apart by crabs and fish. The people of this town gave them Christian burials, sometimes under cover of darkness to avoid the soldiers. Would you like to see?"

I shuddered, imagining it, but said, "Yes. Please."

She stood, still holding the spindle, and beckoned to me to follow her. I did, though my feet were hurting now from all the walking and climbing. We trudged down the hill to a small road. It was late afternoon, and the sun was in my eyes as we waded through the snow. At the end of it was a gate, and we pushed through it.

Before us, in every direction, as far I could see, were graves. Some were regular graves with headstones like I'd seen at home, but many, too many, were marked with simple homemade crosses. I walked among them. Were these the men who had been on the ship with Phillip that night? Could he have been among them?

The woman said, "I check them every day or so, to make sure the markers don't get lost in the snow. We plan to put up proper stones someday, when the war is over."

I nodded. She adjusted a cross that was askew in the snow. I found another and did the same. As I did, I found myself weeping, weeping for George, who was dead, for Jack, who was God knew where, for Phillip, who was ruined and gone.

"What is the matter, my child?"

"Will it never end?" I asked.

She shook her head. "Not for a long, long time, I'm afraid."

She adjusted another cross, which was already covered in gray-green lichen.

When we had checked all of them, she said, "You needed help with something?"

I remembered myself. "Yes. I'm looking for a castle. It is said to be east of the sun, west of the moon. I've already been told there is no castle here."

"Whoever told you that was lying!"

"But how can it be east of the sun, west of the moon?"

She took my hand and turned me in the direction of the low sun. "The sun, it sets in the west. We are east of it now." She turned me the other way. "The moon will rise over there, in the east or southeast. It is a full moon tonight. When it rises, if you stand in the exact place in between them and look forward, you will see the castle."

I looked where she was pointing, to the north. There was nothing but empty land, space for more graves.

"It's not there now?" I asked, wondering if she was insane.

"No," she said, "but it will be, at the moonrise. If you stay here, you will see it."

She handed me the golden spindle she carried. "Take this with you, for your kindness in helping me. You may need it."

Then she was gone.

I stood, waiting, I knew not for what exactly. The air had gone from cold to freezing, and the wind whipped through my body, my hair. I drew my coat around me. The heavy golden objects in my pockets clunked against my legs. I had Kendra's mirror with me as well! I looked to where the old woman had said the moon would rise. It was not there yet. Behind me, the sun was beginning to set over the ocean. The sky was starting to pinken.

When I stopped being able to feel my feet, I saw the full moon, visible through the leafless trees. I turned, and the sky to the west was red as blood.

Then I looked to the center, to the plot of land the old woman had pointed out. Before me arose a castle, tower by tower, turret by turret, from underground. It was dark and grim, covered with dead vines, and it climbed until it reached the darkening sky.

There was a door that faced east, toward the rising moon. A single lantern shone by the entrance. I walked toward it, as if mesmerized. The snow seeped through my shoes, chilling me. As I came closer, I saw that the door was covered in cobwebs, as if no one had entered or left in a long time.

I knocked anyway, and waited. Finally, I heard heavy footsteps approaching, and the door opened.

I looked down at a woman who was short and squat, with a snub nose and big ears. Her hair was a glistening blue, and her face was covered with hairy warts. On her head, she wore a golden crown. The troll princess!

"Why are you here?" she demanded in a voice filled with blood and venom.

"I'm here to see my h—" I did not want to anger her. "I am here to see Phillip Harding. Is he here?"

She blinked but said, "No. I know of no Phillip Harding."

Still, I knew the truth by her face. Her mouth had made an O of surprise when I had said Phillip's name. "Please, I will do anything, give you anything, to see him."

She looked interested. "What do you have to give?"

I thought about it and realized that the heavy objects in my pockets were currency. "I have a golden apple. I will give it to you, but in exchange, I wish to spend the night with him. Alone," I added, lest she insist on staying with her husband. I figured out that staying the night would allow us time to plan his escape.

I plucked the apple from my pocket and held it out high, high enough that she could see it but not touch it, for I was far taller than a troll. It gleamed in the light of the full moon.

"Oooh." She reached for it, but I held it higher.

"You must bring me to my husband first," I said.

The troll princess stomped her foot. "He is not your husband but mine. But I want that apple. I will go to him and ask if he will see you. Sit down."

She gestured to a dark and gloomy living room. I noticed there were no windows. Were the nights black in France too? Or did she just prefer to have no light, because she was so ugly? In any case, I sat on a dusty gray sofa, and she disappeared down a dark hallway.

It was a long time before she returned, maybe half an hour, maybe more. When she did return, she said, "All right."

She beckoned for me to follow her. But I hesitated. It was too easy. Still, I followed her down the black hallway on cold floors made of stone.

Finally, she reached the doorway. In the shadows, I could barely see her hold it open.

She reached for the apple.

I looked into the room. Was Phillip there? Yes. Through the strained moonlight from the window, I saw him. He was asleep, looking as beautiful as he had on the night we were together last.

I took the apple from my coat pocket and handed it to the troll. Then I entered the room and shut the door behind me. I ran to Phillip's side.

"Phillip?" I whispered. "Phillip?"

He did not, would not stir.

I said his name more loudly. "Phillip!"

Nothing. Had this been the troll's trick, the reason why she had made it so easy for me? Was Phillip sick? Even dead? But I touched his wrist, and I felt there was a pulse.

I shook him. "Phillip! Phillip! Wake up!"

But there was nothing, no reaction. I screamed and cried and shook him from side to side. I slapped him on his face, and around his body. He was like a corpse. Finally, I fell, sobbing, to sleep beside him.

When morning came, he was still asleep, and the troll princess was at the door. It was not quite light.

"You must leave now," she said, her voice menacing.

"I must stay," I said.

"You cannot stay during the day, but for the right payment, I will allow you to stay another night."

What could I do? I must try again. I reached inside my pocket and pulled out the comb.

"I have this carding comb," I said. Again, I held it high so she could not reach it.

"Very well," she said. "Come back at moonrise, and I will allow you another night with your beloved." Her face wore a sneer, and she sniggered a bit when she said *your beloved*.

"I wish to see him awake," I said.

"I cannot help if he falls asleep," the troll said.

I thought she could, but still, I agreed. I walked with her to the doorway. I noticed she stood back from the door when she made me leave, and when I opened it, she cringed at the light.

I tucked the comb into my pocket and went to sit in the cemetery. Since I had nothing else to do, I tended the graves as I had before with the old woman. I tended some of the older graves too. I wished there were flowers with which to decorate them, but it was January, and the ground was bare. I was so hungry, but I had nothing to eat, so I simply tried to forget. But around noon, the old woman returned, and she offered me a loaf of bread. I took it and ate, furiously.

Finally, it was dusk. When the moon rose, the castle returned, and I knocked on the door. We repeated everything the same way, and alas, Phillip was still asleep, never to wake.

I knew what had happened. I remembered when I was little and Esther had had her appendix removed. They gave her a medication

219

that made her sleep for hours, despite the surgery, despite the pain. That's what Phillip was like, sleeping despite my screaming, my crying, my hitting him. But for his warm flesh and his heartbeat, he might have been dead. Had the troll princess drugged Phillip to make him sleep so soundly?

After hours of begging and imploring him to rise, hours of singing our favorite songs in his ear, hours of pleading with him, I thought of the mirror in my coat pocket. I took it out and said, "Show me Kendra."

Kendra's face showed immediately in the mirror.

"My dear Grace," she said. "You look awful."

I explained the situation, that I believed the troll princess had tranquilized Phillip. "I don't know what to do," I said. "If only I could leave some sort of message for him, tell him not to eat or drink anything the troll gives him."

She thought about it a moment, and then she said, "Leave the mirror under his pillow. When he wakes, he will feel its hardness, and since he has seen it before, he will know what it is. Hopefully, he will remember and ask to speak to me. If he does, I will give him your message."

I nodded and bade her goodnight. Then I stashed the mirror under Phillip's pillow. I slept better that night, in Phillip's arms.

The following morning, I again begged the troll princess to allow me to stay another night. But, this time, when she asked what I had as payment, I pretended I had nothing.

"Then you cannot stay," she said.

But just as I reached the door, I said, "Oh, oh, oh, I remember. I do have something." I opened the door as wide as I could before reaching into my pocket. "Come see it." I beckoned to her, remembering again how it was said that trolls lived under bridges.

She stood far away from me, cringing at the light but greedily looking anyway. "No. No! What is it?"

I pulled the spindle halfway from my pocket. "Oh, 'tis nothing but a little . . ."

"What? What?" She shrunk farther into the shadows. "Tell me quickly, or I will have to say no!"

I held up the spindle. "A spindle of pure gold! Can I come to lie with my Phillip tonight?"

"Yes." She slunk back into the darkness. "But he is not your Phillip no matter how many nights you stay. He is mine and mine forever."

"But I can come back?"

"Yes! Yes! But now, begone and shut the door on that infernal light!"

Infernal light.

The day passed much like the one before, but this time, when I returned at night, Phillip awakened easily. He had merely been pretending to sleep. "My darling, you are here," he whispered. "Kendra told me, and I didn't eat or drink anything she gave me, but there is nothing you can do. I am pledged to be with her now, forever."

"But I haven't told you my plan, darling."

Quickly, I told him what I had in mind. Then I summoned Kendra in the mirror, and we repeated it to her.

"Do you think it will work?" I asked when I had finished.

"I think it's as good a plan as any," Kendra said. "And I think you are right in your suspicions. I haven't known any trolls, but I have heard they are rather peculiar about light."

"I'm not sure, but we can try," Phillip said. "There is nothing to lose, for I am miserable here. My nightmares have been twice as bad as before, and I love you. I want only to be with you."

"I do too," I said. "I want to be with you, and if I cannot . . . there is nothing to lose. I have no life without you."

It was then that I remembered I *was* with him, and I hugged and kissed him until he said, "Perhaps we should begin."

I nodded, and began to yell his name and cry as I had on the previous two nights. This I did for an hour or more before giving up, sobbing, and falling asleep in Phillip's arms.

But this time, his arms held me tight.

In the morning, I secreted the mirror inside my coat, then had a good cry. It wasn't difficult. All I had to do was think about the men who lay dead in the cemetery just outside the castle walls or think of George or Jack or the pain Phillip had gone through. But this time, there was hope for him, and hope for me.

As I had the two mornings before, I asked the troll princess if I could come back that night. As before, she asked me what I had as payment.

This time, I walked to the door as I spoke.

"Let . . . me . . . see . . . ." I fumbled in my pockets. The troll princess followed me, but when she got close to the door, close to the light, she stopped. I opened the door wide.

"Oh, look!" I said. "Look what I have! This is so beautiful!"

"What?" she screamed with impatience. "What is it? I can come no closer!"

It was then I knew my suspicions were true—that the light was her downfall. That was why trolls lived under bridges or in castles that sank underground in daylight. Outside, it was a brilliant, clear day with the sun streaming forward into the castle.

"It's in here somewhere. . . ." I fumbled in my pockets as she craned forward eagerly. Finally, I pulled out the mirror by its handle. Outside, the sun was rising, and as I held the mirror out, I made sure it caught the sun. Then I angled it so it reflected that sun—right back at the troll princess.

"No!" she screamed. And then she was silent.

I looked back. She had turned to a stone statue.

"It worked!" I shrieked to Phillip. Then I ran into Phillip's room. The door was locked, but I found the key on the wall and let him out.

"It worked!" I threw my arms around him.

I was happy. Not only because I had Phillip back, but also because my own resourcefulness had made it so. I had figured it out myself.

And then we hugged and kissed, and were generally beside ourselves with joy.

We used the mirror to contact Kendra, to share our joy.

"It worked!" we told her. "The troll is turned to stone!"

"Where are you now?" she said.

"Inside the castle. Look!" I angled the mirror so that it showed the stone-made troll. "Your mirror did it! Trolls can't be in the sunlight!"

"I never knew that," she said, "but . . . er . . . I would get out of there right now."

And just as I started to say, "Why?" I felt a rumbling beneath my feet.

I looked at Phillip. A few pebbles fell from the ceiling. He looked at me. "Come on!" I grabbed his hand, and we flew toward the door, the floor rumbling and shifting beneath our feet.

Seconds later, the house slipped beneath the ground.

"Well," Phillip said, "that was an interesting turn of events. Now how do we get home?"

How did we get home? "I don't know. I have my own travel documents, from the old lady at the War Office, but you . . . ?" I looked at Phillip.

"Check your pockets," Kendra said in the mirror.

I did, and I found Phillip's passport and all the documentation we needed.

And so we returned to London, wrapped in each other's arms

and planning for our future. "I'd still like to take you to Paris," Phillip said as we snuggled on the train. "Perhaps we will be able to go some-day, when this cruel war is over."

"In the meantime," I said, "since we can go out in the daylight, perhaps you can take me to Regent's Park."

"I will," he said. "But first, I will take you home, to our home."

But the best of all surprises awaited us when we reached my parents' apartment. I expected to see only my father there, for my mother and sisters had said they were going to live with Aunt Lydia. But when I knocked on the door, it was opened by another man, tall and gaunt and far younger than my father.

"Jack!" I said, and fell to embracing him. "Jack!"

"It was the strangest thing," he said. "Two days ago, I was in a Nazi prison camp. Then, yesterday, I was free and walking along Whitehall. I went into the War Office. I was worried they'd think I was a deserter, but strangely, they seemed to know I wasn't."

After I introduced Jack to Phillip, I said, "So many odd things have been happening." I preferred to wait to tell Jack the whole story. "Haven't they, darling?"

"Yes," Phillip said. "Yes, they have, my love. But happy things."

"Yes, happy things." To Jack, I said, "You must come to see us, at our home. I am a grown-up woman with a house now."

Jack laughed. "I cannot imagine that. I just remember the silly girl who laughed because Ethel and Esther would not share their dolls."

At that moment, a man who had been sitting on the sofa cleared his throat.

"Oh!" Jack said. "How rude of me. I found a friend when I was at the War Office." He gestured to the man, tall and handsome, with dark-auburn hair.

"I'm sorry. I hadn't seen you. Jack, introduce me to your friend."

"Grace, this is James Brandon. He was the bravest man in our unit, saved hundreds of lives in battle, volunteered for every dangerous mission, and he's planning to go back for more. Brave as he was, you'd have thought he had a death wish."

James laughed. "Perhaps I'm immortal."

"It would explain a lot," Jack said. "James, this is my baby sister."

"And my husband, Phillip." I squeezed Phillip's hand, and he smiled.

There was a knock at the door, and I ran to get it. It was Kendra. "Oh, Kendra! He is back! He is back!"

"I thought I'd see you here." She was carrying a mince pie. "Your father said you and your Phillip were back, and I thought I'd just . . ." She stopped, and the pie nearly slipped from her hands.

I caught it. "Kendra, are you all right?"

"James?" Her voice was a whisper.

"Kendra? Is that you?"

Kendra Speaks

"Yes." I was trembling. "Yes."

"I have looked for you for so long," he said.

His hair was shorter than I remembered, likely a product of being a soldier, but still the same copper color. He never truly changed.

"Not long enough," I said. "I found you once, in London. About to be married."

He took my arm and pulled at it. "Perhaps we should talk out in the hallway."

Once out of earshot of the others, he said, "Aye. I was once married, for a time. For forty years' time. She was a mortal, and I had to watch her age and die. I used magic to pretend I was doing the same thing too, while folks marveled at my longevity. Poor Lucy—sweet woman. She never knew our life together was a lie. A man gets lonely when he doesn't find the woman he loves. But I learned it was just as lonely to be with someone who doesn't understand. Poor Lucy has been dead nearly a hundred years. Our son has been gone for more than fifty."

I knew what it was to be lonely. I had not lacked for male companionship either in that time, but I wanted to marry someone who would be with me for eternity. I wanted to marry James. I nodded. "And since then . . . ?"

"No one. I have been waiting for my equal, my darling, my mirror image."

I didn't quite know whether to believe him, but a moment's thought told me I should. "So we can be together forever? And never be alone?" I could wait no longer. I threw myself into his arms and kissed him.

He kissed me back, and in his arms, I found every bit of the passion, the danger, but also something else that I had never had in Salem. Safety. I was safe. No one was hunting us. We could be together.

"Yes, darling, after the war is over, we can be together."

"After the war?" I drew back from him.

"I'm off on another tour in two days' time, this time to France."

"But why?" I asked.

He shrugged. "It's a theory I have, that someone who has been given the dubious gift of immortality, as I have, should use it for good. I've enlisted in every war, always fighting on the side of good. I'm a paratrooper, and nothing can kill me. I could be the one to get Hitler."

I had to admit that this was a worthy goal. I pushed back in my mind the idea that something *could* happen to him. Of course he would survive a war where people were stabbing one another with bayonets, but planes could explode in a ball of fire.

"You have two days?" I pressed my lips together to keep them from quivering. I had only just found him. It wasn't fair.

"I leave Tuesday."

"Well, then." I kissed him, swallowing my protest. "We'd better make good use of our time."

We bid our good-byes to Phillip and Grace and went to walk along the Thames, as I had dreamed of doing so long ago.

"My first war was the American Revolution," he said as we strolled together in the light of the slivered moon. London was dark, and no one was out, but we had nothing to fear. "I wasn't involved in the Seven Years' War. I didn't quite understand what that one was about."

"I see. And which side were you on, in the Revolution?"

"Oh, the American side. I was an American then. I fought in the Battle of Saratoga, along with Benedict Arnold. Nice fellow."

The uniform. The tricorne hat. That was when I had first seen him in the mirror!

"You must have been handsome in your uniform," I said.

"I don't know about that." He laughed.

"I do."

We were passing the Tower of London now. Though it was unlit, I could see it in the moonlight. I was at the exact spot where James had stood that day I had seen him in the mirror. James squeezed my hand, seeming to know this.

"Benedict Arnold is commonly viewed as a traitor, is he not?" I asked.

"Oh, he was a traitor," James said. "He would have surrendered West Point to the British. But in the Battle of Saratoga, he was a great hero. The Americans would not have won it without him, and that was the battle that started their winning the war. It was only later he went bad. I was sorry for it. But people have reasons for what they do, I suppose."

I nodded. No one with my history in Salem, with my history of *history*, could doubt that people did strange things.

Do you have to leave? I wanted to ask, but I didn't.

"What next?" I asked instead. I would be waiting for my soldier, just like all the other girls. That wouldn't be that bad. That is what I told myself.

"Next was the Franco-American War."

"Oh!" He must have been there, when I was looking for him all that time. "Was that how you happened to come to Europe?"

"Yes. And then, the Crimean War, and the Spanish-American War. Oh, but before that, I fought in the Civil War. I was back in America by then. Over fifty thousand men died at Gettysburg. I was one of the lucky ones."

"You were a wizard," I said, kissing him. "But I am sure you were very brave." I remembered how brave he had been for me in Salem.

"A man can be brave when he has nothing to lose," he said, "though, even then, I had hope that I might find you."

This time, I did say my mind. "Then why are you leaving when you finally have?"

"Because I said I would. If only I had but known, my darling."

"But—"

He kissed me. "This war will be a minute in our lifetimes. We have centuries to spend together."

We went back to my flat then and spent two days together, reminiscing and planning our future and kissing and more, before it was time for him to ship out. On that day, I handed him a mirror and explained how to use it.

"Look for me," I said.

"I will," he said, tucking it into his duffel bag.

I did not go with him to the dock. I did not want to see him leave again, as I had seen him fade from view that night in Salem. But we spoke sometimes, though often he could not contact me for fear of being seen. And I wrote to him every day. Sometimes, he wrote back.

But then the contact stopped. His letters stopped too. When I asked to see him, I saw a battlefield, but I could not pick him out.

Had he been burned alive? My James? Or had he simply lost the mirror?

In 1945, I left London to go to the United States. It was peacetime, and I would start a new life for myself. One with no hope of James. I stopped looking for him. If he was alive, if he wanted to find me, he would look. I lived in New York City for a time, because it is a good place for those in hiding. But, eventually, I settled in Miami. Miami is a place for those with nothing to hide, and I realized that is what I was.

I enrolled in school like the obsolete teenager I was. That was how I met many friends, including a boy named Chris, who thought himself an ugly duckling.

1

Amanda Lasky Is a Badass
Miami, Florida, present day

This is the story of Amanda and me. How we met, how we became friends, how we *stayed* friends, and how we stopped being friends. Hopefully, it will have a happy ending.

Like the stories my mom read me when I was a kid.

When I was little, my mom put me to bed with stories every night. Her favorite was *The Ugly Duckling*, which was about a young duck who suffered physical and emotional abuse at the hands of his duck peers and other barnyard animals alike because he was so ugly. But when he grew up, it turned out that he was really a beautiful swan.

As you might have guessed, Mom had always wanted a girl. Since she got two boys, she was big on helping us explore our feminine sides. My brother, Matt, was having none of it, so I got to be the sweet one.

At the time, I thought the ugly duckling story was just a story, like the kid who went where the wild things were, or the one about Sam, who rightly rejected green eggs. It wasn't until I got older that I realized it was more than that. Really, it was Hans Christian Andersen reaching across the centuries with a hand pat and an "It gets better" to homely kids everywhere.

That realization started on the first day of kindergarten.

I didn't go to preschool. Maybe Mom was overprotective, or maybe she just liked having me around. So it wasn't until the first day of kindergarten that I realized I was kind of an ugly duckling.

That was also the first day I met Amanda Lasky.

And the first time I learned that Amanda Lasky was a badass.

I didn't cry that day when Mom dropped me off at school. This was partly because my dad had told me, before he left for work, that only girls and babies cried, and partly because my mother had bought me a Pose and Stick Spider-Man. She said I could take it to school as long as I didn't cry and promised to put Spidey in my backpack when the teacher said it was time to work.

The Pose and Stick Spider-Man was possibly the most awesome toy ever made. It was soft, with wires in its arms to make it poseable and suction cups in its feet so you could hang it on walls. I'd gotten one the Christmas before, but I'd played with it so much and stuck it to the refrigerator and waved it around and hit stuff with it and fought about it with Matt, and eventually, Spidey's arms came out of their joints and the wire started protruding through so it was kind of dangerous, and my mom had to throw it out so I wouldn't lose an eye. I had cried then, quietly in my bedroom, so my dad and Matt wouldn't hear, but anyway, I was really happy to get a new one.

I was sitting at the table with my name, Christopher B., on it. A lot of kids had missed the memo about not crying. There were so many of them, and they moved around too fast for me to count, but it seemed like about a third of them were crying, and half of those were boys. The chair I sat on was cold and hard, but just my size, and I was sitting, sort of hugging Spidey, when a blond boy, who was bigger than I was and looked as old as Matt, came and took the seat by mine. I couldn't read his name at the time because I couldn't read. But now, I know it was Nolan Potter.

"Why'd you bring a doll?" he asked.

At first, I didn't think he was talking to me. But when he repeated his question, and no one else answered, I realized he was.

"It's not a doll." I hugged it. "It's Spider-Man." I couldn't believe anyone wouldn't know the difference.

"Let me see it," Nolan said, and without waiting for my okay, he yanked Spidey by the arm.

"Hey! Don't do that! You'll break it!" I looked around for the teacher, but she'd been swallowed up by a tidal wave of kids and parents.

"I just want to see it. You need to learn to share."

"No, I don't. Stop it." I tried to hold Spidey's elbow with my fingers, to keep the wire from coming out, but Nolan's hands were twice the size of mine, and he crushed my fingers. "Ow!"

I felt my eyes get hot and hurty. I didn't want to cry, not just because I'd promised I wouldn't, but also because I knew Dad and Matt were right. Only babies cried. I didn't want to be a baby, especially since a quick look around told me I was the shortest, smallest boy there. I was smaller than some of the girls. A little runt like the ugly duckling. I looked down so no one could see my eyes getting red, but I was also slowly realizing that the only way to keep Spidey's arms from being ripped from their sockets on the very first day was to let go. I was about to do that when suddenly Nolan lost his grip, and I was tossed back, almost falling out of my chair.

"Let go, Nolan!" a voice said. "Stop being a bully!"

I looked up, hugging Spidey close. In front of me stood a red-haired girl. She was one of the girls who was bigger than me—a lot bigger. Several inches taller and what my mom would call "heavy-set," she'd apparently just karate-chopped Nolan, because he was holding his arm like it hurt.

"Ouch! Why don't you get a Barbie, Amanda?" Nolan reached for Spidey again.

Amanda got between Nolan and me. "Why don't *you* get a Barbie, Nolan, or steal one from a three-year-old girl? If you keep taking other people's stuff, I'll tell your dad, and he'll spank your butt."

"He won't care," Nolan said.

Amanda shrugged. "Then go ahead and take it, I guess."

I hustled to get Spidey into my backpack, but I was sort of amazed Amanda had said *butt* in school.

Nolan sat down. "Aw, forget it."

"Good." Amanda took the seat on my other side, where the name tag had a ladybug sticker and a name that started with *A*. She said, "My name's Amanda. What's yours?"

"Toph—I mean, Chris," I said, remembering that Matt had also said that Topher was a wimpy nickname that would make me have no friends. My name tag said Christopher, so I could say either. "Chris Burke."

I shared my oatmeal scotchies with Amanda at lunch. There were assigned seats in the cafeteria, but I'd have sat with her anyway. I didn't know anyone else.

"These are good cookies," Amanda said. "What are they?"

"Oatmeal scotchies. My mom makes them." I offered her another one. "I think the recipe's on the bag of butterscotch chips."

I knew it was, because Mom and I had made the cookies, but for some reason I didn't want to admit that.

"Oh." Amanda chewed the second one. "My mom doesn't make cookies."

"Does she work?"

Amanda took a second bite and shrugged. "She doesn't live with us." She gestured at Nolan, who was picking on some other kid, the second-smallest kid in class. "Nolan lives next door to me. He thinks he's tough because he's the best hitter on the team, but my dad says I'll be better than him by the time the season starts."

"Oh." When Amanda had said "best hitter," I thought she'd meant fighting-type hitting. Now I realized she meant baseball. "You play baseball?"

"I used to. But they said I had to switch to softball because I'm a girl. It's so unfair, because I'm better than most of the boys. Dad says that's what they don't like." She took a third cookie without asking. I didn't care. As usual, Mom had given me way too much food, hoping I'd bulk up, like Dad said.

"Aren't you one of the best on the softball team too?" I asked.

She snorted like that was obvious. "Do you play?"

"Softball?"

"Baseball. You don't have to be big to play. Lots of smaller kids are fast."

I shrugged. I sort of wanted to play, and my dad would have loved it. But he'd probably be too busy with work ever to practice with me. Matt only played with his DS, and my mother wasn't into sports. I knew there were tryouts, and I didn't want to be the worst.

"You could come over, and my dad would practice with us."

"Really?" It was like she'd read my mind. "You could come over to my house and . . . make oatmeal scotchies with me and my mom."

"Cool."

From then on, like oatmeal and butterscotch chips, Amanda and I were hard to separate.

So that was the start of Amanda and me. People were singing the *K-I-S-S-I-N-G* song about us by the end of the week, and even though Amanda was always the first-picked girl when we played team sports in PE class, while I was the last-picked boy, when she was captain, she always chose me third.

"You have to practice," she told me when I didn't get a runner out in kickball because I was cringing away from the ball. "This is kickball, Chris. Kick. Ball. The ball is soft, so it doesn't hurt even if it hits you in the face. See?" She tossed the ball at me. I ducked it.

She sighed. "What are you going to do when we start softball?"

"Isn't a softball soft?"

"No," she said, like that made sense.

We had our first playdate the Saturday after school started. My mother drove me to Amanda's house. "I'm so glad you made a friend," she said on the way "Would I know Amanda's mother?"

"She doesn't have one." Mom gave me a funny look, so I added, "I mean, her mom doesn't live with them. She lives with her dad. And her sister."

I didn't know why it mattered, but I sensed it did. "She's really nice, and her dad sounds nice, and she says he'll teach me baseball. Please let me go over there. She's my best friend."

Amanda was more than my best friend. She was my only friend. While Amanda knew people, girls from T-ball and soccer who talked about practices, boys whose families were friends with hers, they all pretty much ignored me. Or included me only as Amanda's friend. Even at five, I sensed that. I was too small, too quiet, too insignificant. I was like the ugly duckling, maybe not actually ugly, but just . . . nothing. I didn't know if I'd have made other friends had Amanda not adopted me as her personal project. Somehow, it didn't matter. I'd had no real friends up until then, just playgroups with Mom's friends' kids. Amanda was the one friend I'd made by myself. Amanda seemed like enough.

"So is it okay?" I said.

"Of course it's fine. I just want to meet her father."

I nodded happily. But as we got farther away from our house, closer to Amanda's, I started thinking. I hugged Spidey, who didn't go to school anymore but mostly resided in our car, suctioned to the back passenger window. What if Mom didn't like Amanda? Or her dad? I'd never been to a house where there was no mother. What if it was messy or smelled funny, so my mother would wrinkle her nose? What if they weren't back from Amanda's soccer game yet, so we had to stand outside and maybe see Nolan? What if she had another friend over, and they didn't want to play with me?

Mom pulled into the driveway of a peach-colored house bigger than ours. The front yard had a tire swing and a bunch of equipment for sports. As our car slowed, the white front door flew open, and Amanda, in an orange soccer jersey that said *Hurricanes*, flew down the path, yelling something. When I opened the car door, I heard her.

"Chris! You're here!"

A man with a red beard and a soccer jersey that matched Amanda's came out next. A little girl in a pink ballet outfit followed him, twirling around and trying to run on her toes. The man was laughing.

"Mandy, Mandy, we've been home, like, five minutes. Don't lay a guilt trip on the boy. He's not late."

Amanda reached our car first. I had this weird feeling she was going to hug me, but she detoured back to Mom. Then she stuck her chubby little arm out like someone had told her to. "Hello, Mrs. Burke. I'm Amanda Lasky."

Mom looked dumbfounded, but finally, she held out her own hand with an *Isn't that cute?* expression I knew Amanda would hate and said, "How do you do, Amanda? Laura Burke."

My mom was being totally embarrassing, but Amanda said, "I'm fine, Laura."

I saw Mom decide to ignore her first name, though she'd told me never to call adults by them, even if they said it was okay. Mr. Lasky had reached us by then. "Nice to meet you. Tim Lasky." He held out his hand, realized it was dirty, and wiped it on his shorts. "Sorry. Coaching girls' soccer is messy."

Mom took his hand. "Our children seem to have become fast friends."

"My Mandy's pretty outgoing."

Beside my mom, still holding Spidey, I mouthed, *Mandy?* Amanda scowled.

Mr. Burke invited us in. I figured my mother was dying to get a look inside, and I wasn't wrong. We followed him inside. The house smelled like lemons, and Amanda's sister leaped and spun in front of us.

"Do you do ballet too?" my mother asked Amanda.

"No," she said, and I was glad she didn't talk about ballet being dumb.

"The ballet was more my wife's thing," Mr. Burke explained in a low voice. "Can't say I was devastated when Mandy quit. I'm terrible at buns."

Mom laughed but said, "Christopher thought you didn't have a wife," pumping him for information.

Mr. Burke shrugged. "Like they say, it's complicated." He tousled Amanda's curls. "Why don't you guys go up and play in Amanda's room. We'll play some catch in a few."

Amanda grabbed my arm. "Come on, come on!" She dragged me toward the stairway. Her little sister followed, but when we reached the threshold, Amanda said, "Go to your own room, Casey," and slammed the door. I heard footsteps running downstairs and something about telling.

I looked around. The room was painted the color of cotton candy, with a dollhouse and about five of those dolls with the big eyes. Not what I expected from Amanda. Would there be anything for me to play with? There was also a poster of a women's softball team and a bunch of other softball stuff, including trophies and a batting helmet, which sat on the bedpost of her flouncy pink bed.

She squinted at Spidey. "You brought that?"

"It was just in my hand when I got out of the car. It's cool." I walked over and suctioned it to her wall. "He could play with your dolls. One of them could be Mary Jane."

"Ha!" Amanda picked up a blond doll, who was taller than Spidey in about the same proportions Amanda was to me. She made her voice high and girly. "Help me, Spidey! Help meeeee!"

She tossed the doll down and grabbed my arm. "I've got a ton of Legos in the closet. The nanny just puts them away." She opened the door to reveal thousands of Legos packed in plastic containers. She took out two of the boxes and pulled a pink Lego table from the corner. "You good with Legos?"

I was good with Legos. I totally coveted her Legos, which would have made Matt drool with envy. "My mom says they're too messy."

"Let's make a skyscraper. Last year, we went to New York for Christmas, and my dad took us to the top of the Empire State Building."

"Cool." I started taking out gray pieces to make the building. "Why does your dad call you Mandy?"

"Don't call me that!"

"I didn't. I just asked why he does."

She didn't answer, and I kept gathering grays.

Finally, she said, "It's from some dumb song my mom likes about some girl who gave without taking. I hate it. You're so lucky your name's Chris."

There were three boys in our grade named Chris. "My mother wanted to call me . . ." I stopped. What, was I stupid?

"What?" Amanda was gathering windows now.

"Never mind."

"Wha-at?"

"I don't want you to call me it."

"I won't call you it if you don't call me Mandy."

"I'd never call you Mandy. Okay, she wanted to call me Topher."

Amanda giggled. "Topher! That sounds like an animal."

"I got attacked by a vicious topher. It ripped off all my toes."

"And then I ran into Mandy, and she gave without taking," Amanda said.

We were still giggling, and we'd made about a six-inch tower, when Amanda's dad came in. "Ready to play some ball?"

I looked at the Lego table.

"We can finish it another time," Amanda said.

Mr. Lasky didn't make us put away the Legos, like my mom would've. "Mandy tells me you want to play baseball."

"I guess. Everyone says I'm kind of small for sports."

"Anyone can learn if they try," Mr. Lasky said.

I hoped he was right and followed him downstairs.

At first, it seemed like I was going to be the exception to Mr. Lasky's statement about anyone. He lined me up in front of the batting tee, which Amanda said made it easier, and he showed me how to stand.

I hacked into the air with my bat.

"That's okay. Look at the ball," he said.

"Tell him to choke up on the bat," Amanda said. She had been sworn to silence about instructing me.

"And choke up on the bat," Mr. Lasky said.

On about my fifth try, I hit it so it sort of dribbled off the tee and onto the ground.

"That's good. Bunting isn't allowed in T-ball, but if it was, that was a good one. Just try and swing through it."

After Mr. Lasky worked on my swing so long that my elbows hurt from holding up the bat, with Amanda forgetting herself and shouting stuff like "Tell him to rotate his hips!" I actually hit one that went a few feet.

Then another one. Then about ten more, including one glorious one that sailed over my mother's car as it pulled into the Laskys' driveway.

I dropped my bat and ran up to her. "Did'ya see that?"

"I did. Wow. That was incredible."

Tim—that's what Mr. Lasky had told me to call him—walked up

to Mom. "Kid could be a ballplayer."

Mom looked dubious. "He's kind of small."

"He's got good instincts, good reflexes, follows directions, which is more than a lot of kids. And nothing teaches teamwork like being on a team. Little League tryouts are in December. I could prep him."

Mom smiled like she wasn't really listening. "I wouldn't want him to get hurt."

Tim laughed and gestured to Amanda. "Why don't you kids go over there and throw a few while the adults talk."

Amanda led me over to her pitchback. She stared throwing the ball and catching it, always catching it. "Now you."

"I can't."

"Even Casey can catch a ball." She threw the ball at an angle so when it bounced back, it came to me.

I caught it, then threw it again, copying the way she wound her arm back, then threw the ball over her head. It went a little farther than I'd planned, but I still got it. The next time, I ran back right after I threw it, so I was ready. That's when I realized Mom and Tim were watching.

"Good job!" Tim yelled.

"Is he really any good?" Mom's voice carried even though she tried to whisper.

"He's good. It's his first time, right? He was afraid of the ball at first."

I pretended not to hear, concentrating on throwing and catching, throwing and catching. Finally, Amanda intercepted the ball. "My turn!" After she threw it, she said, "I knew you were afraid of the ball."

"I was not."

"You aren't anymore."

"Never was!"

"Mandy!" Tim said.

"Topher!" Mom said at the same time.

We both burst out laughing. Our parents stood there, staring, with no idea what was so funny.

Then Amanda pitched it, and I caught it again. "Sorry, Mandy!"

I loved arguing with her. It wasn't like fighting with my brother or even people at school. It was more like a sport. Or like having a friend.

Sometimes my brother, Matt, called us Chrisandamanda. Not in a Brangelina type of way, but just because when you saw one of us, you usually saw the other. I went over to Amanda's house or she came to mine almost every day after school. At her house, we played ball, and I actually was kind of good. I thought Amanda would be bored with the baking and art projects at my house, but she seemed to enjoy it.

Mom also read us stories, including *The Ugly Duckling*.

After it was finished, Amanda said, "Aren't most people born pretty or ugly?"

Mom looked at Amanda, probably taking in her chubby, freckled face. "Not necessarily. Some people are just late bloomers. That's what the story's about."

Sometimes, Mom took us to the park near school to feed the

real ducks. We saved our bread crusts all week for the cute little ducklings who swam in the canals. The bigger ducks were black-and-white spotted, with warty red things on their bills.

"Why are they so ugly?" I asked once.

"They're Muscovy ducks," Mom said. "That's just what they look like."

"So the ducklings are going to turn into those big ugly ducks?" Amanda said.

"Just like in the story," Mom said.

Amanda took some bread from the bag. "They seem pretty happy." She tossed a crust to the biggest, ugliest duck of all, the duck with a fishhook permanently stuck in its beak. He ate it fine.

It took a while for Dad to figure out that I had a girl best friend. But when Matt enlightened him, Mom reassured him that Amanda was "a tomboy" and that we weren't having tea parties.

Later that night, I heard Mom whispering about Amanda and her dad. Apparently, she'd asked around to the other moms, who'd been happy to fill her in. I heard her saying things like "mother ran out on her family" and "drugs" and "poor child." I went to bed with my pillow over my face. I didn't want to hear.

In December, I tried out for Little League. "What if I don't make it?" I asked Tim. He and Amanda were accompanying me even though Mom was going too.

"Everyone makes it," Tim said. "Tryouts are just to make the teams fair."

"There are a *lot* of people worse than you," Amanda said.

"Mandy, that's enough," Tim said.

But it calmed me down. Amanda thinking people were worse than me was a huge compliment.

We'd stopped using the batting tee at Amanda's house weeks before, but that's what they used at tryouts. It would be easy. When

Nolan Potter saw me coming, he nudged his friend and said, "Oh brother." I ignored him. I stepped to the tee and hit every ball with a loud thwack, the way Tim had taught me. And when the coaches hit pop-ups and grounders to us, I got those too. When I finished, Tim walked over and flipped up my cap. "Good job, sport."

Nolan wasn't laughing anymore, especially when Amanda said, "Hey, I think he did better than you."

I thought so too. And so did Nolan, I could tell.

I was on my first team that year, the Tigers, with yellow baseball jerseys that I slept in some nights. I finally made friends with some of the boys at school. They were going to play football in the fall, and Tim promised to teach me that too. But Amanda was still my best friend.

Some days, Amanda played with other girls in class, which I hated. I liked having her all to myself. She had friends from softball, so I couldn't be part of that group.

"What do you do when you play with them?" I asked every time she had a playdate.

She'd say something mundane like "Sophie has a trampoline" or "We watched a movie," and I made plans to re-up my trampoline begging or ask for more TV time.

But one day, Amanda walked away from the girls at lunch looking perturbed.

"What's wrong?" I asked, as we sat down in class again.

"Nothing."

"Come on."

"I *said* nothing." Amanda took out the sight-word list and started to study it.

"I can do that with you," I said.

"I'm ahead of you."

"Then do mine with me."

She turned her back. "Just leave me alone."

She stared at the word list for a long time but didn't ask Mrs. Rosner to test her on it. When we went on to the next activity (filling in a coloring sheet about autumn leaves), she broke her red and yellow crayons, the fat kind that were impossible to break.

After school got out, Sarah Rivas came up to her.

"My mom said I could only ask four friends," Sarah said.

"Okay." Amanda put her homework folder and lunch box into her backpack.

"I didn't think you'd want to go," Sarah explained. "It's like a Disney Princess party at a makeover place."

"So?" Amanda said.

"I don't know. I'm sorry."

Amanda looked down. "I have to go."

I followed her out. "What's wrong?" But I knew.

"Nothing. Go away."

We walked to the drop-off not talking. When Mom picked me up, she said, "What's wrong with Amanda?"

"She didn't get invited to some birthday party with makeovers. I don't know why she cares. It sounds stupid."

"Don't say stupid. Say foolish," Mom said. "And all girls like that stuff."

"Why would Amanda want to be a foolish princess when she can be a ballplayer?"

The next day, when Amanda got in the car, my mother said, "I'm going to get my hair and nails done Saturday, Amanda. My friend Stacey can't make it. Would you like to come with me?"

I glared at Mom. Amanda would know I told.

But Amanda was smiling, her face all pink. "Really?" Her face fell. "But I have softball."

"What time is that? We could go afterward."

"I'll ask my dad." She kicked the seat. "Can I do my nails any color I want?" She held out her nails, which were short and ragged.

"As long as your father says it's okay."

"And toes too? Or just fingers?"

"Definitely toes too," my mother said. "Wouldn't be a proper pampering without a pedicure."

Amanda giggled. "Pampering."

I stared at her, incredulous. I just didn't get this part of her at all.

When I got out of the car, I tagged her while she was still sitting down, yelling, "You're it!" because impromptu games of tag were our thing lately.

I ran down the block, and she tore after me.

On Saturday, my mom picked Amanda up after her morning softball game. I had baseball that afternoon, but she got my friend Tristan's mom to drive me. She'd found out that the party Amanda was missing was a Disney Princess theme, so she went to the store and bought a crown with a picture of Ariel on it.

"Amanda doesn't like stuff like that," I told Mom.

"Every girl wants to be pretty. When you see her, tell her she looks nice."

"She'll punch me."

"Say it anyway."

When Amanda and my mom came back from the salon, hours later, Mom looked the same as she always did. Amanda was unrecognizable. Gone were the bouncy red curls that clustered around her face and made me want to touch them to see if they'd spring back. Instead, her hair looked straight and poofed up like Ariel in *The Little Mermaid*, emphasized by the dopey green crown. I knew Amanda thought Disney princesses were stupid. She'd said so. The only Disney movies we liked were *Aladdin* and *Ice Age*. She held her hands in front of her, staring at her shiny pink nails. She had on sandals, and all her toes were a matching color. But the middle was still Amanda in her dirty baseball jersey.

"You look . . . pretty." I followed Mom's instructions and tried to smile.

She didn't look pretty. She looked like all the other girls in school.

"Thanks." She stared at me, staring at her. "Are we going to play something now?"

"Yeah. Tag! You're it!" I ran to the door, relieved.

Mom said, "Maybe you should play something in—"

But we were already out.

Our yard had a hammock section with three black olive trees and lots of bromeliads that filled with water when it rained. We used the part where the trees hung low as a sort of clubhouse, spending days there, playing that it was a cave or a pirate ship or, today, the tree where the Lost Boys lived. Except in our version, Amanda was Wendy, a much cooler Wendy who ran with the boys instead of just sewing and telling stories like my mother.

When it started to rain, I said, "Should we go inside?"

"Nah," Amanda said. "We're not getting that wet."

So we kept playing.

By the end of the day, Amanda's curls were back. The pink nail polish was chipped, and her feet were dirty. "Where'd your crown go?" I asked her when we finally went inside.

"Oh, shoot. It must be in the bushes. Should we go get it?"

My mother walked in and sighed. "Oh, Amanda. I wanted your father to see. Well, at least we took a picture."

"I'm sorry," I said, even though I wasn't.

Over dinner that night, Mom said, "I guess that girl was right. Amanda wouldn't appreciate a party like that."

Dad sort of smiled. "Maybe next time take her to an MMA match."

"I wanted to take her for a girls' day, since she doesn't have a mother to do it with her."

"How was your game today?" Dad asked.

"Good. I got on base twice and threw two men out."

I'd actually gotten a triple and was given the game ball, but for some reason, I didn't want to mention that. Other dads would *know* about that because they'd have been there. "Can you come next week?"

"Maybe when this trial's over I'll have more time. When does the season end?"

"I don't know," I said.

"They play until May," Mom said, "so there are plenty of games after your trial. He might play summer ball too."

I bet Dad wouldn't come. I tried not to care too much. I didn't really want one of those dads who coached, or a dad who had fits when his kid didn't get played enough or got mad if they screwed up. Nolan's dad had started yelling and kicking dirt like a baby the week before. He screamed at Nolan for dropping a pop fly. I didn't want a dad like that. I was sort of glad Dad didn't understand baseball. But it would have been nice if he'd shown up.

4

The next few years kind of blend together in my mind. T-ball melted into Khoury League football into coach-pitched baseball, then football, then baseball again.

I was sort of small for football. Okay, I was really small. But everyone played. People liked me when I was seven and the oldest on the Tiny Mites team, but I knew I'd be the smallest on the Mighty Mites the next year and drag everyone down. Coach Lou suggested I try to "bulk up," so I got Mom to drive through McDonald's after every practice and buy me a milkshake.

It was on one of those days, at one of those drive-throughs, that the song "Mandy" came on the radio. Mom started singing along, "Oh, Mandy, you came and you gave without tak-i-i-ing."

The next day at school, when I saw Amanda, I started singing it.

"If you don't stop, I'm going to karate kick you in the head," she said.

I knew she would, so I stopped.

It was in the beginning of second grade that Amanda showed up at school and ran to my desk.

"My mom's back," she said.

"Back?" I knew nothing about Amanda's mother except what my mother had said in the first place, that she was a druggie. And I'd never met her since kindergarten. There was that.

"She lives in Miami now. She moved in with my grandma, and she's coming to my game Saturday, and I'm seeing her tonight."

"That's great."

I didn't know what I expected Amanda's druggie mom to look like, maybe like the high school kids at the park who always looked a little dirty. Or the skinny homeless person we'd seen downtown, the one my mom wanted to give a dollar to, but my dad said would use it to buy heroin. But when I met Amanda's mom, she didn't look like either. She looked like a normal mom, a little brighter, with her yellow hair, pink lipstick, and aqua workout clothes that fit a little tight.

She came to pick Amanda up from playing over at my house. She drove up in a two-seater red car, which didn't look like a car anyone else's mom drove. We already knew she was there before she rang the doorbell. Mom raced to get it, Amanda and me behind her.

"Hi," the woman said. "I'm Jackie Lasky, Amanda's mother."

"Laura Burke. Nice to meet you." Mom's eyebrows looked weird, frozen in the middle of her forehead.

"Nice to meet you. Mandy, do you have your things?"

Amanda ran to get them. My mother cleared the doorway for Mrs.—Jackie—to come in. "Amanda's told us so much about you."

Amanda had told us nothing until that day. But that day, she couldn't shut up about her. Her mom was living back in town. Her mom was looking for a job at Macy's. Or maybe Bloomingdale's. As one of those ladies with pink or white coats that did people's makeup. Then she'd get a discount there, and she'd take Amanda and me to lunch at the mall. When we were alone, she'd said that her mom and dad were getting back together. My mom didn't know about that one. I didn't think Tim did either.

"She's a great kid," Jackie said.

"She is a great kid," Mom agreed. "Tim's done a great job with her."

Jackie blinked. "Tim's a great guy." She looked at me. "Mandy said you've been friends a long time."

I fidgeted with my hands. "Since kindergarten."

"That is so great, so great that Mandy's got such a nice little boyfriend."

I wanted to tell her mother that Amanda hated being called Mandy, but I didn't think Amanda wanted her to know. Neither of us liked people calling me Amanda's boyfriend.

Amanda came back with her backpack then. "We're just friends, Mom. I'm too young for a boyfriend."

"Of course you are. I was just teasing. Maybe I can take you kids to the movies Saturday."

"I have softball then," Amanda said. "Travel team."

"I know that," Jackie said. "But *after* softball."

"Maybe," my mother said in a way I knew meant no. She didn't like me to go in cars with people she didn't know.

"Or we could all go," Jackie said. "We could meet after the game and all go to the movies together."

"I'll have to check our schedule," my mom said in a way I still knew meant no. I knew our schedule. I had a football game at eight, and Amanda's softball game was usually at ten. So we'd all be done by lunch. Amanda knew it too.

"Please," Amanda said.

"I just have to check," Mom said again.

"Sure." Jackie pulled something out of her wallet, a card. "Call me when you decide, and if you need a makeover, I'm an independent consultant for Aurelia Cosmetics. I could show you what to do about those fine lines."

"I'll keep you in mind." Mom was smiling big. To Amanda, she said, "Why don't you have your dad call me?"

"Okay." Amanda walked to the door.

"Aren't you going to thank them for having you over?" Jackie asked.

Mom laughed a little louder than usual, a fake laugh. "Amanda always says thank you." And then she actually patted Amanda on the head, which was something my mom would do, but not something *anyone* would do to Amanda.

I didn't remember if Amanda actually did always say thank you. But she said it then. Then she took her mother's hand and pulled her toward the little two-seater. They roared off with the top down.

Mom decided we should all go to the movies together even though she hated movies. We planned to meet at Amanda's softball game and see a Dwayne Johnson movie. We went over after my game.

Amanda was playing shortstop. Tim was teaching her, he said, to be a pitcher, and Amanda and I spent hours practicing, her pitching, me at catcher. I knew she spent hours more with her pitchback. But our age played coach-pitched, and Amanda usually played catcher or shortstop.

That day, it seemed like every ball came to her. She got maybe half of the outs, including participating in two double plays. Tim was coaching, but I noticed every time Amanda made a hit or an out, her eyes would go to the stands. After a while, I realized she was looking for Jackie. She wasn't there. So, the next time Amanda looked up, I waved and pumped my fist at her. "Go, Amanda!"

She smiled but didn't wave back.

In the fourth inning, she was at bat with runners on second and third. A hit by her would load the bases. She looked around again and missed one pitch.

"Strike one!" the ump yelled.

"Go, Amanda!" I screamed.

Mom yelled, "Yeah, Amanda! Come on! You can do it!"

The next pitch was a ball, which Amanda didn't swing at.

"Good eye!" Mom yelled, because grown-ups loved yelling *good eye* for some reason. Other people yelled it too.

Amanda looked up.

"Strike two!"

"Come on, Amanda! Swing at something!" I started chanting, "Amanda! Amanda!"

The next pitch, she hit it into the outfield. I screamed as it soared toward Sophie Rodriguez and the runner on third came home. The third base coach yelled for the next runner to keep going. The second runner scored just as Sophie caught the ball.

I was screaming. We were all screaming as Amanda walked back.

"Whoo, Amanda!" I yelled.

"But she's out?" Mom said.

"Yeah, but she brought in two RBIs."

As I started explaining the concept of a sacrifice fly to Mom, I noticed Amanda looking up into the stands again.

Jackie still wasn't there.

Amanda's team ended up winning two to one.

When we went down to wait for her, her mother still wasn't there.

"Great game!" I told her when she showed up.

"It was okay."

"Yeah, okay. They'd have scored zero runs without you. You're the best player on the team, probably the whole league."

Other people were even coming up and patting Amanda's shoulder. No one did that on the boys' teams. Derek Jeter himself could have been playing on our team, and no dad would have admitted he was better than their kid.

Amanda was back to looking around. Kids had finished with snacks, and people were packing to leave. The next team was setting up.

"We can still go to the movie even if she doesn't come," I said finally. "My mom would take us." I knew my mom would prefer it. She was only going because she didn't trust Jackie.

"Like I want to go to stupid *Game Plan* if she doesn't show up. It was a dumb idea."

Beside me, I saw Mom about to tell Amanda not to say *stupid* and *dumb*, but she stopped herself.

"We can play at my house," I said. "Or yours."

"I don't want to." Amanda looked around for Tim, who was talking to a parent behind her. She tugged his arm. "Can we leave now?"

"Give me a sec, Amanda."

"I want to go home!"

"Hold on," Tim said.

That was when Jackie finally showed up. She was all dressed up in a short skirt with high heels, so she stuck out among the other moms in jeans and T-shirts. Her hair looked all fancy too, and her makeup, with bright-blue eye shadow.

"Mandy!" she yelled when she saw Amanda. "I'm so sorry I'm late."

Amanda ran up to her. "You missed the game. It was so great. I made four outs and got two RBIs!"

"What's that?" Jackie looked confused.

"It's where the batter hits the ball where she'll get out, but she brings another runner in." Mom used her newfound knowledge. "It's called a sacrifice fly."

"That's great, honey," Jackie said. "And did you get any runs yourself?"

Amanda rolled her eyes. "No. Those were the only runs we scored. I brought them in. We won two to one."

"Well, that's good anyway. I have some good news myself. I was late because I had a job interview."

No one said anything, and Jackie looked around like she was trying to figure out why we didn't. Then she added, "I got the job!"

"That's great, Mom," Amanda said. "Is it at Macy's or Bloomingdale's?"

"Well, no. Those are my dream jobs, it's true. But baby steps first. This one's at Bed Bath & Beyond, and once I've worked long enough to get a discount, I can use it to fix up a room for you and Casey at Grandma's house."

"One room for both of us?"

"Your grandma doesn't live in a mansion, Amanda."

"Does it have to be pink?" Amanda asked, which surprised me because Amanda's room at home was pink. Then I realized Jackie might have decorated it.

"I will consult you," Jackie said.

Tim finally finished with the parent. "Sorry about that. Everyone thinks their kid should be the star, when clearly"—he leaned over and whispered to Amanda— "my kid is the star."

Amanda giggled.

"Ahem," Jackie said. "Hi, Tim."

"Ah, hey, Jackie." Tim looked at Amanda. "So you still want to go home?"

"No, it's okay. Mom got a job."

"Great news," Tim said. Then he turned to my mother to make sure she was driving and ask what time we'd be home.

Jackie did show up for Amanda's game the next week and some other weeks when she didn't have work. I came once and saw her, wearing green, the team color, including a big bow in her hair. She sat near the dugout with Casey and talked to Tim between plays, like she was his girlfriend. She must have studied up, because she definitely knew what an RBI was and the infield fly rule. She even had opinions on bunting.

"I think they might get back together," Amanda told me, gesturing to them talking after the game.

"Do you want them to?" I asked.

"Sure. Why wouldn't I? You're lucky your parents are both there."

Except that my dad wasn't ever there, but I didn't really have to explain that to Amanda. She knew.

The next year began as a good one for Amanda, but a bad one for me.

Good for Amanda because Jackie moved back in with Tim at Christmastime. When Amanda found out, it was like the times she hit two home runs in the same game, only better because it didn't happen as often.

Bad for me because when we started baseball in the spring, the coach said I should stay in coach-pitched another year because of my size, even though I was almost nine, and everyone else was moving up to the majors that year.

"They don't know what they're talking about," Amanda said when I told her on the way to Chuck E. Cheese's. My mother said I could drown my sorrows in pizza and Skee-Ball. "You're the best player on the team anyway."

"Yeah, well, you're the best player on your team, even though you moved up."

I'd expected to stay in the lower division in football, where they based it on weight as well as age. But I'd been working hard on baseball. Amanda and I practiced almost every day, and I was good enough. At least, I thought I was.

The night before, when I'd complained about it in front of Dad, he'd said, "That's what happens when you give every kid a trophy. They all think they're good."

"You're wrong," I said. "I know I'm good. My batting average is higher than most people, and I'm a good fielder. You'd know that if you went to the games!"

"Watch it," my father had said.

As before, my mother said it was just because I was small. "You just have to grow. It's a safety issue."

"Yeah, right." Like I was some baby who'd get hit with the ball.

When we got to Chuck E. Cheese's, I made Mom order a large pizza, then I ate half of it.

Jackie quit her job at Bed Bath & Beyond when she moved back in with the family, but she still did the Aurelia Cosmetics makeovers, so sometimes, Mom still drove Amanda to practices. She never asked Jackie to drive me.

One day, when I was having a snack before doing homework, the phone rang. It was Amanda.

"Hey, can Casey and I come over your house?"

"Sure. When?"

"Like, right now? Or in a few minutes? We could walk over from school."

I lived about a mile from school. Amanda lived farther.

"Sure. Why are you at school? Do you want my mom to come get you?" I'd never walked from school by myself, and now, it was later, so there wouldn't be as many people out as right after school let out.

"No, I can do it. Just wait outside for me, okay? Maybe you can tell your mom I'm getting dropped off to work on a project for school."

It didn't seem super likely that Amanda would come over with Casey to work on a project. The last time Casey had been over, she'd broken a vase in the living room doing a *tour jeté*, which also scared the cat so badly we didn't see him for a couple of days. And people thought she was the quieter sister just because she dressed in pink and liked dolls.

Still, I said, "Okay," and went to tell Mom. "Jackie's dropping Amanda and Casey off in a few minutes. We have a project to work on, and Jackie has a makeup thing."

I'd never lied to Mom before. Well, not about anything important anyway, just dumb stuff like who finished the toilet paper and didn't replace the roll. Probably that was why Mom believed me.

"Let me know when she gets here. I need to talk to Jackie about driving Saturday."

"Okay." I knew I wouldn't, so that was the second lie I told.

When Amanda got there, I said, "What happened?"

"Shh." She put her finger to her lips. "Let's go in your room."

"Mom never came to pick us up," Casey said.

Amanda elbowed her. "Yeah, that. Now be quiet."

"Oh, did Jackie already leave?" Mom came up to us. "I wanted to talk to her."

"Sorry," I said, "I forgot." So that was the third lie that day.

We went into my room and closed the door.

"I guess she just forgot," Amanda said. "She's forgetful. I called and she didn't answer. I'll try again."

She dialed, and I heard the phone go directly to voice mail.

"I'll keep trying," she said. "I just don't want Dad to know, because . . ."

He'd think she was doing drugs again. Which is what I thought, but I didn't say it. I mean, moms didn't forget to pick their kids up from school. At least, not people at our school. Maybe bad moms in movies. Moms at our school called a neighbor if they were running late and had a secret code word people were supposed to use if they picked you up unexpectedly. But I said, "You don't want him to get mad at her," at the same time Amanda said, "I don't want him to think she's doing drugs again."

"I saw her take that pill the other day," Casey said. "Was that drugs?" She looked all wide-eyed, like little kids do when they talk about something bad. Even though she was only a little younger than Amanda, I never remembered Amanda looking that way. Amanda was born a boss.

And she was one now. "No. I told you, that was a prescription. It was in a bottle with her name on it." She rolled her eyes at me. "I hate dealing with people who can't read."

"I can read!" Casey said. "Mommy was supposed to help me with my AR book. I need to get two more points by Friday."

"I'll help you," Amanda said. To me, she said, "Please don't tell your mom."

"Okay," I said even though I wasn't sure I wanted to add a fourth lie to my list. Or lie to Tim either. I mean, what if Amanda hadn't been able to come over to my house?

I pushed the thought away. She always could.

We helped Casey with her reading book, pretending to work on a project. Then we made oatmeal scotchies. Amanda finally got in touch with Jackie, but Mom said they could stay for dinner, and she'd bring them home.

"What'd she say," I asked Amanda.

"She had an appointment."

"That's what she said last week," Casey said.

"Last week?"

"It wasn't a big deal. Mrs. Garcia brought us home then. I just didn't see her today. Mom forgets things."

"Moms shouldn't . . ." I stopped. I'd been about to say moms shouldn't forget their kids, but I saw the look on Amanda's face.

"I won't call you next time."

"No, it's okay," I said.

Over dinner, my dad remarked I was putting on a little weight. "Maybe lay off the oatmeal cookies," he said.

Amanda and I exchanged a look. "Chris is bulking up for football," she said.

One day, when I was over at Amanda's practicing pitching and catching, her dad came out, singing, "Oh, Mandy, you came and you gave without taking. . . ."

"Stop that," she said.

"Hey, I'm a Fanilow," Tim said, because the guy who sang the song was named Barry Manilow.

I knew better than to sing myself. I knew not to get on Amanda's bad side. Last week, Nolan had called her "Lardass Lasky" out on the playground. A few days later, she'd "accidentally" dropped a pudding on him at lunch. "I think you must have meant badass," she told him after.

"You know there's another Amanda song?" I said when Tim left. "My mom had it on the radio once."

"Yeah, but you're not going to sing that one to me. It's all, 'Amanda . . . I loooooove you.'" She imitated the group that sang it, which my mom had told me was called Boston.

"True," I said.

"Let's play, so you can be a better ballplayer than you are a singer."

"That wouldn't be hard," I said, even though I thought I was actually an okay singer.

"No, it won't," Amanda agreed. "Okay, let's play so you can be way better than stupid Nolan and make everyone sorry they didn't let you in the majors."

"Hey, I'm already better than Nolan."

"That's true."

In summer, Amanda and I spent less time together. That was when Amanda played on a travel team while I went to YMCA camp, where they trapped us inside and made us play dodgeball against teams that included my brother, under banners that said *Best Summer Ever*. But the summer I was nine was the year I started going to sleep-away camp. That year, my mom was having a hysterectomy ("getting her plumbing removed," my dad said), so I went away to Camp Evergreen, in North Carolina. Their motto was, "Fourteen days without a mosquito-related fatality." No, really, it was "At one with nature," which involved paddling canoes, hiking up mountains, and trying to catch sight of a senior girl's boob on pajama day. The best thing about it was that Matt was going to a different camp, a computer camp in a whole different state (not that he'd see it), so no one would be there to tell the "funny" story about how I always had to poop when we went to the library ("It's just something with Chris and books"). The worst thing was that all the hiking and kayaking weren't helping with my plan to bulk up for football season. Dad had even said maybe I could lose some of that baby fat, and by the end of the first week, I knew he was right. My arms took on the lean look of string beans, an athletic vegetable to be sure, but to be a Junior PeeWee in the fall, with Alex and Brendan, I had to weigh at least sixty-five pounds, preferably seventy to make up for my height. Five-hour hikes and "creative" food by the chef, Zetta, who fancied herself a gourmet, weren't helping.

But then I discovered the peanut butter. The camp had a "picky eater" table for kids who didn't like the food. Fortunately, no one had told them about allergies, because it was peanut butter, bread, and this great, gloppy jelly that tasted like the stuff they put in Dunkin Donuts jelly donuts, so every meal, I went through the line, took a serving of yesterday's Hamburger-Marshmallow Surprise, or We-Figured-Out-How-to-Use-Every-Part-of-a-Cow Goulash, choked that down, then ate two peanut butter sandwiches. I also bugged Amanda and both sets of grandparents for care packages. Amanda's was the best. She managed to shove eighteen Hershey bars into a small flat-rate box. I signed up for lanyard making because it involved no exercise, and when I got poison ivy, I spent three days in the infirmary with no hikes. It worked. By the third week, I had to ask Dad to send uniform shorts in a larger size. I told him it was because they'd all gotten ripped or dirty, and he was so happy I was roughing it (he didn't know my original size) that I felt guilty for sitting in the air-conditioning. For the first time, some kid called me fat, but I didn't really care. I figured I'd eventually get taller. That was, after all, a big part of Mom's ugly duckling story, that I was just a late bloomer and wouldn't always be a short little turd. And then I'd be the right weight for my height. For now, I just wanted not to be on the little kids' teams.

When I got home, the first thing I did was weigh myself. Seventy-two pounds. That, along with my athletic ability, should make me a Junior PeeWee. The second thing I did was call Amanda. I hadn't heard from her since the care package. I figured that was because she was too busy setting home run records, getting her fastball up to fifty miles per hour, or making friendship bracelets with ponies on them—whatever girls did on travel teams.

I wasn't ready for what she actually said.

"Can I come over? Please? Like, can your mom pick me up?"

"Um, sure." I didn't think Mom would be too happy to pick her up, considering she'd just driven thirteen hours each way to pick me up from camp. "Can't I ride my bike over? Or can your mom bring you?"

Amanda sniffed. "No, she can't. She's not here anymore. She's gone."

"What? Where'd she go?"

"I can't talk. That's why I want to come over there."

"Okay. Sure."

As predicted, Mom didn't want to pick Amanda up. As predicted, she wanted to know why Amanda's mom couldn't bring her. But, finally, when I mentioned it hadn't exactly been my idea to go away for the whole summer, she agreed.

Amanda was waiting outside when we got there. She was taller since I last saw her, maybe slimmer, and her red hair hung in messy curls around her shoulders.

"Hey," she said when she got into the car. "Thanks for picking me up."

"You're always welcome," my mother said.

Mom pulled away, and no one said anything.

After a few minutes, I said, "Um, how's softball?"

"Fine," Amanda said.

More silence.

"How are your parents?" my mother asked as we passed the school.

"Fine," Amanda said.

More silence.

When we got to the house, Amanda jumped out of the car the second it stopped. Mom yelled something I didn't hear. I was running after Amanda, across our front yard, through the hammock to our old clubhouse. It had been months since we'd been there, and the plants had grown. There were even vines attaching themselves to the table with little clawlike tentacles. Amanda pulled them off and sat down. The table itself was wet and faded and a little small now, even for me but especially for Amanda, who was taller. Soon, we wouldn't be able to sit at it at all. Still, I squeezed into the opposite bench. "So?"

"I'm sure your mother already knows. Everyone knows."

"I don't think my mom knows anything about your mom."

Amanda looked down, playing with a little puddle of water with her finger. "She was arrested."

"Arrested for what? Drugs?" I was picturing Jackie in her cute tops and bright makeup, being taken away by the cops. "I thought she didn't do that anymore."

"We thought so too. I saw her taking pills sometimes, and she'd show me the bottle. It was a prescription from a doctor. But I guess she took too many of them. Like she went to more than one doctor."

"And that's illegal?"

"I guess so." Amanda scrubbed the table back and forth with her hand. "It was bad after you left. Like Dad would take me to travel team because he was the coach, but when I went to a friend's house or something, she would forget where I was and just leave me there for the whole day. I could see people getting uncomfortable, like they didn't want to tell me to leave because it would be rude. And I didn't want to ask them to take me home because, half the time, her car would be out in the driveway. She'd just be asleep. It wasn't like when I come to your house and can just stay."

She drew in a deep breath and scrubbed the table some more. The dirt she was trying to get out was obviously permanent, but I didn't say anything.

"Plus, I didn't want them to know how messed up she was. Now everyone knows."

"Why? What happened?"

"Last week, two police cars came to our house, and they took her away. There were all these lights flashing, and everyone—even neighbors we never see—came out of their houses to look. Then more police cars came. I don't know why they needed so many cars to take away one woman who was half asleep. It was like one of those shows where they bust some big drug dealer, but it was just my mom, and she wasn't fighting or anything. She just looked tired. Even my dad, he was, like, demanding to know what was going on, but when the cop said prescription fraud, he just threw up his hands. Like, he actually threw them up, like he'd expected it. He told Casey and me to go inside. I heard him on the phone with someone, saying something about *again*."

"What'd you do?" I asked, picturing it, sort of wishing I'd been there but also sort of glad I hadn't been.

"I just went to my room and turned on the music and closed my eyes until it was over. I could still see the red-and-blue lights behind my eyelids, though."

She put her hand over her eyes like she was demonstrating, but I thought she was wiping at a tear. I wanted to touch her somehow, but I thought she might hit me, so I just said, "Wow, that sucks."

"So since then, I've barely gone out of the house except if I have to for practice or a game. It's so embarrassing that everyone knows my own mother can't stand to be around us."

"What? What does that have to do with you?"

"That's what she told my dad. My grandmother bailed her out, and when she came to get her stuff, she told my dad she was sorry but it was too much pressure. She said she felt so stressed out, and she needed to take a pill just to play with us."

Wow. She looked down, and I knew she was crying. I reached over and touched her shoulder. She stiffened for a second, and I started to jerk my hand back. But then she leaned forward across the table and pulled me toward her.

"That's messed up," I said. "She's messed up, not you." It was something I'd heard a shrink say on one of Mom's TV shows.

"I know, but—"

"No. It's not you. It's about her. She's . . ." I searched for the right word. "She's weak. You're not weak."

"I guess."

"It's like with my dad. He's always working. He never spends any time with us, and he says it's because he's so busy at work. But other people's dads don't work all the time. Your dad doesn't. My dad just likes work more than he likes us."

"And my mom likes drugs more than she likes me?"

"Yeah."

"Just part of being an ugly duckling, I guess," Amanda said, and I knew I should say she wasn't one. Someone on TV would say that. But sometimes, it seemed better just to be quiet. We sat there a minute, not talking. A car came down the street, but I knew they probably couldn't see us through the trees, not if they weren't looking for us. I heard a door slam from my house, and I wondered if Matt was coming out to bother me. Amanda must have had the same thought because she said, "Do you have a softball?"

"I have a baseball."

"That's fine. I just want to throw it. You can catch."

We went up and got my baseball stuff. It took a while because even though my mom had supposedly been recovering all summer, that hadn't stopped her from cleaning out the closets, but finally, we found it.

"Do you think your mom knows?" Amanda asked.

"I don't think so. She's been in the hospital." I figured if my mom knew, she'd have mentioned it on our drive.

We went to the backyard. Amanda pitched while I caught. Even though it was a baseball, Amanda pitched it underhand like a softball, and it was so hard and fast my fingers ached after maybe the fifth pitch and felt like they might be broken after the tenth. I didn't say anything, though. I just kept catching until Mom said it was time for dinner, and did Amanda want to stay. "I made tuna casserole, Chris's favorite." She knew it was Amanda's favorite too.

"Okay. And my dad says if Chris wants to come over tomorrow, they could run some plays."

"That's nice," Mom said. "Is that baseball?"

"Football," I corrected her. "Tryouts are next week."

Later, after Amanda left, I heard my mom talking to my dad. She said something about "that poor girl." So she'd known all along.

So it turned out to be a bad year for Amanda and a good year for me after all. The year Amanda's mom moved out for good was the year I made the Junior PeeWees. I wasn't big enough to play defense or play much at all, but at least I was with my friends, and Tim said I had potential. "I played high school ball even though I was short," he said. "No reason you can't."

Fourth grade was the year everyone switched best friends. They started realizing they were only friends because their parents were friends or they didn't have anything in common. Or one person shopped at American Eagle or Pac Sun while the other still wore clothes from kids' stores (overheard on the playground: "I'm sorry, but I find it hard to like people who still shop at Justice"). So everyone kind of shuffled, and then, like the solitaire games my grandmother likes, hearts went with hearts, clubs with clubs, everyone finding their own match.

Except us. Amanda and I were matched from the start. We didn't get divorced in fourth grade. We didn't split in seventh either. Amanda switched from pitching to catcher, but she didn't switch best friends. Our friendship was like an old cell phone. Even though there were newer ones that might support more apps, you keep the old one because of the memories, the secret texts it got at night, the emotion of it. Okay, I sound like a girl, but you know it's true.

Of course, we had other friends too. Amanda made friends with a new girl, though, a girl named Kendra, who was shortstop on the middle school's team and also played volleyball, which Amanda had taken up. I stopped hanging with Brendan and Alex so much, after a sixth grade party that involved a really gross game of Truth or Dare, but I met some new guys on the middle school team. By seventh grade, I was playing outside linebacker. It was like Tim said, you could play if you weren't tall, as long as you were big.

I tried not to think about how that meant fat. I was getting fat, as my father constantly reminded me.

But Amanda and I were still best friends.

"What's her deal?" one of the guys, Kamal, said in the locker room after baseball practice one day in eighth grade. "Like, why do you hang out with her?"

I shrugged. "We're friends. I've known her since kindergarten."

"She's kind of fat," my friend Eric said.

"No, she's not," Kamal corrected. "She's fine-looking." He made a gesture I understood to mean big boobs.

I was getting a little uncomfortable with the direction of this conversation. It wasn't that I hadn't noticed Amanda's boobs. They were kind of hard to miss. I just didn't want to *discuss* them with other guys.

"Who?" Darien said. He'd just come over from the shower and was wrapped in a towel.

"That girl Amanda," Eric said. "Kamal thinks she's hot. I say she's a chubbo." He looked at Darien like he was going to break the tie.

"She's hot," Darien said. "Baby got back."

"Guys, gross," I said. "Quit it."

"What, are you in love with her?" Darien asked.

We'd been friends over seven years, and someone asked that question at least ten times a year. Instinctively, I answered, "Of course not."

But the next time I saw her, I couldn't keep my eyes off of her, off her chest, specifically. It's funny how, when you spend a lot of time with someone, you don't really notice how they look. My mom would get mad at my dad for not commenting if she got a new haircut, but honestly, she could have developed a third eye, and it probably would take me a few days to see it. Same with Amanda. I never saw her as hot or not, pretty or ugly. She was just Amanda.

Probably that was why the ugly duckling's friends didn't notice right off that he was a swan. Maybe they'd gotten so used to seeing him as ugly that they didn't notice he was beautiful, even when he was.

But that day, I noticed. The middle school was closer to Amanda's house, and Fridays, when neither of us had practice or a game, we walked to her house together after school. That day, I was waiting in our usual spot, under an oak tree at the side of the school. She was a little late, so when she showed up, she was running. Her face and chest were flushed. She had on a bright-green T-shirt, and when she ran, her backpack bouncing against her back made it pull tight in the chest.

Darien was right. She was fine-looking.

"Um, what are you looking at?" she said.

"What?" I realized I'd been staring right at her boobs, so I pretended I'd been spaced out, gazing ahead. "What? Oh, sorry. You're late."

She shrugged, and her T-shirt pulled tight again. "Yeah, sorry. I was talking to a teacher."

"Sure."

"So what do you want to do?"

"Whatever." I wanted to talk to Tim about football tryouts for high school, which were coming up. Tim was friends with the coach, so I hoped maybe he could give me some pointers, even put in a word. But I didn't want to say that. Amanda and I didn't get much time together, between her two softball teams and volleyball and me playing football and baseball, plus advanced classes that counted for high school. I didn't want it to seem like I was only interested in her dad. Besides, I wasn't.

I said, "I don't know. Go to the library?"

"On a Friday afternoon?"

"Watch a movie and get pizza?"

"That's less type A."

"I'm not type A. I just like to get homework over with early so I don't have it hanging over my head all weekend."

She tapped up the brim of my baseball cap. "That's the definition of a type A personality."

"No it's not." I adjusted my cap.

"Yeah it is." She pulled out her phone and did a search. "Rigidly organized, anxious, and concerned with time management."

"What personality type is it that whips out their phone and looks something up on Wikipedia to win a conversation?"

"I didn't do that." She took my cap off and hid it behind her back.

Instead of trying to get it back, I grabbed her phone and read, "A competitive drive which causes stress and—"

"I'm not that competitive."

"What's your batting average?"

"Point four seven one. But that's not really accurate, because they have moms scoring the games, and sometimes they call it an error when it's really—"

"You're making my argument for me." But I didn't want to argue with her, so I pointed toward the neighbor's house. "Hey, look. How many are there?"

It was a mother duck with ducklings. They must have come from the canal.

"One, two, three, four, five." Amanda shook her head. "They keep moving around."

"They do that." I counted fast. "Maybe eight, maybe nine. Yeah, nine. Four with spots on their sides, two with brown heads, and three completely yellow ones."

"Which are the pretty ones?" Amanda said.

"All of them." I grabbed back my baseball cap when her guard was down.

We approached Amanda's house. There was a car in the driveway I didn't recognize, a blue Toyota with a dent on the back.

"Oh shit." Amanda started to walk away. "My mom's here."

"She sees you."

Sure enough, Jackie was getting out of the car, yelling, "Mandy! Mandy, it's me!"

"Don't call me that," Amanda said.

"Fine, A-man-duh." Jackie enunciated each syllable in an annoying way. "I'm so glad I found her highness at home."

I hadn't seen Jackie in a few years, but I knew sometimes, she randomly showed up at Amanda's softball games. "Trying to act like a mom," Amanda said. Or Amanda would see her when she visited her grandmother.

Now she said, "What do you want, Jackie?"

"Mom. And where's Casey?"

"She's at school. At aftercare. Dad will pick her up after work like the other single parents."

"Okay, smarty pants. I came to see you, anyway. Thought we could pick out a dress for the eighth grade dance."

The eighth grade dance was this sort of mini-prom they had for, obviously, the eighth graders. It had a theme, ranging from Hawaiian to neon, and was held in the ballroom of a nearby office center, with the balcony doors locked so no one would "do anything foolish."

"Oh, I'm not going to that," Amanda said.

"You're not?" Jackie and I both asked at the same time. Everyone went to the dance, even people who sat at home and played computer games every night. People didn't usually have dates, so it wasn't only for people who could get one.

"No, I'm not." Amanda glared at me. "I think it's stupid. Besides, it has a theme, and they haven't announced it yet, so I wouldn't be able to buy a dress even if I was going, which I'm not."

Now I knew she was lying. They'd sent the invitations the week before, and the theme was "Back to the '80s." So Amanda was going. She just didn't want to shop with Jackie.

Jackie knew too. "I know there's a theme. One of the other moms told me. Why do you have to be such a brat?"

"Don't say, 'One of the other moms,' like you're one of the moms. You're not. And I'm not going to some stupid dance if I have to go shopping with you. So just forget it." She started running toward the house.

Jackie ran after her, yelling, "Amanda! Amanda!"

"Leave me alone!" Amanda fumbled with the house keys. She was so angry her hands were shaking, and I could hear the keys jingling. I didn't know what to do, just sort of got between her and Jackie.

"Why can't it ever be nice with us?" Jackie said.

"Because you're not nice," Amanda said. She finally got the door open and went inside. "Come on," she said to me.

"Maybe I should go."

"Come *on*!"

I followed her inside, which was no easy trick with Jackie trying to get past me. Sure, I had defensive experience, but I couldn't exactly tackle her. Finally, I got past her and into the house. Jackie was screaming at Amanda that she was a brat, a bitch, a few other things. Amanda double locked the door, then went into the family room and turned on the TV loud. *Ellen* was on. She was dancing to some rap song. Amanda turned the volume up louder and threw herself onto the sofa.

"No," I said.

"What do you mean, no?"

I gestured for her to stand. "You gotta dance. Dance with Ellen."

I started to dance. I am not a good dancer. To say two left feet is not only a cliché; it grossly overstates my ability, because it would imply that at least one of my feet was competent. That was not the case. But I was a football player, so I'd seen my share of side-line dances. I'd also seen my football brethren excited about pizza, excited about chicken wings, excited about getting the required 2.0 average to stay on the team. With that in mind, I started pumping my fists like Jaden Sanders had when his prealgebra teacher forgot to give a Friday quiz, thrusting my hips like Andy Rodriguez on forty-nine-cent hamburger day, and jumping up and down like my brother when I got in trouble for something he did.

"What are you doing?" Amanda yelled.

"What does it look like I'm doing?" I fanned myself. Like a rapper.

"Having a seizure?"

"I'm dancing." I imitated Ellen, who was doing some kind of hip-hop move. "Come on!"

"Stop it. I don't feel like dancing."

I did the running man in front of her.

"Oh my God, you look so stupid! You're not even doing it right." But she was laughing.

"Then show me! Show me the light of your masterful choreography!" I started doing the Dougie.

"Oh, God. Okay. If it will get you to stop."

She started dancing, locking and popping along with Ellen. When Ellen finished, we both collapsed on the sofa, laughing.

"I wish Ellen could be my mom," she said.

"Yeah, that's kind of the dream," I said. "At least you have Tim."

"I guess."

"You have to go to that dance. You need to show off your moves."

"Don't you mean our moves?" she asked.

"If you seriously want me to dance, I will."

"I just want to stay home."

"Everyone's going," I said.

"Not me."

"How about this? If I make the football team, you'll go."

"You'll definitely make it."

"I'm glad you're so confident. Just go."

In the end, it was my mother who talked Amanda into going to the dance. The following Friday, Dad was working late, Matt was doing whatever Matt did on Friday nights, so Amanda and I went to my house for "taco night." When Amanda got there, my mother said, "I have something to show you."

We went into the living room, and Mom gave Amanda three hangers with dresses on them. "I heard it was an eighties theme. I used to wear these to sorority dances in college. I never throw anything away. Maybe one of these will work?"

Amanda held the hangers apart. One of the dresses was black, made out of a kind of net material with a sparkly top. Another was pink with a big, poofy skirt like a bubble. The third was bright-aqua satin and strapless.

"This one matches your eyes." Mom pointed to the aqua.

"They're really short," Amanda said.

"Yes, and you're taller than I was. But short is in style now. Why don't you try?"

"I don't know. I don't think I'm going."

I was nodding, like, *yes, you are*, and I said, "Just try them. You don't want to hurt my mom's feelings, do you?"

"It's true," Mom said. "I'd be really hurt."

"She'd cry," I said.

Finally, Amanda ducked into my bedroom, just to shut us up.

Then she didn't come out for a really long time.

"Come on," I said. "I want to see them."

"Just your mom. I need help."

"Okay." My mom went in too. Then they were gone forever.

"Should I, like, find something else to do?" I asked through the door.

"That would be a good idea," Mom said.

It was probably a good sign that they were taking this long. I went to watch a rerun of *The Big Bang Theory*. It was the one where Leonard was pretending to understand football. At the end of it, Amanda finally came out.

She wasn't wearing one of the dresses. She was wearing her hoodie, though I thought I noticed some makeup that hadn't been there before. If I was the type who noticed stuff like that.

"I was thinking I'd go if you made the team." She swiped at her cheek to get off the makeup.

"So I guess I'll have to make the team."

"Guess you will."

When I'm forty and have forgotten a lot of things, I'll still remember the eighth grade dance, and who I went with.

I made the team. NBD. And Amanda went to the dance. Also NBD. It wasn't like a date or anything. We were going as friends. But, for a few minutes, when I first saw her, I forgot that.

She chose the aqua dress, the one Mom had said would match her eyes. It probably did, but that wasn't what I noticed.

I noticed what Kamal noticed, what Darien noticed.

And I noticed she was beautiful.

She was. Beautiful.

We were meeting friends there, but Tim drove Amanda and me to the dance, and Mom was going to pick us up. Tim brought Amanda inside so Mom could take pictures. I was wearing a white jacket of my dad's with a bright-aqua T-shirt, which Mom said was the style in the 1980s. So we matched.

"This is stupid, Mom," I said. "It's not prom."

But I was lying. I wanted the picture.

At the dance, we sat with some girls from the softball team, Kendra and Lilly, and some football guys, Darien and Eric, plus this guy Brian and Brian's girlfriend, Sarah, the same girl who'd had the Disney Princess party back in elementary school. We had a great time dancing to silly 1980s music. Dancing, in this case, mostly meant jumping around, but near the end of the evening, the DJ played the Boston song "Amanda." Amanda and I were standing in this photo area they'd made, where you could try on hats and glasses and stuff to take pictures. When it started, I had on a fake mustache and a pirate hat. Amanda wore a tiara. I said, "You need to dance to this."

"It's a slow song."

"It's your song."

She switched her tiara for my pirate hat and plopped the tiara onto my head. "I'm not going to dance to it alone."

"Okay, then." I held out my hand and walked her out, still wearing the tiara.

I don't know how to dance, not really. But slow dancing is just swaying. Some people, the ones who were dating, tried to make out, but I held Amanda's right hand in my left and put my right hand on her back the way my mom (without my asking) had told me to. We swayed.

It had seemed like a good idea at the time. Like, to tease her about the song.

Turned out, though, that if you're not making out, there's not much to do during a slow song. And if you're already a few inches shorter than the girl, and then she wears heels, you end up eye level with her chin.

And you have to crane your neck up not to seem like you're looking, um, down.

Truth told, I wouldn't have minded looking down, but I didn't think Amanda would like it, particularly considering the context. The fact that the song was all about a guy telling a girl named Amanda that he loved her.

Just to break the silence, I said, "I'm glad you came."

She gave me a weird look, which I had to crane my neck to see. "Really? Why?"

I shrugged, a little embarrassed. "I don't know. 'Cause you're my best friend. 'Cause someday, we'll look back on this, and we probably won't even know most of the other people anymore. Because everyone else is sort of . . . temporary. But we'll still be friends."

She nodded, then took her hand off my back. At first, I couldn't figure out what she was doing. Then I realized she was kicking back her feet to remove her shoes, first one, then the other. They were the kind with straps, so she dangled them from her finger. "Better?" she asked.

"Yeah."

"Don't step on my feet."

"Okay."

She said, "It's weird. I'm not friends with anyone else from grade school. Like when I look at the pictures from the fifth grade lunch, I don't even like any of those girls anymore."

"Sooner or later, everyone disappoints you," I said, thinking of her mom, but also kind of my dad. When I told him I made the football team, he said he guessed they needed husky guys to play defense. And tonight, he hadn't been home at all.

"Everyone but my dad," she said, "and you."

We kept swaying. The song was almost over, and for a minute, I wanted to pull her closer, like a *real* slow dance. But that would be all weird, something that couldn't be undone. And I realized I couldn't take a chance, couldn't face the possibility of losing her.

So I just swayed until the song ended, and when it did, Amanda said she had to go to the ladies' room. She put her shoes back on. I watched her walk away. I went back to the table.

Kendra was sitting there. I didn't really know her enough to talk to her, and they were playing another slow song, so I couldn't dance. So I started playing Candy Crush on my phone.

These two girls walked by. One was this girl Sophie, who'd been Amanda's best friend besides me in fifth grade. The other one I didn't really know. As they passed, the girl I didn't know said, "So did you see that girl Amanda?"

Sophie stopped walking. "Yeah. What about her?"

"Um, that dress she's wearing. Slutty much?"

"What do you expect?" Sophie said. "She has to show off her boobs to make up for the rest of her body."

I looked up then, right at Sophie, to let her know I'd heard her.

Sophie glanced back at me, laughed, and looked away. She started walking again.

When she did, she stumbled. "Ugh!"

She leaned down. Her shoe had come off. She went to get it, but it was glued, somehow, to the floor.

"Yuck! What is this?" She put down her foot, and that, too, stuck to the floor.

Beside me, I heard Kendra chuckle. I looked at her, and she was staring at Sophie real hard, like she was concentrating.

Finally, Sophie pried her shoe off, but not before she got her other shoe and foot stuck. She and the girl walked away, talking about how gross the place was.

When Amanda came back a minute later, they were playing a fast song again.

"Hey, do you guys want to dance?" she said.

"Sure. But watch out. The floor's sticky there."

But the weird thing was, Amanda was stepping right on it. It wasn't sticky at all.

I looked at Kendra. She smiled. "Yeah," she said. "Be careful."

Things that happened in ninth grade:

Ninth grade was the year college scouts started looking at Amanda.

It was the year Nolan got busted for smoking weed on a field trip to the planetarium.

It was the year I started the Caveman Diet and worked out ninety minutes a day, gained ten pounds but not an inch of height.

It was the year the Gay-Straight Alliance wanted a day of silence for gay bullying, but the school decided people should be able to do it for whatever cause they wanted. One girl chose lobster empathy. I couldn't make this up.

It was the year I was chosen Rookie of the Year but didn't make varsity. I was too short.

Oh, and it was the year my parents got separated.

Matt and I knew it was coming. Or we knew something was, anyway. For one thing, Dad was actually home a lot more than usual. In a typical week for, oh, most of my life, Dad worked late at least four nights, worked one weekend day, and had an important, work-related golf game on the other. Lately, he'd also started going to the gym at five a.m. so he wasn't home in the morning either.

But then, for a month, he started coming home semi–on time several days a week, and he and my mom locked themselves in the bedroom after dinner.

"Do you think they're doing it?" Matt asked when we were clearing the table.

"I can't imagine them ever doing it."

"They've done it at least twice."

"Mom must have made an appointment."

"Listen at the door," Matt said.

"To see if they're doing it? No thanks."

But just then, something broke in their room. I heard Dad yell, "Shit! Why'd you do that?"

"Must've been an accident. Like that e-mail Julia accidentally sent you."

"I told you, she was just updating me on—"

"I'm not stupid," Mom said. "I'd have to be stupid to trust you after that e-mail. Do you really think I'm that stupid?"

"She was just—"

"I don't even care if you think I'm stupid. I just can't do this anymore."

"Fine. I'm going to the gym."

"Will she be there?"

"For God's sake, no."

Two days later, they sat us down in the family room before dinner or, I should say, instead of dinner, because dinner never happened. Mom said, "Your father and I need to talk to you boys."

"We need to talk to you boys like adults."

"They're not adults, David," Mom said.

"They're fifteen and seventeen. You always coddle them."

"Because you don't coddle them at all. You don't even go to Chris's games."

"Just because I'm not like Tim Lasky, with all this free time."

"God, can you stop it?" Matt had his hands over his ears and was yelling.

Both my parents shut up and looked at Matt.

"It's obvious you're getting a divorce. We've heard all about the e-mail, the girlfriend, not to mention the fact that he's barely been home for—oh, the last ten years.

"I can't believe this," Dad said. "I work to support this family, and I get . . ."

He kept talking, but I stopped listening. He hadn't denied the part about having a girlfriend. I felt like he was cheating on me, on our whole family, not just Mom.

But I also felt like I hadn't really lost anything. Nothing was different. It was like I'd always known he wasn't part of us, but I'd avoided the knowledge. Now it was there, unavoidable, and it was a little bit of a relief not to have to pretend anymore.

He finished his oration, saying, "At some point, I realized I haven't been happy in twenty years. That's a hard thing to realize."

It wasn't a surprise that he felt that way, only that he said it. Did this guy really have no clue?

I said, "Really, Dad? Twenty years?"

That was when I walked out. Dad was screaming after me. I don't know why he cared. So was Mom, but the blood was rushing through my ears, and I couldn't hear what they were saying. I looked back to see Matt applauding me.

I said, "I'm going to see the people who have time for me."

And I took off, running. I wasn't wearing shoes, and the Laskys lived maybe three miles away, so I ran on the street, ran across the neighbors' gravel driveway, across the grass. I felt my phone buzzing in my pocket. I ignored it. There was no one I wanted to talk to. Even though I was barefoot, I could tell I was fast, faster than I'd ever been, and I sort of wished I'd turned on my app, but if I did, it would ruin the pure anger of it, and that was what was pushing me. What a jerk, blaming me, blaming Mom, blaming everyone but himself.

I'd run as far as the park when Matt caught up to me in his car.

"Hey, you want a ride?"

"No. No thanks."

"You're not crying or anything, are you? I can't let you embarrass the family like that."

I started to tell him to screw off, but then I noticed he was crying. I stopped. I said, "Nah, I'm okay."

"I brought your sneakers." Matt held them up, wiping his eyes with his arm.

I took them. "Thanks. I'll put them on for the run home. Want to come with me?"

"Nah, I'm going over Brittney's."

I nodded and took off again.

When I reached the Laskys' a few minutes later, Amanda was already at the door.

"Hey, your mom told me you were on your way over." She looked down at my feet, which were covered in dirt and leaves, but made no comment.

I wondered if Mom had told her why, but I didn't want to ask.

"I was just about to call you, actually, to see if you wanted to go to the batting cages."

I knew Mom had told her then. We never did stuff like that on weeknights, and she seldom went to the batting cages with me during the season. There were already a ton of practices. She probably thought I needed to hit something.

I said, "I'd rather go to the playground."

She smiled. The playground at the elementary school was our happy place. Unlike the park playground, which was always packed with moms who looked at us weird for swinging on swings, the school playground was empty at night. We knew how to get in through a crack in the fence. It reminded me of the old days of Chris and Amanda, playground buddies.

"Are we running there?" she asked.

My feet were actually throbbing. "Can we walk?"

"Good idea."

The night air was cooler now, but still, I was sweating. The moon was a sliver, and the sky was bright with stars. We snuck through the fence and started swinging.

"Do you want to talk about it?" Amanda said.

I said, "Don't get me started."

Don't Get Me Started was a game we'd play where one of us would bring up a topic that was super annoying: boy bands, the Kardashians, people who turned on their flashers when it rained, and the other would see how long they could rant about it. I held the record of thirteen minutes, on the topic of Kendall Fisher commenting when I ate Chinese food with a fork at the food court, then offering to teach me to use chopsticks because she said I used them wrong (which was why I'd been eating with a fork). Then it had sort of deteriorated into a general rant about white girls who think they're Asian because they read manga. I hadn't even been trying.

Amanda made a shooting motion toward me and said, "Start."

"They're splitting up. Which shouldn't be a surprise, which isn't a surprise, actually. I mean, the guy was barely home. I've spent way more time with your dad. I've spent so much time I should be starting to look like him by now. Your dad was there when I hit my first home run. Your dad helped me with my math homework."

"Okay."

I pumped a few times, looking for the right words.

"He said he hadn't been happy in twenty years."

"He said that?"

"Right? That's my entire life, Matt's entire life, and I'm thinking, 'How is that *my* fault?' I mean, did I suck my thumb too long? Did I not get potty trained early enough?"

Amanda kicked her legs higher. "You were awfully fixated on that Spider-Man toy."

"Hey, hey, hey, watch it. That was a *Pose and Stick* Spider-Man toy. That was the ultimate Spider-Man toy in the whole world."

"I stand corrected."

"We wouldn't even be friends if it wasn't for that toy," I said.

She laughed. "That might be true. That would have been tragic for you, really."

"Just for me?"

"Yup. Just for you. I would clearly have been besties with Nolan."

Then she leaped off the swing. She flew through the air a moment, then landed with a thud on the ground. She clutched her arm, screaming, "Ow! My arm!"

"Amanda, are you okay?"

"No. I think it's broken." She clutched her arm.

"Shit!" I jumped from the swing and ran toward her. She looked like she was crying, holding her arm. "Can you bend it?"

"No. No. Oh, wait. . . ." She pushed herself up on the arm. "Yeah, I can." She stood and ran for the monkey bars and hoisted herself atop them. She crawled to the center. "Bet you can't get me."

"Asshole. Of course I can." I ran for the bars myself. I was shorter than her, and not as agile, but they were made for little kids, so I pulled myself up and sat next to her. We were over everything, level with the moss hanging from the trees.

I said, "What would have happened if you hadn't saved Spidey that day, and we'd never become friends?"

"Clearly, I'd have become a very proper girl who dressed in pink every day and did nail art and knew how to use a flat iron."

"What's a flat iron? Is it for clothes?"

"It's for hair, idiot. See how you've corrupted me?"

"Yeah, it's a tragedy, really. And I probably would've been a big, tough guy without you."

"So you're saying I made you *shorter*? Yeah, I think that was genetics, buddy."

"It's my dad's fault."

"Oh, and I'd have been skinny," she said.

"You don't need to be skinny."

She punched my arm. "You're supposed to say I *am* skinny."

I punched her back. "You were supposed to say I'm tall."

We sat there a moment, silent, listening to the coo of doves on the electrical wires. It was such a mournful sound. Then I started thinking about getting down from there, or rather, getting down without looking like a total idiot or actually hurting myself. This was an issue every single time we did this.

Amanda spoke first. "Do you think they were ever in love? I mean, they must have been, right?"

I shrugged. "Yeah, they were college sweethearts. They met at a frat party. She once showed me a whole album of love notes he sent her."

"Weird."

"How about your parents?"

291

"They were in love. He's still in love with her. That's why every few years they start talking, and I think they'll get back together."

"Do you want that?"

"I used to, but now I don't. She says she loves us, but she loves drugs more."

I nodded.

"I wish he'd meet someone else," she said. "Then I'd know they'll never get back together."

"I'm not there yet." The monkey bars were starting to dig into my butt. "I still want everyone to pretend they're happy together, even though we apparently never were."

She touched my hand with her fingers. I don't know if it was intentional, but I sort of started a little at the unexpectedness, and she pulled her hand back. But I grabbed it.

"Thanks for coming here with me," I said.

"I didn't have anything better to do."

"Sleep, homework, answering BuzzFeed quizzes about which Hogwarts house you belong in, watching . . ."

Down the street, I saw a flash of red, followed by blue. A police cruiser. Did I mention we weren't, strictly speaking, supposed to be on the playground?

"Shit," Amanda whispered. "The neighbors must have heard me screaming."

"You think?" I whispered back.

"Come on. Jump down. We can go before they see us."

I gaped down at the black hole that was the playground. In the occasional strobing light, I could see the ground, some patchy grass, mostly hard, brown dirt. This would be where I died. Or broke my leg, then got arrested, then needed my dad to bail me out. Or died.

"I have to climb down. You go." I started to pull my hand away from hers.

She clutched mine. "Never leave a man behind. Come on. When I count three, jump, and then we'll split up. You go left, I'll go right."

"I can't."

"One . . . two . . ." She tugged at my hand. "Three."

And I jumped, knowing she'd pull me off with her if I didn't. I landed, mostly on my feet, my whole body jolted like a punch to the gut, but okay, still holding her hand.

She yanked it away.

"Run! Text me when you get home."

We both ran in opposite directions just as the police car stopped.

When I got home, I saw she'd already texted me.

Same time tomorrow at 9?

I texted back:

Yeah

A moment later, she texted back:

Do you ever wonder if you have a doppelganger?

Clearly I do. It's Ryan Gosling

No, that's not true. There couldn't possibly be 2 such great-looking guys on the planet

But if you had a double . . . what would you do with one?

Send him to take my SATs for me if he's smarter

Boring

If he was from another country and spoke another language I'd send him somewhere to speak it and really freak people out

What about you?

I'd send her to take my classes in school so I could sleep in

Now who's boring?

Okay, I'd make her have Thanksgiving dinner with my mom and grandmother. She'd probably behave better

As usual, we texted all night.

That summer, I went to camp for the first four weeks so I could be back for football practice. In that time, Mom and Dad separated. Dad moved in with his new girlfriend, Chelsea (turned out Julia was just temporary), and Mom had five garage sales to sell off twenty years of memories so we'd fit in the condo we were moving to.

"Will you still go to school here?" Amanda asked one night at the school playground. We'd been going there every night since I got back. The possibility of getting caught just made it cooler, though we'd found that, if we refrained from screaming, nobody called the cops.

"Mom said she'd try to find a place in the district," I said, not adding that most of the condos and townhouses were on the other side of the district. I wouldn't be able to walk or run to her house unless I was planning on joining the cross-country team. But maybe I'd get a car.

"You could always move in with us," Amanda said.

"Matt too?"

"Sure, why not?"

"You wouldn't say that if you lived with him. The smells alone . . ." I pretended to shudder.

"Or your mom could marry my dad."

I laughed. "You want to be my sister?"

"Why not?" she repeated, and even in the darkness, I could see she was looking at me, like she was daring me to say why not. And I wondered what would happen if I just leaned over and kissed her.

It would ruin everything, that was what.

I slapped my arm. "It's really buggy here."

"Yeah, I wish they'd spray."

"Don't get me started."

"I won't," she said. "Unless you want to talk about . . . why people feel like they have to yell when they talk into their cell phones."

"Right?" I said. "Like, do they think the person needs to be able to hear them without the phone? And why do they especially do it when they're someplace like Starbucks, where you want it to be quiet? Do they think everyone is interested in their conversation? Thank God they don't allow people to talk on their phones on airplanes. You'd have murders. And since people can't bring weapons on airplanes, you'd have people being beaten to death with copies of *SkyMall*."

I went on like this for another minute or so before I started repeating myself.

"How long was that?" I asked.

"Only two minutes, forty-five seconds. You're losing your touch. What should we do now?"

I reached out and grabbed the monkey bars, using them to swing down, then across, rung by rung. "Come on. I want to show you something."

"What?"

"Just something."

She scrambled down too and ended up beside me. I tried not to notice I only came up to her nose. I grabbed her arm and pulled her toward the park that adjoined the school. The walking paths were unlit, but there was a full moon we could see by. I led her to a giant ficus tree that stood by the canal, its gnarled roots making a pattern on the ground like one of those Irish knots. I walked around, looking. "They're usually right here at night."

Then I spotted them. The mother duck was sleeping, head tucked under her wing. Her babies, seven of them, slept the same way around her.

"Remember when we used to come with my mom to feed them?" I said.

"Like it just happened."

"It's been half a lifetime."

"Weird." She looked at the ducklings in the moonlight glinting off the canal. "They're so cute. No swans to make them feel bad about themselves."

"I don't think that's how the story goes."

"Yeah, but you know that's what would happen in real life. Did you know that the term *pecking order* came from stronger chickens pecking at the weaker ones to achieve social dominance?"

"I didn't need to know that," I said. My phone was buzzing in my pocket, but I ignored it. There was no one I wanted to talk to.

"The more you know. Wonder what happened to the fishhook duck?"

"Probably long gone."

"I guess. He was a fighter, though."

"Good old Fishhook," I said. Amanda moved closer to me, but also closer to the ducks. My phone was buzzing in my pocket again.

Probably just a text about practice or something. One person texts, then ten people have to respond. I said, "Hold on. Let me turn off my phone. I keep getting texts."

I took it out of my pocket and looked. It wasn't texts. It was five missed calls from my mother.

I called her.

"It's your brother. He's been in an accident." Her voice sounded shaky.

"Is he okay?"

"I don't know. I don't know. They took him to the hospital."

I said to Amanda, "My brother's in the hospital."

"My dad can take you."

I said to Mom. "Go ahead. Tim will bring me. Where is he?" We were already walking back to our bikes. What if it was a bad accident? What if Matt was dead?

I felt Amanda's hand on my shoulder. I tried to unlock my bike, but I couldn't because my hands were shaking. Finally, Amanda did it for me.

"Are you okay?" she asked.

"I don't know. Guess I'll have to be."

My brother, Matt, my phenomenally stupid brother, who later insisted he was neither drunk nor texting but just tired at ten at night, had fallen asleep at the wheel and plowed through a traffic circle with an ornamental obelisk at its center and giant bronze fish swimming around. The fish were fried and Matt was knocked out for two days, so he got to miss my first meeting with Dad's girlfriend, a twenty-two-year-old blond yoga instructor who wished me *Namaste* when we met. I wished I'd been so lucky.

But at the hospital, Dad told Mom, "I can't believe you let this happen."

"How is it my fault?" Mom asked.

"He was in your care," Dad said.

"Because you ditched him. He has a curfew, eleven o'clock. It was ten."

"That's just like you, always making excuses."

"She's not always making excuses," I said. "She never makes excuses. You're the one who's always blaming everyone else for everything."

Amanda took my hand and squeezed it.

"I don't have to listen to this," my father said. "I just want to see my son."

"The one who never made you happy in twenty years?" I muttered.

"And what's he doing here?" Dad gestured at Tim.

"He drove me here," I said, "and he's being supportive, like you never were."

Dad hitched his fingers in his pockets and glared at Mom. "Should have known you'd turn them against me."

"No, Dad, you did that yourself." I tugged at Amanda. "Let's see if there's a Coke machine around here."

As soon as Dad figured out that Matt wasn't going to die but probably was going to have to pay for the ornamental fish, he cleared out. Mom and I stayed at the hospital all night. Tim and Amanda stayed with us.

Matt showed up the first day of school in a wheelchair and with his jaw wired shut. The Great Fish Encounter was the stuff of legend. Mom made him apologize to the mayor of our town for breaking the statue. She never made me apologize to Dad.

11

When we were little kids, Amanda was the best at hide-and-seek. The reason was, she was patient. Other people might find a good hiding spot, but the second the person who was it passed by, they'd run for base, revealing themselves, and usually get caught. Not Amanda. I still have no idea where she'd hide, but she could outwait anyone. Probably it was because of softball. She was used to waiting her turn at bat, waiting for someone to hit the ball so she could get them out. So Amanda waited. And waited. She waited in whatever hiding place it was she found, and just when everyone had been caught and I was ready to give up, Amanda would come flying out of nowhere and make it to base. She snuck up on you.

That's how it was, falling in love with her.

Or maybe realizing I'd been in love with her all along.

She snuck up. One day, we were friends, doing homework or texting, talking, ranting, playing catch. The next day, I was waking up at five in the morning, waiting until it was late enough to text her to see if she was awake, waiting to see her blue Civic picking me up for school.

Her dad had gotten her the car for her sixteenth birthday, in December, which was two months before my birthday. I'd avoided the question of whether I'd get a car when I turned sixteen. Matt had, and I bet if I was nice to Dad, I would too. But if I got one, I couldn't go with Amanda.

I knew I'd never act on it, though. Saying I liked her as more than a friend would kill our friendship. Probably she wouldn't feel the same way. Or if she did, we'd date a month or so, then break up. Then we wouldn't be friends anymore.

Part of me said maybe we could beat the odds. After all, we'd beaten the odds with our friendship, which had outlasted everyone else's playground relationships.

But I wasn't willing to take the chance. I couldn't lose anyone else right now.

Besides, she probably didn't feel the same way.

Even if she did magically know each day if I wanted to drive through McDonald's or Starbucks, and even if she had memorized my order at each place. But a friend might know that stuff too.

That day, we had taken a trip through McDonald's drive-through (number three Egg White Delight McMuffin combo with a Coke and an extra hash brown) when Amanda mentioned sort of casually, "Coach says there's going to be a scout from UCF at our game tonight."

"That's great." There were often scouts at their games.

"Coach says she's there for me."

We were only sophomores, so it wasn't time to sign yet, but that didn't stop colleges from looking at the best girl catcher in the county. I knew Amanda wanted to stay in state to be near Tim and Casey.

"That's so great!" I said, and I meant it, although for sure no one was recruiting me. Softball was Amanda's life. I wanted to make the varsity teams because it was fun and it would look good on college applications—especially if I was captain. Everyone liked me, but I knew I was too short to go farther than high school.

"Think you could go and, like, yell nice things about me, maybe bring some friends?"

"You won't need it, but sure."

So that night, I recruited Brian and Darien and a few of the other guys, as well as my mother, and we all went to see Amanda.

I was right that she didn't need us, though I'd have gone anyway. Softball wasn't usually a big draw in high school, but our baseball team was having a losing season, and everyone knew how good the girls were, particularly because of Amanda. Also, we were playing Kenwood High, our biggest rival.

At the top of the eighth, the score was tied at three, and Kenwood, the visiting team, was up. Amanda had had a good game, getting on base once and one RBI, but it wasn't her best game. Now Kenwood had two girls on base with two outs and one strike.

Kendra, the pitcher, pitched a curve ball, which the batter missed.

And Amanda dropped the ball. It rolled away from her.

The coach at third screamed at the runner to go, go, go! She started running. Amanda scrambled for the ball, got it, and tagged the runner out at home.

At least, that's what I saw.

What Mom saw.

What all my friends saw.

What a stand full of fans screaming Amanda's name saw.

But the home plate ump saw the Kenwood runner safe at home.

That's how he called it.

Our coach came out to argue the call. We were booing. The whole crowd was—well, except the Kenwood crowd. I watched Amanda. Tim had taught us not to yell, certainly not to cry, but even though she had on a catcher's mask, I could tell she was having what her dad would call "a moment." A dropped ball was bad enough. A run scored on it was tragic.

Kendra struck the batter out on the next pitch, but the damage was done. The score was three to four, and it was Amanda's fault. I saw Kendra go up to Amanda in the dugout and put her arm around her.

When it was time for Amanda to bat, there was one out and the bases were loaded. The perfect opportunity for Amanda, who led the league in RBIs, to hit a sacrifice fly and tie up the game. Hopefully, another demonstration of Amanda's RBI brilliance would make up for the dropped ball.

The pitch, and then I saw Amanda hit it perfectly, low and into left field, just out of reach, just like she had about a thousand other times.

And then suddenly the ball lifted up. Like, it made a dramatic right angle up and sailed over the right fielder's head and toward the fence.

The runner on third came home.

The third base coach told the next runner to come in.

She did too.

The ball cleared the fence, somehow.

The runner who'd been on first came home.

Then Amanda, looking completely dazed.

We were screaming her name, everyone was, even people who hadn't known her name an hour before. I noticed a woman sitting alone, taking notes on an iPad. The scout. She was smiling.

Four runs scored. Game over. A win.

Maybe it was my imagination. Maybe no one else noticed because they were watching Amanda or watching the action on the field.

But the instant before the ball tilted up, I could have sworn I saw Kendra staring at it. And then, not taking her eyes off the ball, she gestured toward it, like she was lifting it.

It was like magic. Witchcraft.

Crazy. The witchcraft was Amanda. Her talent. Her awesomeness. Nothing more. I ran onto the field with everyone else. I found Amanda and hugged her.

"That was incredible!" I screamed. "That was so great!"

"I know! I know, right? I wasn't even trying to do that. I was going for the sacrifice. It must have been the wind."

It was a windless night in a windless week in a largely windless month.

But I said, "Yeah, it was the wind. Or you're just the best hitter in the league!"

"You think so? You think the scout noticed?" She was holding my hands, shaking.

"Unless she was comatose. You got a grand slam! In front of a college scout!"

"Eek!" She screamed, and then she put her arms around me and squeezed me hard, making me wonder if she might feel the same way I did.

Then about twenty girls pulled her away from me into their vortex of girl energy, screaming her name, and I knew she was just excited. She was a star, and I was her short, pudgy best friend. I was lucky, but that was it.

12

After that game, I started noticing that when Kendra was around, stuff happened. Weird stuff. Things like Mr. Cardenas losing a stack of pop quizzes before he got a chance to grade them, or Nolan slipping on a banana peel no one had previously noticed when he was onstage for a pep rally. Things like the marching band bizarrely switching from a *West Side Story* medley to Suicide Silence, then back without missing a note of "I Feel Pretty." Nothing too Stephen King, just middle school weird stuff, stuff like Sophie's shoe getting stuck to the perfectly clean floor or Amanda hitting that grand slam after that unfair call.

More scouts were looking at Amanda now. She still played on two softball teams along with her classes, community service projects, and driving Casey around in her car. I had most of those things too. But every morning, we drove to school together, and every night, we lay in bed and texted.

Sometimes, the subject matter was about serious things.

I'm really overwhelmed lately

Yeah, I bet having to talk to college scouts and sign autographs must be a pain

It was just that one girl who wanted an autograph. I think Celia put her up to it to mess with me

Just ONE autograph

I'm serious Chris. What if I fail all my classes and can't even go to college?

Are you failing?

No. It's just hard. I'll probably get a C in algebra 2

Maybe take math for college readiness next year instead of pre-calc

Everyone would make fun of me

Remind them that you have a bat and you're not afraid to use it

I think the school would frown on that . . .

You're Amanda Lasky. They can't make fun of you. You're a badass softball queen

True . . .

Other times, it was less so.

I really want a slurpee

Now? It's 10:30 on a school night

With a bendy straw

A purple one

Who do you think invented bendy straws?

I thought Google was your friend.

Checking

Enlighten me

Ancient sumerians invented the straw in 3000 bc. They were made of leaves

Interesting

A guy named marvin chesterstone invented the modern straw made of paper because he didn't like leaves in his drink

Makes sense

Then a guy named joseph friedman invented the bendy straw in the 1930s to help his daughter drink her milkshake

Nice dad

I still want a slurpee

Would your mom let you go if I picked you up?

Yeah

I'll be there in 10 minutes

And sometimes, we still went to the playground and sat on the monkey bars.

Generally, things were going pretty well for me. If you don't count that I barely spoke to my dad and was in love with a girl who had me permanently in the friend zone. But I had good grades, good friends, and a surprisingly decent relationship with my brother (his near-death experience seemed to have mellowed him). Until Coach Tejada posted the rosters for next year's team, and I was on JV for the third year in a row.

And all my friends made varsity.

"Man, that sucks," Darien said after he finished celebrating his own position on the varsity roster long enough to notice I wasn't on it. "What are we gonna do without you?"

"Maybe it's a mistake," Brian said. "You should ask Coach if he forgot you."

"It's no mistake." I pointed to the JV roster. "He didn't forget me, just remembered me on JV."

We stood in awkward silence for a moment, then Darien said, "Tough blow, man."

"Yeah, tough blow," Brian agreed.

"Maybe next year," Darien said.

"Yeah, maybe next year," Brian agreed.

They kept repeating the same things until I wanted to punch one of them to see if the other would bleed. I needed to get out of there, so I said, "Yeah, I need to go. I've got a doctor's appointment."

But I didn't. And I did go talk to Coach Tejada, and he said exactly what I knew he'd say. "Sorry, Burke. You're a great kid. You've got great heart, and I love having you on the team. But you're just not big enough to play varsity. If you were only a few inches taller. Maybe next year, if you grow a little."

I nodded. "Maybe."

But I knew I wouldn't.

I wanted to see Amanda. But I knew she probably had practice for something, homework for something, a game that night where she'd be the star and no time for her short, toady little friend who'd probably still need her to save his Spider-Man toy from a bully, if it came up. So I didn't call her. I walked home.

On the way, I stopped by the park. It was spring, and the mother ducks were there with their babies. I sat by the canal and took my shoes off, then rolled up my pants legs. They were a little too long. Mom had gotten the wrong size, and now that she was working, she wasn't as on top of returning things, or shortening them, so I'd just worn them like that, dragging slightly on the ground. I fished out the wadded-up peanut butter sandwich from my backpack and threw it, bit by bit, into the water. I was an ugly duckling, too small for sports, too insignificant to make a move on the girl I loved.

We ducklings needed to stick together. I noticed a crow nearby and threw it a crumb. It was ugly too.

"Hey there. Everything okay?"

I looked around, at first seeing nothing. Then I found her. Kendra.

"What? Yeah, everything's fine." *I'm just short, and I suck.*

"Oh, okay. You looked kind of . . ." She stopped, then peered into the water as if something had caught her eye. "Hold on."

She stalked toward the canal near where the ducklings had congregated. They scattered, making little peeping noises. Kendra reached her arm below the surface. She pulled something out, brown and wriggling. A snake! It writhed around, but she held it firmly away. Then she flung it as far as she could. It flew through the air and landed on the opposite canal bank. She shook off her hand, then came back and sat beside me.

"What was that?" I asked.

"Water moccasin." Her voice was totally calm.

"What? Aren't they poisonous?"

"Uh-huh. It would have gotten those ducklings."

"But . . . how did you . . . ?"

She shrugged. "Confident hand. Don't try this at home."

"I won't." I looked across the canal, trying to find the brown snake, but it was too bright. I couldn't see.

"So do you want to tell me what's wrong?"

I had this weird feeling she already knew, and it was a little embarrassing. But I said, "Nothing. First World problems. Didn't make varsity, and all my friends did."

She looked at me, really concentrating on my face like she was trying to place me.

"You're Amanda's friend, right?"

I nodded. That was apparently my whole identity.

She looked me up and down. "What would get you onto varsity?"

I laughed. "If I grew six inches."

"Six would do it?" Her tone was light, but her voice was weirdly serious, like she was a doctor, questioning a patient.

"Eight would be better," I joked.

Kendra nodded. "I need to get going." She stood and walked away.

"Sure. Good . . . talking to you. I'm just going to finish feeding these ducks."

"Give some to the crows too. I like crows."

"Sure." I threw one to a duck. A moment later, I turned to wave good-bye, but she was already gone. I threw the last crumbs to the ducks and that one crow who showed back up. There was a strange chill in the air even though it was May. I figured I'd better get going.

I stood, gathered up my shoes, and rolled down my pants.

When I stood, the pants were the perfect length, as if I'd grown an inch.

Which I had.

By the time I left for camp that summer, I was already three inches taller. I grew one inch more each of the four weeks I was there.

But it wasn't just height. I maintained my weight, so I got slimmer, but my shoulders were broader. My arms got bulkier. I'd had to borrow Matt's clothes to take with me. Then, for the second time, I wrote home from camp to get larger shorts.

When I arrived at practice in late July, I'd gone from five seven to six three, exactly eight inches taller, and twenty pounds heavier, all muscle.

"You're looking good, Burke!" Coach Tejada said. "Amazing growth spurt."

"I know, right?"

"Wouldn't have recognized you." He was shaking his head.

"So, you said I could make varsity if I grew."

"If your playing's still on the same level, I'll see what I can do."

But my playing was on a completely different level. I learned that size did matter, at least in this case. I got five sacks in practice that day. Of course, it was easy against JV players. But I had a feeling that would be remedied soon.

I'd become a swan.

13

So everything changed after that, including me and Amanda.

People at school noticed the difference in me. Of course they did. It's not like I was ever bullied, not really. This isn't one of those stories. I know lots of other people who could tell it, but I've always been medium popular, as Matt's dorky brother or Darien's fat friend. I mean, yeah, when girls talked to me, it was usually because they wanted Brian's number or because they felt comfortable asking me for the homework assignment. But at least they talked to me. I was never a pariah.

Now they talked to me because they thought I was hot. Short, fat Chris would have laughed at that. New Chris kind of enjoyed it, though I wouldn't necessarily admit it.

I noticed it in the first period on the first day of school. I had

AP Biology, a class that was almost completely seniors, so I didn't know that many people. This girl Sydnie, a tiny blonde, who I knew because she was the cheerleader who did lines of backflips along the sidelines at football games, took the seat beside me.

"Hey," she said. "It's Chris, right?"

"Yeah." Baffled that she was talking to me.

"I'm Sydnie."

"Yeah. I know."

She looked around. "I don't know anyone taking this class."

"Okay." I found that very difficult to believe.

"No, really. Most of my friends have serious senioritis. They're not taking any hard classes. But I want to get into Syracuse, and they look at your schedule."

I nodded.

"Anyway, my mother is sort of involved in my life. Like, she still checks my homework and stuff. Anyway, she promised she'd stay on her helipad if I got a phone number in each class, so I'd have someone to text about assignments and stuff."

I nodded again, since I had no idea why she was telling me this. When she didn't continue, I said, "That's a good idea."

Palpable silence.

"So can you give it to me?" she said.

"Huh?" I fiddled with my phone. I'd been sending a text to Amanda. I hadn't seen her that day because I'd driven myself to school. My dad had bought me a car for my birthday, an Audi, which put me in the top ten percent at my school. A guilt car, Amanda had called it. Truth was, I missed going with her. I was texting her my schedule.

"Your phone number?" Sydnie said.

She reached over and took the phone from my hand. The gesture was surprisingly intimate, like she had some right to touch my phone. Then she went one step further. She exited the text

I was sending, pressed the phone symbol, then dialed a number. I assumed it was her number because her phone (in a hot-pink case that said *Love fades, Cheer friendships are forever*) immediately vibrated. She grabbed it, added me to her contacts, and handed my phone back.

"Add me too," she said. "It's Sydnie with *y* and then an *ie*."

It took me a second to figure that out, but she was the only Sydnie I knew with any spelling. I added her.

"Text you tonight," she said after class.

That happened in all six classes. Well. Some version of it happened. It happened with girls I didn't know at all. It happened with girls I'd known since kindergarten, who'd never spoken to me except to say, "Excuse me could you please get out of the way" or, "Stop eating all the cupcakes that are for the whole class." It happened with Jessie Alvarez, who I'd sort of considered a friend, but who now wrote her phone number on my hand in pink Sharpie with a heart around it. And it happened with Megan—"Berkie"—Berkowitz, who had once cried at being assigned as my partner on an eighth grade science project but now wanted to be "study buddies" in American history (I'd politely declined that one).

By the end of the day, I had six girls' numbers in my phone, not counting the one on my hand.

And when I got to practice that day, I found out that not only was I on varsity. I was the starting middle linebacker.

I never did text Amanda, but walking out to the parking lot after practice, I saw her. I ran up to her to tell her about making varsity. My car was parked next to hers anyway.

"Hey! Think I'll be able to get the assigned space next to yours?"

She laughed. Her hair was a little sweaty. She'd just come from volleyball practice, and her face was flushed pink. "It's really only fair."

"So guess what?" I said.

"I heard! I'm so happy for you!"

She was smiling, walking toward me.

"Chris!" Sydnie was waving blue-and-white pompoms in my face. I didn't even know how she got there without me seeing her, except that she was so tiny that she sort of just showed up like a cat.

"Hey, Sydnie," I said. "Amanda, do you know Sydnie?"

Amanda smiled. "Sure. Hey."

"Hey." Sydnie turned her attention back to me. "Any way I could get a ride with you? I usually go with Ireland, but she had a doctor's appointment."

"Um, sure." I looked at Amanda and shrugged. "Can I text you later?"

"Sure. But I'll be driving Casey around, so I might not be able to text back. 'It can wait' and all." I saw her eyes flick to Jessie's number on my hand.

"Okay."

Amanda and I always had a long talk on the first day of school, to compare schedules. This year, we had no classes together. That had only happened once before, in seventh grade, and I'd actually switched my elective to chorus so we could be together there. It turned out I was actually good at singing, and I stayed in it for eighth and ninth grades too, even getting a few solos and an invitation to join Matt's garage band, but I'd dropped it last year to take weight training. Amanda had dropped it too.

"I'll text you late? Maybe ten?"

Sydnie sighed and was pulling on the door handle. I clicked on the lock button so she could get in.

"Sure." Amanda waved. "Gotta go. The princess doesn't like when I'm late."

"Hey," Sydnie said when I got in the car. "Do you want to come over for a while? Our maid, Minnie, makes these incredible conch fritters, and we could organize our notebooks for Perez's class."

"Uh, sure." I looked back at Amanda, but she'd already gotten into the car.

"This is such a cool ride." Sydnie stroked the leather seat, her hand accidentally brushing my shoulder. "You're so lucky."

"Thanks."

We ended up going shopping for school supplies. When we got to Office Max, the whole school was there, and I got to tell everyone I made varsity. Then we went back to Sydnie's house and organized our notebooks. Or, rather, she organized mine for me.

"Let me write the dividers for you," she said. "I have super-neat handwriting."

"Won't it look girly?" I said.

"Yeah, like a girl did it for you." She giggled.

Her mom invited me to stay for dinner, but I told her my mom always had a big first-day-of-school dinner. "My brother started at FIU today too."

"That's so cute," Sydnie said. "Can I text you later?"

"Sure."

She did. So did Jessie. And Berkie. And Emma Jordan. And Ally Garcia. Seven different girls texted me, all wanting information about the nonexistent assignments, all congratulating me on making varsity.

By the time I realized I'd never texted Amanda, it was eleven.

I texted her.

Hey

She didn't text back.

I tried:

Do you think there are alternative universes?

Nothing. I figured she must have been asleep.

314

* * *

In the next few weeks, I found out what life was like for a swan. It seemed that there were tons of parties at my school, parties I'd never heard of, much less attended. The first was an apparently annual back-to-school beach bash on Saturday.

"Are you going to beach bash?" Sydnie asked me on Thursday. She'd started hanging around after cheerleading practice to grab a ride with me. So we were walking to my car, and she was gushing about how great I'd played.

"I don't know. I haven't been invited."

"You're so cute." She brushed my shoulder with her hand. "It's not like a wedding with invitations and stuff. You just hear about it from someone who's going and show up."

"Okay." I nodded like I got it.

"*I'm* inviting you, stupid. You can pick me up at eight Saturday."

"Okay, then. It's a date." I paused. *Was* it a date? I'd never actually asked a girl out or particularly thought about asking Sydnie out. She seemed nice enough. She just wasn't the girl I wanted.

She laughed. "It's a date."

Between that day and the next, three other girls asked me if I was going. I said I was. I still hadn't talked to Amanda, but Friday, I saw her in the activities office when we were buying our parking passes.

"Hey," I said.

"Hey." She looked up at me. She looked up. It was so weird being taller than her for the first time in, well, ever.

"Um, how's everything going?" I asked.

"Good. Great. Hey, we've got a regional game Saturday. Can you come?"

"You made it to regionals?" This was something I should have known about, would have known about if it had happened a few months earlier.

"I know, right? We've never gotten this far. If you come, you could sit with my dad and make sure he doesn't, like, explode with pride all over the infield."

"I don't think I'd be able to prevent that. Sorry."

"Yeah, probably not. Come anyway."

"Sure. When is it?"

"Saturday at seven."

The office aide called the next person, and I handed her the money for the parking pass.

"Driver's license?" she said.

"Oh, sure." I put my binder on the counter and fumbled for my wallet. When I finally got it out, I noticed Amanda staring at my neatly labeled tabs.

"I'm sorry," I said. "When did you say the game was?"

"Seven on Saturday. It's okay if you can't—"

"No, I want to go." I really did. I wanted to see Tim and be with Amanda like I hadn't been all summer. But I'd already told Sydnie I was going to the party. And for some reason, I didn't want to tell Amanda about it. "Oh, wait—did you say seven on Saturday?"

"Yeah. Maybe a little later if the game before goes long."

"Shit, I have . . . there's a family thing, my uncle's in town." Groping for an excuse I didn't really want to have to make. "Really boring."

"Oh. That sucks."

"I know." The office aide handed me my parking pass and asked for Amanda's forms. "But if you win that game, there's another one, right?"

"Yes. *When* we win, there'll be another game on Sunday."

"Okay. I'll definitely go to that."

"Cool." Amanda took her pass from the office aide. "It'll be at noon at Tropical Park, and the finals are on Sunday night."

"I'll see you there."

Saturday night, I texted Amanda:

Good luck, I know you'll be awesome

Then added and deleted a heart emoji three times before I went to pick up Sydnie.

14

You know those television shows about high school students where all the actors are actually twenty-five, have cool cars, thousand-dollar outfits, and names like Trey and Denali? High school students who bear no resemblance to anyone you actually know? Well, once you filtered out the ninety-five percent of people at my school who didn't get invited to the cool parties, my school kind of looked like that.

At least, in the dark.

"I've actually never been to the beach at night," I told Sydnie as we walked from my car, which was parked like six blocks away at a meter I'd had to pay with my debit card.

"You are so cute," Sydnie said. "The way you get all excited about regular things. It's great. You don't have to worry about getting a sunburn." She took my hand. She was wearing a bikini top

318

made out of two scraps of fabric the size of toilet paper squares that barely covered anything. She'd had on a tank top, but she took it off as soon as we left her house.

I said, "Yeah, I guess that would be a real worry in that bathing suit."

"Do you like it? They had an end-of-season sale at Victoria's Secret."

"Cool," I said, because I didn't know how to respond to that. I wondered how Amanda's game was going.

"I love Victoria's Secret, don't you?"

"Sure."

She laughed. "You're such a guy. You don't know anything about fashion."

"Well, not girls' fashion. Okay, maybe not any fashion."

"Such a guy. People say I look like this one model, Kate Grigorieva. She's Russian. Do you think I look like her?"

I was about to say that I had no idea what Kate Grigorieva looked like when Sydnie stuck her phone in my face, showing me a photo. She looked like a generic pretty girl. Her hair was slicked back, so I couldn't even tell what color it was, presumably the same color as Sydnie's, but I said, "Yeah. Yeah, you look a lot like her."

We passed a pickup truck that had about a dozen bumper stickers on it, but the funny thing was, they weren't the usual pickup-truck bumper stickers. Other than the expected *My President is Charlton Heston* (I was pretty sure Charlton Heston was dead, but it was an old truck), it had two Darwin fish and mostly liberal sentiments like, *If you're against abortion, get a vasectomy* and *The road to hell is paved with Republicans*, along with a neutral *I'd rather be flying* plate holder.

I said to Sydnie, "How many bumper stickers do you think you can have before you look crazy?" This was a topic Amanda and I frequently debated. Amanda said no more than two. I said you could have more than that as long as some of them were politically neutral "My child made the honor roll" or "Go Gators" type stickers. This guy would have too many by any standard.

Sydnie looked at me like I'd spoken a foreign language, but finally, she said, "Don't they mess up the paint on your car?"

I nodded. "Yeah."

We reached the beach. People were standing around in clusters of shadows, drinking something out of Solo cups. We took some. Coke. Drew Bailey, one of the seniors, offered us something from his flask.

"Oh, no thanks," I said. I'd had to beg to be allowed to drive to the party, on account of my brother's legacy. Part of that begging had included promising not to drink.

"You're so cute." Sydnie accepted a shot into her own soda. "Such a cute nerd." She peeled off her shorts and left them lying on the sand.

"You know what's bad about going to the beach at night?" she said.

"What's that?"

"We can't rub sunscreen on each other."

Someone wanted to take a picture, and Sydnie hung on my arm. I thought I was hallucinating. This was my life. This was me. On the beach at a party with people who looked like extras on a CW show, with this girl who sort of looked like some model saying she wanted me to . . . rub her?

I said, "That's unfortunate."

"Unfortunate." Sydnie burst out laughing. "God, you're funny!"

"Okay." I didn't really think I'd said anything funny.

"I always thought you were really funny and nice."

"Really?"

"Sure. Everyone always knew how funny and nice you were." She moved, if possible, even closer. Someone had on music, and she held my shoulders, sort of dancing, but sort of not.

I wondered, if everyone thought I was so funny and nice, why I'd never gotten invited to parties like this before, why she'd never even spoken to me. I mean, it's not like I wasn't friends with all these people. But I knew the answer, of course. I'd been a duckling. I hadn't been fit to party with the swans. I wasn't really sure how I felt about that. I mean, weren't people at least supposed to *pretend* they liked you for you, not just because you looked a certain way?

But I pushed the thought back when Sydnie stroked my arm and said, "Let's go into the water."

"You want to . . . swim?"

"Yeah, silly. I want to swim. I'm thinking about trying out for the swim team."

"You have time . . ." I started to ask if she had time for swimming with cheerleading. Then I realized she was being sarcastic. Short, fat Chris used to get sarcasm. Tall, thin Chris apparently had no sense of humor, not even enough to keep up with a girl who had photos of Victoria's Secret models on her phone.

She stood on her toes and whispered loudly in my ear, "I want to make out with you in the water."

So I followed her into the water. She wasn't really who I wanted to make out with, but she was pretty and she was there, and she wasn't my best friend, and I'd never kissed anyone before, so I followed her, and we made out in the water. And I may have had a couple of drinks after all, but I was big enough and we stayed late enough that I didn't get drunk. At least, I didn't hit any public art. But I did forget to charge my cell phone, so when I woke up the next morning at eleven, it was totally dead.

And it was almost noon before I charged it enough to get Amanda's text that said:

Hope you had fun with your uncle

And then I saw about twenty photos online of Sydnie and me at that party. Including one of me with my tongue fairly obviously in Sydnie's mouth. I guessed Amanda knew about those parties even if I hadn't. Amanda knew everything.

And, by then, it was too late for me to make it to Amanda's noon game.

And since they lost, it was the last one.

And she didn't answer any of my texts saying I was sorry.

Or any of the others.

And I was too ashamed to go knock on her door, even though I should have.

On the Monday-morning announcements, they said the Lady Lions had come in third in the regionals. Amanda was MVP.

I was probably the only person in my class who even heard the announcement. Sydnie held up her phone, then pulled me toward her for a selfie. I tried to smile.

I saw Amanda in the hall on the way to lunch. Okay, I took a different route to lunch in an attempt to run into her, and it worked.

"Hey, congratulations." I tried to pretend everything was okay, that she hadn't ignored eight texts in the past twenty-four hours, which was the maximum number I felt I could send without a reply.

"On what? Coming in third? Yeah, that's impressive." She started to walk away.

"Third at regionals is good. And you were MVP."

"We almost won. If I'd gotten one more hit, we'd have won. Of course, you wouldn't know that since you weren't there. But forgive me if I'm not all that excited about this tiny victory." She walked faster.

"You always congratulated me on my tiny victories." I tried to keep up with her.

"Yeah, cause that was all you had."

I stopped, stunned. It had always been unspoken between us that she was more athletically gifted than I was. She was the star. I wasn't. She was the winner. I was just a player, and a mediocre one at that. I thought of all the times she'd made a big deal when I got a most-improved trophy or made second string. Had she been lying all those times?

"I don't get why you're so mad." I ran to catch up with her. "I went to a party for, like, the first time in high school. I made the plans before I knew about your game."

"So why lie about it? Why tell me you had a visiting uncle?"

"I guess the same reason you lied when you made a big deal about me making JV and stuff. I didn't want to hurt your feelings."

"Well, that worked."

And she turned and walked away.

I didn't follow her that time.

15

So that was how we stopped being friends.

I didn't see Amanda for a week or two. Our schedules were different, and she had a different lunch. And she was avoiding me.

And maybe I was avoiding her too, but only because it felt too bad to see her, like getting my arm cut off with a chainsaw.

Some people, like my mother, want to wallow in bed when they're upset about something. My mother spent two weeks in pajamas when my dad left. I'm not like that. I like to fill my schedule with so many activities that I don't have time to think about whatever's upsetting me. When my dad left, I started playing volleyball at the Y in addition to football at school, and I ran for sophomore class president (which, fortunately, I lost), took a class in stand-up comedy, and briefly considered joining a barbershop harmony group before

I remembered, oh yeah, I wasn't seventy-five years old. I did join Matt's garage band. Sometimes, I still sang with them. And I spent almost every day at Amanda's house.

And then I got over it. At least enough to function.

When I lost my best friend, I decided to get over it by making twenty others. I started dating Sydnie, going to all her cheer competitions and driving her to dance classes, and partying with her—now my—friends, who roped me into entering the Mr. Lion King homecoming contest.

A month later, I still wasn't over it.

Most of Amanda's friends who had, I thought, been my friends too, sort of looked through me these days. It was like I was their friend's cousin who they might have met at a birthday party once, but they weren't sure. That was when Amanda wasn't around. When Amanda was around, they formed a sort of girl wall around her like they might just lift her up on their shoulders at any second. And once, I heard her friend Callie whisper something like, "Ignore him."

I felt like I'd become my dad. Amanda and I were divorced, and I got the hot new girlfriend and all of the blame while she got all our friends and righteousness on her side.

Except we weren't married. I hadn't cheated on her. We were just friends, and I'd gone to a party. Why was she being like this?

The only one who'd still talk to me was Kendra.

"Hey, I saw that interception," she said in the parking lot the day after a particularly stellar game. I was throwing myself into football, and it showed in the amount of play I was getting—and the results.

I nodded.

"It was great," she added. "You're a star."

"Yeah. A star." I saw two girls from my bio class. One of them, the one whose name I didn't know, leaned over to the other and whispered something ending in "hot." The other one—her name was Emily—yelled, "Great game, Chris!"

"Thanks," I yelled back.

"You don't seem too happy about it," Kendra said.

"I'm not. I'm a star, and I can't share it with my best friend. This wasn't what I wanted."

"Sometimes, things don't work out like you think they will. A wise man once said you can't always get what you want."

It took me a second to place the line. Then I recognized the lyric from an old song. I said, "Yeah, but he also said if you try sometimes, you get what you need."

"So what do you need, Chris?" She put her hand on my wrist. It felt weird, like when the blood pressure cuff tightens at the doctor's office, even though she was only touching me with her fingertips.

"I need Amanda." I had to catch my breath to choke the words out. "She's my best . . . person. I'd give up"—I gestured to my body, my swan body—"all of this for her. Can I do that? Can you do that?"

"Do what?" Kendra removed her hand from my wrist, and the weird, throbbing, intriguing feeling stopped. "Give up what?" she asked.

"This. Being tall. Being a starter. I don't care about any of it. It doesn't matter."

"How could you give it up?" Kendra looked confused. "Your height is your height. You can't change it."

A wind swept by, whipping up dirt and leaves and pebbles. I remembered once Mom took me to this play, a musical called *Damn Yankees*. She thought I'd like it because it was about sports. I sort of did. It was about this old guy who sold his soul to the devil so he could be young and athletic and lead his favorite team to victory.

Was that what I'd done? Was Kendra the devil? Had I sold my soul to be a few inches taller, to make a team, to be a hero?

I said, "Can't you put me back the way I was before?"

She said, "I don't understand what you mean. How could I do that?"

No, she wasn't the devil, but she was a witch. And no one ever said witches were nice or that they did anyone favors.

She put her hand on my wrist again, and again, I felt weird. I wanted to flinch away, but I didn't, couldn't. Instead, I said, "What do I do?"

She said, "Figure out what you really want from Amanda. Then figure out how to get it."

"Oh, okay. That's easy."

"After all these years, it should be." She took her hand off my arm.

I had no idea what she meant.

So I went to school and went home and did homework and hung out with Sydnie and her friends and played football (well, amazingly well), and I never saw Amanda. She didn't come to my games.

Until she did. With Darien. She was going out with Darien.

And then I knew the answer to the first question Kendra had put to me: Figure out what you really want from Amanda.

What I wanted was not just to be friends with Amanda. I wouldn't want to ball Darien up in my hand like a used McDonald's napkin over a girl I just wanted to be friends with. I loved her. Like, *love* loved her.

But I didn't know the answer to the other part: how to get what I wanted. What I needed.

I broke up with Sydnie. It wasn't fair for me to date her. I tried to be nice about it, but when she screamed that I was just doing it to get out of taking her to homecoming when homecoming was a month away, I was over it. Done. She only liked me because I was a tall, good-looking football player. But I didn't even know who that was. The guy she liked wasn't me. In my heart, I was still a short, fat, funny guy who sometimes played football but mostly liked math and sending goofy texts.

Other girls flirted with me, but I didn't flirt back. I didn't want anyone else. I knew who I wanted.

I wondered if swans ever looked into the water and wondered who that was, looking back.

Probably not. They were birds. You could only carry a metaphor so far when it involved birds. Birds weren't really that smart.

I tried to text Amanda, but now she'd blocked my number.

I left a note on her car, begging her to meet me. She ignored it.

I wanted to do more, but when you're a guy, there's only so much you can do before you get arrested for stalking.

Then, one day, I came home and my mother was cooking ziti.

Mom never cooked ziti, not anymore. Since my dad left, she'd been on a health kick, lost forty pounds, and pretty much only ate dirt. Or quinoa, as some people called it.

Now she only made ziti when someone died, to take it over to the family. One time, it was a woman from her book club. Another time, my uncle Dave.

So, weirdly, I associated the usually pleasant smell of sausage and onions with death.

I walked up behind her. "Everything okay?"

When she turned, I knew from her face it wasn't. "Oh, Chris. It's Tim Lasky. He's had a heart attack."

"Tim . . . what . . . is he . . . ?" I looked at the ziti, boiling in the stockpot.

"He's okay. I mean, he's going to be okay. I heard from Stacey Rankin, and then I called Amanda. She said he was doing better. He's in the hospital, though."

A landline. She'd gotten hold of Amanda on a landline. I'd

forgotten such a thing existed. We'd stopped answering our own because it was only robo-calls.

Mom was still talking. "I tried to get her and Casey to come stay with us, but she said they were okay. So I thought maybe you could bring this over there?"

Mr. Lasky. Tim Lasky could have died, and I wouldn't have talked to him in the past four months. Shit.

"Tim's really okay?" I noticed I was shaking.

Mom nodded. "Yeah, that's what Amanda said. Can you bring this over there? I know you're busy."

"She's home?"

"I can call and make sure."

I half expected to see Amanda's car roaring away down the street when I showed up, but she was there. She opened the door.

"Hey," she said. Then, maybe realizing there was no way simultaneously to take the proffered ziti and slam the door in my face, she stood there a moment, doing neither, saying nothing. Her hair was messy, and she had on a T-shirt that said, *You wish you could throw like a girl!* She looked the way she looked when we were kids.

And, stupidly, I said, "It's ziti. My mom made it."

She said, "I know. She called and told me."

"Can I maybe put it in the refrigerator?"

She moved aside, and I walked in. I hadn't been there for months, and the smell, a kind of air freshener I'd never really noticed but that had always been there, a smell like lemons, brought back every memory of being there, every Halloween, every day after school, every weekend swimming there. I could barely hold up the casserole dish. My arms felt too weak.

"How is he? He's going to be okay?" I needed reassurance on this point.

"Yeah, he's fine. Or he will be. I think. They say he'll be home in a few days."

It had never been awkward to talk to her before. Before, I'd barely had to speak at all. It was like she was inside my head, hearing my every thought through headphones.

I wanted to tell her everything, everything from the car with all the bumper stickers to how much I missed her every single day, but I said, "I'd like to go see him." I put the dish into the refrigerator. That, too, was so familiar. Takeout rotisserie chicken, stacks of Oscar Meyer cold cuts, and a six-pack of Sam Adams.

"They're only allowing family."

I turned on her. "He is my family. He's the only one who ever played ball with me, the only one who cared about . . . anything."

"Yeah, he asks about you, why you don't come around anymore."

"Yeah? What do you tell him?"

"I tell him the ugly duckling grew up to be a huge asshole."

"Why? Why are you so angry at me? Because I missed a softball game, because I messed up once? You're throwing away an eleven-year friendship over that?" I'd been over and over it in my head, and I still couldn't believe she wouldn't give me a second chance.

"It wasn't the baseball game. It's that you lied about it. And . . ." She shook her head. "Forget it."

"No, what?"

"You'd rather hang with those people, people like Sydnie, people who make fun of people like me, now that you're good enough for them."

I couldn't even answer her. Was that what I'd done? I'd just been freaked out that things were happening for me, making varsity, having girls actually come on to me when I was used to being the fat, funny kid everyone mostly ignored. Maybe I was star struck. Was that the same as what she'd said? Probably was.

330

"We don't all get to be swans, Chris," she said.

"I don't want to be a swan. God, I'm sorry. How can I tell you I'm sorry so you'll believe me? I just want it to be like it was with us."

We were standing in front of the open refrigerator. Maybe that was why I shivered when she said, "I'm just stupid. I thought maybe we'd be more than friends, and now I feel so stupid and embarrassed for thinking that."

Was she saying what I thought she was saying, that she had felt the same way? Was that why she'd gotten so mad at me? I looked in her eyes. "There was never anything more than our friendship. Our friendship was the biggest thing in my life."

And then I leaned over and kissed her.

It felt like the right thing to do. I loved her. She was the single most important person in my life, always had been since that first day with Spidey. She'd said she wanted to be more than friends, and I did too. I knew, just knew I had to kiss her. I thought she'd kiss me back.

Instead, she pushed me away. "Really?" She backed up until she was on the other side of the open refrigerator door, then held it in front of her. "You really thought it would be okay to kiss me? When my dad's in the hospital, and we haven't talked in a month?"

"I don't know. You said—"

"I know what I said. You thought it would be a good idea to take advantage of that, of my feelings?"

"They're my feelings too. I have the exact same feelings, Amanda. I need—"

"You need to leave. You need to . . . I can't look at you anymore." She slammed the refrigerator and started toward the front door.

I followed her. "Amanda."

"Please leave."

"I'm sorry." I knew now it was a stupid thing to do. God, I'd just gotten her to talk to me again. What an idiot I was. "I'm sorry."

"I wasn't just waiting around for you to decide you like me, you know."

"I didn't think that."

"Go away!" she said.

She was gesturing toward the door, then out the door, and I knew I should shut my mouth, but I had to say, "I'm sorry."

I was on the doorstep now, and she started to close the door behind me. I looked at her face. It was pink and beautiful, and I could tell she was trying not to cry.

"Tell your mom thanks for the ziti," she said.

"Yeah, tell your dad—" But she'd closed the door and couldn't hear me. Someone down the block was mowing the lawn, and it drowned out my voice, but it didn't drown out Amanda's voice, what she'd said, her voice in my head. I was a huge asshole. But that didn't mean I had to keep being an asshole. I admitted to myself that I'd *wanted* to go to the beach party and not her game. It wasn't because I'd committed to it first. It was because I was flattered by the attention, that people wanted me there, the varsity players, a hot senior girl. Amanda was right: I was flattered to be good enough for them.

But I'd always been good enough. Better, because I'd been good enough for Amanda, and she was the best there was.

Now I wasn't good enough for her anymore.

How could I get to be good enough for her again?

When Tim came home from the hospital the following week, I made sure Amanda had practice before I called.

Then I went over and told him everything. Everything.

"Wow," he said when I got to the part about kissing Amanda. "Yeah, son, you don't touch my daughter when she doesn't want to be touched. That Darien kid found that out the hard way."

I laughed, more than a little relieved to find out that Amanda had broken up with Darien. Tim crunched a carrot stick from a bowl by his chair. "Can you see if there's any ranch dressing for these? My daughter—I mean, my doctor—has me on a pretty strict diet."

"Sure." I walked over to the refrigerator, trying not to remember the last time I stood there. I opened it and searched the shelves for salad dressing. When I finally found it, I saw someone had written

Not for Dad and a dead smiley face in Sharpie on the ranch. Next to it was a bottle of low-fat sesame ginger. That one was labeled *Okay for Dad*. I noticed the beer was gone too. I poured the sesame ginger into a bowl and brought it back to Tim.

"Looks like you're out of ranch. I brought this one."

"Shit. She got to it." He dipped his carrot into the dressing. "It's actually pretty good. Have one."

To be polite, I took one. Tim was right. It was pretty good. I took another. When I reached for the third, he said, "Hey, hey, slow down there, son. That's supposed to last me until dinner."

"How do I get . . . ?" I stopped. I'd been planning to ask how to get Amanda to stop hating me, but instead, I said, "How do I get to be good enough for Amanda?"

Tim smiled. "Well, no one's really good enough for my daughter, but maybe . . . I've got this football team I'm coaching, kids without dads to help out." I nodded. It sounded familiar. "I can't run around as much as I used to, apparently. Maybe you'd want to coach?"

"That sounds great." Then I remembered football practice. I was almost ready to quit the team. I mean, I hadn't made it fairly anyway.

But Tim said, "We can schedule around your football practices. I'll call Coach Tejada and ask him."

"That'd be great."

So, two days a week, in addition to school and practice, I helped Tim with his team. Amanda wasn't there. I didn't expect her to be. I wasn't doing it to show off. But I wouldn't have minded if she'd noticed.

A few weeks later, she did. She showed up to watch a game. Tim introduced her to the team. "This is my daughter, Amanda. She plays high school softball, and she's gonna play college."

The boys acted politely impressed.

Amanda looked at me and raised an eyebrow. I hadn't seen her since that day, not even at school. It was like she'd dropped out or found an invisibility cloak or something.

Tim said, "Chris has been helping me out."

Amanda said, "Cool," in a tone that indicated it wasn't.

I picked up my clipboard. I'd wanted to type the lists on my phone, but Tim insisted that football was traditional.

"Okay, so here's the starting lineup. DeMarco is offensive guard, Sebastian's offensive tackle. . . ."

"I'll see you later," Amanda told Tim.

But, as she walked away, I noticed she looked back.

"Zephyr is, um, quarterback," I said, trying to pretend I didn't see her.

The team won but, more important, this kid Davis, who'd never caught *anything*, caught a pass. I'd spent most of the last two practices working with him.

I really wished I could tell Amanda about it. I wished she would care.

Tim did, at least. "Hey, good job with Davis," he said as we put away the equipment.

"I know, right? It's weird how proud I was about it. You'd think I was his dad."

"Nah." Tim shouldered a bag of pads, gesturing for me to take the cooler. "That's how I felt when you got your first hit."

I remembered the hours he'd spent, standing behind me, telling me to follow through, and I smiled.

We walked to his truck. I wanted to ask him if he thought Amanda would ever forgive me, but that would be too selfish. Also too bare. So I said, "How're you feeling?"

"Hungry. My daughter's been feeding me tilapia. Apparently, it's a fish."

"I've heard that," I said, opening the tailgate.

"It didn't exist when I was a kid. I think they created it in a lab."

I laughed. "You should come over our house. My mom makes a no-calorie, no-carb, soylent green casserole." It was a reference to a science fiction movie I'd watched at his house once, where the food supply was all this weird green compound.

"Soylent green is people!" Tim said, throwing everything into the back. "Seriously, whatever you're eating, it's working."

"Practice Tuesday?" I said.

"Same as usual."

On Tuesday, Amanda showed up to help too.

She didn't really pay attention to me. Tim explained that she was helping because one of the other coaches couldn't come. Then he divided the kids up, and Amanda worked with the better kids while I helped the ones who were struggling. But she didn't elaborately *not* pay attention to me either.

When she showed up Thursday, we had an actual conversation about which one of us should make the kids run sprints and whether certain kids were shirking their cleanup responsibilities, but still, I considered the dim possibility that she might, sometime in the not-too-distant future, unblock my phone. But I didn't ask. Too soon.

And Saturday, when the Bluejays pulled off a surprise victory against the much stronger Cardinals, she actually high-fived me.

But then, she also high-fived Tim and Craig, the coach who hadn't shown up all week.

So, whatever that meant.

"Hey, what happened to your little girlfriend?" Matt asked me one day.

I hadn't seen much of Matt lately. He'd started college locally, but he'd joined a frat. So he pretty much only showed up at home to sleep, eat, and tell me how easy I had it.

I pretended not to hear him.

He paused the football game I was watching on TV. "Yeah, your friend, whatserface. The girl who whipped your ass in baseball. I haven't seen her in, like, a month."

It had been closer to five months. I tried to get the remote back from him. "I don't know who whatserface is."

"Sure you do. Whatserface. The annoying one. Amanda!" He held the remote up away from me, and since I was too lazy to get up, that worked. "What, did you have a fight with her?"

"Something like that. Can I watch the game now?"

"Spoiler alert: The Gators lose." He still held up the remote. "Really? I was right? You had a fight with her?"

"Yeah, why do you care?"

"I dunno. I just got used to seeing her around here, I guess. What, did she get jealous of Sydnieeee?" He made his voice high-pitched and annoying when he said Sydnie's name.

I stood and walked around, looking for the other remote. "Why would she be jealous of Sydnie?"

He looked at me like I was brain-damaged. "I don't know. Because she's totally in love with you."

"She is not."

"Yeah, she is. I always thought it was weird that she'd be into a toady-looking kid like you, but she was."

"Right."

"Yeah. She was always sticking up for you, telling me how much better you were than me."

"That's just her having eyes." I found the remote, but now I didn't use it.

"Yeah, but one time, after Dad left, she actually called me."

"She called you?"

"Right? I didn't even know any ninth graders had my phone number, but she got it, and she called, like with her *voice*. She sounded really nervous, but she said she hoped I'd be a little kinder to you. That was the word she used, *kinder*—because you were going through such a rough time."

I put down the remote. That was so weird.

"I don't have any friends I'd do that for," Matt said. "I was so freaked out by it that I actually did try to be nicer—for about a week."

"I do vaguely remember a week when you didn't throw my clothes into the shower."

"I'm the best." He gave me a thumbs-up. "Anyway, that's when I knew she was in love with you."

"Okay, so if she's so in love with me, why'd she rip me a new asshole when I kissed her?" I unpaused the TV. The Gators' quarterback was in the process of getting sacked. I fast-forwarded through it.

Matt said, "You kissed her? Like out of the blue with no warning?"

"Yeah." Hearing him say it like that, I could see why it was a bad idea.

"Dude, that only works in TV shows Mom likes, and not even always then."

I shook my head. "What do you mean?"

"If there's anything I've learned in my long and storied history with girls, it's that they want to think you really care, like you put some thought into making a move on them."

"Okay."

"Like when I asked Brittney to prom, I knew she was going to go with me, but you can't act like you know. So I bought a couple bunches of roses from one of those old guys who sells flowers on the street. I pulled all the petals off one and made a trail going to her car.

Then I left the other bouquet on her car with a note that said, 'Will you go to prom with me?' It's what they call a romantic gesture."

I paused the TV again and stared at him, stunned as the UF quarterback. I couldn't imagine my goofy brother doing something like that.

And then he Matt-ified it by saying, "It worked, if you know what I mean."

I did know. "You're such a douche."

"I may be, but I know you want that girl, for some strange reason. And I know what you have to do to get her."

I unpaused the TV. He was right about me wanting Amanda, of course. I wondered if he was right about the other thing too.

Problem was, if he was wrong and I left a trail of rose petals leading up to her car, she might break my nose.

But maybe you had to be in it to win it.

As the Gators definitely weren't tonight.

I watched the Gators flounder (figuratively) and fumble (literally) for another hour, and I knew I had to make a big gesture. But before that, I was going to make some smaller ones.

The first was, I went to her volleyball game the next day. This might not seem like a big deal, but no one in our school went to girls' volleyball, even if it was a choice between that and sitting home watching reruns of *Say Yes to the Dress*. The game wasn't even listed on the school's website. I had to ask around.

I took Mom, and we sat there in a crowd that was basically everyone's parents, and we cheered every time anyone did anything, but especially at anything Amanda did.

After the game, Amanda came over, because she couldn't ignore my mom waving and cheering. "Hey," she said.

My mom was all excited. "Hey, you were great." They'd lost in straight sets.

339

"I'm just tall. If you're tall, you have to play volleyball."

"Tall and incredibly athletic," I said.

Amanda glanced at the scoreboard. "Well, volleyball's not really my sport."

There was this silence where I figured if anyone wanted, they could have heard the small voice in the pit of my stomach screaming, "Help me! Help me!" and just as Amanda was about to excuse herself, my mom said, "So, how's your dad?"

"Oh, he's a lot better," Amanda said. "He's taking blood pressure meds and watching his diet. Not too happy about it, but I threatened not to let him go to any of my games if he wasn't careful. Wouldn't want to excite him too much." She was gesturing animatedly as she said all this. I hadn't seen her happy in a while.

"Oh, look, here he is." My mother pointed out Tim, who was walking toward us with Casey, engrossed in her phone. "I was just about to tell Amanda you three should come over for dinner one night. I have a great recipe for ginger salmon with brown rice—very healthy."

"My mom's on a health kick lately," I said. "You should be thankful she doesn't want you to eat the quinoa."

"Oh, I love that stuff," Amanda said, "but my father hates it. He calls it dirt."

Tim and I exchanged a glance at that.

Mom asked what would be a good day for them, and Tim suggested Friday night after practice. "Then we could go over Saturday's roster."

"Sounds good," I said.

"Don't you have a date with Sydnie?" Amanda asked.

I glanced at her. I figured she had to have heard that Sydnie and I broke up. News like that didn't go unmarked at our school, especially with Sydnie's mouth. But maybe she wanted details. "No, I broke up with Sydnie a few weeks ago." When she didn't ask why, I added, "I decided she wasn't really the person I wanted to hang with."

She nodded.

"And what about you?" I asked. "No date with Darien?"

She looked down. "Same."

"Okay." Tim clapped his hands together. "Sounds like we're all dateless and free Friday at, um, seven?" He looked at Mom.

"Sounds good," she agreed.

Over salmon, we mostly talked about the food. And college admissions. Because that had become my life.

After dinner, Mom suggested a board game.

"Monopoly, maybe?" I said, because I wanted to keep them there as long as possible.

"I don't have six hours," Matt said. "How about Cards against Humanity?"

"With a little kid and our parents?" Amanda said. "No thanks."

"Who's a little kid?" Casey said.

"Me," I said. "I'm super immature. How about Taboo? Me, Tim, and Amanda against the two of you?"

I chose the game because Amanda and I always won as a team. The object, if you haven't played, was to get your team members to guess a word written on the card. Trick was, the person giving clues couldn't use any of five "taboo" words on the card—the most obvious clues. So, if the card word was lifeguard, you had to get your team to guess it without being able to use words like "pool" or "save."

It was hard—unless you had such a long history with your team members that you could practically read one another's minds.

Our team's first word was "seagull." I looked right at Amanda and said, "Mrs. Wynne at the Seaquarium."

"Seagull!" Amanda screamed, laughing because we both remembered the birthday party at the Seaquarium, the one where Tori Wynne's mom got pooped on by a seagull.

Next was, "Nolan put them up his nose."

"French fries!"

"Right. Made me want to . . ."

"Puke! No? Barf!"

"Right." Next card. "That short substitute always smelled like it."

"Garlic!" Amanda yelled.

"Shelby Ladis was obsessed with them."

"Vampires."

"The thing I hated to do at camp every summer."

"Hiking." Amanda turned to my mother. "He used to write to me, complaining."

"I never knew," she said.

"We're on the clock." I tapped the next card. "If I threatened to tell everyone about your ninth grade crush on Paolo, the exchange student, it would be this."

"Blackmail."

"Good! My mom once totally humiliated me by walking into one at Hot Topic."

"Dressing room," Amanda yelled just as the timer ran out.

"Yes! Yes!" Amanda did a victory dance but came just short of taunting my mom. "How many points was that?"

"Eight," Tim said, "and I'm feeling kind of invisible."

My mother's team went next, and it took them a full three minutes to get the words *octopus* and *brunch*.

We let Tim be the clue giver the next time, and we still got five points.

"We had these in the rice last year," Tim said.

"Moths," Amanda said. "Don't tell people that. It's gross."

"Since when is he people?" Tim gestured at me.

"I knew about it anyway." I was happy she thought of me as people. She wouldn't have cared what I thought a week ago.

When it was Amanda's turn, she said, "They made us do this in PE."

I winced. "Square dancing."

For her last one, she said, "You acted like one."

I knew it because I'd seen the card before. "A jerk. I'm sorry."

We won, twenty to eleven.

When Amanda was on her way out the door, I said, "Is there any way you'd consider maybe unblocking my number? I have some things I've been wondering about."

She laughed and pointed to my phone. "Try it."

I texted her:

Do you think anyone understood the irony of naming the Miami airport MIA?

I heard her phone vibrate.

"I unblocked it a week ago."

Five minutes after she left, she texted me:

People in Miami don't understand irony

Don't get me started

We texted all night.

And, after that, we were friends again.

But I knew, now, I didn't want to be friends with Amanda. I loved her. I wanted that big gesture.

It was Sommer Hernandez who reminded me I'd agreed to do the Mr. Lion King contest for homecoming.

At first, I'd planned on begging off. I didn't run with Sydnie's crowd anymore, and they were the ones who'd put me up to it. Plus, the contest had a talent component, which sounded like a lot of work.

Not that the word *talent* was, strictly speaking, accurate. Last year, Stephen Richardson played his stomach.

I told Matt this, and he said, "But you do have a talent."

That's when I realized it might be an opportunity.

I told Sommer that I absolutely would like to be part of the grand tradition of the Mr. Lion King contest.

Then I got to work.

I didn't tell Amanda about it. She'd think it was dumb. It was dumb. I didn't tell many people about it. Strictly on a need-to-know basis.

I did tell Matt.

The night of the "pageant," I was sixth out of eight contestants, a pretty respectable placement since they seemed to have put it in reverse order of coolness. Only two seniors were after me. I sat out in the audience with Amanda, watching the first of the talents, Garrett Greenstein, giving a karate demonstration. We were in the front row, which was good because we had a good view, but bad if Garrett happened to fly out into the theater.

"Okay, okay, guys," he said. "These are the basic karate stances. *Kiba dachi.*" He stood with his legs apart. "*Kokutsu dachi.*" He leaned most of his weight on his back leg. Then he shifted. "*Zenkutsu dachi.*"

"Wow," Amanda whispered. "What would make someone agree to do this—blackmail?"

"Maybe he wants to impress a girl. That's what motivates a lot of human conduct."

"Here's some strikes," Garrett said and started hitting and kicking.

"I hope someone's filming this for YouTube," Amanda said.

"Yeah." I was getting a little worried.

For his big finale, Garrett kicked a board. It didn't budge, and Garrett tumbled back.

"Wait! Wait! Do-over!" He rubbed his legs, then tried again.

This time, it worked. The crowd went wild. Okay, they stopped laughing and clapped politely, especially Garrett's friends. Which was more than they'd done when he fell on his ass.

"Good job, Garrett," Alex Pacheco, who was announcing the show, said. "And now, Josh Wilson!"

"Hello, everyone!" Josh was on the football team, varsity, even though he was only a freshman. Huge cheers.

"I'll be doing a dramatic reading"—he held up his phone—"of Kanye West's tweets."

He scrolled through them, reading, "I'm so lucky." He scrolled some more. "Dreams are worth more than money."

"Hey," I whispered to Amanda, "I'll be back. I told Andrew I'd help him with something for his act."

Onstage, Josh read, "I'm so lucky."

"Okay." Amanda was staring at the stage, where Josh was reading, "I want to steer clear of opportunities and focus on dreams."

The next act was Harrison Garcia in a wig and grass skirt. Two more before me. I might regret this.

But I'd definitely regret it if I didn't do it.

When I got backstage, Amanda had texted me:

You're missing the best part

I texted back:

The best part is coming

I hoped that was true.

Don't leave

I texted that as the next act started. It would so suck if she got mad at me for leaving her alone and ditched.

Finally, it was my turn.

"Contestant number six," Alex announced. "Chris Burke."

I came onstage. I didn't have a costume or anything, just jeans and a T-shirt. I'd spent all my energy on the other elements of the act. I looked out into the audience, and for a moment, the lights hit my eyes, and I couldn't see anything. Then I did see, and it was so much worse. I'd done all sorts of scary things in my life, from oral presentations in class to starting in football to just showing up every day as a short, fat kid. But this was the bravest thing I'd ever done. If it didn't work, I'd be totally humiliated.

I found Amanda in the audience. Sure enough, she was half standing, like she'd been about to leave, but now she was rooted to the spot. I met her eyes, saw her mouth, "What the—?"

I took the mic from Alex. "So I'm Chris."

People cheered, which was encouraging.

"And I'm gonna sing. I wanted to dedicate this to a girl." I couldn't look at Amanda. "She's my best friend, and she's the most badass girl I know."

Even though I was trying not to look, I saw Amanda do a face-palm in the audience.

Possibly bad, but it was too late. The music was starting up.

I'd thought about using karaoke, but then I'd have had to be onstage alone. So I decided to go all in, and I asked Matt's garage-band guys to play. I'd had to promise to do a gig with them on a date of their choosing. Between practicing with them, writing lyrics, and making a slide show, I'd barely slept in two weeks.

Behind me, Matt was strumming his guitar. I couldn't look at Amanda. She'd know the Boston song as soon as she heard the first notes.

I hadn't changed the beginning, so I started with the first line:

Babe, tomorrow's so far away
There's something I just have to say

Then I went into my version.

If I say where I'm at
Would you hit me with a bat?
Or would you let me
Tell you I love you?

I pressed the button to start the slide show with photos of me and Amanda, Amanda and me in baseball uniforms and zombie cos-tumes, at fifth grade awards, the eighth grade dance. I looked at the screen while I sang. In the audience, people were clapping along.

I'm gonna make myself a fool
In front of the whole school, Amanda

I wanna be more than your friend
Cause I hope it never ends, Amanda.

Just as a photo of her and me holding hands on a field trip to the zoo flashed on, I decided to sneak a glance down, just to make sure she hadn't left.

She hadn't left. She was smiling. But she still had her face in her hand. Was she laughing at me?

Or was she crying?

I sang:

I'm gonna take a chance
And ask you to the dance Amanda
I love you!

She was shaking her head, like in disbelief. At least, that's what I hoped it was. We were at the little musical interlude part where I didn't have anything to do but look into her eyes. But I was scared. What was she thinking?

At that point, I realized almost everyone else was looking at her too. God, she'd kill me.

Finally, the music part was over, and I sang:

You and I
We've been together through the years.
Softball, football, and baseball,
Through the laughter and the tears.

You can tell I'm really trying
Because I've got to admit I'm dying.
I hope you'll answer
Because Saturday will be too late.

Out in the audience, Amanda was nodding yes.

Yes? I mouthed.

She put her hands over her heart and mouthed, *yes*. "Yes!"

Matt had been right about the big gesture. It had worked.

I finished the song with a dramatic "I'm in love with you!" The crowd was going crazy. I called her onstage.

She gestured no. I should come down.

I did. People cheered even more. I heard a girl tell her friend I was "the cutest thing ever."

Then I found her, and the world blurred. She said, "Shit, you really went to a lot of trouble to prove me wrong."

"I really did."

She was too beautiful not to kiss, but this time, I knew she wouldn't want to hit me. I put my arms around her and kissed her, kissed her like I'd been wanting for months, maybe years.

Which I did all through David Castillo's tap dance routine and Jacob's rap about the school. Then it was time for me to go back onstage for the interview portion.

I don't remember what the question was, so I'm pretty sure I was incoherent.

I won anyway.

Kendra
One Night Later

"Do you think the cheerleaders actually know what's going on in the game?" I asked my friend Amanda as we watched the homecoming matchup between the Lions and the Tigers (oh my!). "Or do they just wait until the crowd cheers and act excited?"

"Probably a little of each," she said. "I mean, Sydnie . . ." She pointed to a girl who'd just done about twenty-five backflips. "Her brain's probably too scrambled to keep track of what's going on on the field, but some of them are pretty smart."

As if to prove it, the squad all started cheering just as the wide receiver caught a tough pass for first down. I noticed the name on the back of his jersey. BRANDON.

Brandon?

"Who's that guy?" I asked Amanda. "I never saw him before."

"Yeah, it's weird," she said, pumping her fists. "He's new. One day last week, he was just at practice. No one remembered him from before, but he had a jersey and he was on the roster, and since Spencer broke his leg last month, they were happy to have him."

A strange thing, to be certain. But I was no stranger to strangeness.

"He just . . . appeared?"

"Yeah. He's really good."

"He is." It couldn't be him. Brandon was a common enough name. No, not really. "What's his first name?" The team was lining up again.

Amanda shrugged. "I don't remember. John, maybe?" She was watching the game—watching her boyfriend—and wanted me to shut up.

I couldn't stop watching the player. Brandon. So was everyone else when he ran the next pass in for a touchdown. The graceful way he caught the ball, the way he ran, all of his movements were so familiar.

So familiar.

Nonsense! I had never seen James play football! There was no football in seventeenth-century Salem! However, I dimly recalled having seen him play at lacrosse, a game that did exist then. He was a Shakespeare sonnet at that.

My eyes followed him as he high-fived his teammates, then took off his helmet to drink blue Gatorade.

His hair was bright auburn.

I fidgeted in my seat, clenching my fists, waiting for the game to be over so I could see him, though it might only lead to bitter disappointment. "I'm going to sit closer," I told Amanda as the fourth quarter began.

"Okay. I never knew you liked football that much." She followed my eyes. "Ohhhh, that new guy's kind of hot, huh?"

"Kind of." I moved closer. The helmet was back on, but his movements, even the size and shape of his hands were what I had been seeking, seeking for so long.

Could it be him?

Finally, it was over. Of course, there were many girls wanting to congratulate the football hero, hoping to meet this new boy. I was in a crowd of them when suddenly I felt a tap on my shoulder.

"Excuse me," a voice said. "I'm looking for . . . is there a girl named Kendra here? Sort of strange and wonderful? Pretty, but rather old?"

His very voice. I felt a bit hot, but it must have been the crowd streaming out. I always feel a bit claustrophobic in crowds. I felt my throat tighten and tears come to my eyes.

I turned. "I'm Kendra," I said, then stepped back.

It was him. It was James.

My heart was a ball of rubber in my throat. I was choking. Finally, I got out, "I thought you were dead."

"I thought I was too. I stopped getting your letters, and I thought I'd die from that. I started taking greater and greater risks."

"I wrote every day."

"I know. I found out, eventually. But that was after my plane was shot down in the battle of Normandy."

But he was immortal. "How—?"

"I wasn't killed, obviously, but I was unconscious, burned, disfigured."

I looked at his perfect face, his perfect, perfect face.

"They took me to a hospital," he said.

"Hey, James," a blond girl said. "Great game!"

"Back off," I told her. "He's mine."

She muttered an unkind word under her breath, but James sort of smiled at her. "It's true." He looked at me. "Do you want to go someplace else?"

"I want to know where you've been the last sixty years—sooner, rather than later."

"I couldn't find you, Kendra! The mirror disappeared in the wreck, and when I finally got back to London, you were gone. I asked all around."

And he had not shown up in my mirror either. I had experienced this with it. Often, someone was missing, and I seemed not to be able to find them. I had tried it with kidnap victims, missing persons. Sometimes, as with Grace's brother, Jack, I could find them, but other times, it seemed beyond my magic. James must have been "missing" at the time I looked for him, his whereabouts unknown to the British government. And I hadn't tried after that, assuming him dead.

It was just starting to sink in to me that I was truly seeing James, talking to James, for the first time in so many years. I held my icy hands to his cheek. "Are you real?"

He grasped my elbows and lifted me toward him. "I'm real." He was sweaty and smelled it, which made him all the more real. He kissed me.

"You two have gotten acquainted, I see!" a voice said. It was Amanda.

"Oh yes." I felt my face grow hot. I was blushing as I had not since I was a girl the first time. I turned away so they could not see me shaking with unshed tears. "James is an old friend, from Boston. That's why I was asking about him."

"Very cool," Amanda said. To James, she said, "You should take Kendra to the dance tomorrow."

"I should," he agreed, adding, "I should also probably take a shower," after Amanda and Chris left.

"But I don't want to let you out of my sight," I said. "How did you find me? It's not just a coincidence, is it?" I wanted to touch him, hold him, keep holding him so he couldn't leave again.

"Hardly. I found you the way everyone finds everyone—on Facebook."

I laughed. "Only old people use Facebook now."

"No one's much older than you."

It was true. I'd made a Facebook profile only recently. I finally realized that here in Miami, no one cared if I was a witch. There were people calling themselves witches who weren't even witches and plenty of voodoo ceremonies involving dead chickens in the woods. Probably no one would even believe me if I said I was one.

"I didn't think they'd let a person list 1652 as a birth year," he said. "That was a dead giveaway."

"I may have used some magic for that."

"And you listed this school. So I came here. I've been looking for you for a few days now."

"Sixty years and a few days."

"Maybe three hundred years and a few days."

"And now you've found me."

"And I'll never leave," he said.

"Never? No more wars? There's always a war somewhere."

"I'm too old. I've done my part." He took me in his arms. "I used to fight because I had nothing else to live for. Now I have you, finally."

"Finally!" I pulled him close.

I took James home with me that night. After three hundred years, I decided I was allowed to do that. And that Monday, we were married, secretly, at the courthouse. We had to ditch school, but it was okay. I'd been to school before, ten or twenty times.

Still, we decided to stay in high school a while longer. And then, maybe someday, we'd go to college. Take five years, maybe ten. It didn't really matter. We had forever.

The End

Historical Note on Beheld

Kendra, James, and most of the people they encounter are fictional, but several of the people in the stories (and everyone else in the first one) are real—though there is no evidence they had magical experience.

The Salem Witch Trials have always interested me since I played Martha Corey in an eighth grade play, *Reunion on Gallows Hill*, and Ruth Putnam in the opera version of *The Crucible* in college. Both appear in this story, and both were real people, though Arthur Miller renamed Ruth Putnam. Her real name was Ann, and she was one of the principal witnesses in the Salem Witch Trials, sending many women, including Martha Corey, to their deaths at the scaffold.

Ann interested me because she was the only one of the various "crying out girls" who ever apologized to the families of the women she'd hurt. The text of her apology is included after this note, and it made me feel that, somehow, she was swept up in something she didn't entirely understand. She was twelve at the time. Thus, this is a peer pressure story of sorts, with grave consequences as some peer pressure stories have. Ann's real story played out as Tituba said it would in my story. Her parents died when she was nineteen, and she was left to raise her siblings. She never married and died at thirty-seven. There is no evidence that her father could morph into a wolf, though.

Prince Karl Theodor of Bavaria was a real person. There is no evidence that he was a cad or was involved in any gold-spinning activities. He married twice and fathered three children. He was a second son and, thus, not heir to the throne.

The baby hatch or "foundling wheel," which Rumpelstiltskin describes to Cornelia, was also a real thing. In that way, a young woman could leave an unwanted baby so that it would be taken in. In modern times, all fifty states and numerous other countries have "safe-haven laws," which allow young women to leave unwanted babies less than thirty days old in a safe place, often a fire station. Many of the older foundlings died, but this is not the case in modern times.

The HMT *Lancastria* sank in 1940 with at least four thousand fatalities. It was the greatest British maritime disaster in history, worse than the *Titanic* and *Lusitania* combined. However, it was largely kept secret and out of the presses because the British Prime Minister, Winston Churchill, ordered a media blackout, fearing the effect on morale of the British citizens if they knew about the tragedy. This distressed many survivors. A memorial to the ship was placed in Scotland in 2015.

The stories adapted in this book were *Little Red Riding Hood*, *Rumpelstiltskin*, *East of the Sun and West of the Moon*, and *The Ugly*

Duckling. For the historical versions of each, I recommend the website www.surlalunefairytales.com.

The text of Ann Putnam's apology follows. She read it in church in 1706.

"I desire to be humbled before God for that sad and humbling providence that befell my father's family in the year about '92; that I, then being in my childhood, should, by such a providence of God, be made an instrument for the accusing of several persons of a grievous crime, whereby their lives were taken away from them, whom now I have just grounds and good reason to believe they were innocent persons; and that it was a great delusion of Satan that deceived me in that sad time, whereby I justly fear I have been instrumental, with others, though ignorantly and unwittingly, to bring upon myself and this land the guilt of innocent blood; though what was said or done by me against any person I can truly and uprightly say, before God and man, I did it not out of any anger, malice, or ill-will to any person, for I had no such thing against one of them; but what I did was ignorantly, being deluded by Satan. And particularly, as I was a chief instrument of accusing of Goodwife Nurse and her two sisters, I desire to lie in the dust, and to be humbled for it, in that I was a cause, with others, of so sad a calamity to them and their families; for which cause I desire to lie in the dust, and earnestly beg forgiveness of God, and from all those unto whom I have given just cause of sorrow and offence, whose relations were taken away or accused."

Acknowledgments

Thanks so much to my editor, Antonia Markiet. I often feel lucky to have you as an editor because you (along with my late agent, George Nicholson) connect me to a lovely bygone era in publishing when the reader and the beauty of the story reigned supreme. Also, to her assistant, Abbe Goldberg.

Thanks also to my agent, Erica Silverman.

My critique group, Christina Diaz Gonzalez, Stephanie Hairston, Alexandra Jorge, Danielle Cohen Joseph, and Gaby Triana, are there, sometimes for advice, sometimes for cookies. Mostly cookies.

I always appreciate the Florida SCBWI and Linda Rodriguez Bernfeld for making it happen. Special thanks to Debbie Reed Fischer and Marjetta Geerling for being Patty and Maxene to my LaVerne—Andrews Sisters forever!

Thanks to my family, Gene, Katherine, and Meredith, for putting up with the, um, clutter while I'm writing.

JOIN THE

COMMUNITY

THE ULTIMATE YA DESTINATION

◀ **DISCOVER** ▶
your next favorite read

◀ **MEET** ▶
new authors to love

◀ **WIN** ▶
free books

◀ **SHARE** ▶
infographics, playlists, quizzes, and more

◀ **WATCH** ▶
the latest videos